THE SIXTH SUN

TED BARBER

A Prehistory of Man's next 4300 Years

Words Matter Publishing
P.O. Box 1190
Decatur, IL 62525
www.wordsmatterpublishing.com

ISBN 13: 978-1-962467-89-6

Library of Congress Catalog Card Number: 2025939429

Certainly, religion must be granted to be one of the
greatest inventions ever made on earth.

–H. L. Mencken

A wise and courageous prince, with money, troops, and laws, can
perfectly well govern men without the aid of religion, which was made
only to deceive them, but the stupid people would soon make one for
themselves, and as long as there are fools and rascals there will be
religions. Ours is assuredly the most ridiculous, the most absurd,
and the most bloody that has ever infected the world.

–Voltaire

Dedication

Dedicated to my daughter, Jenna, who learned about life through Daddy's stories.

And to my Muse, Lauren Jakes, who I first met in Egypt during the Fifth Sun

Acknowledgements

With the encouragement of my (then) wife I left my career of fifteen years in 1999 to accept a position at half the pay but double the free time (work) hours and began my research on this project. One to four hours a day I researched, outlined, and wrote a 175- page first draft of this novel while working a university job that encouraged workers to "do homework during downtime." Thinking I was done, I took the project to my mother (a career teacher) to review and edit. After she finished her review, we spent a wonderful eight-hour day tweaking my word usage and character building. My dad came in, asked for a ten-minute synopsis, and asked a few key questions. That experience inspired me to expand my research and expand the novel to its present length.

Due to an endless stream of tragedies that struck my family including births (not tragic, time consuming), injuries that left me bed ridden hardly able to hold my newborn for more than five minutes, cancer scares, major operations, job changes (I.E. life) the first edition of this novel was postponed to 2011. During this time the characters you will meet came to life in my head. They are as alive as anyone I know and many of the conversations they have in the novel they had with me or were witnessed by me (in my imagination). After The Sixth Sun was released, their conversations with me never ceased. They requested their story continue and it has. This series is called The Infinite Quest. Look for book two soon.

I would like to thank the authors Tom Clancy for stating it's okay (and beneficial to the creative process) to have out loud conversations with or between characters and Stephen King for encouraging other writers (in On Writing) to explore the "what ifs" in life.

My ex-wife, Daphne Gill, and daughter Jenna Barber for first encouraging me to pursue my talent and second for putting up with all those hours locked up in my office writing. Jenna, I had a lot of fun when you came in to do your homework at my feet. Daphne, sorry I wouldn't let you type it up for me. I felt I needed to experience the whole process.

My deceased brother, Tim, for taking ten minutes out of his day to come over and draw my maps from my descriptions of the islands. They worked out great and were right for someone who'd never read my story.

My sister-in-law, Autumn, for photographing the painting The Prophet for me.

To my mom and dad who were invaluable with suggestions during my first and second drafts. Dad, the extra two hundred pages added were inspired by your questions.

And to my fans who continually ask me "When's the movie coming out?" And to my "super" fan who cornered me at a luncheon one day and knew more about the book than I did! To you all, you inspire me to be my best!

Finally, I would like to thank the band Zebra for asking, Who's Behind the Door?

Indeed, let's find out....

TABLE OF CONTENTS

HISTORICAL CHARACTERS

Through test readings of this story, I found that people could follow the sequence of events easier with a list of characters to refer back to. Since the story encompasses about 4400 years of man's prehistory and future (with a short note on the past 40,000 years), many characters were needed to tell the story with as much accuracy as possible. Pronunciations are provided as most names are foreign to the reader.

GAIANS (Guy ons)

Tian (*Tee on*): colonial recruiter

King: Gaian king

Farmer: Amateur scientist

CHARACTERS FROM OSIRIAT (*Oh seer ee at*)
The Immortals- the parents of the "Gods."

Wolvernix (*Wool ver nicks*): Governor of Lonix (*Low nicks*)

Oblivia (*Ob li vee ah*): Governess of Lonix
    -parents Mercianiax and Marsax

Cronix (*Crow nicks*): Governor of Isoloquat (*Eye sol oh qwat*)

Sate (*Sae tee*): Governess of Isoloquat
    -parents of Uryxs and Satetan

Petex (*Pee ticks*): Governor of Crystalia (*Cri stae lee a*)

Dolphinia (*Doll fin ee ah*): Governess of Crystalia
    -parents of Nepeta and Vienusia

Tarus (*Taur us*): Governor of Gosiria (*Go seer ee ah*) and King of Osiriat

Elysia (*Ee lee see ah*): Governess of Gosiria and Queen of Osiriat
    -parents of Jupoler, Arop, and Planex

(The above immortals participated in the fifth expedition and were responsible for all pyramid-type structures built on Earth at the dawn of civilization)

THE "GODS"
(All but the last God: members of the sixth Earth mission)

Jupoler (*Jew pole er*): Co-captain of Osiriat VI; first prince of Osiriat

Arop (*A rop*): Co-captain of Osiriat VI; princess of Osiriat

Planex (*Plan ix*): secondary prince of Osiriat; specialty is relating to children

Mercianiax (*Mer see on ee ax*): first son of Lonix, future governor

Marsax (*Mar sax*): first daughter of Lonix, future governess

Uryxs (*Yer ix ees*): first son of Isoloquat: future governor

Satetan (*Say tee tan*): first daughter of Isoloquat, future governess

Nepeta (*Na pet ah*): first son of Crystalia, future governor

Vienusia (*Vee en oo see ah*): first daughter of Crystalia, future governess

Hermax (*Her max*): revered as the 'one true God'

CHARACTERS FROM EARTH
B.D. Era: ancestors of John

45 B.D.: woman, great-grandmother of John

25 B.D.: John and Mary, grandparents of John

6 B.D.: Jane and Bob, parents of John

6 B.D.: John is born

B.D. Era: ancestors of Daphne

72 B.D.: woman, great, great grandmother of Daphne

47 B.D.: woman, great-grandmother of Daphne

29 B.D.: woman, grandmother of Daphne

5 B.D.: Steve and Susan, parents of Daphne

5 B.D.: Daphne born

Earth 0 to 4196 A.D.
218 A.D.

Veon (*Vee on*): fisherman, John and Vienusia's line

Saara (*Sarah*): captain of the Marsax soldiers, defenders of Gosirius (*Go seer ee us*)

Neta (*Neh tah*): food stores keeper on Veon's ship

Hadim (*Hah deem*): adventurer/explorer from the Far East

1050 A.D.

Vernax (*Ver nax*): mining slave

Nocix (*Know six*): laboring slave

1234 A.D.

Ronix (*Row nicks*): metalworking slave, upper-class caste

Vinx (*Veeinks*): laboring slave

Uria(*Yer ee ah*): Vinx's daughter, Ronix's love

Ury (*Yer ee*): laboring slave

1238-2138 A.D.

Joplo (*Jop low*): spokesperson for the Delegatia (*Del ah gae see ah*), part of the triumvirate

Etan (*Ee ton*): Leader of the Gosirian (*Go seer ee* an)priests

General Zearn (*Zern*): Heroic conqueror of Hermatia (*Her may see ah*), part of the triumvirate

Mercor (*Mer core*): wealthy merchant, member of the Delegatia, part of the triumvirate

Zearnanine (*Zern ah nine*): eighteen-year-old emperor, great-grandson of Zearn

The Laara (*Laura*): Leader of Laarisia (*Lore ee see* ah)and Hermatia, religious world leader and emperor of the Holy Laarisian (*Lore ee see an*) Empire

Lord Rapta (*Wrap ta*): Landowner, ruler of the city Crono (*Crow no*), Uryxia (*Yer ix ee ah*)

Lanx (*Lanks*)family: servant/tenant farmers of Lord Rapta

Ales (Alice) Lanx: concubine of Lord Rapta

Titys (*Tie tus*): head of a family of servant/tenant farmers of Lord Rapta

Onix (*Oh nicks*): son of Titys

Taes (Tae es): daughter of Titys

Captain Nepusia (*Nea poo see ah*): seaman, adventurer, explorer

Cronon (*Crow non*): head priest of the temple of Uryxia

Emperor Upol (*You pole*): the last emperor to be spoken of as a duality; He is Laara John VI; all future emperors or empresses referred to as Laara only

Tatan (*Tae ton*): new arrival on Nepusia; military duty; lookout

King Nepusia: Leader of Nepusia when Laarisia attacks

General Risi: Laarisian General in command of the Nepusian campaign

Laara Daphne I: Laara, who conquered Nepusia

2220-3220 A.D.

Axiax (*Ax ee ax*): Leader of the Alpanian (*Al pain ee an)*tribes (hordes)

General Maar (*Mar*): Axiax's head General

Laara John VII: Faced Axiax in Laarisia

Linx (*Links*): Aropian (*Ah rope ee an*) sorcerer

King Herme(*Her mee*): first king of the unified Stonland (*Stone land*)

3220-3620 A.D.

Captain Edion (*Ee dee on*): Herme's most senior captain, explorer

Captain Nies (*Knee es*): Alpania's (*Al pain ee* ah)most senior captain

King Surat (*Sir ought*): Alpanian king, the enemy of Herme

Laara Daphne VIII: Negotiator of peace between Stonland and Alpania

Xar (*Zar*): King Herme's administrator

Herme II: Stonland's king of peace

Noxon (*Knocks on*) Prince of Stonland, King Herme II's son

Ursia (*Yerf is see ah*): Princess of Alpania, marries Noxon to secure the peace

Noplod (*Know plod*): Poet/playwright

Celes (*Sell es*): warrior of Stonland, inventor, scientist, astronomer

Nyxs (*Nicks es*): Celes' blacksmith

3620-4120 A.D.

Phaol (*Fall*): Science officer on first circumnavigational voyage, biologist

Haden (*Hay den*): Inventor, improved farming techniques, father of the industrial revolution

Taria (*Tar ee ah*)family: displaced farming family)

    Tepex (*Tee pecks*): father

    Pinodol (*Pin oh doll*): mother

    Wilix (*Will ex*): son

    Obvia (*Ob vee ah*): daughter

Captain Wolv (*Wollf*): Pirate

King Jopol (*Joe pol*): King of Stonland

King Syal (*Sigh all*): King of Nepusia

King Sikm (*Seek em*): King of Andenan (*An dee nan*)

King Rasu (*Raw sue*): King of Alpania

4124-4196 A.D.

Taval-pan (*Tah vole- pan*): son of Taval (*Tah vole*), world historian

Taval: Representative of Nepetan (*Neh pet an*)in the Senate

Miska (*Miss caw*): Daughter of the representative house of Kashim (*Cash eem*)

King Jopol IV: King of Stonland, ruler of the Empire

Head priest of the temple of Hermatia: Taval-pan's mentor for five years

Laara Daphne XV: Taval-pan's mentor for ten years

Senator Reesar (*Reese are*): protests Taval-pan's research

Solgas (*Sole gas*): Supervisor of the monument complex, keeper of the monument of the sun

Tarta (*Tar tah*): Taval-pan's cynical cousin, artist

PLACES IMPORTANT TO THIS HISTORY

GAIA (*Guy ah*): Suggested birthplace of humanity long forgotten in the conscious minds of humans

SIRIAN BINARY SYSTEM:

Sirius a- Osiriat's main sun

Sirius b- Golas, the dwarf star that helps balance the system

OSIRIAT: a planet in the Sirian binary system

populated centers of Osiriat:

Crystalia: undersea city
Lonix: island chain, forested
Isoloquat: forested mainland country
Gosiria: mainland city-state; world government seated here

EARTH: third planet of the Sol system, 8.7 light years distant from Osiriat.

Populated Earth centers:

Gosirius: city on the Antarctic continent; formerly Osiriat V
Laarisia: Himalayan island; religious center of the world
Hermatia: Himalayan island; religious center
Islands of the Alps:
Alpania
Marsia (*Mar see ah*)
Ciaxian (*See ox ee an*)
Vienus (*Vee en oos*)

Uryxia
Sateland (*Sae tee land*)

Aropia/Stonland: southern portion of Great Britain
Islands of the Andes spine:

Andenan
Kashim
Nepetan

Nepusia: Island of the Cascadian range

IMPORTANT WATERWAYS

GALACIA (*Gall a see ah*): Name of Earth's one ocean
HIMAL (*Hymn all*): Laarisia's holy river

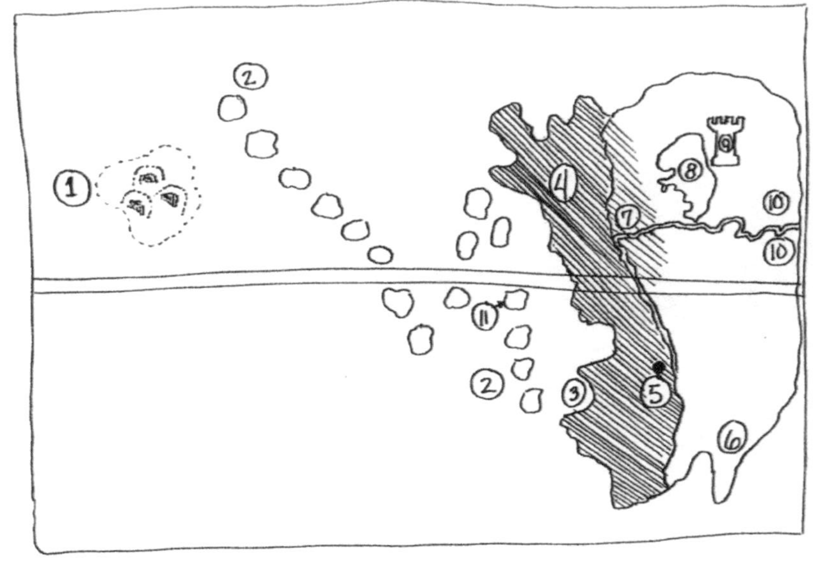

MAP OF OSIRIAT

KEY: PLANET OSIRIAT

1. undersea island of Crystalia (cave/mound city)
2. island chain of Lonix (capital city of Lonix NE island
3. harbor and cave entrance to Isoloquat
4. heavily forested mainland area: Isoloquat
5. Uryxs and Satetan's village
6. Gosirian mainland
7. River route to capitol city (Gosiria)
8. Royal lake
9. Castle
10. imperial farmlands
11. Earthia

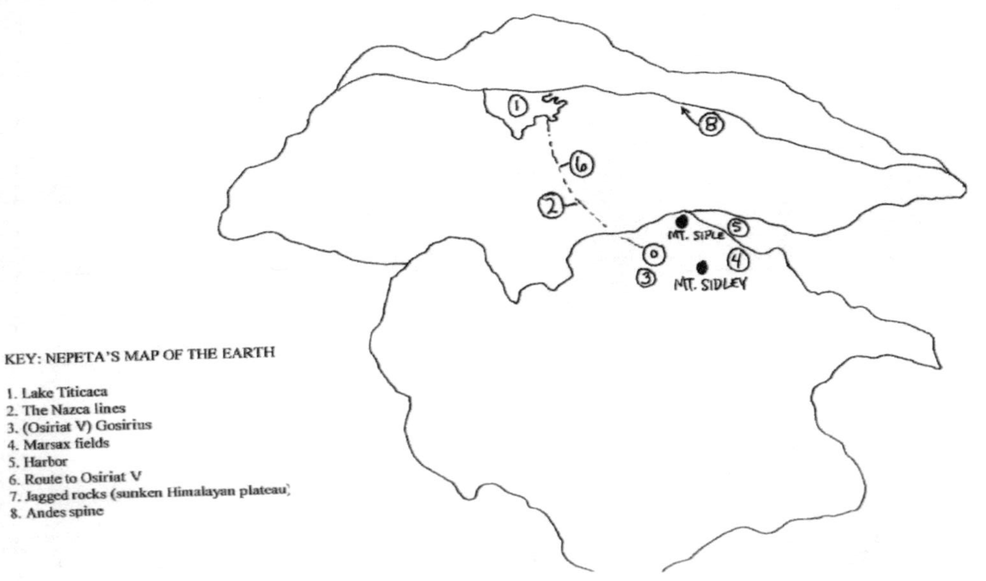

MAP OF GOSIRIUS

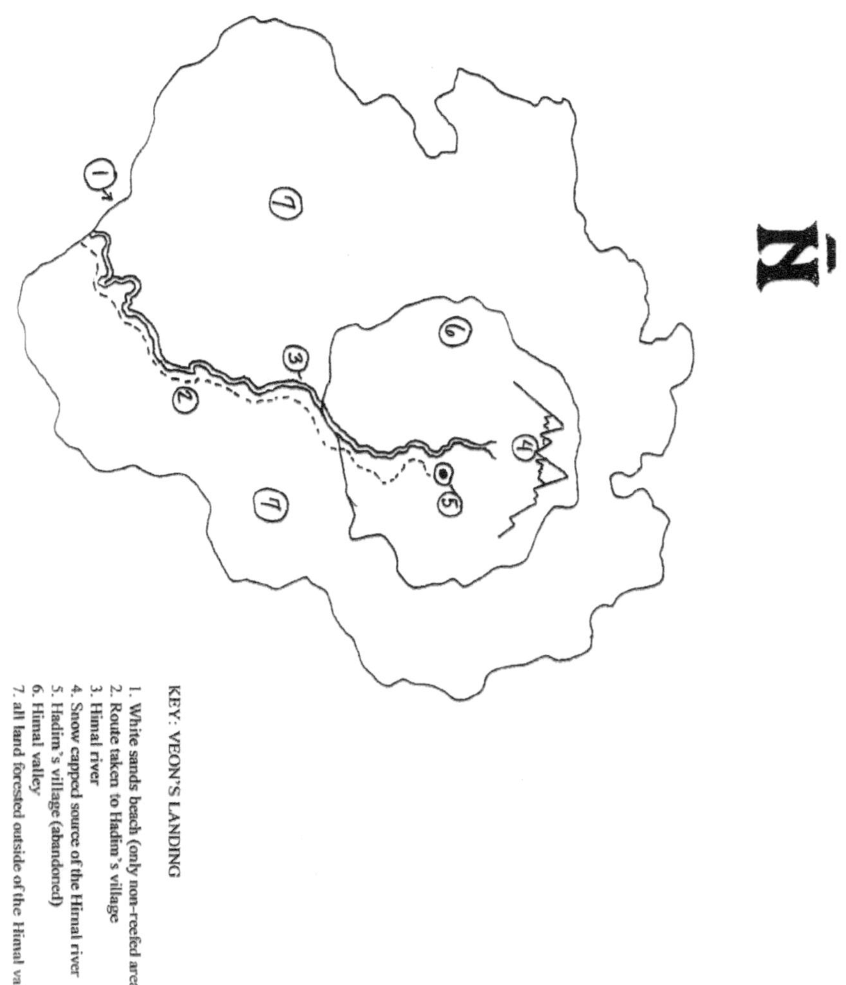

MAP OF VEON'S JOURNEY

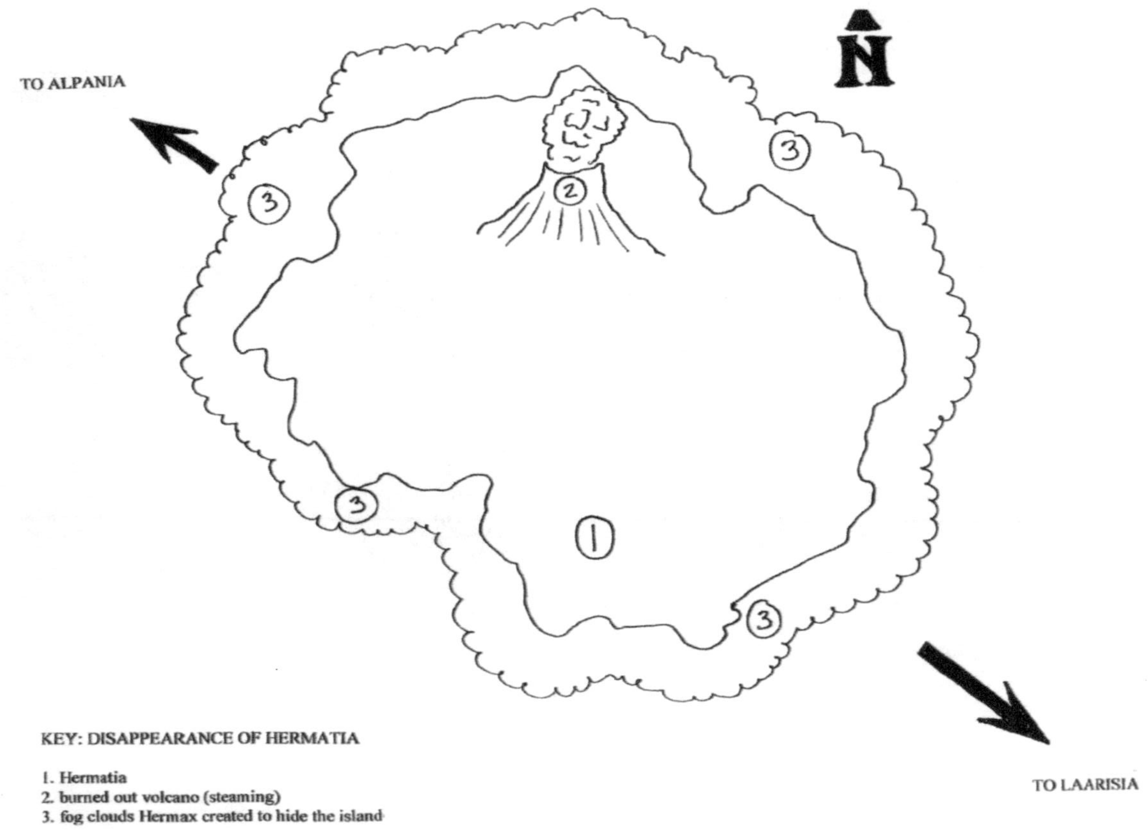

MAP OF HERMATIA

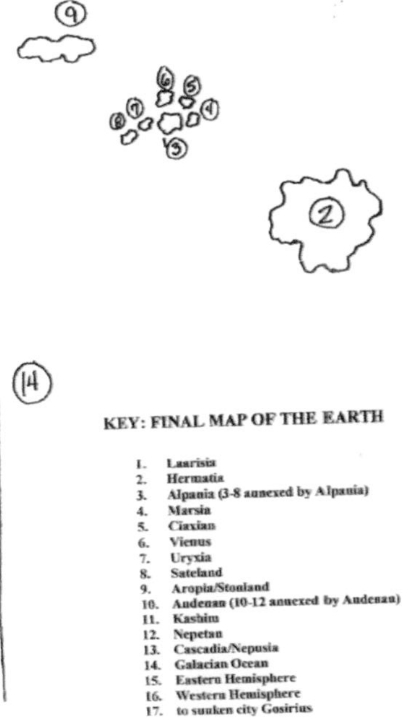

MAP OF THE WORLD

CHAPTER 1

COMMENCEMENT

Graduation Day

".... And to these people, you will be seen as gods. Never forget that; encourage it. You must remain above them to keep absolute control. Be warned, however, they must not revere you, for religion has continually destroyed them."

The commencement was over. Nine graduates, the eldest seven years old, scanned the audience, found their parents, rose, and walked toward the lavish reception area. Dignitaries from Osiriat who had participated in the last five missions filled the room. They walked down the plush, carpeted staircase toward their waiting parents. Waves of enthusiastic supporters surrounded them. As the others found their parents, Jupoler and Arop braved the gauntlet to continue toward the row of plate glass windows. Planex, the toddler of the group, tried to follow only to be scooped up happily by Vienusia, his favorite crew member, who, to his extreme delight, began playing with him. The others sat quietly with their parents, enjoying the view. Families of the chosen had major celebrations at home when their children, picked for the mission, received their orders to report to Osiriat's space station learning center. Now, the parents beamed proudly.

Jupoler and Arop were standing at a window looking down at the planet, wishing their parents, Tarus and Elysia, had come. They claimed the pressure of ruling the planet restricted them. Jupoler knew better. The mission his dad had begun sixty years before was failing miserably.

1

Osiriat's region, Gosiria, sent four previous observation missions to Earth before they sent his 'Tarus' group. The first mission left Osiriat twenty thousand five hundred years before. When they reached Earth, it was, by future Earth calendars, 20,238 B.C. They observed man rise from savagery to thatched hut societies over four thousand years. Then, Earth violently rose against man, destroying society with an epic flood four thousand and eight years after it began.

The next three missions witnessed similar fates. When mankind was on the brink of a major strive forward, always four to five thousand years into the observation, disaster struck.

Directed not to interfere, the second mission watched in horror as violent winds destroyed most of the life on earth. Mission three witnessed the earth engulfed in a great fire. Mission four watched helplessly as life starved after a deluge of blood and fire caused by great regional battles.

Reviewing these four similar, well-documented reports, Osirian royalty learned over the next five thousand years that, in each case, these disasters had been foretold by the earth's heavens. Mankind ignored the warnings. Even if he had noticed, he was not technologically advanced enough to save himself. What interested them was that after each disaster, two humans, one male and one female, survived. In them, mankind's knowledge survived. Man was proving to be resilient.

The rulers of Osiriat changed the goal of the fifth mission. They felt they had observed long enough. Humans proved their resiliency, and the Osirians felt if they could teach the race to read the signs, they could save them and create a powerful ally in the galaxy.

Earth was the first inhabited planet they found in the galaxy. Normal colonization took place on uninhabited planets. The challenge they faced was whether or not to expose themselves to these primitive humanoids. The accepted theory became "exposure will frighten them to the point of submission." Submission was not acceptable. If these humanoids were to become allies, they must prove to be as strong-minded and intelligent as the Osirians.

The Osirians suspected they themselves had come from humble beginnings such as these, but thousands of years on Osiriat had erased any memories of life on a home planet. They believed observing these humans might provide the key to their own past. With that knowledge, they would be able to identify why they left their home planet if one had indeed existed. Clearing up that mystery could lead to insights designed to direct their future, as they were, as a society, at a standstill.

Jupoler and Arop's father, Tarus, were sent to Earth in a craft named Osiriat V. His mission was different. The Osirians knew disaster would strike Earth in the year of earth calendars 2012 A.D. in the form of major plate shifts, floods, and fires. Tarus' mission was to warn them.

Osiriat V's destination was the earth year eighteen eighty A.D. Mankind misinterpreted the Egyptian monuments that Osiriat IV had encouraged them to build through cryptic signs. The monuments had fallen to ruin within one thousand years. Mankind let them sit as a reminder of Pharaoh's failure. Tarus' group was to build "obvious" monuments. To survive, mankind must decipher them within the next one hundred thirty years.

While they slept, the computer on Osiriat V slightly altered their course to miss a comet. When it did, it forced Osiriat V into a time wave. They traveled this rare reversed wave five thousand years back in about one year. When they were released, they continued on to Earth. Upon arrival, they scanned the earth for the monument locations and were shocked none existed. Based on Osiriat IV records, they determined it was about three thousand B.C. on Earth. Tarus was excited. He saw in this error an opportunity to vindicate Osiriat IV and elevate himself to a hero.

His mission had a rule of non-interference, with one exception: bring the signs that were in the sky down to the earth's surface. Osirian command suggested he involve man without interfering with his natural growth. It was suspected that if man had a hand in this task, he might, in the future, more readily understand the signs.

Mammoth monuments were created on several continents. They were constructed quickly and precisely using tractor beams and laser cutters. He was not to reveal their purpose to mankind. Figuring out their purpose was the only way man could be saved.

Before they built the monuments, his group had to decide how to involve man without physically making their presence known. They found societal groups already gathered in the proper locations. The Osirians sent the leaders of these societies cryptic visions of great monuments. Visions, waking dreams, seen as mirages or, sometimes, in pools of still water, excited the leaders. Strong leaders enslaved people to quarry stones. Man's vanity allowed him to take credit for the building of the monuments. Two religions, one of the slaves and one of the masters, grew. Mankind spent centuries wondering *how* they were built instead of determining *why* they were built. Mankind was destined to fail again. Extreme pressure was on Jupoler's group. This mission was important because it was considered man's last hope, as even the immortal Osirians could not change Earth's fate.

40,000 years previous: Immortal evolution

Tian nervously approached the palace, the symbol of Gaia's power. His task was dangerous. If presented wrong, his findings could mean his life. Would the king believe? He hardly had at first, but the idea grew on him. If they were to be saved, this was the only sensible choice.

Ten thousand years of progressive societal growth was a glorious thing, but to believe that disaster would not one day strike was foolish. Scientists, naturally inquisitive, provided answers to all the questions Gaians had ever thought to ask. Science was religion. Recently, it had propelled society into space. They explored their solar system and found no life. Space was continually monitored for sound; any messages from other worlds. Gaian scientists were constantly disappointed. Powerful telescopic arrays that could see many light years distant had found no signs of life. Unable to accept that they may be the only intelligence in the Universe, they were developing long-term transports in order to colonize other planets they suspected could support life. They theorized that the farther they ventured out, the more likely it would be that they would meet other intelligent life. The scientists recommended ten planets to colonize.

The king had sent Tian in search of possible colonists. He was the official court historian and was directed to enlist people rich in knowledge of Gaia's culture and history.

The ageless monument stood on a flat plain located in the exact center of three hills that formed a natural isosceles triangle. No one could recall how or when it first appeared or who built it. It was a gigantic, circular obelisk that stood perfectly vertical to the ground. Early farmers depended on it as it acted like a natural clock, accurately predicting the onset of the seasons. Farms and ranches naturally sprang up near it.

The first scientific community formed around the monument. In the beginning, the area provided basic clues that led to mathematical invention. The site was abandoned after a millennia. Science took a new direction. Exploring the planet became paramount. The monument, its mysteries assumed understood, became unimportant to science. It became a tourist attraction. Plants and domestic animals important to the planet's survival were still raised here.

On this plain, in the shadow of the monument, he had gone daily to review his list of colonists from the region. On one of those occasions, a man found him and profoundly changed humanity's future.

"You are Tian, the one who's compiling the list of colonists?"

"Yes. Why are you on my list?"

"Yes. You will choose me. It is my destiny."

Agitated, he said, "I will choose no one. I only recommend people to the king."

Undaunted, the farmer said, "When you hear what I have to say, you will make sure I'm picked."

Curious, Tian asked, "What could you know that would make me recommend you?"

"I know two things. I know what planet we'll be successful colonizing, and, more importantly, I know we have to go because soon our sun is going to destroy our beautiful Gaia."

"How-?"

"The monument told me."

"The monument! This old relic? Everyone knows it's only good for telling time."

"That is correct. Time. But what time does it tell?"

"Seasonal time, of course!"

"Yes, but it tells much more than that. Our scientists abandoned it too quickly. It gave them knowledge, and they turned their backs on it. I have studied this monument for thirty years. I wondered if it calculated more than seasonal changes. I knew it must, but I couldn't figure out how. One day, I decided to distance myself from it. I looked at a picture of it taken from space. What I noticed was this: If I took the measurements of the distance between the three hills and multiplied the area by 2π, I had a 1:500,000 scale model of the area of our planet. Then I realized the monument wasn't just a gigantic obelisk for show; no, this beam was pointing at something. It seems that every year at midnight, on the vernal equinox, this beam points to the Sirian system. These hills represent the Sirian system well. There are two suns and an inhabitable planet waiting for us."

"Yes, Osiriat. It is on the list of ten possible planets to colonize."

"Osiriat. Is that what we've named it?"

"Yes. There is something I don't understand. Why haven't our scientists discovered that the sun is going to destroy life on the planet?"

"They are too busy looking out into the Universe."

"How did the monument tell you? What is your proof?" Tian wondered.

"I observed. At sunrise, on the equinoxes, the shadows have lengthened considerably. That tells me either the planet's orbit is creeping closer or the sun is increasing in size. Either way, life on this planet will be eradicated."

"If that is so, we must colonize all ten planets."

"You may, but I'm convinced only Osiriat will accept us. It is the chosen planet, the prophetic choice."

"But who gave us this sign, this choice?"

"Does it really matter?"

Now, as he stood outside of the palace recalling that conversation, his fear peaked. He knew he must tell the king what he had learned, but he also knew if he angered him, he could be executed. The king must accept the theory of Osiriat because it supported colonization. But the theory of the sun? Everyone on Gaia was mortal. People lived and died; that was natural. It was also slow and easily acclimated into everyday life. This represented a sudden upheaval; it would spread fear and panic. He was not a scientist but was about to present a report like one when, after all, the "facts" had come from a common farmer.

As he debated with himself, he gazed over the serene scene below. The palace sat on top of a hill. It was purposely built here so the royalty could ceremoniously rise above their subjects. Laid out before him were acres of fruit orchards, grain fields, produce fields, and livestock ranges. Though they appeared wild, they were well-planned and maintained. Centuries before, by royal order, all domestic animals and plants had been ordered to be grown and raised here to symbolically represent the balance between nature and man. Looking upon it now, he realized this serene planet would soon perish. The colonial missions, full of plant and animal cargo, must survive if humanity was to remain intact.

He decided, as he walked in, to leave the theory of the sun out of his report. Although he had come to believe it as he pondered the evidence, he did not fancy the risk to his health. To survive, he would volunteer for colonization.

He was greeted warmly by the king, "Tian, it's good to see you. I trust your journey went well?"

"Very well, Sire. Here are my lists of applicants for colonization."

He handed them to the king, who handed them over to a secretary to be reviewed at a later date.

Tian asked, "Are you not going to pick today?"

"No. Choosing will be a long process that will involve a meeting of the council of territorial governors." He went back to his reading. A few moments later, he sensed a presence, looked up, and saw Tian still standing there.

"I'm sorry. Was there something else?"

"" Yes, if you don't mind. I found an extraordinary man I would like to sponsor for colonization."

"Is his name on the lists?"

"No, I have removed it."

"Why do you hold it back?"

"I must tell you about him if you have time."

"Go ahead." The king set his official document to one side. He was bored with paperwork, and this might prove interesting.

"He discovered that only Osiriat will be successful when we colonize."

"How does he know that?"

"He studied the monument for several years, took measurements, and learned that it represents a message telling us to travel to Osiriat."

"Is he a scientist?"

"No, Sire, he is a common farmer, but he is self-taught. I have examined his theory and am convinced he's right. I think we should send our best and brightest people to Osiriat. If it is the best chance, we should send the best people."

"His not being a scientist worries me. Can we really risk our best people on some rogue theory?"

"I've thought of that. I want to volunteer to go as an observer. If I see his theory is wrong, I'll demand we return to Gaia. If we are successful, I will return with a report."

"You may go, but please abort if things look bad. We will give you a second destination just in case. You're dismissed. Go. Inform this farmer that he has been chosen."

Without a word, because the king had gone back to work, he left the building. He worried that he had not mentioned the sun theory and justified his hesitancy by assuming the scientists would wake up in time and discover the disaster looming. He had made up his mind. Once gone, he was never going to return.

Six months later, he and the farmer, whom he had kept hidden, were ready to board their transport to Osiriat. Transports were being loaded with every seed of every species of plant and animal on the planet. The mission parameters included planting familiar plants in order that the colonists would be instantly comfortable in their new home. They would also thaw and combine the eggs and sperm of domestic animals in case none existed in their new home. The farmer, when he questioned the restraint, was told that everyone was being isolated to make the launch more emotional.

"How long will it take to get to Osiriat?" The farmer asked.

"Fifty-nine light years."

"How will we survive?"

"The shuttles are equipped with hibernation chambers that will slow down our metabolism. We will only age six years in the next fifty-nine light years."

"At the speed, they say we'll travel, we'll be traveling for six hundred years. How is it possible that we'll only age six years?"

"If we arrive alive, does it really matter how?"

The king came out to wish each shuttle crew well. He thanked each for their personal sacrifice; as volunteers in an untested process, they were sacrificing their lives for the good of Gaia. Whether they succeeded or not, each individual was considered a hero. He finally arrived at the Osirian transport.

"You are about to embark on a historic journey. If you succeed, the chances for our race to survive increase tenfold.

"You can see there are ten couples per ship. Ten ships heading to ten different planets. I wanted all the others boarded before I talked to you. You are the best, and the brightest Gaia has to offer. We have chosen you for the Osirian mission because this farmer," whom he nodded toward, "claims Osiriat is our best hope for success. I am sending Tian along to make sure it is a prudent choice. Please keep accurate records, as he will be returning with a report."

The farmer burst forward and proclaimed, "-But he can't return. Twelve hundred years will pass, and you'll be gone-"

Tian gave him a look that silenced him. The king saw the look and questioned Tian, "What does he mean?"

"Sire, he means nothing. I will simply report to whoever is king when I return. I think he is worried you'll be dead."

"That's quite true, but my line will be very much alive."

As the king walked away, the farmer said, "But-" and was abruptly silenced as Tian pushed him up the ship's ramp.

As they walked to the hibernation chambers, Tian told the farmer, "Do not be upset that I silenced you. I didn't tell the king about the sun. He has no idea how quickly he will die."

"But why? If he'd known, he could have sent more ships out."

"No, there were only the ten. More likely, he would have canceled our trip until he could investigate the theory, thereby stranding us on the planet. Your prediction about Osiriat made sense. I didn't want to confuse the issue. Besides, word of the sun destroying the planet may have caused worldwide panic."

"But you've condemned a whole planet to death. What will become of the race?"

"I guess that's up to us."

They opened, climbed in, and lay in the hibernation chambers. Before the ship launched, they began their six-hundred-year sleep.

The vessel monitored life internally and externally, constantly receiving signals from the other ships. As the flight neared completion, the computer noted eight external failures. One external success was noted; however, the signal was lost when it passed the new planetary atmosphere.

They awoke in orbit around the fourth planet of the giant sun. They studied Osiriat, found no humanoids, as expected, and proceeded to evaluate the best area to start their new lives. There was a major landmass and a series of islands to choose from.

They then focused their attention on the giant sun. Estimates determined the surface temperature was about sixteen thousand five hundred degrees and that it was around one million three hundred thousand miles in diameter. It lay almost one hundred forty-two million miles away from the planet, so temperatures were ideal for humanoid life. However, a sun this size was going to produce an alarming amount of ultraviolet rays, so they looked for an area to start society that was well-covered with forest growth. The western most island in the series was ideal because the greatest concentration of sea life surrounded it. Starting out on the heavily forested mainland was preferable, but game appeared too scarce. The decision made, they left the shuttle in a high orbit and electronically transported themselves, their food and seeds down to their new home.

"This is a paradise. When will you report back to the king?" The farmer asked.

Tian didn't answer. Instead, he called the ten couples together and made an untrue announcement.

"I will not be reporting back to Gaia. They have all died. The sun was changing. Life was destroyed soon after we left. The king sent the colonists out so that our race would have a chance to survive. We must forget our home and move forward. I know you're sad, but mourning won't honor our ancestors. We must build to honor their memory. Though they died, they would have wanted us to survive. We are the hope of the race. Only one other shuttle made it, but we don't know where because our ship lost the signal. We should look forward to the day we find them."

The audience stood stunned. They admired the king's bravery, sacrificing all so that they may live. A vow was taken to always remember Gaia, but three generations later, it was believed to be a myth, and three generations after that, it disappeared from the collective memory.

They soon acclimated to their new home. Fish provided the main source of nutrition. Tian invented a three-pronged wooden trident sword and was the first to attempt to spear fish in the sea while swimming. Wonderfully clear blue seas finally became dark about one hundred feet down. Tridents became the weapon of choice. Soon, everyone was using one. Over the next two thousand years, the citizenry spent more time in the sea than on the land. They evolved tails, allowing them faster hunting speeds. Tails also allowed them to swim deeper.

Another evolutionary change came about because they spent so much time in the water. Their lungs began to store oxygen, allowing for longer hunting periods under the surface. Hunters braved deeper waters. Groups stayed close to each other in order to protect their members.

Eventually, evolution added another gift. They developed an undersea, high-pitched, chirping, sonar-type language that allowed hunters to spread out. Hunters never harmed each other because the sonar pinpointed locations.

Near the end of the second millennium, the island was abandoned. Hunters stumbled upon an undersea mountain where a series of caves existed. These caves had a natural oxygen spring that had formed millions of years after the planet had cooled. Society settled here and future generations learned that it began here.

In two thousand years, the second sun of Osiriat, the dwarf star the people named Golas, appeared close to the planet's orbit forty times. Every fifty years, as it came as close as it would, its gravity slowly changed these new Osirians into immortals. The gravitational pull of Golas eradicated the microorganisms that when left alone, cause death to come to all creatures.

Not understanding their fate and having plenty of territory to inhabit if they wished, the Osirians reproduced at an alarming rate. Ten thousand years later, they had settled the entire planet. They were running out of space and very few people were dying accidentally. A law was passed by the king that no Osirian couple could produce more than one child and there was a reward for remaining childless. Animosity arose amongst the populace because this law infringed on the basic humanoid desire to reproduce. An ugly fact of the law was that the governors and king were not required to observe it. A solution was needed.

The Osirians, having long ago lost their past, concentrated intensely on survival. Space travel, a long-forgotten memory, they looked longingly to the stars. A hunter/gatherer found the original shuttle. Long ago, its orbit had decayed, plunging it into the sea. Witnesses thought that it was merely a shooting star. Osirian scientists studied it and, though they could not salvage it, figured out how to build another one.

Osiriat entered a colonial age. Colonists would be sent to find other habitable planets. Since it was suspected that immortality on Osiriat was a freak of nature, people were warned that they might lose it if they colonized. The volunteers did not care; the chance to be free to procreate overshadowed the advantages immortality offered.

Colonists, successful or not, were moving forward, whereas the Osirian immortals were stagnant. Osiriat was a paradise, but when you had forever to enjoy it, it lost its excitement. The immortals suffered the quandary of all immortal races: in order to move forward, they must create, but the laws concerning creation were very specific.

One day, a colonial shuttle came back. This was odd. Colonial shuttles never came back. Once free of Osirian rule, the euphoric colonists succeeded or failed on their own merit.

"Why have you returned?" The king asked.

"We had no intention to," their leader started. "As a matter a fact, when we found it, we almost decided to move on, but then we evaluated the situation. It is so exciting; the possibilities are so numerous-"

The king was slowly becoming agitated.

"Well, what is it, man?"

"We found humanoids!"

"Humanoids? Where?"

"We found a planet just over eight light years away. We named it Earth. The people there are primitive; however, they resemble us almost completely."

"Did you contact them?"

"No, we only observed. We considered them too primitive to contact."

"You say they resemble us. Are they immortal?"

"No."

The king dismissed the colonists.

He called a meeting of the governors.

The king announced, "We have a report of a primitive humanoid race on a planet called Earth. Because they are primitive, I've decided not to contact them. I seek your approval for an experimental plan.

The report states that they are very similar to us. I propose that we watch them until they become a technologically advanced society. This will serve two purposes. One, we may discover things about our past that we have forgotten. Also, when we are ready to contact them, we'll understand them. They may prove a powerful ally. Together, we will spread humanoids throughout the galaxy. Do you approve of this?"

A unanimous "yes" filled his ears.

"Then I ask each of you to pick a team to observe Earth."

Five observation missions were considered failures because mankind never advanced enough to survive.

CHAPTER 2

TRAINING THE GODS

Jupoler and Arop, both lost in thought, continued staring through the window at Osiriat. One year ago, the group came to this space station to prepare for their mission, carrying the stigma of the five failed missions. It was Jupoler and Arop's burning desire to prove themselves. This was especially difficult because Tarus insisted that their little toddler brother, Planex, be included in the mission, adding the extra burden of "babysitting" to their already strenuous schedules. In spite of the extra demands on their time, they excelled in every part of the training and earned the co-captain status that had been handed to them because of who they were.

Training consisted of space flight procedures: when and where to hibernate, earth mathematics and mechanics, geography (where to land and where to settle), monument erecting and why, how to find survivors, and most importantly, non-theology classes. Classes were toned down for Planex who spent most of his time playing, inventing games and stories he would use to relate when they reached Earth.

Jupoler remembered the final day of classes. The exams that day would determine if anyone was to be left behind. He was proud of his crew.

Everyone knew when and where he or she was to hibernate. All seemed comfortable with the theory, however, none had experienced it;

they had only lain in the containers as a comfort test. The real test would come the night before the launch.

When quizzed about earth mathematics and mechanics, noise levels rose as everyone fought to be the first to answer:

"Earth speeds through space at sixty-six thousand miles per hour!"

"A day is 24 hours long!"

"Their year is three hundred sixty-five days!"

"They have four seasons!"

The instructors were satisfied the math had been retained.

Nepeta asked to explain the geography and launched into a speech complete with elevation levels, city layouts, the process they were considering for rescue based on geography, how they were going to attempt to find Tarus' city, and how they were going to know where to land. Everyone nodded in agreement, assuring the instructors they all understood.

The question of monuments was directed to Uryxs because he had an architect's mind. Again, everyone nodded in agreement as he spoke. Officially, they were to hold back monuments as a last resort. Tarus' group had used them to warn man that there was going to be a major catastrophe, but man chose to ignore the signs.

Instead, his vanity had allowed him to take credit for building the monuments with slave labor. Two distinct religious bases, one with many gods, created by those in power to justify their excesses, and one that raised one true god, created by those enslaved to add hope to their otherwise hopeless lives, grew around the monuments. Clashes over belief systems caused continual strife. Man suffered the centuries battling over ideologies and ignored the message inherent in the monuments.

Because of man's blindness, he was destined to fail once again. The experiment Jupoler's group was conducting pivoted on the hope that the new race they created would be smart enough to read the stars, but if not, monuments would again be erected. Hopefully, they would have a clearer message than Tarus'.

Uryxs, in his speech, had brought up the question of religion. The head instructor asked, "Does everyone understand why we don't want religion to form?"

"Because of what happened after Tarus' group built the monuments," Satetan answered, supporting her brother's last statements.

"That's partially true," the instructor conceded, "anyone else?"

Mercianiax stood and said, "Their race has always had gods. They put too much faith in their gods, believing the gods will take care of everything in life, when, in reality, they are just a figment of the people's imagination. The gods who arose during Tarus' mission were just the newest in a series."

"And what have these gods caused?" The instructor asked.

Vienusia answered, "They blinded man's eyes. He saw the world around him as belonging to the gods and, therefore, didn't see the warning signs."

Arop added, "My father discovered, through his observations, that man naturally revered gods because he sought out answers to the mysteries of life. Tarus' group inadvertently added fuel to this natural fire. He was not supposed to interfere with man's natural evolvement, but he made a serious mistake. Instead of basing his group in space, he stationed them, for their comfort, on an uninhabited continent. He built a wonderful city equipped with gravitational machines that kept his group immortal. When a lost Greek sailor found the city, Tarus, instead of killing him, befriended him. He introduced the sailor to his group, told him they were immortal gods, and warned him that they did not wish to be revered. When he was caught revering them, Tarus ordered the city destroyed and covered the continent with a veil of ice.

"The Greek sailor barely escaped with his life. The first port he stumbled upon was Egyptian. He told his story about the gods. The king was summoned. He kept this story of the gods in his mind, and when the monuments appeared, he formed a religion in their honor.

"Meanwhile, in Greece, the sailor had told his story. When news of the new monuments arrived, the gods were also revered here. The sailor had been too long at sea and had forgotten Tarus's name so he'd made names up. That is how the mythical Olympian gods were invented."

Jupoler interrupted.

"We will emphasize non-religion to the humans as part of our goal to suppress this basic human desire. We have every confidence that Osirian blood will dominate and that the quest for knowledge will lead to science rather than religion. So, although we'll teach non-religion, it is only as an added precaution that we do.

"Mankind has failed every four to five thousand years for at least the last twenty-five thousand, mostly due to these false gods." He turned to face his peers. "Osiriat has, for many millennia, sought an alliance with these humans. Up until now, one has not been possible or practical. Our royalty is tired of dealing with these incompetent humans. We will create a new race. This grand experiment will prove, finally, if the problem is inherent to the planet or the species. If we succeed, we will have created another strong, space-faring planet. Our society frowns on us procreating on Osiriat, so we will procreate elsewhere."

"Very well put, Son."

Jupoler, surprised, turned to the door.

"Father, what brings you to the training station?"

"I wanted to witness your final exam. Since I ordered this mission, I wished for proof that it would succeed. Listening to you all has proven it to me beyond a doubt. Do any of you have any concerns?"

"I do, Father," Arop said. "My question concerns the new race we are to create. If they are half Osirian, shouldn't we do everything we can to help them? We have learned that we can guide them toward the signs, even create events on Earth that will cause them to believe in us as gods, but why can't we actually help them."

"Arop, the reason is simple. Yes, they will be half Osirian. Regardless, we have to know if the inability of humanoids on the planet to read the signs is inherent in the planet itself. In other words, is there something about the planet, its beauty perhaps, that blinds humans? Our ultimate goal has always been to have a partner in space, but that partner must prove worthy; he must succeed or fail on his own merit. If we held his hand as society expanded, he would eventually expand into space as we wish, but he would be too weak to make decisive decisions. You will find that occasionally, you will need to guide him onto the right path. If he loses faith in you nine, he will seek faith elsewhere. Do you understand?"

"Yes, Father. It is clear to me now."

"Remember, Arop, if it becomes blurry during your mission, you can always contact me."

She felt they had been staring at Osiriat for an eternity. Arop turned to face Jupoler. He was taller than she, close to Tarus's height, and destined to surpass him; otherwise, he had the same black hair and blue eyes as his father. He was deep in thought, and she decided to try to cheer him up, "You know that father is proud of us-."

"Yes, he is very proud of you." The deep voice, odd for one so young, indicated to him that it was Uryxs who interrupted Arop. His hand rested upon Jupoler's shoulder. "We are all proud of our captains."

He turned to see them all standing there. Completely engulfed in their thoughts, they had not heard the group approach.

He took in the three pairs, the new graduates. Nepeta and Vienusia visibly struggled. He knew they would rather be in the sea than at this reception. Mercianiax and Marsax seemed more comfortable because they preferred neither water nor land. They were confident in any environment. Uryxs and Satetan, pale skin inherited as part of their forest lifestyle, looked as if they wanted to hide or at least blend in; the attention was taken off of them. He thought, "My friends, you may need to hide where we're going. They truly can't know we're..."

His thought was interrupted by Planex, who ran across the room, hugged him, and, looking up at him with hopeful, mischievous eyes, asked, "Wanna play, Brother?"

"Not now, little brother, there will be time for that at home." Planex frowned then quickly brightened as Vienusia laid her hand on his shoulder.

Jupoler's attention again turned to the three pairs of siblings.

"Are you all going home before you come to the capital for our bon voyage party?"

Vienusia answered, "Oh yes! We must all go home and wrap up our affairs in case something goes wrong."

Arop, sensing an awkward moment, said, with as much enthusiasm as she could muster, "Then we shall see you all in two weeks at the castle!"

Earth: May 1940

The delivery room was cold dreary. The window cooler was set on high, combating the summer heat, feeling uncomfortable, she thought about asking the nurse to turn it off but then concluded that cold was exactly what her life was. Although she'd been in labor for nine hours, her husband was not there. He was in England helping plan a way to stop the most ruthless man history had ever seen -- HITLER.

It was a cold, harsh, cruel world that she had been impregnated in, but she could still hope because all babies brought hope. When, at last, the pain ended, and the little girl was in her arms, all of her bitterness toward the world left her. She quietly whispered to her daughter, "Yes, you will make a difference."

CHAPTER 3

DEPARTURE

Crystalia

The morning following the reception found them in the transport bay. Five airlock bays led to five planetary shuttles. Departure signs above the bays listed Crystalia, Lonix, Isoloquat, and Gosiria as the intended destinations. Two bays were labeled Gosiria. Shuttle technicians scurried about conducting last-minute safety checks. The earth mission could not be jeopardized now. The passengers thought it overkill, but the techs had their orders. A shuttle accident among these passengers would mean a death sentence. Their parents had arrived earlier. Each set of children bid a sad farewell to them as the elders boarded the first shuttle bound for Gosiria. The children then walked morosely to their separate transports, sad because their final home visit would not include their parents. Planex was fixated on the stream of blinking lights. Arop picked him up to get them moving.

Once they boarded, the transport coordinates were locked in. A memory chip recorded the facts and auto-launched the transports in sequence. The passengers had no way to control the descent, so they leaned back, relaxed, and planned their two-week furloughs at home.

Nepeta and Vienusia launched immediately after the parents. The trip was short. To the observer it would have appeared they were going to crash land in the middle of the ocean, far from any civilization. The transport, designed to dive three hundred feet below the surface and then automatically flood the interior, landed perfectly. As the water came in, their legs fused into tails, and they took one last deep breath. Nepeta pushed the ejection button when Vienusia indicated she was ready, and they were flung out into the sea.

Swimming north, instinctively, through pitch-black waters, the ocean floor rose to meet them. Soon, they found themselves in one hundred feet of crystal blue water. The combination of the white sandy bottom and the brightness of the giant sun allowed them to see as if in perfect daylight.

Vienusia, at four, was constantly learning from her older brother, Nepeta, now six. She watched him now, swimming ahead of her, as he led them out of the darkness. He was a long child, typical of males from Crystalia, built hydrodynamically correct. He had no body hair except for a few blonde patches on top of his conical head. Like her, he had webbed feet and hands, allowing for faster speeds in the water. As the water became crystal-blue, she broke the silence using the high-pitched, chirping, sonar-like language they used when under the sea.

"Nepeta, how will we see in the darkness of Earth?"

"What do you mean?"

"Don't you remember from training? They don't have two suns, and the sun they do have is one and a half times smaller and thirty-five times dimmer than our own Sirius," she emphasized, obviously very worried.

"I remember. Father taught me that although they have fewer crystal blue seas, sight shouldn't be a problem as long as we use our undersea language when swimming. Our natural sonar will allow us to locate each other."

They continued, in silence, swimming north. The first sign of civilization was the work of the sea harvesters, each armed with a trident sword for self-defense, busy gathering vegetation and checking traps as they did daily. Working beneath a canopy of seaweed to protect themselves from the sun, they were responsible for feeding the entire city. Harvesting was an art form that created a surplus. The surplus was the catalyst that allowed this first civilization to travel and colonize the planet. Over millennia they spread first to the beach areas, then to the deep forests, finally expanding inland, creating a beautiful castle and planetary capital they named Gosiria. Over time, a certain isolationism formed between the four groups of civilization. There were sporadic wars until, finally, Gosiria brought them together in peace.

Below them, three hundred feet below the surface, they saw the murky outline of the great city. They saw it as a city anyway; it was simply a mound of dry caves. The caves had been formed millions of years ago in a series of volcanic eruptions that had opened an oxygen spring that filled the caves making them ideal for the formation of intelligent life. They were located deep enough to prevent the sun's rays from harming the inhabitants. Because much of their lives were spent underwater these humans adapted tails. In training, they learned that the only real physical difference between them and the humans they were going to help was the tail.

Closer to the caves, children were playing. Mothers taught them how to swim, how to recognize danger, and how to identify plants and animals to help them as they grew into workers in this society of gatherers. Even they carried mini tridents as predators frequented the outskirts of the city, waiting for a stray Crystalian to expose himself. Numerous past tragedies had convinced the people to become well-trained trident experts. Each civilized region of Osiriat used basic training techniques similar to those first developed by the Crystalians. As a result, most children, although not mature in body, were highly responsible and dependable by the age of four.

Nepeta and Vienusia found the cave entrance to their home, swam in, and up toward the stairs. Once there, they climbed out onto the dry deck, lost their tails, and regained their human form. Clothes were hanging next to the entrance. Vienusia slipped into a dress adorned with seashells and crystals that gave a shimmering effect, highlighting her beautiful blonde hair and blue eyes. Nepeta wrapped himself in a white toga; he preferred white because all of his color came from his piercing blue eyes and sea-tainted blue-blonde hair.

Nepeta went to his room. Someone would be living here soon. Crystalia operated on a communal basis so most of the fixtures in the room would stay; however, he did need to pack up personal belongings. He would entrust these to his parent's care until he returned.

Almost finished packing, a group of friends appeared. They waited outside of the entryway to his room, swishing their tails, treading water, separated from Nepeta by an oxygenated force field. When he looked up, their leader shrieked, "Nepeta, why are you wasting your sea leave doing that? Let your parents do it."

"I cannot. They are too busy running this city and have assured me they will give away anything I leave behind."

"Then do it later. Thick clouds have rolled in. We're going to surface."

"I'll be right behind you. Go on without me. It's going to take me a few moments to locate my trident."

He turned away from them and continued packing.

His friends did not hesitate, sped to the surface, and broke it with magnificent jumps. The farthest arched twenty-five feet up. Gravity corrected this breach and brought him rushing down with a great splash.

Nothing was more exciting to a Crystalian than a good surfacing day. Thick clouds allowed it. Festivities always started with jumping, followed by tail surfing. No wave was a bad wave, but storm waves were the best. A Crystalian catching a storm wave could surf all the way to Lonix. The greatest surfer, it was said, rode a wave all the way into the mainland. No one alive had ever met him, so he was regarded as a surfing myth. When they tired of surfing, they slowly headed home. Armed with tridents, this was a chance to hunt top water delicacies that were normally out of reach.

Nepeta found his trident, programmed the force field to allow him five seconds to pass, and dove out of his room into the sea. Slowly, he rose to the surface. He was excited about surfacing, but he wanted to impress these friends he had not seen in a year. Out of the corner of his eye, he saw movement. He loved animals and had modified his chirping to talk to them; he asked for and was granted a ride to the surface on a dolphin. Together, they rose, each swishing their powerful tails. The treading surfers located, they broke the water in the middle of them, flew thirty-five feet into the air, parted in opposite arches, each performed a triple summersault, and landed. Nepeta speared a fish and gave it to the dolphin as thanks. The dolphin rose vertically out of the water and swam backward using his tail, and happily chirped goodbye to Nepeta.

Already behind the other surfers, he attempted the first big wave that came to him. Unaccustomed to surfing because training had left him dry for two years, he failed to catch it. Angered by this inanimate object, he flung his trident violently toward it. Another surfer retrieved the trident, returned it to him, and told him to relax. Everyone understood he might not have his sea fins back after spending so much time in space. Embarrassed, he caught the next wave, surfed until he was alone, and then, saddened, dove deep to go home. He forgot to hunt as he was scolding himself for his violent outburst.

Vienusia had not seen her brother for four days. She finally caught up with him at the great feast the city prepared for their heroes. Vienusia heard about his violent outburst and was not surprised to see him sitting alone, pouting. She knew what she had to do.

Forming her brightest smile, she swam up to him and chirped, "Nepeta, cheer up, this party's for us. Don't spoil it."

He looked up. She interrupted his deep thought, and he did not recognize her right away, "Vienusia?" He chirped as if she were someone he had not seen in years, "Oh, Vienusia! How can I be happy? I tried to kill a wave and almost killed one of my friends. Will I ever be able to control my violent temper?"

"You must relax, Nepeta. That is the only way to control your violence. We're about to hibernate for sixty years. Maybe you'll grow out of this violent stage. Then again, maybe violence will be an asset on Earth.

Right now, let's have fun. Look at your friends, they don't look worried about the incident," she chirped. He looked up at her and was disarmed by her sweet, engaging smile.

He rose, and, hand in hand, they swam around the party. Well-wishers late into the evening overwhelmed them. The next day, one week before the reception, they started their swim toward the mainland. Once there, they took a transport to the castle, arrived a day early, and decided to sleep that day away.

Lonix

They watched the Crystalian transport leave, braced their bodies in expectation, but still noticed the tremendous jolt as they took off. From this height, Mercianiax and Marsax could see home, the long island chain located in the eastern ocean, almost reaching to the mainland. From space, it appeared to represent a bolt of lightning. Starting in the northwest, the islands spread in a straight line southeast, turned northeast for about a quarter of the original distance, and then turned southeast again only to stop abruptly, shy of the mainland.

The main island was the trade port of Lonix. Other islands, spread across the ocean, supplied the main island with produce, grains, and domestic meats.

Each island specialized in climatic production. Tropical islands exported fruits, coffee, beans, sugars, and opium. Opiates were widely used in medicine. Opium had arrived on the original transports, but was lost upon landing. The Osirians had discovered opium and its medicinal quality soon after the first few Crystalians were attacked at sea.

Domestic animals, including cattle, sheep, and pigs, were raised on the northern islands. They were grain-fed as wheat, barley, rye, oats and rice thrived in the north.

The southern sub-tropical islands were the homes of wild horses. Never domesticated in this sea-traveling society, they were hunted for meat and turned into glue. Natural to these islands were tobacco, olives, and hemp. Tobacco was used only ceremoniously, and hemp helped create the shipping industry.

All products were shipped to the natural port of Lonix. Well-centered, Lonix provided ninety percent of Osiriat's food sources.

Their transport was programmed to land in a deep cove just outside of the city of Lonix. It filled with water; they formed tails, took a deep breath, and ejected. Since it was a clear day, they swam along the over-grown shoreline until they entered the river that fed the lagoon. They exited where the triple canopy let in minimal damaging sunshine. Nude, they walked into the forest, their nostrils assaulted by the lingering scent of rotten leaves, a scent they had not forgotten while in space.

Massive ferns, tall and thick, wrapped through and around larger conifers, creating the first canopy. The second and third canopies consisted of deciduous trees at different developmental stages. Seasonally, they lost their leaves. Those that fell to the ground through the first canopy disintegrated in the rain, adding a layer of mulch. Soft mulch allowed them to travel barefoot and stealthily through the jungle.

On their way to Lonix, they did not worry about dressing. They exited into a clearing occupied by thatched-roof huts constructed of cane, resting on stilts. From each hut hung a rope ladder used to access the living quarters. Because of the giant sun's harmful rays, a thatch canopy constructed long ago on cloudy days covered the clearing.

The village was deserted because it was a clear day. Clear days were reserved for activities that took place under the forest canopy, which included hunting and gathering wild fruits and vegetables. The forest provided such an abundance of food that farming never developed here. These days were also used to explore their island, and over time, coupled with cloudy days, they worked their way to the mainland. Society eventually spread onto the mainland and into the deep forests. Each new community was set up as a trading center, but a four-year drought created too many cloudless days and the island society lost touch with the mainland five years after Tarus' mission launched.

Usually they brought back a surplus of game. On cloudy days, they headed to the ocean to fish or, if they had a surplus of food and game, they traded with Crystalia for seafood delicacies. Surfers, landing on Lonix, would be sent as messengers, and soon, Crystalian goods would arrive. Trading for seafood took place in the sea, and game took place on land, thus honoring each other's lifestyles. Trading slowed in the era when Lonix was expanding onto the mainland, and over time, Crystalia was forgotten. The last war had changed that, and trading resumed.

Mercianiax and Marsax climbed the rope ladder into their house, each to his own room, and got dressed. He found a pair of animal skin shorts and wore nothing else because of the heat. She did the same with a two-piece. She quickly gathered her spear, torch, and scarf to camouflage her blood-red hair. She found Mercianiax on his way out of his room with his wand. He used his enchanted wand to hypnotize small animals, tricking them into rushing Marsax.

They walked to the edge of the village. As Mercianiax was pulling on a camouflaged hat to cover his bright red hair, Marsax came up with a plan.

"The way I figure it, Mercianiax," she began, "is our villagers have headed to the other side of the island to hunt wild boar and elk. Moving as a group they will have frightened most of the small game back to this side of the island. With my skill, we will bring many trophies home," she stated vainly. "When we find game, I will depend on you to flush it out."

"Don't worry, Sister. If I get their attention, they'll be sitting ducks for you."

They located a trail and headed out amongst the ferns. At a clearing, Marsax hand signaled Mercianiax. He quietly edged his way over to the far side. In the mood for fun, he chirped like a squirrel and rolled a hunk of wood out into the clearing. Marsax, adrenaline rushing, threw her spear and "killed" the wood. Mercianiax laughed so hard he fell into the clearing. He abruptly quit when her spear landed inches from his head.

Marsax pulled the spear out of the ground.

"Mercianiax, you are a funny boy. You and I both enjoy a good joke, but don't ever mess with me on the hunt! Now, go. Scout another clearing, and, this time, be serious."

He smiled. "Okay, Sister. I just wanted to have a little fun. Let's go fill up your game bag." He ran into the forest, making as much noise as possible, continuing the joke.

She followed his trail but soon lost sight of it. The trail ended at another clearing. There was no sign of him anywhere.

Then she heard a rustling of leaves across from her. Mercianiax stood and yelled, and as he did, a squirrel ran out into the clearing. Marsax waited. Mercianiax then chirped like a squirrel and held up his enchanted wand. When the squirrel turned toward the noise, the wand began to work. Mercianiax was very inventive. A chameleon-like hologram turned him into a large squirrel. The squirrel was mesmerized. Now Marsax acted. A quick toss of her spear skewered the squirrel.

The pair encircled the village, hunting as a team. Marsax's game bag was so full she could not close it for their return. They had done the right thing. It was impolite to return to the village without game.

The village compound was full of people processing the day's hunt. Marsax poured her game bag onto the processing skin and boasted that she and Mercianiax were a brilliant hunting team. An elder gave her a stern look.

"You have brought us many fine small animals, but look around you. This whole village has been successful. Every one of us is a great hunter. We shall have a feast to celebrate this hunt and to welcome you home. Maybe we shall even trade with Crystalia for seafood, but after the feast, we don't wish to deprive our own people."

Mercianiax and Marsax excused themselves. They, like Nepeta and Vienusia, collected keepsakes and took them to their parent's house. That evening, in the enclosure where there were no longer any signs of meat processing, a great feast was held. A wild boar and an elk were cooked over an open pit. Fruits and vegetables were laid out as appetizers.

As the people began to eat, a night surfer from Crystalia landed on the beach. He said the smell of meat had lured him ashore and asked to join the feast. As he was eating he informed the elders that clouds were forming in the east and, in a couple of days, Crystalia would be ready to trade if Lonix could gather more meat. The elders sent Mercianiax, his name meant the messenger, with the Crystalian back to Crystalia to set up the trading day. Mercianiax was happy to go because he wanted to see Nepeta and Vienusia. He asked Marsax to come along, but she declined.

Marsax did not want to go. The elders announced at the banquet that tomorrow, another hunting trip would go forth to produce enough game to trade with Crystalia. Marsax eagerly volunteered. She and a group of friends were going to help. This would be her last possible Osirian hunt for thousands of years. Let Mercianiax waste his time in Crystalia; she could not miss this. Who knew if she would be allowed to hunt on Earth?

The elders split the villagers into groups; each group was assigned a job. Marsax's group of three boys and three girls was assigned the task of rear guard. Any animals that slipped through the ring of "real" hunters were to be frightened to return by these screaming, arm-waving kids.

Marsax, naturally the leader of her group, put her foot down. "These spears you carry aren't just symbols. Did you guys see all the game I brought back yesterday? We are on a hunt. We must kill!"

"But that was small game," one of the boys protested.

"Small or large, my spear will down them all."

Through her confidence, their decision was made. They would disobey orders and kill whatever came their way.

Moments after the decision was made, a wild boar broke through the line and headed toward the children. Excited by the large pig, a rare thing happened; Marsax missed. Easily enraged, her emerald green eyes turned a dark jade, illuminating her blood-red hair. The others were frightened. They backed away, afraid she would take revenge on them for not moving against the boar quickly.

When she calmed down, she invited the others into a conference.

"I'm not angry with you," she assured them. "I'm angry with me. I'm not used to missing."

She laid out a plan where each individual would act like a barrier to trap the next beast. Once trapped, she volunteered to kill it.

They did not wait long. A frightened elk burst through the trees. Little hunters quickly encircled it. Fear, panic, and antlers could have done much damage were it not for Marsax's bloodthirsty actions. She leaped at the beast, first spearing it in the side, then, when it stumbled, slicing its throat. She made a quick cut and stood up, holding its dripping heart for all to see. There were none to see. Her vicious action scared the others. They were running back to the village. Alone, she dragged the carcass back home. The elders returned with their own game later. They congratulated Marsax and scolded the others. Though Marsax had broken the rules, running from the field was a worse, cowardly offense.

Marsax, alone because the others blamed her for their punishment, was excited when Mercianiax returned. He had learned much about trade but barely missed Nepeta and Vienusia. A couple hours later, they boarded a transport to Gosiria. The transport stopped on a mainland beach to pick up Nepeta and Vienusia. Although separated for only a short time, it was a joyous reunion spent talking about what they would do before the reception. Of all the ideas, sleep won out.

Isoloquat

Uryxs and Satetan braced for impact. They detested water landings, preferred solid land to the sea, felt more comfortable on two legs, and considered their tails an atrocity.

They ejected and quickly swam to the cliffs. Long ago, the islanders found this cave entrance they were using to enter the mainland. It safely opened up, out of reach of the giant sun's harmful rays, into a deep, triple-canopied forest. At the mouth of the cave, they climbed out of the water. Quickly fanning their tails, they recovered their legs.

Isoloquotions had left them clothes at the exit to the cave. Uryxs put on a sky-blue robe that fit like a glove. Still only six, people were certain he would grow up to be a finely cut sculpture of a man. The robe helped to highlight his pale features and white hair. His dark blue eyes offset his nearly albino appearance. Satetan's brown eyes neatly contrasted with her pale skin and white hair. She slipped into a brown dress, and they walked toward Isoloquat.

He let her walk ahead. She was five and needed to develop her leadership skills. It was his habit to allow her to learn whenever possible because he was already well-practiced in leadership.

Isoloquat's capitol city, a small village, lay two days due east of the canopied cave exit. Satetan led them north. All other directions were lightly covered. Because of their pale skin, they could not risk exposure to the giant sun. If they could have journeyed directly east, they would have arrived in the village later that same evening, but she was forced to choose a zigzag path that ran constantly under thick cover.

Slowly, they picked their way under the triple canopy. Trails didn't exist here. Often, their clothes snagged on the thick underbrush.

Ferns hid the forest animals that chose to live on the floor. Occasionally, as she brushed past a fern, panicked animals would bolt across their path.

Uryxs, sensing danger, signaled Satetan to stop. They lay on the forest floor, waiting. Quick as a flash, a tiger sprang out and captured a panicked rodent.

Uryxs directed Satetan to cautiously encircle the tiger. Busy playing with its food, it did not notice them.

Picking their way home, they soon came upon a thorny hedge surrounding a small hill. They walked along the hedge until they came to a small river.

Satetan laughed, "Look, Uryxs! Everyone came out to greet us."

Uryxs soaked in the scene. What he observed looked less like a greeting party and more like a picnic. Children were swimming in the river, some adults were washing clothes, and still others were processing game. A smell wafted by him, and he realized he was famished. A giant fire pit was being stoked while a water buffalo turned slowly on the spit. No one had seen them arrive.

"Come, Satetan. Let's walk up river and swim into the festivities. We'll swim in underwater, surface, and see if anyone notices."

They walked west up the river. When they turned, they saw what most travelers did not. Since they had grown up here, they knew what to look for. Similar to Crystalia, the city was a series of caves. These caves were covered in jungle underbrush. The village was so totally camouflaged that most travelers simply missed it. Individual caves were simple to spot by natives. Little things like small breaks in the brush or small plumes coming out of nowhere, carrying barely distinguishable cooking odors, told them where the inhabited caves were.

Within five years of discovering the mainland entrance, the Lonixians had moved east and discovered these caves. The first settlers were here to serve Lonix. They processed cane and thatch for island dwellings. Lonix paid for these building materials with Crystalian seafood and Lonixian processed meats and produce, grateful that they did not have to deplete their own limited island resources.

Villagers named their new home and forest that surrounded it Isoloquat, which meant hidden home. Not everyone was employed in building material processing; a select few were employed as hunters.

Over time, these hunters discovered new territories. They built a trade route east to the edge of the forest, overlooking a natural lake. At each important stop, villages were built and castle-dominated trading centers naturally built up around them.

Trade with Lonix prospered, despite sporadic wars, for many decades. Then, a four-year drought hit. Cloudless days were in abundance. Lonix and Isoloquat lost touch. Trading continued between the villages but eventually faded as superstitions arose concerning the cause of the drought. Villages became islands. No one from the outside was trusted. A thirty-year period of isolation began. The people of Isoloquat lost touch with the world. When the Lonixians "rediscovered" the mainland, they sent emissaries to contact any people they might encounter. Outsiders were seen as evil. These emissaries were killed. A sporadic, stagnant war was fought between Lonix and Isoloquat. The people of Isoloquat retreated deep into hiding, abandoning the trade route. When Gosiria ended the war and became the center of world government, the trade route was reopened to secure the peace.

Uryxs and Satetan waded into the water and swam downstream. Underwater, they worked their way into the middle of the villagers. Uryxs signaled Satetan to abandon the surfacing plan. They continued on to the caves.

When they reached the shore at the base of the hill, Satetan asked, "Uryxs, why didn't you want to surface?"

"I remembered we have one more job to do. We need to empty our caves of personal possessions and transfer them to mom and dad's cave. When we finish, we'll be able to join the party."

Completing their task, they walked back to the water and swam back out to the party. When they broke the surface, cheers arose from the villagers.

The feasting continued all night. "Farewells" and "good lucks" flowed. When dawn rose, they set out again for Gosiria. Slowly, they worked their way north along the river. When it cut east, so did they.

They rested at different trade castles, feasting nightly with excited Isoloquans. Ten days, and no incidents with predators later, they arrived at the edge of the forest.

They stopped here, under the canopy, to dress. As they pulled on their coverings, they each began to itch. There had been a tiny incident. Satetan had led them into a batch of poison fern. They had shed and burned their infested clothing. Uryxs, as they walked naked to the next castle, scolded himself for allowing Satetan to lead them into the ferns. The castle physician bathed them in a solution that nearly cured them. Clothing was provided. Uryxs assured them it would be returned once they reached Gosiria.

Covered completely as protection against the sun's violent rays, they resumed their walk along the river, following it until it emptied into Gosiria's lake. Choosing to remain on dry land, they avoided the lake entrance. The castle was a new experience for them. They spent a couple of days touring it, never running into their parents. The day before the reception, they decided to rest.

Satetan said, "Uryxs, I spoke with Vienusia and Marsax when their shuttle arrived. Everyone believes that the reception tomorrow may be slightly overwhelming. The others are going to relax in quarters and probably sleep the day away. What do you think?"

"I think we deserve a day of rest."

Gosiria

They splashed into the deep lake east of the castle. Thousands of years ago when the last glaciers retreated north, a five hundred foot deep canyon several miles long formed. Over time, rain created a natural lake. A river, which began as a stream at the southern end of the glaciers, flowed into the lake and emptied at the southwest corner, continuing to the ocean. The river was a natural trade route and the lake was the natural place to build Gosiria.

Isoloquat's hunters established the trade route from the edge of the sea to the edge of the forest. One day, the governor of Isoloquat, on an inspection tour, came to the edge of the forest. There, he looked out across the plain. The shimmering lake intrigued him. Here, he would build the grandest castle on the line. He called the city and lake Gosiria.

Volunteers, infected with his excitement, built it. First they built a village at the edge of the forest for workers. The workers slept during the day and built at night. Stones quarried from the mountains to the north of the plain formed the walls of the castle and the wall surrounding the castle. A wall, four hundred acres in diameter, encircled fields, which, when properly irrigated, produced an abundance of food. This was the Osirian's first agricultural experimental acreage. Farming and ranching ideas originated in Lonix and were implemented here. Once it was determined every domesticated crop and animal flourished here, crossbreeding began. New breeds resisted spoiling once harvested. This allowed them to be delivered along the trade routes without being cooled or preserved. Immortal Osirians were normal humans in that sickness could invade their bodies. Eating these new foods they effectively neutralized all viral and bacterial strains. The surplus created, in both plants and animals, and the added bonus of fresh fish, quickly transformed Gosiria into the world trade center.

People from each region came here to trade. Isoloquans were seen more frequently than Crystalians and Lonixians as Isoloquans were middlemen.

The castle was the grandest in the world. Isoloquan workers who built it related to it and began calling themselves Gosirians. Gosiria's castle consisted of living quarters for the farmers, ranchers, and house staff, a trading center larger than any on the route, and government offices. The governors became incredibly wealthy and took on royal airs.

The city began to feel privileged. It had risen in the middle of a plain, a direct challenge to the giant sun. No other region had dared challenge the sun. Eventually, being the trade center of the world was not enough. Citizens complained to the governors that Gosiria was dominant and should control all trade. The governors, always willing to add to their treasury, formed and trained a military force. Isoloquat's closest trade castle was the first target.

The transport did not stop until it reached a depth of three hundred feet. Jupoler gave Arop a relieved look and turned to see Planex sound asleep, too young to realize he should have been worried. Lake landings could turn dangerous.

Arop shook Planex awake as Jupoler prepared to eject them. Water rushed in. As they grew tails, Jupoler reminded them to take deep breaths, ejected and they quickly swam westward until they found a cave. Arop kept Planex focused. Each time he saw a school of fish, a mischievous smile spread across his face and he sped swam into them, laughing as they scattered. Arop's duty was to rein him in. Shortly after the last incident, they surfaced in the cave and walked a distance to the castle. Reaching a dead end, they dove back into the water and swam under the wall, into the moat, and into the castle.

They climbed out of the water with their hands, waited until their legs reappeared, slipped into waiting togas, and each went to his assigned room. Jupoler and Arop packed for the trip and headed off to the ship to do a final maintenance check. Planex stayed in his room and played.

His eyes adjusted after a few moments. He could have turned on a light but preferred darkness. Shapes began to form.

"Cool, my toy box!"

He ran over to it and dumped it out. Remembering his lessons, he used wooden blocks and seashells to build a monument. He fell asleep when he completed it, the day's excitement finally catching up to him.

The next morning, he rose, took a tired look at his work, ran over, and kicked it across the room.

"Take that, you stupid humans! That'll teach you not to ignore Tarus' monuments. What? You're not afraid of me? You will be!"

He gathered up his plastic figurines, stuffed animals, and all the things that lived in his mind.

"Now I will destroy Earth. What do you think about that?"

Silence.

"Stubborn to the end, huh? Now you must die!" He yelled as he kicked them across the room.

Over the next two weeks, except at mealtimes, Planex stayed in his room replaying the games he learned in training. They were not always morbid. He played with numbers, letters, and symbols, too, as he was the crewmember assigned to first contact the children. He was a mess when Arop came to fetch him.

Arop saw that Jupoler had things under control. She excused herself, intent on walking through the castle. It amazed her that her ancestors built this gigantic complex, a warning to the giant sun that humanity could survive anywhere. She could not look out the windows because it was a clear day. The windows automatically blackened on clear days and cleared at dark or on cloudy days.

As she walked the halls, people gave her knowing glances of approval because of the upcoming mission. Occasionally, someone would avert his eyes. She was six and no longer bothered by this behavior. It did, however, bring back memories of her younger days.

At age four, she had finally been allowed to walk the halls alone. People knew she was royalty and naturally averted their eyes as she passed. Not realizing this reaction was natural, she became quite upset.

She felt wounded and demanded that soldiers escort her, and, to humor her, they did. Two people who averted their eyes were arrested by her soldiers. Once imprisoned, she had the soldiers destroy their homes. The soldiers did not hesitate; child or no, a royal order could not be refused. However, they did report the incident to her father, who quickly intervened. He sat her down and explained to her that the citizens averted their eyes because she was royalty.

"I have even heard, Arop, that the citizens believe your paleness represents the power of our sun. They consider you bright, pure, and holy and believe it is a sin to gaze upon anything so holy."

Because of her father's explanation, she no longer let the peasant's actions bother her.

She spent the day visiting friends and relatives. She needed to today because she was required to stay in her room out of sight until the reception.

A group of friends met her in the recreation room. They, as a group, were upset; they wanted to go on the mission with her. A couple cried because they were going to miss Arop.

She consoled them, "Oh, my friends, I will miss you, too. I am told my mission is so highly important that it can only be trusted to royalty, but I'm not the only one with an important mission. You left behind on Osiriat, must keep the planet pure. When I come back after successfully saving Earth, I will check on your results. If you have kept this planet pure, I will hire you as my councilors. Whatever my title when I return, I'll need people surrounding me who know the pulse of the planet. Don't be sad. Your job is just as important as mine."

Her friends reassured her, and she went to visit her relatives. One elder gave her a similar speech. When darkness fell, she excused herself and hurried back to her room. When she arrived, she found her window had cleared. Nighttime was the only healthy time to work outside, and she hoped...

Yes! There he is! She stared out at the work being done in the fields. He was much older, tan, strong, and manly. As she watched him, she daydreamed, hoping the mission would bring her as fine a man as this.

Jupoler turned away from the window, tired of watching the workers. His entire day was spent slaving away on the ship. It should not have taken so long, but friends and relatives, assuming he would be there, had come to visit.

The visitors took time away from his work, but he loved the ship and truly did not want to go home early. He ran diagnostic checks on the navigational systems, the engines, the hibernation chambers, the expandable cargo holds, checked the gravitational storage capacity, and checked the chambers for leaks. Stellar cartography maps were carefully inserted into the computer.

The total workload was about two hours. Each visitor set him back as he felt he needed to entertain. His entire focus was never on the visitor, though. Phrases were slipped into the conversation that required his visitor to help him work. For example, when his uncle, whom he knew was a qualified navigational expert, visited, he dispensed with the small talk:

"Uncle, how did your computer perform when you navigated our solar system?"

"It was tricky staying out of Golas' grip. We did get close enough for Golas to play hell with our magnetic directional gauge. Have you solved that problem? After all, you will be using Golas."

"Yes, the scientists installed a demagnification unit around my directional gage."

"Uh-huh. Look, Son, I have to go. I didn't come here to work."

In this way, Jupoler encouraged his visitors to leave. If it was their idea to leave, he was not being rude.

The visitor he looked forward to and would not allow any interruptions of was the computer's builder. Together, they ran a final diagnostic check. Three systems were stripped and rebuilt to create a more efficient computer. When the doctor finished, he asked the computer, "How do you feel?"

"I feel brand new. My efficiency is up twenty percent. Thank you, doctor."

Finished, Jupoler locked up the ship and headed back to his room.

He settled down now and contemplated the next two weeks, which would be spent getting his affairs in order and the affairs of the mission. He recited the mission specifications in his dreams.

Thirteen days later, Jupoler wrapped up the last details and started to truly relax and think about the reception. The others had arrived today and were sleeping. He decided that was a good idea and went to bed.

He saw tails floating in the water, looked closer, and saw the mangled bodies. Much of Crystalia was destroyed. It saddened him because they had created civilization.

"Why has this happened, father?" Jupoler asked.

He knew Tarus was there, but some unknown force kept him on the fringes of sight.

"I told you before, son. Your memory at seven should be good enough to recall it."

"Father, it's the pain. My mind can't see past these people's pain. Please tell me what happened."

"Alright. When Gosiria was built to protect us from the giant sun, the people began to feel superior. 'We have conquered the sun. Now let's conquer the world,' was the cry that went up. We decided to use the abandoned mainland trade routes to achieve victory. Most castles agreed to join us peacefully; the others we took by force.

"When we arrived in Isoloquat, we found that they were already in a war with the islanders. They were trying to stop them from spreading inland. They saw our superior numbers, joined us, and helped us take

island after island until we took their capital city of Lonix. From Lonix, Crystalia was easy prey, so trusting they didn't realize we wanted a fight.

"We gazed upon the carnage, each wondering how we descended from such a weak society. Then a lady surfaced and swam towards us. She saw the dead and shrieked at us, 'Why!' We couldn't answer; her sheer beauty had knocked the breath out of us.

"We came to realize that we had come to land out of beauty, not weakness. The four ruling families decided at that moment to sign a peace treaty. We agreed to have the planetary capital in Gosiria, reopen the trade routes, and rule equally. As king and queen, your mother and I make the final decisions, but we always consider the ideas of our governors. Your friends from the mission are all the children of my co-rulers."

He started awake, looked around, and realized he was in his room. He would have to ask his father who that woman was in a few hours. It was almost reception time.

Arop was very tired. She stayed up late every night preparing for this mission. Last night was no different. When she awoke, it was already midday on reception day. She rushed to get ready, and as she did, she recalled the dream that awoke her:

"Mother, why have I been chosen for this mission? I'm only six."

"You've been picked because, as royalty, it is your duty. We must send you while there is still time for you to do the job," Elysia answered enthusiastically. Her skin seemed to brighten when she was enthusiastic. "Why? Don't you want to go?"

"Of course I want to go. Castle life is so boring.

"Mother, you have the sight. Am I going to succeed?"

"Arop you know my power doesn't reach into other systems. You will no doubt succeed because you will remain immortal. That is why we are sending you children. It should take sixty years to get there in which time your bodies will have aged only ten years. You will have until you're fifty to get the job done. Being Osirian royalty you should be able to finish the job in time."

"Mother, why is it so important to colonize this planet anyway?"

Arop saw Elysia sigh, "As I said before. It is important that we colonize any planet we can. Most planets take to us right away, but this one has eluded us five times. Our immortality makes overpopulation a real problem on Osiriat, so the king of Gosiria decided long ago to colonize.

"Our citizens are only allowed one child before they become immortal at age fifty. Some citizens don't like this rule because it doesn't apply to the governors. They are the people who usually volunteer for colony duty. We know that our second sun, the dwarf Golas, has a gravitational pull that actually prevents our bodies from degenerating. Our bodies are perfect by age fifty. The people who colonize are aware that over time, with no exposure to Golas, they will die.

"After five Earth missions observed mankind fail, colonization of Earth lost favor and was abandoned. Gosiria decided to colonize our own planet. The Great War that united the planet was as much about Gosiria's colonization as it was about overpopulation. Wars kill, and we needed to diminish our numbers. When we united and colonization was discussed, everyone was in favor of it. Earth surfaced again as the best choice."

"But Mother Earth has no dwarf star. Is my team destined to die?"

"We don't think so. We have spent years harnessing the dwarf's gravity. As long as your team doesn't spend too much time away from the ship, you should retain immortality."

"What do you mean? You don't know for sure? What about the other missions? Did they fail because of the immortality question?"

"We're not sure why they failed. One theory is that these observation missions traveled to and from Osiriat routinely because the technology for retaining immortality while traveling in space was unknown. We think people on Earth simply forgot our lessons, went their own way, and failed. That's one of the reasons we're sending your little brother Planex...."

Planex, she suddenly remembered. I'm supposed to make sure Planex is ready for the reception.

When she entered his room, Planex was playing a game he had invented about the earthlings. There were figures decapitated and mutilated all over his room. He sat in the dark. She turned on the light and saw his gloomy expression.

"What are you doing, Planex?"

"I was playing 'shields up!' Look at them. They're all dead!" He shrieked proudly.

"Oh, Planex, you're so morbid for a two-year-old. You should be playing happy games. Hurry up and dress so that we can go to the reception and have fun."

Planex dressed slowly. He pouted because Arop stopped his game. She was his sister, and he loved her, but she could be so mean. Only if Vienusia had fetched him. She would have played for a while. He smiled whenever he thought of Vienusia because she was his best friend. Excited by these thoughts, he quickly put on his shoes and ran out of the room. Arop ran to catch him.

"Why are you running, Planex?"

"Because, Sister, we're going to see Vienusia. Hurry up!"

The Reception

Arop and Planex rushed down the hall toward the reception room. Approaching a line of guests, they ducked into an anteroom before anyone spotted them. Planex smiled shyly when he saw Vienusia. Every one of the honored guests was in anterooms. The children were using the room on the right; the parents using the left. The anterooms exited into the hallway outside the entrance to the reception hall.

Two hundred guests had been invited. As they flowed in, they chose one of the twenty tables provided: four rows of five round tables, each able to seat ten people. Tables were encircled by a moat with aquarium-quality glass walls that were ten feet high and ten feet apart except in front of the tables, where they declined to three feet high. At the lowest point, a bridge had been built over the moat. Beyond the bridge, a semi-circular seventeen-seat table was reserved for the honored guests. Their seats faced the party guests.

Behind the table of honor, the wall was decorated with a mural of life at Gosiria. Opposite, at the entrance, a mural of Crystalia hung, and, hanging on each sidewall, were murals of Lonix and Isoloquat. The murals represented the progression of society on the planet. Gorgeous fountains located in the four corners of the room fed the moat. The moat drained into the floor to the outside moat which, in turn, pumped water to the fountains.

The moat was a party favorite. People could swim in it and usually, if they preferred, live food could be eaten in it. Tonight, however, there was a note at each place setting:

Food will be served from
all regions of the planet.
You may use the moat after dinner-
NO LIVE FOOD TONIGHT!

Bells sounded, signifying the start of the festivities. Everyone turned as the reception doors swung open, and an announcer said:

"Please welcome the governors of Lonix: Wolvernix and Oblivia!"

As they walked in, the guests stood and bowed.

Wolvernix looked about forty years old, yet he was actually fifty-four. Like the rest of the immortal men, he was gray at the temples only; otherwise, he had blood-red hair. It had been a lighter red in his youth. War had turned it a darker red as if the blood of his enemies transfixed itself into his hair to continually remind him he had killed. His eyes, though they had seen the horrors of war, somehow retained their original youthful green. He could only attribute this to the beauty he now walked with. Because of the war, he had waited to impregnate Oblivia until he was forty-nine years old, which was cutting it rather close.

He walked with a staff that never left his side. In a mischievous moment, he had crafted a staff for his son and told him that it was magical. To his surprise, it seemed to be. He thought his son inherited some of his own trickery and cunning and that it somehow transformed itself into the staff. Representing Lonix well wearing a robe of mixed animal skins, he looked over at Oblivia and smiled.

They first met training for the Osiriat V mission Tarus led to Earth. Lonix's governor picked them because they were the highest qualified and they were from different islands. His thought was that familiarity bred contempt, and his theory that strangers would bring out strengths in each other worked.

Above Earth, they were constant companions. They developed cargo holds, both dry and wet, to hold two of each of Earth's species so that it could be repopulated after the coming disaster. They did not interfere, however, with humans who would have to depend on their resiliency or fail. In case of failure, Tarus' group would repopulate Earth along with the saved animals.

Tarus' decision to build a city on Earth was met with mixed emotions. Wolvernix and Oblivia concentrated on helping the animals find homes and, therefore, stayed clear of the emotional turmoil. When the Greek sailor found them, they knew they were doomed. Foreseeing Tarus' decision to destroy the city and abandon Earth, they walked one last time through the magnificent city they had built.

Oblivia began to cry. When Wolvernix squeezed her hand, she lost all control, shaking as she cried harder. Wolvernix, concerned, asked, "What's wrong?"

"Tarus is a fool! We could have succeeded had we stayed in space. Now we must leave, and this beautiful city, and maybe this planet, will be destroyed."

"We still can succeed. There's bound to be another mission. We'll send our children."

She looked down at him, astonished. The shock of his statement dried her eyes. She began giggling, "What children? Are you asking me to marry you?"

"Yes, I think I am, but let's wait until we get back to Osiriat and do it right. We'll get married in the grandest of island traditions."

They had not been away long enough to truly age and were only thirty years old when they married. Planning to have children within a couple of years, they postponed that dream when news of the war between the southern islands and Isoloquat broke out.

The governor went to Isoloquat to command his forces. Isoloquans, adept at guerilla warfare, wiped out his command post. In his will, he had left instructions that Wolvernix and Oblivia should be elevated to his gubernatorial post if he should die. They concentrated on the war effort for the next nineteen years. When it ended, they kept their promise to each other and gave birth to Mercianiax and Marsax. On friendly terms with Tarus again, they secured their children a place on Osiriat VI.

She looked down at him and smiled. She had always liked her men stocky, a little shorter. Though smaller, Wolvernix was one of the few men stronger than she. They were the same age. She insisted on waiting to have kids because of the war. She was tall, strong, and vain. Vanity produced overconfidence. She had once thought, "I am so beautiful the ugliness of war can't touch me." She leapt into battle like she had a taste for blood. When the combined armies defeated Lonix, she was heartbroken. When she saw the destruction of Crystalia, she embraced peace, working first with Sate and then with Dolphinia.

Tonight, she wore a dress of animal skins adorned with seashells and starfish, as well as a jungle vine rope belt. The dress symbolized her peaceful relations with Crystalia and Isoloquat. She also carried a battle spear and burning torch, symbols of Lonix's power over the islands.

They walked past the bowing masses onto the bridge. Almost halfway up the bridge, where it passed over the first moat wall, Oblivia touched her torch to it. A flame spread quickly along the entire inner wall. She then proceeded over the bridge and lit the other wall. The crowd cheered the symbolic demonstration of Lonix's power.

Exiting the bridge, they turned left. They walked to the left end of the table, sat in the first two chairs, and waited.

"Please welcome the governors of Crystalia: Petex and Dolphinia!"

As they started toward the front, everyone again stood and bowed.

Petex looked forty but like Wolvernix was actually fifty-four. He had also waited to have children. He finally impregnated Dolphinia at forty-eight.

Petex and Dolphinia served on Tarus' Osiriat V mission; assigned to interstellar mapping. Constantly together, surrounded by the beauty and majesty of space, they fell in love. In the observation lounge where they worked, the stars watched as they fell together.

Once they settled on Earth, they asked Tarus to allow them to marry. He denied them, "You must wait until we return home. I would've agreed, but humans thrive here. There is no need to populate the planet. I need you two to study the sea creatures. Your tails will prevent you from making love; I want no Osirians born here. I accept your love, but please, wait until we get back home."

They were in the sea, playing with a group of dolphins when they spotted the lost Greek sailor. With the dolphin's help, they pushed the ship to land and reported their find to Tarus. He rushed to the beach to meet the Greek, excited because he wished to evaluate man's progress. Soon after, when the sailor broke the only rule given him, they were off again to Osiriat. Leaving prematurely, they doomed man to failure.

Petex and Dolphinia were married the day they returned to Crystalia. The governor, soon after, was trapped and killed by sharks. Petex and Dolphinia became governors. Hunting all sharks that threatened their boundaries was their first order. They put off starting a family because they had a society to run. Eighteen years later, she gave birth to Nepeta, and two years later, she gave birth to Vienusia.

The family was exploring the sea, teaching the children, when the combined forces attacked their city. Returning to Crystalia, Dolphinia sensed danger. She asked Petex to watch the children as she raced forward. When she saw the mass destruction, she shrieked. The victors were humbled, and a peace was arranged.

To protect the peace, Petex always carried his trident. Tonight, he let the trident gently touch the ground as he walked. Each time he did, a slight tremor was felt. He was demonstrating Crystalia's power over the elements. Those who dared look at him were held in awe by his appearance: blue piercing eyes, sea blue-blonde hair, and a golden robe covered in sea creatures.

Dolphinia was the same age as Petex. People could not look at her directly because of her beauty; they would simply forget to breathe. She was wearing a shimmering robe covered in bird and sea life depictions; she wore many sparkling jewels and a golden necklace. When Crystalia was destroyed, she brought peace and always dressed so gloom could not affect her. She also carried a trident. When they were on top of the bridge, she struck the water with it. The waves she created symbolically proved their dominance over the sea. The crowd applauded. They exited the bridge to the right, took the first two chairs opposite Wolvernix and Oblivia, nodded to them, and waited.

"Please welcome the Governors of Isoloquat: Cronix and Sate!"

Again, the crowd rose and bowed.

Cronix, like the others, was immortal. He was fifty-five years old and wore a dark blue robe sprinkled with stars, which matched his dark blue eyes. Contrasting his robe, his pale skin and white hair shone like the brightest of planets and moons. It appropriately represented night because he preferred dark isolation to this public spectacle. He was secretly glad that the people bowed because he abhorred staring. People admired his short, stocky, powerful frame, but the admiration embarrassed him. He looked toward the moat and gave a sigh of relief as he hated the barbaric ritual of hunting and eating raw seafood. They had left the moat empty to please him.

He glanced up into Sate's eyes and could see her relief. She wore a dark dress to highlight her white hair and carried a sickle. It also highlighted her hourglass figure that he loved, but it was her deep brown eyes, as brown as the trees in the forest they lived in, that had originally attracted him to her.

Tarus chose Cronix and Sate to run engineering on Osiriat V because Isoloquat was a society of builders. They sent beautiful building materials to Lonix and, built the castle at Gosiria. Before Tarus took his crew to Earth, he ordered Cronix and Sate to build monuments near established farming communities and the city they would inhabit.

Once on the surface, they were put in charge of farming. They successfully fed the city until Petex, Dolphinia, Wolvernix, and Sate were allowed to hunt and fish once the animals regenerated. The sickle they always carried became their symbol.

They were shy people. When the Greek ruined their mission, and Tarus insisted on leaving, he also insisted that they marry when they returned home. They were shocked. Everyone knew what they barely acknowledged.

Married as soon as they returned home, to their surprise, they found Isoloquat had broken contact with the outside world. Its citizens were very superstitious of strangers and, in some cases, of each other. The governor was killed when he visited one of the trade castles. Cronix and Sate were elected. They spent the next eighteen years trying to realign the trading villages. They started their family late. At forty-nine, he fathered Uryxs, and at fifty, Satetan.

Gosirian troops arrived and easily toppled Isoloquat. Cronix agreed to help Tarus invade Lonix on the condition his children would be selected for the Osiriat VI mission. Tarus agreed, and Lonix was taken.

Sate's sickle represented Isoloquat well. Not only had it defeated the forests, but it had allowed crops to be cut, therefore allowing the inland expansion and final building of Gosiria. When they reached the top of the bridge, she stopped to slice the air with the sickle. Witnessing this demonstration of Isoloquat's power, the audience cheered. Cronix and Sate then walked off the bridge, walked to their right to the end of the table, took the seventh and eighth seats, nodded to the others, and waited for the trumpets.

Momentarily, the trumpets sounded. "Please welcome the Governors of Gosiria, your King and Queen: Tarus and Elysia!"

The crowd stood and applauded as the reception doors swung open, quieted, and bowed as Tarus and Elysia came in. He was the oldest of the parents. The doctors could not explain it. Somehow, his immortality was delayed.

Tarus was the leader of Osiriat V. He was already an adult of twenty-eight years when he was picked to captain Osiriat V. He chose children, as he had again chosen them for the Osiriat VI mission, to give them time to succeed.

A mate, a female child from Gosiria, was sent in case they needed to repopulate Earth, but she died in a horrible accident involving a computer malfunction. Her hibernation chamber was the only one to lose life support. The computer glitch was quickly corrected, but too late to save her. When they awoke and found her dead, they buried her in space.

Tarus was greatly upset. As the others fell in love, he became more withdrawn. He assigned duties. Everyone performed flawlessly. He directed the work, taking particular interest not only in the placement of the monuments but also in patiently sculpting the art that would adorn them.

Still, he was lonely. His state of mind caused him to make a tragic mistake. No one could talk him out of relocating to Earth. He hoped to meet a woman there, although that was forbidden by the rules of conduct of the mission.

He denied the others the right to marry based on his own misery. When the Greek sailor came, he befriended him, hoping to find out how to approach earth women. When the Greek figured out what Tarus was trying to accomplish, he decided to flatter him.

"Any woman would be proud to sleep with a god, my Lord."

Tarus, realizing his mistake, ordered the Greek to go back to his ship. "You will sail or die."

The Greek had barely provisioned his boat when the rumbling started. He witnessed the city fall and watched the land as it was covered in a veil of ice. A blast knocked him to the deck. As he recovered his senses, he watched a contrail streak across the sky.

He related his story to both the Egyptians and the Greeks, "I saw a glorious city, a city of the gods, sink into the ocean. The continent it was on also disappeared. I saw the gods ascend to the heavens. In Egypt, the gods were developed into benevolent gods who had power over the people through the great pyramids. In Greece, the gods were thought to have settled on Mt. Olympus. They were used to describe life's mysteries. Tarus, mispronounced by the Greek sailor as Zeus, was supreme, father of all the gods.

The crew were teenagers when they arrived on Earth, and had conditions been ideal, they would have reached full Osirian maturity on Earth. The Greek sailor's mistake shortened their mission to five years. Each crewmember, therefore, only gained ten years over the following sixty. Tarus bitterly lay in his hibernation chamber, wondering if he would mature and never reproduce.

His last act, a desperate gamble, was to order the computer to locate the time wave and reestablish the proper timeline with Osiriat. He hoped this would slow his maturity. Nature was kind to him in the end.

When Tarus' mission returned to Osiriat, he allowed each couple to return home to be married. His own father, the king of Gosiria, master of the trade route, welcomed him home. Upset, his son returned without a mate, and he introduced him to Elysia. Within a year, Tarus married Elysia. He was sixty-three, and all of the women his age were no longer fertile. The forty-year-old Elysia was the perfect match. He did not know when his infertility would kick in, but he knew she would be fertile for ten years. His father, absent on a trade mission in eastern Isoloquat, was not in attendance.

Three days into their honeymoon, Tarus was informed his father had been killed in Isoloquat by a radical faction, and he was now king. Tarus declared war on Isoloquat. Three years later, he forced the surrender of the governors his friends Cronix and Sate. When they learned Tarus was king they ordered their army to surrender; they would not fight their captain.

Tarus, after a long negotiation, secured the loyalty of the Isoloquan forces. Combined forces were sent against Lonix. During negotiations, he promised to end Isoloquat's conflict with the island nation. Sixty-six now and tired from the war effort, he took a break, returning to the castle to celebrate his victory over Isoloquat. Nine months later, Jupoler was born. He took a three-month leave to return home to enjoy his baby. Before leaving to continue his fight for Lonix, he visited Elysia again. Nine months later, Arop was born.

As a gift to Elysia, he swiftly crushed Lonix. He brought Elysia and the children to the field. He created a friendly peace with Wolvernix and Oblivia. They encouraged him to take Crystalia and form a world government. The three armies crushed Crystalia. Surprised by their easy victory, they looked on the carnage in disgust. Then Dolphinia broke the water and shrieked. Tarus learned that Petex and Dolphinia were Crystalia's governors. He could have annexed her peacefully.

Dolphinia swam up to Tarus, crying.

"What have you done?"

"I'm sorry, Dolphinia. This war made me overzealous. Where's Petex? If he's alive, bring him here."

Dolphinia fetched Petex. She told him Tarus was king.

"He summons us. He destroyed Crystalia."

"Why? We are a peaceful nation."

"That is why he summons us into his presence. I think he wants to apologize."

"Did he appear calm?"

"He appeared confused."

"If he summons me, I will go," Petex conceded. "But I will not take the children."

He turned to the guards, asked them to watch the children, and swam off to Crystalia.

Petex was infuriated by the carnage. He calmed when he saw his friends crying. Tarus ordered a crew to clean up the sea and forced his leaders to watch.

Petex forced himself to calm down and gathered as much strength as he could.

"So Tarus, you are the king of Gosiria? Is this slaughter what it means to be king?"

Tarus wept loudly.

"I made a mistake, my friend. Please forgive me."

"How can you fix this, Tarus?" Petex demanded, waving his hand over the scene.

"By securing the peace. I'm asking each of you governors to support me as king of all Osiriat. In return, I will rebuild your lands, and I will set up a council of governors to help Elysia and me rule fairly. We will not make a decision without first consulting you, and if any of you disagree with a policy, I will not implement it."

The countries were rebuilt. Tarus ordered guest palaces built for the governors. Lonix and Isoloquat's palaces were built at the forest edge. Crystalia's was built in the lake. The governors spent so much time in Gosiria that these palaces became second homes.

The world was at peace. A new Earth mission was on everyone's mind. Tarus predicted mission preparation would take about five years. The space training facility had degenerated during the war. It had to be remodeled. A new transport ship was constructed. Populating the mission were the leaders' own children. This gesture of trust sealed their bonds of friendship.

Tarus and Elysia were euphoric that the people approved their mission choices. Their personal celebration turned wild, and nine months later, Tarus received another surprise. Because he was seventy-one, he should have been infertile. He worshipped Planex as a sign of his powerful fertility; he knew he had caused friction, forcing Planex onto the mission, but he only wanted the best for him. There would be no others. Elysia's immortality and subsequent sterilization came at fifty as expected, and his, well overdue, came on finally at seventy-three.

They wore simple white robes because any design might show favoritism to a certain region. They had to remain neutral and impartial, ruling each region equally. They had a regal walk. Tarus held his head high, not betraying his gloom. His children were going away. He had a headache and the trumpets, which he had previously ordered silenced, were not helping.

Reaching the top of the bridge, they turned and bowed. The crowd ceased cheering when they reached their chairs. Centered, they were taller than the governor's chairs and carved with scenes from the war. Minor stirring stopped when Tarus raised his hand.

"Thank you, citizens of Osiriat. We appreciate the applause, but it's not us you are here to applaud. You will notice that there are five empty seats on my right and four on my left. These seats shall be filled with heroes. Ladies and Gentleman, may I present the heroes of the next Earth mission, our children!"

The reception doors flew open. From the back of the anteroom Jupoler watched as out came, hand in hand, Mercianiax and Marsax. When they had gone a few steps, out came Uryxs and Satetan. Planex tried to exit with Vienusia. Jupoler caught and scolded him; his attention diverted from the procession at that moment. He did not see Nepeta and Vienusia walk to opposite back fountains, climb in, and sit dangling their feet in the running water. After the first four had cleared the bridge Nepeta and Vienusia dove into the moat. Already fully tailed because of the fountain's water, they sped swam to the bridge, hurdled it, caught each other midair, softly landed on the bridge, fanned their tails, and walked to the table.

Before Nepeta and Vienusia dove into the moat, Jupoler and Arop walked out with Planex proudly beaming between them. Jupoler was confused when he saw Uryxs and Satetan ahead of him. Then he heard the dual splash and chuckled to himself, "I should've known Nepeta and Vienusia would do something to ease the tensions."

As they approached the bridge, Jupoler squeezed Arop's hand. Although they had attended many royal functions in this room, they had never had a seat reserved at the table of honor. At the top of the bridge, they stopped and bowed as Tarus and Elysia had. They then turned to face their friends. Jupoler was amazed at how similar his crew looked to their parents. Each boy and girl was a miniature picture of their mom or dad. Clear of the bridge, they walked to the back of the table, past the kitchen staff that stood at attention and took their seats. As Jupoler, Arop, and Planex sat, they completed a perfect representation of the planet's regions. The outer families, evidenced by the still-dripping Nepeta and Vienusia, represented the sea and islands, while the inner families represented the forest and mainland. The royal family was naturally at the center, or the head, of the table.

Everyone was asked to take a seat, and dinner was served. The head table was served first, but the leaders patiently waited until all other tables had been served. Tarus lifted his cover off of his dish, signaling everyone the feast had begun. Dinner consisted of seafood from Crystalia, wild fruits from Lonix, wild meat from Isoloquat, and vegetables from the crops surrounding Gosiria. As people finished eating, the fire died around the moat.

Music started. A few people came over the bridge to dance on the huge dance floor. Others decided to swim in the moat. The favorite sport was speed swimming towards the bridge to jump it.

The ruling families sat and watched their people. Tarus bet with Wolvernix, Petex, and Cronix on these informal races. Petex, naturally a swimmer himself, had a good eye and won many bets. Tarus loved these informal races and was never angered over his losses.

When it was appropriate, the children rose, walked to the front of the table, and waited. Their parents, meanwhile, rose and grouped into sexes. As usual, the men talked of the war, new growth, and trade while the women discussed peace initiatives.

The children were busy with lines of well-wishers. Out of the corner of his eye, Jupoler saw Planex run to the bridge and jump into the moat. Vienusia offered to go after him. She quickly caught him.

"Planex, why did you dive into the moat?" She was smiling because she loved swimming. Chasing Planex had given her an excuse.

Planex pouted.

"I was bored. No one is talking to me. Everyone loves Jupoler and Arop. Besides, you and Nepeta did. Why shouldn't I?"

"What we did was part of the show. You know you can't swim right after dinner. Come on." He was helpless against her grip. She grabbed him around the middle and speed-swam to the bridge. They shared a private laugh at the bridge, delaying the inevitable as their tails vanished. She turned serious and brought him back to his scolding parents.

Seeing a royal child scolded was not comfortable. The well-wishers went back to their seats. The children took the opportunity to head back to the other side of the table. Only Jupoler remained. Planex's pouting made him uncomfortable. He walked over to the group of men.

The girls sat with Planex. He was mad and wanted to go home, but they put a smile back on his face when they told him dessert was coming. Arop explained to him that Mom and Dad had to punish him to show the crowd they were in control. Secretly, they probably admired his boldness.

Jupoler interrupted the war conversation, asking Tarus, "Father, I had a dream last night. You were explaining the war to me. Who was the woman who swam up and yelled 'Why!'?"

The group of women was close by, and before Tarus could answer, Dolphinia did.

"Jupoler, I was that woman. With my sheer beauty and sadness, I shamed these warriors and brought the peace. Your father is the symbol of victory, and I am the symbol of peace."

"Yes, and Wolvernix is the symbol of the messenger because he spread the word of the peace, whereas Cronix is the symbol of patience because he thought the peace would spread naturally," Tarus added.

"You forgot my husband. He is the symbol of the flowing seas," Dolphinia continued. "We women are symbols also, and you need to remember our symbols, for it may be the only way to communicate on Earth. We have found that symbols are the easiest way to communicate with alien races because pictures break down language barriers. As you can see, I am also the symbol of beauty. Oblivia is the symbol of fertility, for it is said that as she spread the message of peace with Wolvernix, the very fields blossomed. Sate is the symbol of time because time is what it would've taken to spread the peace naturally. She became an advocate with me against her husband. Finally, as you can see by looking at her, Elysia is the symbol of brightness. She persuaded the entire mainland to embrace the peace and it is said that the suns shone brighter on that day than on any other since."

"Listen to Dolphinia, my son. It was her idea to paint and etch symbols on the monuments we built on Earth. Mankind, unfortunately, has ignored the symbols. The message we left told him to live and work in peace, yet even now, three of their countries are attempting to take over the world. They are of mixed races; none are supreme, for they all sprang from two, yet they kill and destroy for 'racial purity.' They will be destroyed. Hopefully, the symbols you use will be better understood by the next race of humans.

"Now, go sit, Son. It's time for the toast."

Jupoler did as his father asked. He sat next to Arop, still busy comforting Planex.

The adults sat. Only Tarus and Elysia remained standing. An announcement sounded:

"There will now be a royal toast!"

All activity ceased. Waiters came out of the kitchen, located behind the main table, and headed to the fountains with empty pitchers. Seeing this, the swimmers slowly worked their way back to the fountains. When everyone was in place, wine replaced the water flow in the fountains. The waiters first served the main table and then spread out among the guests. When everyone had been served, Tarus raised his glass and, with a booming voice, proclaimed:

> Earth has eluded us
> five times.
> Earth flung us into
> world war.
> Earth will not elude
> us again.
> To these young heroes!
> To a successful mission!
> May they come back alive!

Cheers arose, and the wine flowed. The children left early and headed to mission control. The scientists insisted on one last safety check. Tonight they were to sleep in the liquid system, one night in quick hibernation.

The Launch

...Waking. Instinct forced a deep breath of air from their facemasks. This signaled the system to remove the masks, drain the water, and finally open each sleeping chamber. The scientists, satisfied with their flawless experiment, directed the travelers to the changing rooms.

The crew sat quietly, eating their final meal. Then they slipped into their spacesuits for the launch. As they walked out toward the ship, Planex, not able to contain his excitement, asked Jupoler, "Are we leaving now? Are Mom and Dad going to watch? Will we be able to see home? Are-?" Jupoler put his hand over Planex's mouth.

They boarded the ship and each went to their designated launch seats. Jupoler and Arop went to the captain's chairs. Planex, pouting, sat next to Vienusia.

"Vienusia, why didn't Jupoler answer my questions?"

She had heard his yelling.

"Our march to the ship was supposed to be a solemn, silent occasion."

They felt movement as the ship rose off of the surface and leaned upwards into a forty-five-degree angle.

"Look Planex! The screens are on now. The cameras are on the audience. See, all of our parents are there!" Vienusia's excitement brought him out of his pout. He was happy to see his parents, but before he could react, he heard:

"10...9...8...7...6...5...4...3...2...1... We have ignition."

With a jolt, they lifted off. Knowing she would not be able to be heard, she pointed at the screen again, and Planex watched, his smile growing.

He saw the castle from above, fast-moving away. As the ship rose, Osiriat fell. He had slept last time when they came up to train. This time, he refused to miss anything. The planet awed him; everything connected from the mainland to the islands to the hidden undersea city of Crystalia. His smile told Vienusia everything.

Jupoler also smiled. He focused one camera on the planet and one on the crew. He was pleased to see Planex smiling, happy his many recent punishments had not scarred him. He patted Arop's leg and pointed to the camera. She smiled also, glad Planex had the proper perspective.

Arop flipped the communication switch and asked the crew.

"Is everyone okay? Does anyone feel strange?" She took their silence to mean no. She then asked, "Is this an appropriate time?"

Everyone nodded 'yes'.

Marsax said, "You tell him, Arop."

She turned to Jupoler and said, "Last night, at the party, while you spoke with Father, we unanimously elected you commander of Osiriat VI."

Jupoler gaped. When he regained his senses, he said, "But we are co-captains."

"And co-captains, we shall remain. We need a true commander, though. I can pilot the ship, but you, you are in love with the ship. It makes sense that you command. We want the son of the king represent-ing Osiriat in space to be king of this vessel."

Jupoler thanked everyone.

"I will try to be as worthy as Tarus."

When they had cleared the planet's atmosphere, Jupoler turned the ship on a course away from Earth. They planned this launch to coincide with the closest pass of the dwarf star Golas. It took fifty years for the dwarf to encircle their main sun, and it was closest to the planet this year. He steered far to the left of the star. One mistake would send them hurling in the wrong direction.

It took most of the day at the speed Jupoler set. While they were wait-ing, everyone except Jupoler and Arop went to their quarters, stripped off their suits, and went into the hibernation chambers. None of them would be awake for the trip around the star. Hibernation provided equi-librium- the force of the speeds they had to achieve to travel a distance of eight point seven light years would kill them without it.

When the arc around the star began, Jupoler asked Arop to check on Planex and then get into her chamber. She left, and he set the course. He then went to check that everyone else was secured.

His final check was done; he went to a terminal and quizzed the computer. One wrong answer, and he would immediately abort.

"Are we going to be close enough to Golas for this to work?"

"By my calculations, yes," the computer answered mechanically.

"How fast will we travel?"

"Once the gravitational pull of Golas grabs us and slings us around, we will be traveling at thirty percent of the speed of light at two hundred million eight hundred eighty thousand miles per hour, to use the Earth term."

"How will our speed decrease?"

"The ship has a controlled rate of declination of point five percent of light per year. I am to regulate it by using boosters either to slow us down of speed us up. Other gravitational forces may affect us, so I will constantly monitor our speed."

"How fast will we be traveling when we reach their solar system?"

"You will be at point zero five percent of light or, again, to use an Earth term you need to be familiar with, three million three hundred forty-eight thousand miles per hour."

"Will you wake us up then?"

"I will have to. It will be your decision whether or not to slow us down."

Jupoler was satisfied. The computer had answered all of his questions correctly.

"I am going into hibernation now; please give me fifteen minutes before you shut my chamber."

"Yes, sir. Have a good sleep, sir."

Jupoler double-checked everyone. He then checked the computer's mainframe airlock; without it the computer would fail. Satisfied, he went to his room. He stripped, climbed into the chamber, put on his oxygen/feeding tube mask, and waited. Eventually, water began to fill the chamber. As the lid closed, he thought he felt...

He truly did not feel it. One hour passed after Jupoler fell asleep. As expected, the dwarf star's gravity locked onto the ship and flung it into space. Two hours later, headed towards Earth on its sixty-year journey, the screens showed a very small sun behind the ship.

Earth 1965- U.S.A.

"A difference, my ass!" She thought to herself. She was alone in the delivery room. She regretted everything now. Her parents could not help. They did not know where she was.

She thought about Peter. They had left in a rage, pissed off about Johnson's war. They set off for Canada, but one hundred miles out of town, the car broke down. They were rescued by hippies and were quickly assimilated. She was in love, not just with Peter, but with the whole free love movement. When Peter found out she was pregnant, he abandoned her in the night. The note was accusing, 'You'll only slow me down, and it's probably not mine anyway.' That really pissed her off because the only free love she practiced was *with* Peter.

She thought now of her parents. Mom was a typical mom, but she shared in the proud feeling. A career soldier recently retired, her dad constantly talked about how he helped stop Hitler. They were dumbfounded that she was in love with a "traitor."

Her mom conditioned her with those words her entire life. She was forever telling her the story of her birth, and the first words she said to her, "You will make a difference."

Pushing in agony, she thought, "The only thing I'm going to make is a clean getaway before I have to pay for this hospital stay." Finally, the baby came, and she collapsed.

Two days later, as she was enjoying her new daughter, she received a visitor. The lady from the hospital administration wanted to know who was going to pay the bill.

"My parents. Here's their number," she answered, handing over a piece of paper.

Expecting this sort of answer, she hurried back to the phone in administration. By the time she confirmed the suspected lie, the patient had opened the first-floor window, escaped, hitchhiked, and luckily found some more hippies.

Earth 1967- U.S.A.

She never dreamed that she would be sad in the delivery room. They had been married for three months when John was drafted. He impregnated her the night before he departed.

His last letter from Vietnam was hopeful. On what they called short time, he had only three and a half months before he would be home. Thrilled at the prospect of fatherhood, he brought cheer to his whole unit. Men would gather around as he read her letters aloud grasping a tiny bit of heaven in the hell they were living. . ". . .In two weeks, I have my last point duty, and then my colonel has promised me rear echelon duty: training new arrivals on what to expect."

Today was his last point day. She did as the doctors asked, pushing and breathing. At the end, she yelled and cried. When she saw her new son, she named him after her husband. His entire life, she would tell him, "You have your father's spirit. I know he died the moment you were born."

Osiriat VI- Earth Date: June 1967

The computer spoke. Nobody heard:

SPEED: sixteen point five percent of light at one hundred ten million four hundred eighty-four thousand miles per hour.

DECLINATION RATE: Standard; forty-five percent of the original thirty percent

YEAR: twenty-seven begin

HIBERNATION: Chambers sealed

VITALS: Normal

AGING: Within parameters

COMPUTER: airlocks sealed.

SELF-DIAGNOSTIC: O.K.

... And the earth continued its conflict. Destroying nations is an art form.

Earth 1983

Eighteen years old now, the girl had run away from her mom and the hippie/welfare lifestyle at the age of twelve. She knew her mom would not find her in the city streets; the hippies preferred communal life in the country.

Instantly hooked into the profession like a child being tricked with candy, at least she had a good pimp. He said he would rather have them on birth control because a pregnant bitch cost him money, and his bitches cost him enough already.

She took after her mom, only her mom was not paid. She ran the day her pimp found out. He beat her, screaming, "Goddamn pregnant bitches cost me money!"

The cops she ran to sent her to a home. When the time came, her caretakers brought her to the hospital. The home promised her a job and education if she would stay with them and raise the child. As she pushed, she made her decision. Holding her new son, she said, "You will never meet your grandmother. We're going to a home where we'll be fine."

Earth 1987

John was twenty years old. Named after a dad he never knew, he was, according to his mother, a living memory of him. Tall, short-cropped brown hair, brown-eyed, very strong, perfect in every way to follow his father into the military, but he did not choose it. He married his high school sweetheart, Mary, the day after graduation. He had fallen in love with her in their early high school days. Her blonde hair and sparkling blue eyes that so effectively contrasted his own dark features first attracted him. Withdrawn, probably because of the lack of a father, she had brought him out of himself with her outgoing, perky wit. Almost instantly, he wanted to marry her. To honor his grandfather's wishes, he went into the family business and was already a vice president in the box factory. His friends thought it would bore him, but the orders for specialty boxes kept him on his toes. Special orders meant higher pricing. As a result, they already had their first three-bedroom, brick-constructed house half paid for, two brand-new cars bought with cash, and a well-stocked baby room.

Invited into the delivery room! Something dad would have been denied. He felt her pain mainly in his right hand- she had a super grip he never knew about. When it was time, he watched in pure awe. Cutting the cord was the icing on the cake. The doctor put his daughter in his wife's hands. As she cried, his tears welled up. He promised himself he would be the ultimate dad because he had never had one.

Mary's parents were in the room two days later. When a nurse came in and asked how this was going to be paid for, John could not answer quickly enough.

"How's cash?" asked Mary's dad. He looked at John and said, "Consider it a gift."

Osiriat VI- Earth Date: June 1987

Again, the computer spoke out into empty space:

SPEED: point six five percent of light at forty-three million five hundred twenty-four thousand miles per hour

DECLINATION RATE: Standard; seventy-eight point thirty-three of original thirty percent

YEAR NUMBER: forty-seven begin

HIBERNATION: Chambers sealed.

VITALS: Normal

AGING: Within parameters

COMPUTER: Airlocks sealed

SELF-DIAGNOSTIC: O.K.

There would be silence for another year as they continued to sail through space.

CHAPTER 4

ARRIVAL

Osiriat VI- Earth date: May 5, 2000

The silence was broken. The computer announced:

WARNING!

Forward sensors show a strange anomaly in the Sol system. Data confirms that the first, second, fourth, fifth, and sixth orbiting planets are aligned with Earth. Earth is on one side of Sol. The planets are on the opposite side.

The computer continued (voice and printout):

THEORETICAL ASSESSMENT

THEORY: inner planets will have minor gravitational effect (tides may rise).

THEORY: Sol, fifth, and sixth planets will have a combined gravitational pull on Earth.

RESULTS: IMMEASURABLE. However, be advised that unstable magma pockets may rise.

63

Earth date: May 6, 2000

John had read about doomsday. He worried that he had brought his daughter up only to die. Relieved, he read today's headline:

DOOMSDAY FAILS/ PLANET FINE!

All reports said there were no unusual events on May 5th. Okay, so the tides rose one millimeter; that was not going to put any beaches out of business.

Still, he knew Jane would benefit from her teachings. As a baby, he had played her language tapes creating a fluency, at twelve, in English, Spanish, Russian, Japanese, and French. An excellent mathematician, which was as abstract as some of her languages, he had made sure she was well educated. If she survived she may have to deal with many different languages and cultures.

Deep below the Arctic Ocean, bubbles of heated oxygen began to rise. The gravitational pull of the planets and sun opened a weak spot in the ocean floor...

Osiriat VI: Earth Date: June 2000

Each chamber was activated. A stimulant caused the sleepers to breathe deeply, signaling the automatic removal of their facemasks. Water rushed out as the chambers were opened.

The computer's voice echoed through the ship:

SPEED: zero point five percent of light at three million three hundred forty-eight thousand miles per hour

DECLINATION RATE: standard; ninety-eight point three percent of the original thirtypercent

YEAR: sixty begin

HIBERNATION: chambers opened

VITALS: normal

AGE GAIN: ten years

COMPUTER: airlocks opened. Please sign on...

"Please sign on, Please sign on, Please sign on..."

Jupoler hurriedly dressed and found the closest terminal to sign onto. His head pounded. He desperately needed the message to end. The last message was still displayed on the screen. "Good, everyone made it," he thought.

He found the intercom. "Arop, please meet me at the helm." Walking down the hall toward the helm, a blinking warning light caught his attention. Knowing the trouble must be in this sector or the light would have been deactivated, he pushed the warning button and read the assessment.

As he was reading, Arop entered.

"Is that going to be a problem?"

"I hope not. We didn't anticipate it. Almost immeasurable tidal risings. Magma stirrings, possibly. I'd say the only problem would be if it geometrically progresses toward the next planetary-"

As Jupoler answered, he turned toward her. What he saw abruptly silenced him. Arop was as beautiful as Elysia, and for a moment, he thought his mother had come along.

He had never really noticed his sister; had not seen her in sixty years, and his memory could only draw on the little girl he had once known. Fully blossomed sixteen, wearing a white dress, fair and pale, she shone like a sun against the backdrop of space. He blinked several times. Finally focused, he noticed her blue eyes focusing on him like piercing stars. He knew they would all grow, but he did not expect her to be as beautiful as Elysia; he found himself envious of the male they might save.

He stood and moved toward her. She gaped. Seventeen years old, dressed in a toga, she could see the beginnings of his masterful body. There was a lot of exercise designed to counter the debilitating effects of long-term hibernation in their future.

"It's true! We are ten years older. Jupoler, call everyone in. I want to see them all."

He keyed the intercom. "All crewmembers to the conference room, please."

He motioned her to lead. They came in first, and soon, almost everyone was there.

"This is amazing," Arop said, her skin brightening with enthusiasm. "We all resemble our parents down to the most minor details. Even Planex looks like a miniature Tarus."

She looked around the room, trying to guess. Nepeta was a tall sixteen. Mercianiax was fourteen years old and looked awkward next to the fifteen-year-old Marsax, whose full breasts enhanced Arop's feeling that Marsax's whole body could be used as a weapon. They both took after Wolvernix being of medium height. Uryxs was sixteen, while Satetan was fifteen and slightly taller than he. The only person missing was...

Gasping filled her ears. She turned toward the entrance, and her throat froze, stifling her breathing. Vienusia had the same effect on them as Dolphinia. She was only fourteen but a heavenly sight, as tall as Jupoler. Her shiny blonde hair fell slightly below her waist, her body mirroring Dolphinia's. Her sweet, engaging smile was transfixing. As she realized the effect she was having, she quit smiling and turned slightly. The trance broken, they all turned away, once again able to breathe.

Jupoler broke the silence. "We've had a warning about possible gravitational effects on Earth. I'm sure it's nothing, but we'll keep the computer on it.

"We called you in here to assign tasks. Uryxs and Satetan, you're assigned to run engineering. Mercianiax and Marsax, please check and maintain the cargo holds. Remember that we'll need two each. Make sure the holds can handle the stress modifications if they have to be enlarged. Nepeta and Vienusia, you're assigned to innersolar mapping and assistance with any aquarium work Mercianiax and Marsax may need. Planex, you see to the children's quarters. Arop and I will concentrate on getting us to Earth safely. I expect everyone to be in the gymnasium two hours a day, as we need to be in top physical shape when we arrive. At our current rate of speed we will be there in forty-four days. I will decrease our speed to give us approximately one hundred seventy-eight days to prepare." Jupoler took Arop's hand and walked briskly out of the room. Each pair headed to their assigned departments.

Jupoler and Arop went back to the helm. "Computer decrease speed to eight hundred thirty-seven thousand miles per hour," Jupoler ordered.

"Done, sir; we will decelerate to point zero one two five percent of light within minutes," The computer answered.

He turned to Arop, "You and I will need to spend twelve hours each day on duty. We will start our shifts together each morning. I will start my shift here, and you will spend four hours monitoring the departments. We will then spend four hours here together. When my helm shift is over, I will spend four hours monitoring the departments while you spend the last four hours here. I will join you here at the end of your shift. After you've turned the controls over to the computer, we'll go to the gym."

The following six months sailed by Jupoler as he coordinated his crew's efforts to prepare the ship for Earth orbit. His first afternoon walk found him in engineering. Ozone filled his nostrils. He guessed Uryxs was working on the power systems. When he found him, Uryxs was covered in grease. Satetan was busy handing him tools and guiding him using a computer-printed specification sheet. She saw Jupoler at the door.

"Uryxs, I have to greet our captain. Yell if you need help."

"I'm on this power line for at least another half-hour. Go ahead. I'll be fine."

Satetan wiped her hands on a towel as she approached the door. She extended her hand to meet Jupoler's. "It's good to see you captain. How can we help you?"

"I'm out on my afternoon walk. Arop suggested I stop here first today. What are you guys working on?"

"Plenty. Sixty years of sporadic use can take its toll on any engine. Of course, constant use would've run us out of fuel. Engine maintenance is much preferable to that. Our first priority when we took over engineering, was to check the computer. It detailed the weakened areas."

"What's Uryxs working on now?"

"He's replacing the fuel intake valves. Our drop to quarter speed has slowed the flow, allowing him to shut down one valve at a time."

"Let's take a look." Jupoler was already walking toward the panel Uryxs was encased in.

"Uryxs, how's it coming along?"

Uryxs, covered in grease, crawled out to face Jupoler.

"Did Satetan tell you about the fuel valve?"

"Yes. What else needs attention?"

"According to the computer schematics, there are multiple light repairs to address. Seals everywhere are leaking. Some components have quit responding; these I will address first. Also, our sudden speed decrease yesterday may have shocked the system. We will run a complete diagnostic and have the engines fully repaired. I estimate sixty days until we're fully functional again."

"Any chance of finishing sooner?"

"Not if we want one hundred percent efficiency."

Jupoler could tell he did not wish to be bothered. "Uryxs, Satetan, proceed. I will not interfere. I'll be back to check your progress in sixty days. Each morning, however, Arop will check in. Please tell her if you have any problems or need assistance. In that case, we'll be glad to help. I'll leave you alone now. I need to check on the other departments."

He walked out. Uryxs crawled back into his hole, and Satetan resumed her position in front of the schematic. Satetan noticed the relieved look on Uryx's face. She knew he did not want anyone meddling with HIS engines.

Jupoler walked down the sterile metallic hall to an elevator. Once inside, he selected level two. When the doors slid open, he walked out into the cargo bays, which incorporated all of level two. The cargo bays were built directly above the engine level. They were designed to expand in each of six directions, depending on the load needs. At the moment, the holds were laying in their standard positions, streamlining the ship.

Jupoler's inspection took him to the left of the elevator doors. There was light in that quadrant he decided to investigate. He found Marsax and Mercianiax talking and waited patiently in the shadows. Mercianiax was saying, "This glass wall is ten feet thick. Do you think that's enough?"

Marsax looked up from the schematic she was reading.

"Yes, if this is to be the freshwater aquarium, I'd say that's adequate. The salt-water aquarium walls should be twenty feet thick, though."

"I think they will be. Past mission diagrams show that more pressure is applied to the walls of the salt-water tanks. Your diagram shows known predators, doesn't it?"

"Yes, but there may be new animals. I think we should compartmentalize the aquariums for the protection of each animal."

"Agreed," Jupoler said, walking toward them.

Mercianiax greeted him.

"Captain, what can we do for you?"

"I'm checking with all of the departments today. I want to get a feel for the work that will be accomplished over the next six months. I like your idea of compartmentalizing. Are you going to do the same in the land animal areas?"

"Yes, we're checking the record right now. Tarus' crew entered every known animal into the computer, but more species could've evolved after five thousand years."

"Will there be roofs on the compartments?"

"That depends on the animals. The aviary for birds of flight will have a roof, and climbing animals will be roofed. Flightless birds will be in the aviary, also, but not roofed. We also learned from past missions that natural enemies must be housed on opposite ends of the bays. For instance, lions and antelopes have to be split, or the scent of the antelope will drive the lions to destroy their environment. We are also going to create a frozen environment for any polar animals we encounter."

"Where are you going to build it?"

Mercianiax turned the question over to Marsax.

"We've agreed that the center of the floor is the best spot because the cold air may diminish predator's senses and quell violent behavior."

"Where are you going to store food?"

Marsax continued. "Forward. The computer suggests storing it well away from the animals as it will cause them to act crazy if they can smell it. We will store it in a double sealed environment so that when we fetch their food, they will remain calm."

"Have you checked the seals on the expandable walls yet?"

Mercianiax answered, "No. We intend to check a different wall each week for the next six weeks. Opposing walls will be fully extended to keep equilibrium. We will wear our space walk gear as we check for seal breaches, as a precaution. The computer hasn't detected any, but we still feel we must check manually."

"When will you build the compartments?"

"The computer will set them up according to Tarus' logs. We will modify them ourselves, closer to Earth, as we receive an accurate animal count."

"Are there any other tests that need to be performed?"

"Yes, as soon as we have checked the holds for leaks, we are going to test the waste removal system. The computer should register waste and transport it to the dung bins above the thrusters at the rear of the cargo hold. Waste dumping into space will correspond with thrust bursts instantly vaporizing the waste when it's released into space."

"Very good. How long do you estimate until you clear the system?"

Marsax said, "Shouldn't be more than sixty days."

"Okay, I'll return in sixty days. Arop will drop by daily to check with you. If there is anything you need, don't hesitate to ask."

Jupoler turned and headed back to the elevator. When he entered, he selected level one, the life/crew activities level. The elevator serviced three areas, the gym, cargo bays, and engine room. The ship consisted of only three levels, but each level housed multiple activities. The lowest level, level three, consisted of the transport bays in the nose of the ship, the shuttle bay in the middle, and the engine room, which controlled the thrusters in the extreme rear of the ship. Level two housed the cargo bay. Empty now, in six months, it would be a bustle of activity.

Level one was the "brains" or life of the ship. Up front, above the nose, sat the bridge. Two exits left the bridge. The first, on the floor, opened to a staircase leading into the crew quarters. Ten cabins sat directly above the aviary/food storage area of level two. Each room had windows that provided an excellent view of space. The front room, reserved for the humans, had a semi-circular bay of windows in the nose lining the floor. This restricted their view to Earth only.

The second door leading out of the bridge exited into innersolar mapping. This room was capped with a dome window that provided a one-hundred-eighty-degree view of space. It was also utilized as the conference room. Meetings, social gatherings, and meals were taken here.

The innersolar mapping room, room five, exited into room six. Room six housed the elevator and the gymnasium. There were workout machines, a computer massage booth, a small pool and spa, and showers for those who wanted to feel refreshed after visiting room six. The showers were sometimes used before working out when crew members, such as Uryxs, arrived covered in filth.

Exiting the gym, one entered the computer's mainframe. Room seven was rarely entered, as the computer was self-maintained. Occasionally, the computer would ask one of the captains to check an outward component, but truly, the only reason to enter was to check the computer's airlocks for travel.

When the elevator door opened, Jupoler stepped out into the gymnasium. He walked forward, opened a door, and entered innersolar mapping.

Nepeta and Vienusia were staring out the window. Jupoler walked up to them and said, "Do you have this system mapped already?"

"Yes, Tarus' mission records are a duplicate of what we're seeing. We printed a star map and a planetary map. Our course won't take us close to any of them; we're going to encircle the asteroid belt to avoid damage."

"What work do you still need to complete?"

"We are studying planetary movement to determine whether the alignment theories are correct. About sixty day's observation should give us sufficient data."

"Interesting. I will come by daily to help. These theories are the key to our mission success. I need to go back to the bridge. Keep up the good work."

Jupoler walked ahead and opened the door. Arop, silhouetted against space, still surprised him with her exceptional beauty. He walked over to her and asked, "Problems?"

"No, we're approaching the eighth planet's orbital path; otherwise, everything's quiet."

"Good. Computer?"

"Yes, captain?"

"Please take helm control on my mark. Mark."

He immediately asked, "Is the ship in your control?"

"Yes, you may retire. I'm counting down twelve hours on your mark. Goodnight, my captains."

Jupoler turned to Arop. "Shall we go to the gym?"

They exited the bridge into room five, asked Nepeta and Vienusia to join them, and continued on to room six. Exiting the elevator were Uryxs, Satetan, Marsax, and Mercianiax. Uryxs, covered in grease, and Satetan, slightly dirty, headed toward the showers. Everyone turned toward the unexpected splash. Planex, fully tailed, was swimming in the pool.

Jupoler walked to the edge of the pool. Planex swam up to him, a mischievous grin on his face, and asked, "How was your first day, Brother?"

"Very productive. Yours?"

"Not very exciting. I looked into the children's quarters as ordered. The Osirian symbols are in place, but there's really nothing I can do until we pick the two. I'll want to utilize their items to make them comfortable. Until then, I guess I'm free. I've been swimming for the last half-hour. Wanna join me?"

"Not today. We'll discuss your freedom at dinner. Carry on."

Jupoler was angry, but inwardly, he smiled. Did this child really think he had nothing to do?

As everyone casually worked out, Jupoler, anxious to keep Planex working, asked each crew team if they needed outside help. He took everyone's suggestions and then took Arop to one side to hear her opinion. Together, they agreed he would prepare the shuttle since the departments did not particularly want Jupoler hovering.

They spent one hour in the gym, showered, and then sat down to their first group dinner, provided by the computer. The computer transported the food, already cooked, from the food storage bay.

Jupoler waited until everyone was finished eating. "I have come to a decision on the fate of Planex. Each team has provided me with a heavy workload. I want Planex to know this ship as well as I do, so I'm assigning a rotating schedule. He will spend two weeks in each department. His first duty will be engineering, then cargo, then mapping. After six weeks, he'll go down to engineering again. This schedule will continue until Arop, and I decide that he needs to concentrate on the children again."

Planex smiled. Jupoler expected him to pout, but he was not two anymore and was excited to be handed these responsibilities.

A routine was established over the next sixty days. Arop visited the departments every morning to check progress. During their shift together on the bridge, she reported to Jupoler. Rarely were there complications to report. Uryxs was correct about the sudden speed decrease causing maintenance issues, but all systems were nearly back online. Mercianiax and Marsax directed the computer to section off the cargo holds and to roof the aviary. They still had some aquarium work to do, but it would be addressed closer to Earth. Nepeta and Vienusia finished their calculations and found that the alignment would proceed as predicted. Gravitational effects were unknown and would remain so until the incident occurred.

Jupoler called a progress meeting after the first sixty days. "According to my last report, you have all completed the tasks you originally set out to accomplish. What's next? Engineering?"

Satetan answered. "Engineering is developing a cloaking device because Earth's scientists have the ability to see into space."

"Good idea. We cannot be detected. Cargo?"

"We need to start aquarium stress tests. May we have Nepeta and Vienusia's help?" Marsax asked.

Nepeta and Vienusia nodded. Vienusia said, "We have the next sixty days free; of course, we will help."

"When will the cloaking device be functional?"

"Give us sixty days."

"Okay, we'll meet here again in sixty days. Planex, again, spend two weeks in each department," Jupoler ordered.

The crew easily fell into another sixty-day routine. Nepeta and Vienusia spent most working hours in the aquarium testing the compartments for stress and comfort. Uryxs and Satetan worked with the transporters to transport spatial images around the ship. The results were impressive.

Arop, after witnessing a system test, reported to Jupoler.

"It's amazing. Anyone looking at the ship will see only stars. The computer runs a moving picture of space like a blanket surrounding the ship."

"Are you sure we won't be detected?"

"Engineering is confident we won't."

The weeks flowed by quickly.

Jupoler decided to call another meeting.

"We're fifty-eight days out from Earth, approaching Saturn. I'm very proud of the work you've all completed over the last one hundred twenty days. I want you each to share your goals for the next thirty days.

Engineering?

Uryxs answered. "We are going to spend the next thirty days modifying the transporters against the stress we are going to put on them."

"Good, Cargo?"

Mercianiax answered. "We are done in cargo until we get closer to Earth. We have volunteered to take over shuttle maintenance from engineering."

"Excellent. I've laid some groundwork. I'd like to know if it's going to work. Mapping?"

Nepeta answered. "We were going to work with Uryxs and Satetan but decided instead to work with Mercianiax and Marsax. It is critical we determine which orbit will preserve the immortality chamber on the shuttle."

"Alright. Planex, I want you to spend one rotating week in each department. Arop and I will continue our monitoring walks."

Again, the ship fell into a productive work routine. Jupoler especially enjoyed watching Planex. The deeper the problem, the more excited he became. He began to worry, though, because sometimes Planex would miss gym time and, occasionally, dinner.

Jupoler, after his daily walk, pulled Planex out of level two. They entered the elevator in silence. Planex, older now, knew to keep quiet until Jupoler spoke. They arrived at room six. The doors opened, and they stepped off. Jupoler sighed. He stopped, looked around, and then turned to face his brother.

"Planex, do you remember this room?"

"Of course, Brother. Why?"

"Because lately, you haven't been spending enough time here."

"But I don't have time! The shuttle propulsion system isn't working right, and the math involved in plotting the right shuttle course is occupying my entire mind. I don't know what to do."

"It's all the same problem, Planex. You can't think because you're not utilizing your brain. You have to relax your mind. I ordered everyone to the gym daily on purpose. I think you'll find that if you work out, your brain will relax, and the solutions to your problems will naturally appear."

"But I don't have time -"

"You've been ordered to exercise and you will, daily. Brother, look at Uryxs. Do you think he has time to exercise? Do you think he needs to? He is a beast of a man. No, he exercises to relax his brain. When he's relaxed, he has pleasant dreams. I'm sure they involve power converters and engine schematics, but they don't overwhelm him because he is relaxed. You see, each morning, he wakes up fresh and utilizes the ideas he dreamt up. By the time his day is over, he is once again stressed and out of ideas; therefore, he needs to relax. Do you see the pattern?"

"Yes, Captain. I will quit work when the rest of the crew does and join them in the gym. I can see the benefits of relaxation."

"Good. You can start now. I suggest you swim first to refresh yourself."

Planex dove into the pool. Smiling, Jupoler started toward the bridge. True to his word, Planex balanced out his days properly. When thirty days passed, Jupoler called another meeting in the observation lounge under the stars.

"How have we progressed? Engineering?"

Satetan stood.

"I will answer for all departments. Planex is our hero. He not only solved the shuttle propulsion problem, but he also solved the orbit problem, apparently, in his sleep."

"Planex?" Arop curiously asked.

"Yes, Sister, in my sleep. Jupoler forced me to respect the diet/exercise regimen he has ordered and, like he predicted, the formulas came to me in my sleep."

Jupoler beamed.

"I told you, didn't I?"

Arop scolded him as only his mother ever had.

"Jupoler, I'm sure we're all happy that you were able to direct Planex into good work habits, but isn't it time you stopped worrying about everyone else and started to think about the role you're going to play with our guests?"

Jupoler thought about her comment. Hearing her speak in that manner, he longed for Elysia. "You're right, Arop. I do need to prepare for our guests. I have overstepped my bounds, but only because I care so much about this mission. Until we reach Earth, Arop will tour your departments and check your progress. She is right. I have many preparations to make. Planex, I need you to stay on call. I may need your help.

"Now then. We will arrive on Earth in twenty-eight days. I want everyone to concentrate on your departments only. Planex, download any games the computer has stored for the children. Uryxs, Satetan, double-check all your systems. Same orders for Mercianiax and Marsax. I want to see weekly diagnostic reports. Nepeta and Vienusia, keep an eye on space. There's no telling what kind of craft they may have out there."

An air of excitement developed as the meeting broke up. The crew retired, anticipating the quick pace of the next twenty-eight days. The next morning, everyone headed to their departments as ordered.

Planex, after receiving permission from Jupoler, entered the computer's mainframe located in room seven.

"Computer. Do you have my educational games prepared?"

"Yes, I have developed association games based on Osirian symbols. I also have developed number and language games to help them understand the complexities of life on this ship."

"Are you prepared to incorporate Earth games into the learning programs?"

"I have left a blank area in my mainframe to be used as a collection and storage point for Earth information. I assume the crew will feed it to me as fast as it comes in?"

"Yes. When we interrogate the children, we will probably load more into your systems. Please load the games program for me."

"There are many. I estimate twenty-one days to play them all."

"I have time. Run the first program."

Engineering and Cargo sent diagnostics to Jupoler through Arop, once a week. He was satisfied the shuttle would perform and was impressed with the pathways, feeding, and cleaning systems Mercianiax and Marsax had developed. They tested the waste transport system using their own waste, leaving it on the cargo floor and asking the computer to dispose of it. The system worked perfectly; the waste disintegrated as it hit open space. They also modified the system to direct the computer to feed all of the animals simultaneously, thus preventing panic that would ensue if they were fed slowly.

Nepeta and Vienusia kept a close watch on open space. Fourteen days out, they detected flight patterns around Earth. They informed Arop when she stopped by. She reported to Jupoler. He decided to announce the find at dinner.

While they were exiting room five, Jupoler said, "You can't see them with the naked eye, but Nepeta and Vienusia have discovered objects orbiting Earth."

Planex was anxious.

"What are they? Are they dangerous?"

"We don't know yet," Vienusia answered honestly. "They could be sentries, first warning systems, or exploratory craft. We will monitor them as we approach Earth."

Dinner ended. Everyone was excited. Objects orbiting Earth could mean they had solved the mystery of the pyramids. In that case, they would be saved, and Osiriat VI could make first contact.

Eleven days later, they were approaching Mars. Arop was at the helm. She called engineering.

"Engineering, Uryxs speaking. How may I help you today, captain?"

"We are approaching the fourth planet in the Sol system. May I initiate the cloaking device?"

"Yes, it is ready. All systems are functional."

"Thank you. Arop, out."

Arop pushed the button labeled CLOAK, and the ship disappeared from the heavens. Then she made another call.

"Innersolar mapping, Vienusia speaking."

"Vienusia, have we discovered what is orbiting Earth yet?"

"We have only been able to determine that the craft are metal-based. Most are tiny. Some travel at quick speeds, and some travel only as fast as Earth, effectively isolating themselves over one point. There is one that is rather large. We suspect it may be a station of some sort. Unfortunately, we are too far away to take proper scans. We'll be on Earth in three days. At that time, we should be able to gather more pertinent data."

Three Days Later- December 2000 Earth Time

Jupoler ended his rounds in innersolar mapping. He exited the elevator, saw Nepeta and Vienusia huddled at their computer terminal, and walked over to them.

"Nepeta, what have you discovered about those orbiting objects?"

"It's very exciting. We've discovered they are called 'satellites.' They are transmitting data to and from points all over the planet. We should be able to intercept the transmissions and learn enough about them to avoid sending a team to Earth."

"Excellent. Get right on it. What about the large one? What's its purpose?"

"We think it's a station. Maybe it's designed to acclimate humans to space. Or maybe it's a stopping point for space missions. We haven't closely investigated it yet. We do know it's manned, so we should go into a high orbit where there's no danger of being detected."

"Okay, I'll go tell Arop to put us into a high orbit. It wouldn't do to have an accident with one of those satellites."

At dinner that night, Nepeta told everyone the good news. "I've calibrated our computer with the satellites. Each department will be sent pertinent information to its departmental terminal. Over the next eleven years, you should be able to discover all the information you need to make our mission a success."

Much was accomplished over the next six years. Planex spent all of his work time in the children's quarters. He downloaded games, cartoons, lessons, and numbers into the two personal computers that were housed here. He had no idea how old the two would be, but he assumed young since they would have so much to learn from the Osirians. He found educational materials to teach any child up to the age of eighteen.

Arop, from her personal computer in her quarters, spent her off-bridge time, previously used up touring the ship, exploring the backgrounds of as many male and female children as she could find. She came close several times to the right choice but disqualified them for various reasons. Her first six years revealed to her no real candidates.

Mercianiax and Marsax spent the next eleven years as biologists and botanists. Every known species, their habits and habitats, were available to them from stolen satellite information. Pictures of the planet helped them to determine where the animals were located.

They had to be botanists, also, because food supplies for many animals, came from plant life. They took samples of each plant they would need and told the computer to dissect them. The computer did and, as a result, gathered enough information to synthesize plants that would later be used for food. The computer also synthesized meat products for the predatory animals and rotten meat for the scavengers.

One of their most important jobs was to try to figure out how to house microscopic bacteria. They did not want to upset nature's delicate balance so they determined they had to save bacteria. Each pair of animals transported up would be cleansed of any bacteria to prevent sickness amongst them. They decided, finally, to deep freeze the bacterium so there would be no danger of contamination.

One day, they asked the computer to transport food to each chamber as if the animals were already there. They left the food overnight and came back to a terrible stench; they had not considered what the cargo bay would smell like. This would not be the only stench. How would the mixture of animal scents smell? They did not want to find out. For sanitary reasons, they programmed the computer to constantly filter out bad air. The computer disposed of it as it would any other waste.

Uryxs and Satetan first programmed the shuttle's orbit and made sure it was fitted with enough fuel for its lonely journey. They then spent their days maintaining power. Their lives would not significantly change until it was time to transport everything up.

Earth 2006- U.S. Embassy (Moscow)

Jane had worried whether her dad would approve of her marriage. She was seventeen, and Bob was twenty-five. As her father was the image of his father, so was she the image of Mary. Like Mary, she had brought Bob out of himself. She found him, like so many other withdrawn, lonely males, surfing the Internet. They exchanged pictures. She had always looked for a man with somewhat similar features to her dad. Bob's sandy brown hair and eyes to match seemed to fit her dreams. When she met him in person, as real people finally must, she quickly fell in love with him. Her dad gave his blessing because he liked Bob; he liked the security of his job with the CIA. He could not understand how she fell in love over the Internet, though.

Jane thought, "If that's a fault, it's his only fault. He is such an awesome dad." She missed him so much these last three years, but Bob had his job to do, and luckily, they had requested a translator.

She remembered her dad's excitement when she told him she was pregnant. Now, it was time to concentrate on that. Push. Breathe. Push. Stop. Relax (Who are they kidding!) One more push. Crying. Baby. A boy! She was slightly disappointed with his blue eyes and blonde hair; she really hoped he would look like her dad. Dad? Of course, Dad!

"John. I want to name him after Dad."

"Okay, Honey." Slightly disappointed, Bob agreed. His fleeting thought was that Robert was a good name, too. He thought then of his son's future. "One good thing, with all the countries we're bound to work in, he'll certainly be multilingual."

"And I'll school him at home. He'll be the smartest kid we know."

Earth-2007

Steve knew his life could have been very different. If his mom had stayed on her path, he would have been nothing more than a juvenile delinquent. Instead, she had taken the home's offer and he was raised right. He did not know whom he took after. Mom was a short blonde woman with deep, thoughtful blue eyes. He supposed his red hair, green eyes, as well as his tall/skinny build must have come from his father's side;

however, he had no way of really knowing as he had never met any of his relatives.

His mother worked herself to death as a cleaning lady for the home. He earned a full-ride scholarship to Scripps Institute of Oceanography and told her not to work so hard, but she insisted because she wanted him to concentrate on his studies. Now she was dead and could not be here with him in the delivery room.

Steve was magnetically attracted to Susan's hourglass figure and medium height. A woman taller than he would not do. Her brown hair and eyes closely resembled the dry California hills they picnicked in on occasional weekends. The final approval, of course, came from his mother. He need not worry. She only wanted to see her son in love. He married Susan in his last year of college. He graduated at twenty-four with a degree in marine biology and was hired by an oil company to study the effects of oil production on sea life. They were required to staff a biologist as part of a settlement with the U.N. after too many spills. The oil companies had to give back in ecological ways, and it paid very well.

Steve was twenty-four years old, holding a great job, and was holding his new baby girl, Daphne. She was smiling at him as if she knew Daddy would show her the world, which he would because his family usually traveled with him. She had his own green eyes with just a touch of brown in a circle around her pupil and a mixture of both of their hair that appeared a curly auburn. Susan had curly hair as a child also but had grown out of it. Susan would teach her many languages. He knew she would be smarter than he was. Reviewing his family history, he said quietly to his mom, whom he thought might be there in spirit, "We finally pulled out of the trap."

Earth 2011- November

There was no question about it. The sea here had progressively warmed during the past four years. Also, the tide had risen a meter over those four years. Steve tapped into a site that confirmed his suspicion. There it was in black and white- the tides had risen one millimeter on May 5, 2000. The ice melts, and the force of the moon had caused the tidal shifts to increase over time. It was time to find out what was causing the ice to melt at such a rapid pace.

The probe slowly descended into the Arctic Ocean for one half-hour. He was glued to the monitor even though no picture would appear until it hit the sea floor.

Suddenly, there was light where light was an impossibility. What the? He saw it but could not believe it. A crack in the ocean floor leading directly north into the polar ice cap. No wonder the tides were rising. A magma gash this size would melt the ice underneath rather than from above, and the warm surface water would break off chunks.

He was glad he had left Susan and Daphne at home- this could turn dangerous. He quickly raised the probe, planning to call the sister ship in Antarctica when he was done. He never got the chance. The entire line of magma blew, destroying any evidence that the ship had ever been there.

Earth 2011- November 3 Days Later

"Momma, why are you crying?"

Susan wiped away the tears. She tried to reassure herself as well as Daphne. "They've lost contact with your daddy's ship. They say everything will be okay." She did not believe it herself. Ships just do not disappear, and in those waters-.

The TV took her attention. The news anchors were having a good laugh, momentarily brightening her mood. It seemed there was going to be another planetary alignment on December 24. They were laughing hysterically because they remembered the "warnings" from May 5th, 2000.

The lead anchor regained his professional composure for sign-off.

"Really, it's okay. Celebrate Christmas Eve, but don't stay up for Santa, or the planets will get you!"

They could hardly say goodnight because they were laughing so hard.

"Honey, let's pack some stuff and go to Grandma's for Christmas." She needed family comfort right now, and the mountains would be nice- just in case.

Earth- December 2011

Bob and Susan had come to Peru six months ago to work at the U.S. embassy in Lima. Finally, they chartered a plane, and here they were.

She was upset because they decided to leave Johnny with his Grandpa in the U.S.

They flew over the Nazca lines.

"Oh Bob, I wish we had Johnny with us; you know how he likes shapes and animals," she said longingly.

"Honey, we discussed that. Peru is no place for him." He could see her disappointment. "At least we'll have pictures for him."

"I guess that'll be okay. What do you think these lines mean? You can't see them when you're on the ground, and there are no mountains close by."

"Ooh! Maybe they're pictures aliens drew so they'd know where to land," he joked.

"Oh, Bob, stop joking. You know that's not true."

"Folks, I hope you've seen enough. It's time to go." The pilot glanced back. "Would you like to fly over the Andes on the way back?"

"Yes!" They both shouted.

As they were flying over, a dormant volcano blew, erasing the plane from the face of the earth.

Osiriat VI- December 23, 2011

Jupoler found Arop at the helm.

"Arop, have you chosen two?"

"Yes, they are highly qualified."

"Was it a difficult process?"

"Yes. The first ten years of my search yielded nothing, but I knew isolating two from billions would take time. Reviewing children was especially hard because their potential rarely surfaces early.

"I decided to change my search parameters. I searched births from about five years ago. I found healthy babies and then concerned myself with the parents. I found two sets of parents fluent in many languages and in mathematical concepts. These particular parents, from the beginning, were determined to teach their children all they knew and weren't afraid to travel with them. World exposure and their quick learning abilities determined my choice of these children. He is five, and she is four. They seem ripe for our lessons."

"Will they be hard to retrieve?"

"No, satellites have kept track of them. They're both in remote mountain regions. Only one of their four parents survives, otherwise, they are with grandparents."

"How did you find them?"

"I used the satellite downloads. They have something called 'cell phones.' I accessed the location of the children using stored data in the satellites. Nepeta did a good job downloading the data stream."

Satisfied Jupoler called Uryxs.

"Uryxs, do you have the coordinates of the children locked in?"

"Yes."

"When can we bring them up?"

"That's hard to say, Jupoler. There is the matter of the humans they are living with."

"Kill them!"

"I'm sorry, What?"

"I said kill them! They're all dead anyway. Transport them to their rooms asleep."

He called Nepeta. "Are the aquarium and dry cargo holds ready?"

"Yes. Mercianiax, Marsax, Vienusia, and I determined the spatial requirements of each animal. The four of us drew up compartmentalization plans, entered them into the computer, and it sectioned off everything for us. Also, the polar area is properly sealed, and the temperature has been set to freezing."

"What about food?"

"We retrieved a wealth of information on the subject from Earth. We have a twenty-year supply of food, real or synthesized. The computer will also continue to synthesize water for all of us."

"Thank you, Nepeta."

Everything was ready down to the last detail. Relieved, he called Planex.

"Planex?"

"Yes, Captain?"

"Are the children's quarters ready?"

"Not completely. I have filled them up as much as I dare. I have asked Satetan to transport their bedrooms up intact to help acclimate them." He looked at Arop. She nodded, indicating she was satisfied.

She knew Planex had made the children's quarters as earth-like as possible. They were filled with all kinds of toys, games, and books that were designed to be fun as well as educational.

"Jupoler, I think it's time."

He barked into the intercom, "Engineering!"

"This is Satetan."

"Satetan, begin transporting all of our selections now."

"Yes, sir."

Satetan and Uryxs were in the transport bay. Normal transport would be ship to surface or surface to ship originating or ending in this room. They had modified the system. The transports they were about to initiate they would not see as they arrived. Each specimen would go straight to its cargo area. Mercianiax and Marsax were busy in the cargo bay directing the transport. Nepeta and Vienusia were helping, each manning one of the water tanks. The animals were systematically transported according to location. The process ended in the polar regions.

When the cargo bays were filled, causing a full six-sided expansion, Uryxs located and transported up the children along with their possessions. Planex was in their cabin when they arrived. They were sound asleep. Their toys and books impressed him. He knew he had a problem when he saw their personal computers. He called Jupoler.

"Captain, these children have their own computers. Why?"

Arop answered. "They were schooled at home. I knew they had computers. Can you retrieve the information?"

Planex checked. After a thorough search, he called her back.

"Lessons and games. Very similar to those I developed for them. I'll need to go to room seven tonight and download all the information I programmed into the mainframe into their computers. May I have access?"

"Yes, we'll let the computer know you have clearance to enter."

Everyone gathered for dinner. Quietly, they ate, each absorbed in the events of the day. As dinner ended, Jupoler took Vienusia to one side.

"In your mapping of Earth, have you been able to tell what the effects of the coming alignment will be?"

"No, sir. We have never been able to calculate it."

"What do you suggest we do?"

"I suggest we leave soon. We need to order the computer to reaccelerate to point zero five percent of light in a direction perpendicular to the alignment. When it is safe to return, we can recalibrate the engines and adjust for any gravitational effects."

Satisfied they should leave, the captains returned to the bridge. Arop set the speed to point zero five of light with orders for gradual acceleration as they exited the system. She then plotted a course out of the system.

Jupoler called engineering. "Satetan, is everything secure?"

"We're done here."

Arop said, "All departments have checked in. Each one is closed and secure."

"Thank you. Arop, get us out of the path."

"Yes, sir."

"Computer, Shields up!"

Earth- December 24, 2011

The doomsayers had cried wolf once too often. No one took them seriously. That was a mistake.

Much activity had taken place on the earth since May 5th, 2000. This nine-planetary alignment was the gravitational pull that was needed.

One by one, the 'ring of fire' volcanoes reactivated themselves. Minor earthquakes rattled several continents. Tides rose considerably. Ships were caught in tsunamis. Beachfront properties were underwater. Mountain homes slipped, crashed, and burned. White bolts of lightning appeared out of nowhere. Two hundred thousand people died that day. Bad, but not doomsday.

CHAPTER 5

TRAINING

Osiriat VI- December 25, 2011

"Attention, crew. Our recent acceleration may have stressed our engines. If a problem arises, I would like all hands available to help Uryxs. We are circling back to Earth. We estimate we will be back in orbit in forty-five days. Any contact with the children is forbidden for the next year. Their only contact shall be Planex."

Jupoler hesitated, waiting for questions.

Silence.

He keyed the intercom once more, his voice muted only in the children's room.

"Planex, to the bridge, please."

"Planex, go wake the children."

"What is my assignment?"

"Introduce our guests to the reality of their situation. Order them to observe Earth as it changes. They must watch and understand the destruction.

"Tell them they are the chosen ones. Prove to them Earth's only choice was failure. The entire story is available on their computers. Show them that this isn't the first time Earth has failed. Stress this is a natural event.

"You will be their only contact this year. Slowly introduce them to the Osirian ways and mention us so that they're not afraid when they meet us. They are the sixth sun rising. They must be prepared to take responsibility. Brother, I do not envy you your job."

"It is still early. Are they sleeping?"

"Computer, status of children?" Jupoler asked.

The mechanical answer was almost surreal.

"Children are sleeping. Estimate natural waking time: one hour."

"Planex, wake them up. I don't want them to wake up in a strange environment alone. Instant exposure to a humanoid will be less stressful."

"As you command, Captain."

Exiting the bridge through the floor hatch down into the crew quarters, he walked forward down the hallway in quiet anticipation. This was the moment he had trained for, yet questions flooded his mind. What will they be like? Will they be angry? Will they smell different? At the end of the hall, he hesitated for a moment and then quietly entered.

Planex ducked through the door jamb into the darkness. He preferred darkness to light. As a toddler in the castle, he had a difficult time dealing with open windows. Space, mostly dark, felt natural. He was wearing a black toga decorated with cypress and narcissus leaves, two plants he had grown fond of over the past few years. It also had outlines of dark animals he had seen in the cargo bays. His hair was black, long, and hanging almost into his blue eyes. Reluctantly, he switched on a light.

The room illuminated. Nepeta located the children by downloading the satellites, and Planex had used the information to make the children's quarters as livable as possible.

A few hours before, Planex had transported all of their belongings to the ship. The children had been asleep for six hours and had no idea of their fate.

As Planex looked around the room, he was satisfied. One side of the room was full of her books, toys, videos, clothing, and, of course, a portrait of her parents. The other side of the room was full of his belongings and a portrait of his parents and grandparents. Both children's computers were now compatible with the ship's system. No data had been destroyed in the transfer.

He looked up at the series of plate glass windows. These windows would always face Earth on Osiriat VI's continuous orbit. The children would be able to have the comforts of home as they watched their real home below them. He hoped they would be happy when he announced his presence. Only two years ago, his voice had been cracking uncontrollably; now, it was a deep, booming voice.

"Arise, children!"

They woke, startled.

"Who are you?!" Johnny demanded. "Why are you in my room?"

Daphne heard the strange noise and sensed she was not home. "Where are we? Where's my mommy?"

"You are on Osiriat VI. You are the chosen ones. I am one of the gods, Planex, the lord of the dead." He added 'lord of the dead' to impress upon them his power.

They looked at each other for comfort, though they had never met.

Daphne turned to face Planex. "Gods? What do you mean? Everyone knows there's only one God!"

"Yes, one God. That is why the earth dies. Humanity chose to be blinded by myth instead of learning the facts."

"What facts?"

"You shall see."

Johnny listened carefully to Planex. He spoke when he thought he would not be interrupting.

"You said we were the chosen ones. Chosen for what?"

"The earth is dying. You have been chosen to make it live again."

Johnny looked out the window. He saw streaks of light but no evidence of Earth.

"You say we are to make Earth live again. How come, when I look out the window, I don't see Earth? Where are we?"

"We are in space, en route to Earth. We've been orbiting Earth for the past eleven years, studying."

"That's not possible. We would have seen your ship."

"It is possible. We have the ability to make our ship invisible. We studied Earth until yesterday. We chose you two and then left Earth to her destroyer."

"Her destroyer?"

"Yes. All the planets and the sun aligned creating a gravitational pull that will tear Earth apart. You will soon see. We are returning to Earth now. We'll be back in forty-five days."

"Where are you from?" Daphne asked curiously.

"We are from the planet Osiriat."

"Where is that?"

"According to Earth's satellites, you call our sun Sirius A and our dwarf star Sirius B. Osiriat orbits between them. They give us life. We have come eight point seven light years to rescue you two."

"Why us?" Johnny insisted. "And if you're from another planet, why can we understand you?"

"You understand me because we arrived in June 2000 and have studied your languages. You were picked because you are the most intelligent children we observed."

"What will happen to everyone else?" Daphne asked, her voice quivering.

"The answer to that question lies in your lessons over the next year. We've downloaded information to your computers to help you understand. Use these next forty-five days to learn why Earth continually fails. We Osirians have observed five failures over the last twenty-five thousand years. They are well documented. Please study them. What you learn will help you to prevent another catastrophe.

"When we reach Earth, you will be required to observe. Even from space, you should be able to see the natural disasters that will plague your planet.

"I will check with you occasionally. Food will appear on these tables three times a day. We can provide whatever you desire; just ask."

"How long will we be here?" Johnny asked.

"I'm not sure. That is up to the earth. Your observation assignment lasts one year. When the year is up, we'll invite you out to meet the crew."

"Why can't we meet them now!" Johnny demanded.

"Patience. They are going to be very busy for the next year."

Forty-five days later, Planex returned to the chosen ones.

Daphne cornered him. "Why are there no satellites orbiting Earth?"

"We believe the gravitational tug-of-war caused them to plunge back to Earth. Even your space station disappeared.

Do you understand the last five Earth failures?"

"We think so," Daphne said. "Were the signs really present?"

"The signs are ever-present. Man has twisted the signs into gods or supernatural objects in each period, blinding himself to the reality of his situation. We have named each new rise of man a 'sun.' You are the dawn of a new civilization, of the sixth sunrise. We will teach you to read the signs."

Daphne's voice had a slight tremor. She was worried because Planex had just laid out an awesome responsibility she was not sure she could handle.

"But you are gods. Won't society be blinded again?"

"Not if you pay attention to our teaching. Continue your assignment. The captain will be excited you understand."

Planex left to report to Jupoler. He visited the children once a week. Each visit found them more morose than the previous. He thought they were being extra studious. When the year ended, he would find out the truth.

The rest of the crew stayed busy over that year. Mercianiax and Marsax visited the animals daily. The animals were content. Several hours a day, they spent observing bacterium under their microscope. Unchecked, they would replicate faster than was desirable, so, occasionally, a batch would be isolated and sent with the waste out to space.

Nepeta and Vienusia were depended upon to run daily checks on the aquariums. They thoroughly enjoyed this duty because they loved the water. The animals responded kindly to them, comforted because Nepeta and Vienusia took the time to learn their languages. Once the whales, dolphins, and porpoises understood they were being saved, they spread a calming effect through the rest of the aquarium.

Uryxs and Satetan, under orders from Jupoler, staged accidents on the surface. Earthquakes lasted a little longer, tidal waves were a little higher, and storms were a little more violent. Jupoler was not taking any chances; humanity could not be allowed to survive if the mission was going to succeed.

Because of the constant changes on Earth, Nepeta and Vienusia had the responsibility of creating new earth maps. Slowly, the continents drifted or sunk, creating islands. The mapping department observed humans trying to escape. Alarmed, they contacted Jupoler.

"Captain, human activity suggests they are going to try to launch escape craft into space."

"I'll watch for them, thanks."

He turned to Arop. "Arop, shoot to kill any craft leaving the surface."

Over the next year, all spacecraft fortunate enough to leave the planet were destroyed. No one, except Daphne and John, survived.

Earth December 24, 2011-December 25, 2012

Two hundred thousand dead the first day. Six point two billion total. A sad loss but a necessary one. Things calmed a little, but the seas were rising. People sought high ground, and boat sales went through the roof.

Within six months, water covered most of the world. Antarctica and the Andes spine were above water, the only habitable areas left. The Andes spine included Peru, a section of Bolivia that bordered Peru's southeastern corner (from the area around La Paz west to the Peruvian border), Chile, and southern Argentina. Antarctica quickly drifted north toward southern South America, slipping, ice melting rapidly, adding to the already high sea levels. Undersea volcanic activity melted the north polar ice cap. The Himalayas were mere islands; the continent had sunk.

Only the people on boats survived. Everyone was trying to get to southern South America. Osiriat VI destroyed those fleeing into space.

The one million people on Earth no longer laughed about doomsday. Many fears developed, the most prevalent of which was the fear of lightning. Jupoler used the ship on December 23, 2012, and sent directional storms to Earth, an electrical storm intense enough to strike all human and animal life down.

Osiriat VI December 24, 2012

Planex entered the children's room as they awoke.

"Hurry children. Today, you will meet the other gods."

The children, sadly, slowly dressed.

Planex was concerned. "What's wrong? Why are you sad?"

Johnny glared at him, "We've spent the last year watching the earth destroyed, and you want us to meet those responsible!"

"I told you when you first arrived these events were natural. We are not responsible for your planet's failure. Human ignorance is the reason it was destroyed. We picked you two for your intelligence and potential, but even you couldn't have saved it. Now let's go."

They arrived at the conference room located in innersolar mapping. Directly across the entrance were a series of plate glass windows encompassing the entire wall. The view was much different than their quarters, where they were only allowed to see Earth. Here, they were allowed to view the grand celestial majesty of space.

The walls were decorated with paintings of a strange ocean, different types of cities, castles, a planet, and a dual sun system. There was also a wall map showing the advancement of civilization from its beginnings on Crystalia across the islands and mainland to the royal capital of Gosiria.

They entered the room cautiously, walking toward the semi-circular table where eight of the 'gods' sat in full regal dress. As ordered by Jupoler, they appeared regal to the chosen ones. The 'gods' sincerely smiled, attempting to reassure the children. As they slowly approached, Vienusia, sensing their caution, rose.

"Welcome, children. Please sit."

She directed them to chairs opposite of the crewmembers.

As they sat, Jupoler stood. "Please introduce us to these children."

Planex was sitting on the children's far left. "Next to me are Uryxs and Satetan, our engineers. Next to them are Mercianiax and Marsax, our cargo maintenance crew. To the far right are Nepeta and Vienusia, our cartographers and sea life experts. In the middle, we have Jupoler and Arop, our co-captains."

Johnny asked, "What kind of gods are you? What God would destroy people trying to save themselves?"

Jupoler's pleasant face changed to a stern glare.

"Don't give me that look. We saw you destroy the spacecraft that tried to escape Earth."

Jupoler controlled his anger well. "They weren't meant to live."

"And our parents?" Daphne asked.

Jupoler was well rehearsed in this lie.

"They died in natural disasters. You no longer need parents; you ARE the parents."

"What do you mean, 'we are the parents?' We're kids. How can we be parents? Does this have anything to do with what Planex said the day we arrived? Something about us being the chosen ones?"

Arop quickly interceded, trying to help her brother. "Yes, we picked you to reestablish the human race."

He gave her a stern look and continued the orientation himself. "As you read, in the past Earth failures, there were always two survivors. We decided this time to save the 'right' two people. We feel that earth picked two based on luck and survival skills. These people didn't retain the lessons imparted on earth and doomed their offspring to be lost. They were resilient, yes. That is an important trait, one of the main reasons we're here, but they didn't learn from humanity's mistakes. We believe you will."

"So we are to accept that we are the last humans and that you are here to see to it that we reestablish humanity. If we accept this as fact, as it would seem we must, what would we have to do?" Johnny asked calmly. He glanced at Daphne. She seemed resigned to her fate.

Arop, undeterred by Jupoler's earlier rebuke, answered. "What you have to do is learn. As you learn, we will find a place where you can settle and rebuild humanity."

"But we are only two. Genetically, we would fail," Johnny said.

Vienusia stood. "Correct, that is where we come in. We will all go to Earth together in about eighteen years. Genetically, we match close enough. We will all create a strong, diverse human lineage. As it will be half human and half Osirian, it should have a better chance to survive and excel."

"Wait a minute. Daphne and I are human. You are Osirian. If we breed, genetically similar or not, we won't be creating a human race; we'll be creating a half-human race."

The others allowed Vienusia to continue.

"Right. That is why we are here. We've allowed humanity to procreate and propel itself after each disaster, but, as proven, it continues to fail. The people of our planet want to know why. There are two theories. The failure is either inherent in man or there is a problem with the earth itself. We've always wanted to colonize Earth, but we can't if Earth is causing the problem. You're correct; mating with us will destroy humanity. But it will also destroy Osirians. We wish to create a new race with all the finest qualities of the two. We've theorized that this will forestall any more destructive periods."

Jupoler, edgy, regained control of the meeting.

"Enough of this. You will understand soon enough. I'm assigning teaching duties.

"Nepeta, you will teach letters, figures, mathematics, astronomy, and memory retention.

"Vienusia, you will teach love and peace using the history of Osiriat.

"Uryxs, you will teach architecture.

"Satetan, you will teach farming and harvesting techniques.

"Marsax, you will teach defensive warfare to be used in the event that society breaks down.

"Mercianiax, you will teach animal care.

"Planex is your free time partner. He has developed games that are fun yet continue your education. He will also be your gym partner.

"Arop will teach purification of the soul through helping and respecting others, medicine, and fair, impartial governing.

"And I will oversee all of your studies as well as teaching anti-theology. After eighteen years, you should be prepared to begin society anew."

They looked at each other, then back at Jupoler. Johnny spoke their shared thought. "Why anti-theology? Aren't you gods yourselves?"

"Why anti-theology? Consider Earth's history. Every time man failed his failure correlated with his blind faith in gods. Those gods weren't like us. We are not irresponsible. It does us no good to have you blindly follow us. We want you to succeed. The race we create must believe in itself to survive.

"We are here to help you. As gods, we shall guide this new race we'll call humanity, since that name suits Earth, into a bright future. It is our goal to once again create a space capable planet; this time, one capable of reading the signs. If there is to be another catastrophe, they will need to be able to escape.

"Yes, we are gods," Jupoler lied. "But you mustn't let yourselves or society revere us. Mankind must believe and trust in itself if they are to survive this time. There has been too much faith put in the hands of gods. We can't do it for you! We are only here to guide you."

Planex broke up the meeting by standing and walking to the children.

"Before we get too serious, let's go introduce you to the animals that will be your friends on Earth."

Jupoler and Arop returned to the bridge. The rest of the crew exited into the gym. Uryx and Satetan decided to use the gym. Everyone else boarded the elevator. When they exited on level two, Mercianiax and Marsax left to tend to the land animals. Nepeta and Vienusia headed to their aquarium duties.

Planex took the children along the observation path. They were both familiar with zoos, but this was something extraordinary. Every animal ever discovered was here, and even a few thought to be extinct. The Osirians did their research and found animals hiding well away from mankind. Planex said, "This is where your education begins. These animals will help you repopulate the earth."

"This polar area is outstanding! How did you get it so well partitioned off?" Johnny asked.

"How do you feed them and clean up after them? This is so overwhelming," Daphne admitted.

"The computer handles all of the chores. It synthesizes food. It also transports waste and odors into space."

They turned to look at the salt-water aquarium. Most animals were visible, yet two odd-looking ones were slightly blurred. Daphne did not recognize them.

She was shocked. "What are those?"

"That's Nepeta and Vienusia. They care for our water creatures."

"Why do they have tails?"

"All Osirians have tails. It's one of the only differences between our races."

As they contemplated this new information, their mouths formed smiles. Planex felt they might be accepting their destiny.

Osiriat VI: 2012-2030- Education

Daphne played with a doll. John read a book. Both wore far-off looks. Meeting the gods shocked them into a contemplative stupor.

Johnny broke the silence. "Daphne, what are you thinking about?"

Daphne snapped out of her daze.

"I'm overwhelmed. It all seems too crazy to be true. Why us? Why would the gods thrust upon us this great honor and not let us worship them?"

"Jupoler will teach us why. I believe we don't have a choice. They obviously picked us for our intelligence. This past year, locked up in this room with you, has taught me one thing. We need to trust each other and stick together. Maybe, through these lessons they will teach us, we can gain insight as to how and why we are here."

They slept, comforted in the knowledge that they had each other. A high-pitched shrieking woke them. Nepeta repeated himself in English. "It's time for your first lessons."

Johnny asked, "Why were you screeching at us?"

"I told you 'it is your first day of lessons' in my language. Soon, you will understand. Over the next two years, I will be your main teacher. I will teach you the basics. Over the next eighteen years, unless you're invited to a department, you will visit the departments only in the presence of Planex. Eighteen years won't be enough time for you to grasp the intricacies of space travel. We don't want to add confusion to your already busy schedule. When you get dressed, meet me in innersolar mapping."

Intrigued, they quickly dressed. The excitement of learning new information propelled them. Daphne ran down the hall with Johnny on her heels, scaled the stairs, and burst onto the bridge breathless.

Jupoler, startled, turned toward them.

"What's wrong?"

Daphne was first to catch her breath. "Nothing. We're excited. Nepeta is going to teach us today. We want to understand why we were chosen. We hope learning is the key."

"You prove why you were chosen. Your excitement is encouraging. Nepeta is through there." Jupoler pointed at the exit behind him.

They entered the innersolar mapping department. Nepeta gestured for them to sit at the dinner table. Across the room, enclosed for privacy, lay the conference room. The doorway to the gym exited through the conference room. Next to them, under a gigantic dome window that held a magnificent view of the stars, Vienusia worked. She acknowledged them with a smile and returned to her duties.

Nepeta was standing behind a projector.

"I am going to show you a series of pictures. A few of them you won't recognize."

"What is the purpose of these pictures?" Daphne asked.

He dimmed the lights.

"They are an introduction to our language and culture. You will also see our attempts to communicate with humans in the past."

The projector sent images to a screen. Their own alphabet appeared, followed by the Osirian alphabet. The next images showed both alphabets side by side. Figures quickly flashed by. Some were familiar, images carved in earth monuments they had learned about in school. Other figures were Osirian images unknown to them. The next images were space-oriented. Galaxies and planets flashed before them.

As the presentation came to a close, Nepeta turned on the lights.

"Tell me the images you remember."

John's answer was vague. "I remember seeing our alphabet, some strange symbols, and some space pictures."

Daphne nodded her head in agreement.

Nepeta sighed. "Two years from now, you will remember it all. You will also be accomplished in the four Osirian dialects."

Nepeta asked them to stand. He screeched at them as he pointed toward Vienusia. Understanding his actions, they walked over to Vienusia. He thought they understood him and smiled. Vienusia argued they understood his gestures only. He was not upset; soon enough, they would understand. To survive, they would have to.

"The rest of the day we'll spend here. Most of your lesson time will be spent in this room watching space. We've repaired and utilized the abandoned craft called the Hubble Telescope. We linked it to our computer. The images can be seen clearly through this dome. Vienusia is monitoring other galaxies. She simply enters the galaxy name and the dome focuses in on that area of space.

"I will teach you all known astronomy first. Next, I will teach you the math necessary to determine spatial distance. Your homework will consist of memorizing the film I showed you earlier, which I have loaded into your personal computers in your quarters. Each day, we'll study several new letters and figures."

Two years later marked their final class with Nepeta. During their free time, they had traveled the ship with Planex who took them to each department for observation. He played letter and number memorization games with them. His lessons exposed them to the different dialects of Osiriat. The hardest language, the chirping of Crystalia, was learned through hours of listening as Nepeta and Vienusia maintained the aquariums.

Nepeta gave them their final exam in Crystalian. He ran the projector for the last time. As each picture appeared, John and Daphne were required to chirp its name.

They passed the test flawlessly. Nepeta chirped, "Go sit at the empty work station next to Vienusia. You will notice the computer is off. I will enter telescopic sites that will appear in the view dome. I want you to tell me the diameter and light-year distance to each site."

This test lasted six hours due to the vastness of space. Nepeta was confident of their memory retention, but he had to test that they had knowledge of the process, not only memorization skills. Interspersed in between known sites, he inserted unknown sites. These, he expected, would stall them, as they would need time to figure out the answers on paper. He was surprised; the process was so ingrained in their brains that they could work out the calculus in their heads and quickly answer.

Nightly, Daphne and John dined with the Osirians. Tonight felt different. Jupoler kept a close watch on their progress. Nepeta sent him regular reports. Not at all surprised they had aced their test, he ordered this dinner to be a celebration of their talents. Everyone asked them questions in natural dialect, which the students answered perfectly. Jupoler knew they were now ready to learn from any crew member. He sent them to Vienusia next.

Vienusia's class met in innersolar mapping. They received two years of instruction from her in the conference room. Here, they learned Osirian history against the backdrop of space. The wall-facing space was constructed of a series of thick plate glass windows. The solid walls provided Vienusia her lesson plan. One wall was painted with a linear map of Osiriat. On a second wall, a mural of the principal cities and castles. The third wall housed a mural of Osiriat and its two suns, as they would appear from space. She spent eighteen months teaching them, using the murals as her main tool. During the last six months she taught them about relationships.

The first day of class, Vienusia walked over to the mural of the planet.

"You can see here that Osiriat is a planet of island nations. Intelligent life began here at the undersea mound of Crystalia. . ."

The first six months were spent documenting the movement of society from island hopping to mainland settling. She was unaware, as was every Osirian, that society actually started on Lonix and had moved to Crystalia for safety reasons. She did not document any villages or castles; she documented only the slow process of Osirian expansion.

The second six months focused on the mural of the cities and castles. She developed each one, from Crystalia to Gosiria, slowly, emphasizing peace.

"These people expanded because of a surplus of food. As they discovered different varieties of food, trade flourished. In the beginning, everyone was related, so love and peace dominated. As society spread, relationships were lost or strained, and war resulted. I will leave war theory to Marsax. Know that Gosiria united the planet, and peace once again dominated. There is simply no reason to fight when everything is provided."

As the second year started, she taught them from the mural that pictured her planet as seen from space.

"This is the great mystery of Osiriat. For all time, we thought we were born on this planet, then, a spacecraft was found in the ocean. This craft, when dissected, gave us the technology to travel space. We've colonized many planets and watched Earth for centuries. The mural represents our mastery of space and the mystery of where we came from. We colonize planets to try and solve this mystery."

Using their imaginations and mathematical abilities to plot where all the colonies were located, they used Osiriat as their central source. They were required to plot Golas' orbit around Sirius a. After plotting the fifty-year orbit, they determined the gravitational effect of Osiriat through the fifty-year cycle. Gravity changed tidal flows. These changing flows provided seasonal hunting and farming patterns. A four-season cycle lasted fifty years, and slow changes occurred over twelve to thirteen years.

They easily passed Vienusia's test covering their knowledge of Osiriat. The test came eighteen months into their training. Daphne asked a question they both were contemplating. "Vienusia, how are we going to spend the last six months?"

"You are supposed to spend them with Planex. I have decided to join you because I enjoy Planex's company."

"What will we study?" Johnny asked.

"We are going to observe each department at work. You will learn the intricacies of this ship. Also, most important to my lessons, you will observe how everyone works together in peace and harmony."

Over the next six months, they rotated to each department every week. They began in engineering. The smell of grease, fuel, and ozone was difficult on them. Concentrating on the bigger picture caused most of the annoying smells to be forgotten.

Satetan and Uryxs were a quiet team. They were nervous when people observed. Working in harmony and speaking only when necessary, they were so efficient they were in demand in other departments. Occasionally, they would team up with others on cross-departmental projects. In these cases, they changed to cordial, talkative team members. Planex sat Daphne and John out of the way to observe. Planex explained the technical details to them as best he could and joked to keep them from getting bored.

The second week of each rotation was spent with Mercianiax and Marsax in the cargo hold. The responsibility level here discouraged observation. Here, one observed by working. Planex made the work fun. The environment, though it tended to be stressful, felt peaceful.

The third and fourth weeks were spent on the ship's upper decks. Four hours a day, they sat in the rear of the bridge, watching the captains interact. Jupoler and Arop did not seem to notice them. Constant course corrections, adjustments, incoming radio waves, and Earth monitoring kept them on their toes. Planex beamed. He enjoyed watching his brother and sister work.

The remainder of the day was spent in innersolar mapping. Here, Vienusia left them in Planex's care and went to work with Nepeta. These two talked constantly. There was never a quiet moment. Daphne and John loved the chirping, sonar language they used. It reminded each of them of a soothing, relaxing song.

At the end of each day, no matter where they were in their rotation, they ended up in the gym. Here, they watched the entire crew interact. Everyone enjoyed the pool except Uryxs and Satetan. When John asked them why, they honestly admitted they did not like 'tail' activities. Jupoler and Arop, natural leaders, led the group in exercise. Mercianiax, Marsax, and Nepeta usually teamed up, as did Vienusia and Planex. Daphne and John, in this room, were allowed to interact with everyone.

After everyone cleaned up, they would eat dinner under the dome. Jupoler, nightly, evaluated their progress. He was pleased at the celebration dinner after they had completed their term with Vienusia because they were still hungry to learn.

"John, Daphne, do you understand that Osirians prosper through peace and harmony?" Jupoler asked.

Earlier, they discussed this issue in their quarters. John nodded to Daphne. Her point needed to be discussed with the gods.

"Vienusia taught us Osirian history. Observing this crew working and playing, we have gained insight into how and why you work in peace. We can't fathom why war existed on Osiriat?"

"I will answer that," Marsax interrupted. "Over the next two years."

Jupoler approved. The next morning, they began Marsax's class. Workload allowed only four hours a day of teaching time. Class met in the gym. A walkway between the men's and women's shower rooms led to the computer room. Orientation was scheduled at the computer terminal located at the entrance to room seven. Marsax ran late due to an open hatch in the cargo. Daphne and John were seated at the computer when she came running up.

"I see you found the Osirian history program."

They turned to see her bent at the waist, hands on her knees, trying to catch her breath.

Daphne was sitting at the terminal. "Yes, this is a program Vienusia used."

"Select the LIVE ACTION option."

Daphne pushed it. The selections included: city building, castle building, social structure, and open warfare.

"Select OPEN WARFARE."

Daphne obeyed. They watched the entire history of Osirian warfare. The presentation first showed minor primitive battles. Most of the program concentrated on the Lonix/Isoloquat guerrilla war and the world war that united Osiriat under Gosiria's rule.

When the program ended, Marsax excused them for the day. "Think about what you saw. We will discuss it tomorrow."

Two weeks were spent analyzing why the war was fought on Osiriat.

Marsax wrapped up the lesson.

"These primitive tribes fought each other for food. We believe this is why Lonixians island hopped. When the guerilla war between Lonix and Isoloquat started, there was plenty of food and land. The reasons to fight were more psychological. The Isoloquans were very superstitious and fought to eradicate the strangers.

Now, we will discuss the war that united the world. This war was officially fought because of overpopulation and the need to colonize. It was actually fought for greed. Greed is the final reason humanoids fight. I will prove this later.

The rest of this year I'm going to explain tactics to you. We'll start tomorrow."

The next day, at the start of the third week of classes, Marsax found Johnny sitting at the computer. "Select: GUERILLA WARFARE."

The screen showed a group of soldiers on the southeastern island of the Lonix chain. They appeared well disciplined, ready to march into battle, spears, and shields ready. Then, the picture panned to the western forest near the cave entrance of Isoloquat. Nothing but dense forest revealed itself.

"Isolate the area around the caves."

Johnny did. Only forest filled the screen.

"Magnify until you spot the soldiers."

John magnified two hundred fifty times. Daphne saw one first. "There, I see one. Wait, I lost him. There he is again," she shouted, excited at her find. "He is heavily camouflaged. Only his eyes give him away."

"He is a bush," Johnny noticed.

"Run the battle."

Johnny selected BATTLE, and they watched as the Lonixians dove into the ocean. They formed tails and sped to the entrance of Isoloquat. When they exited the sea, they were murdered. Fully tailed, they were easy prey.

Daily, they watched Lonix take a beating. Lonix halted its invasion to regroup. The Isoloquans retreated to their homes. They left a small guard contingent at the cave entrance.

The Lonixians waited. They prepared an invasion squad and, without any fanfare, sent them to Isoloquat. The force was small and, therefore, had room to de-tail in the cave. Then, slowly, they secured the perimeter, eradicating the Isoloquan guard. The perimeter secured, they sent a messenger back to Lonix.

Marsax stopped the lesson.

"Computer hold. Class is dismissed for two weeks. Planex will come to your quarters to play a military game he invented. You are to stay in your quarters, except for gym and meals. I want you to strategize, to figure out how the Isoloquans stopped this invasion."

Planex spent the next two weeks with them. As promised, he had developed a war game. The board was a three-D map of Osiriat, complete with foliage. They enjoyed playing with Planex. His playful, positive attitude relaxed them. Learning was easier if they were having fun. Planex revealed nothing to them. By the time class resumed, they thought they knew what the Isoloquan's reaction to the invasion would be.

"What have you decided?" Marsax asked.

John answered for them. "We thought it would be wise for the Isoloquans to station guerrillas in the trees and bushes along this path." He pointed to a path on the screen.

"You are partially correct. Observe." When she said 'observe,' the computer recognized the command and restarted the program.

They watched the screen. The Lonixians cautiously proceeded down the only covered corridor leading away from the cave. They were on their guard, expecting to be hit at any moment. The Isoloquans, however, were unaware of their presence.

A foraging Isoloquan spotted them and ran back to his village. The elders had not expected Lonix to be so bold. Quickly formulating a plan, they sent guerrillas to the trees as Daphne and Johnny predicted. These were decoys placed on the main path to the village. When the Lonixians were in position these decoys rained down out of the trees. Most were sacrificed, but the effect was achieved. The Lonixians decided against the direct route. Instead, they chose to swim up the river because they knew Isoloquans had an aversion to water, swimming into the trap the elders had set. Many Isoloquans, forgetting their fears, lay in waiting under overhangs for the Lonixian force. They let them swim by, surrounding them, then swam out of hiding. Surprising the Lonixians, they killed many with their trident spears. Up and downstream, any survivors who tried to exit the water were cut down by Isoloquans hiding in the bushes and reeds.

Marsax said, "That was a brilliant tactic used by the Isoloquans. There was not another major battle between them until they attacked Lonix with Gosiria's aid.

We are finished for today. Tomorrow, we will discuss Gosiria's domination of Isoloquat." They went to the gym, worked out, showered, and went to dinner.

Jupoler glanced at Daphne and Johnny, then to Marsax. "How are they coming along?"

"They are approaching Osirian's thinking patterns. I ran the guerrilla exercise, and Planex played war games with them. They almost predicted how the Isoloquans were going to defend themselves."

"Almost?" Jupoler asked, worried.

"Don't worry. Before the year is up, they will think like Osirian warriors."

The next day, per Marsax's orders, Daphne selected LIVE ACTION, WAR, GOSIRIA, THE ATTACK OF ISOLOQUAT.

"Push enter."

The crowds cheered as their military marched across the field onto the forest. They immediately stopped at the old abandoned construction quarters. Here they changed clothes designed to make them appear as a large group of traders.

Several groups started out separately and traveled joyously to the first castle on the abandoned trade route that ran from the castle to the ocean. When the first group arrived, they were imprisoned. The duke of the castle allowed superstitious panic to dictate his decision. When waves of traders began to arrive, he considered what he had done and released the first group. In doing so, he committed a fatal error.

The traders revealed themselves as soldiers. Securing key positions, they unleashed their weapons. Caught unprepared, the Isoloquans surrendered.

Each castle of the line fell to the Gosirians in similar fashion. Emissaries were sent to the capital of Isoloquat. The elders of the village decided to surrender on the condition that Gosiria would treat them fairly and help them defeat Lonix.

"That is how Gosiria took control of Isoloquat. It was advanced guerrilla warfare; the villages were successfully infiltrated, resulting in a smaller loss of life. Take a couple more weeks off. Planex is going to play war games with you again. Your assignment is to figure out how Gosiria and Isoloquat took Lonix."

Marsax resumed her duties in the cargo hold. Planex visited Daphne and Johnny daily. He brought the same strategy game. This time, they figured it out. Planex was very excited. At dinner, at the end of the two weeks, he whispered to Jupoler. "They are starting to think like us. They have solved the problem of conquering Lonix."

"Good. They're developing quicker than expected."

Back in class, Marsax asked them to lay out a battle plan for the occupation of Lonix.

Daphne handed Johnny a blank map of Osiriat. He drew the battle plan they had agreed upon. Marsax was shocked.

"You have the correct strategy there. Let's see how it worked for the combined armies. Select: LIVE ACTION; WAR; GOSIRIA AND ISOLOQUAT vs. LONIX."

The sequence ran. They watched as the Gosirian and Isoloquan forces entered the cave and swam into the ocean. A small force attacked the newest island on the east side and allowed itself to be repelled; it acted as a decoy while the true invaders landed on the west side. The unopposed landing team stealthily spread over the island and surprised the defending Lonixians from the rear. Each island was taken in this manner. When the northwestern island was reached, the capital city, Lonix, surrendered quickly. Like Isoloquat, they were treated fairly and allowed to ally with their victors.

"Now Crystalia was the only country left to oppose Tarus' world government. Take another two weeks off. When you return, we will discuss how it fell."

They spent two more weeks with Planex. On the strategy board, they massed the allied troops. The attack on Crystalia, they assumed, had been massive.

Two weeks passed. Marsax had them run the sequence: ATTACK OF CRYSTALIA. Daphne and Johnny were right; it was a massive attack. What they had not realized was the totality of the attack. The aggressors faced no resistance. Everyone in the area of Crystalia was wiped out.

At dinner that night, Jupoler filled in the gaps, "Marsax tells me you've reviewed each of the major battles in our history. Do you have any questions?"

Daphne said, "Yes, I do. Why did each region surrender on such friendly terms with Gosiria?"

A nod in her direction from Jupoler allowed Arop to answer. He enjoyed hearing her recite this story. "They all surrendered easily to Gosiria because they all loved and respected my father, Tarus. Every couple on his team from the last Earth mission had, unbeknownst to the rest, become governors of their countries. Each governor knew he was fighting the greedy monarchists of Gosiria and fought hard because they hated the idea of a monarchy. When they realized they were fighting Tarus, they lay down their arms peacefully. They all trusted Tarus. Government under him would be tolerable. It was senseless to invade Crystalia. They would have accepted Tarus had he communicated with them.

He realized it too late. Vienusia and Nepeta's mom, Dolphinia, opened his eyes. She was enraged by the carnage she witnessed.

"Tarus realized his mistake and called a meeting of the various governors. At the meeting, they appointed him king of the planet. He rewarded them for their acceptance and sacrifices by asking them to serve as a council and govern with him. This worked well because the councilors knew specifics about their regional needs that a centralized king would have difficulty comprehending."

The next day, the class was held in the gym. A large mat was laid out, and the weight machines were removed to a corner. This open space would be their learning center for the next year and a half.

The first day of class, Marsax introduced weaponry. A stockade rested against the wall. Marsax picked out a weapon. "This is Osiriat's first weapon. Crystalians developed it to defend themselves and to hunt. It's called a trident sword. As you can see, the shaft is three to six feet long, dependent on the user. Resting in the hilt of the shaft is a three-pronged blade. Of stone or metal construction, it is equally effective. The trident allows for kills that are out of the reach of an enemy.

Next, we have the spear, which is a single-bladed variation of the trident. For close contact, the short sword and long knife were invented. Over here, we have the shield which is used for self-defense."

Planex entered the room as she was talking. He walked over to the stockade, picked up a trident, and hurled it across the room at Marsax. She dodged. It stuck into the wall behind her. She turned, pulled it out of the wall, and lunged at Planex. He grabbed a shield to defend himself. They fought for a few moments. He finally knocked the trident out of her hands with his shield. He drew a knife. Defenseless, she surrendered. Then they shook hands.

Marsax rose, nearly breathless. "Planex will be joining us every day. Usually, he will be the enemy. As you saw, he is a very learned opponent."

Over the next year and a half, they soaked up all the techniques Marsax and Planex could teach. They became fast experts at thrust and parry, reverse and regroup, sword fighting, knifing, and underwater tactics.

Jupoler watched their progress. At the celebration dinner, Marsax and Planex marveled everyone with stories of Daphne and Johnny's military expertise. Uryxs listened quietly. When dinner was over the ship rule stated that everyone was to relax. Not tonight. Uryx said, "I would like to see these two fight."

Jupoler would not allow it. "No, it is rest time."

Uryxs lectured him. "Battles don't happen on a time schedule. I challenge these two. They have learned tactics, but have they fought against brute force such as mine?" Marsax knowingly looked at Daphne and Johnny. They nodded.

Marsax kicked her chair away. "The fight is on!"

Everyone stood and walked over to the gym. They watched as brutish Uryxs disarmed and knocked the students down one at a time, repeatedly. The battle ended with Uryxs facing two tired, worn-out opponents. Overconfident, he lunged after Johnny. Johnny dodged. Daphne jabbed him in the rear with a trident. He fell to his knees in pain. Johnny jumped on his back and put a knife to his throat.

Jupoler laughed. "Congratulations, Uryxs. You have proven these two are master fighters. Even I can see they're not tired. They lulled you into believing they were beaten. Okay, everyone, it's time to rest. Daphne, Johnny, report to level two tomorrow to begin animal training."

The next day, they woke casually and walked up through the bridge, innersolar mapping, and to the gym. They were filled with the confidence that comes with knowing you can defend yourself.

At the elevator stood Marsax, Mercianiax, Uryxs, and Satetan. They had breakfasted together and were on their way to work. When the elevator doors closed, the normally quiet Uryxs spoke.

"I am rarely beaten. Marsax is the only woman I know with that kind of skill. She has taught you well. I look forward to our time together in engineering. My job is much more complex than fighting. You are quick studies; I shall enjoy teaching you."

Johnny stifled a smile. "Thank you, Uryxs. We hated to defeat you, but that was the goal. No disrespect intended."

"None taken. Remember your defensive lessons. You may need them in dealing with your next class."

The elevator stopped at level two. Mercianiax, Marsax, Daphne, and Johnny exited. The doors shut, and it continued down to level three. Marsax beamed. "You have impressed Uryxs. He rarely compliments. I am off to work. Enjoy learning from Mercianiax."

Mercianiax laid out his curriculum during their grand tour. "We will spend three months discovering each section of this hold. We will begin with predators, then herbivores, polar, salt water, fresh water, and finally aviary animals. The last six months will be spent in the bacterium lab.

Planex arrived on level two after the tour. He joined the class, anxious to explore the environment he was going to live in. Mercianiax dismissed his students soon after. They spent the day in the gym.

The next three months were spent in the predatory containment hold. The animals were content because, instinctively, they knew they were being saved. Class members were allowed to touch and befriend each animal, for the comfort of everyone. The Osirians did not want the animals of Earth to fear them.

Twice incidents arose. If touched wrong, an animal will snap at its offender. The female lion snapped at Johnny one day. His military training saved him. Uryxs was correct; he possessed an instinctive quickness.

The three months spent in the herbivore containment area were not quite as incidental. After meeting all of the animals, they were required to watch computer-generated, live-action predatory chases. None of the chases featured a victorious predator. The lesson was meant to show how each individual's defense mechanism worked. Their final days in herbivore containment were spent goading the animals into defensive postures. Studying the reality of these postures allowed them to develop hunting techniques for Earth. Exercises with animals that used scent as a weapon were discontinued after Johnny's incident with a skunk. Classes were dismissed for three days while the computer deodorized that pungent smell of death. Johnny spent the better part of a day lounging in a synthesized tomato bath, and his clothing was ejected into space with the rest of the cargo waste.

Parkas were provided for the three months spent in the polar habitat. No films were required here. The predatory and passive animals were housed close together. Offensive and defensive habits came alive here, although glass barriers prevented contact.

The next six months were spent in the water. They switched daily from the salt water to the fresh water tank to not overexpose the animals. Nepeta and Vienusia joined the class on a regular basis because they loved the aquatic lifestyle.

Predatory and passive behaviors were studied on the computer as they had in the other containment areas. Not quick enough in water,

Nepeta and Vienusia goaded the animals for them. Extensive time was spent exploring coral, seaweed, and other undersea plant life.

The next six months found them in the bird aviary. Birds were split into three sections: those who ate seeds or flowers, those who were predatory, and those who were scavengers. The only birds missing were those better adapted to polar climates.

Here, they were able to see predators in action. Enough mice and rabbits were born on the ship to supply the birds and snakes with real food. No animal was allowed to keep offspring until they inhabited Earth unless their lifespan was less than twenty years. Scavengers were also seen in action because Mercianiax and Marsax left rotting mice and rabbits for them. Birds who ate seeds and plants received synthesized meals. These birds were passive/aggressive, as Daphne found when she put her finger too close to a parrot's food. The computer's medical aid option healed it quickly, but she still felt residual pain in her finger and forever feared parrots.

The aviary classes ended one month early. Mercianiax prepared for this contingency before he became their teacher. He knew they might excel. "Jupoler has approved my plan. We are going to study nocturnal beasts. Marsax is taking over all cargo duties. We are going to sleep all day and work all night."

That last month, they worked only at night. Mice and rabbits were supplied to all land creatures. Mercianiax taught, "The main lesson in watching these animals is the knowledge of how the earth cleanses itself while you are asleep."

The final six months under Mercianiax's tutelage were spent in the bacterium lab. Bacteria were the only organisms allowed to constantly reproduce. They would be discarded into space if they mutated or overpopulated. In the end only two each would be allowed on earth. The Osirians wanted them to be the newest, strongest strains. Asexual animals, found in many species, stopped reproducing as if they knew instinctively they should not until they returned home.

Daphne and Johnny spent their days looking through microscopes at the wonder of cellular reproduction. What they discovered shocked Mercianiax. He went to Jupoler.

"Jupoler, my students have discovered a new species of bacteria. What shall we do?"

Jupoler thought for a moment. "Destroy it. We are not here to create new species. We must return only natural earth species to the planet."

Mercianiax went back to his class. "We must destroy your discovery. Captain's orders."

Johnny asked, "May we study it?"

"No, it must be destroyed before it contaminates the other samples."

"What if we study it in the discard chamber?" Daphne asked.

Mercianiax thought about that. "Why not! If it can be shown that we tried to discard it, why not study it?"

They put it in the discard bin with the other mutants. When the day was over, they examined the contents of the bin. To their surprise, only the new bacteria remained.

They were frightened. Any predator that killed that fast had to be destroyed. The computer was ordered to dump the bin into space. Jupoler was right. These new bacteria, introduced on Earth, would have caused immortality. They developed by overexposure to the immortality generator on the ship. Immortality was not a natural state on Earth; these bacteria would upset the delicate balance.

At the celebration dinner, Jupoler made the announcement. "Our students discovered a new form of bacteria. We, of course, were required to dispose of it. If everyone agrees, I believe they should continue researching life. Satetan, I believe it is time for your farming class." Jupoler carefully avoided the word or idea of immortality. He brushed the bacterium off as another genetic fluke.

Satetan acknowledged Jupoler's order with a nod. "Daphne and Johnny, class starts tomorrow here in the conference room. After you wake, come on up here and we will share breakfast. I can think of no better way to begin our talk of food production than consuming the end product."

The next day, Daphne and Johnny arrived ready to have breakfast with Satetan. She ordered the computer to synthesize food from every known food group. "As you eat, notice the variety of your food's construction. Dissect it as you eat."

They felt awkward. This was the first time they had played with their food since they were three. Satetan laughed.

When breakfast ended, she directed them to the same computer terminal they had used in Marsax's class. Daphne sat. She selected HISTORY OF FARMING before Satetan told her to. They spent the day watching mankind develop, from harvesting wild plants to isolating them in fields to building societies around the fields. The next day, they watched mills, machines, and commercialism take over farming. The day ended with a lesson on genetic splicing.

When the Osirians saved the animals, they also collected seeds. Satetan taught them over the next year, in an enclave of the transport room, how to plant, cross breed, water, and fertilize all species of edible plant. She ordered the computer to synthesize soil and spread it in the storage room below the transport room. Here, underneath the transport room, was a greenhouse, its walls and flooring made up of windows.

At the end of the first year, she had them plant crops, one type of plant per row. Then class moved back up to the conference room. Here, they learned harvesting techniques. The techniques they learned were man-powered. Machines did not exist on Earth. They learned that some plants were easy to pick by hand, while others needed specific sickle or machete swipes to be harvested correctly. The computer provided materials and Satetan taught them to build rough food storage bins.

The crops they planted each matured at different rates. At maturity, Daphne and Johnny were required to harvest them. Carefully, they set aside seeds they would need on Earth. After each harvest, the crew was served special treats of 'real' food. At the end of the second year, when the majority of the crops matured, a celebratory meal was planned.

Satetan presented her new farmers to the group. "No one will go hungry at the new colony. My students are now masters of agriculture."

Everyone nodded their approval. Dinner was excellent. Arop conveyed new assignments before Jupoler could. "Satetan, go back to work tomorrow. I am going to take over their education for the next two years. Daphne, Johnny, tomorrow morning, meet me on the bridge."

The next morning, they met Arop on the bridge and spent the day shadowing her. The first four hours they visited every part of the ship. The following eight hours were spent observing her working on the bridge. The last few hours were spent in the gym and at dinner.

The following day, classes started. "Yesterday, I showed you what a leader does. The ultimate responsibility for the smooth running of this ship is on my and Jupoler's shoulders. Yesterday went very smoothly, yet there may be days that my presence is required outside of class. Planex has agreed to take over on those days. I am going to ask him to join our daily classes. I want him to learn how to associate with people and govern fairly. My class is designed to teach you the purification of the soul. My main topics will be helping and respecting others, fair and impartial governing, and medicine."

"Why medicine? What does that have to do with purifying the soul?"

They all turned as Planex answered for Arop. "Simple, Johnny. A healthy body allows for a healthy soul. You will find, as we proceed, that helping others and impartial government complement each other."

"Hello, Planex," Arop said as he joined them. "Okay. We are going to spend four hours a day, every day for one year, touring the departments of this ship. At least one-third of the time, we'll run into technical difficulties. In these cases, we must help solve the problems. About one-half of the cases will be dual-departmental. This is where class becomes difficult. We must respect the needs and wishes of each department while maintaining the integrity of the entire ship. You will see how helping and respecting others works hand in hand with fair and impartial governing.

After the first four hours, I will return to the bridge. If we have discovered no problems, you will return with Planex to the computer learning center in room six to study medical technologies. The computer will self-guide you through this program.

Planex has also developed a basic governing game. The goal is to become a fair and just king and queen. There are many pitfalls in this game that will lead you into evil, despotic rule. You must learn to overcome the evil in order to win the game.

If we have located problems, you will attend to them until it is time to report to the gym, exactly twelve hours after class starts. If a problem poses a threat to the ship, we have a containment field that will allow you to leave it for a day. There are only a couple of problems that can't be contained; in those cases, everyone will pitch in to solve them."

They spent the next year in this manner. A short in a conduit in the transporter bay caused the lights to go out in the cargo bay. The animals became hysterical, upsetting Marsax and Mercianiax. Daphne helped calm the animals while Johnny helped Uryx fix the short.

Innersolar mapping lost contact with the Hubble telescope. Daphne, Johnny, and Planex helped solve this situation over the course of a week. The problem was not on their end. Nepeta transported over to the telescope to fix a power outage.

Minor glitches occurred, but none so drastic that kept them from studying each department. Their time was split equally between learning medicine and playing with Planex. When the year was up, they knew how to avoid the pitfalls of evil, promised to be good leaders and had learned enough medicine to start the next section of classes.

Arop met them in the gym. She spent the day quizzing them. She laid out bottles and tablets, unlabeled. They had to identify each and relate its uses. These were all natural medicines they could easily locate on Earth. They knew them all.

The next day, Arop beat them to the gym. They saw bodies sprawled out everywhere in graduated states of injury.

"The computer-generated these dummies from real disaster scenarios. They each have unique symptoms. You can see some are missing limbs, there are a couple of open wounds, and the rest appear okay but complain of internal problems. We will spend the next three months teaching you how to handle each contingency."

They proved themselves natural doctors over the next three months. To prove that their knowledge had become second nature, Arop surprised them. At dinner, the night their medical training ended, Jupoler and Uryxs' conversation developed into a heated argument. Uryxs became enraged and threw a knife at Jupoler. The knife slashed his arm. Instinctively, Daphne and Johnny rose and treated Jupoler. They were oblivious to the danger Uryxs still posed. When they finished, to their surprise, Jupoler clapped.

"Excellent response! Arop, well done. Where are they going to train next?"

"On the bridge with us."

"Excellent. I look forward to spending time with them."

The final nine months of Arop's class were spent on the bridge. The first week was spent strictly observing. The rest of the time, they were required to answer all incoming calls from each department. They solved many problems from the bridge. A few required their direct help. Planex was still partnered with them. He had a grasp on the more complicated problems. Working together, they all became stronger problem solvers and leaders.

As the celebration dinner upon completion of Arop's training course ended, Jupoler congratulated them. "You have become natural leaders. I am going to take over your training now. As leaders, you must know when to lead and when to follow. I am going to concentrate on anti-theology. We must prevent you from traveling the wrong path. You will report to me on the bridge tomorrow."

The following morning found them on the bridge. Arop greeted them and then went off to her daily rounds. She knew this was their observation day. When she returned, she was stunned.

Jupoler was standing by the door, anticipating her arrival. She nudged him. "What's this?"

"This is Daphne and Johnny piloting the ship. They picked up the basics rather quickly. I decided to let them try. There's nothing out here to hit anyway."

Arop walked around the pilot seats and looked at Daphne and Johnny. "Are you having fun?"

"Yes, Arop. This seems rather easy," John answered confidently.

"It can be deceiving. Step away."

"But, I told them they could-"

"I know you did, and they seem to be doing a fine job navigating normal space. I want to give them real problems. They've had enough time today."

"Okay, take the rest of the day off. Tomorrow I will start your classes. I will be your guide for the next three years."

Daphne and John found Planex, and together, they explored the ship. The next day, they met Jupoler in innersolar mapping.

He began class. "Children, every day, in the morning, I want you to come here and explore the majesty of space. Nepeta and Vienusia will allow you to use their computer. I want you to use the Hubble information and your own naked sight to judge the vastness of the universe. After three months, you should have an idea of its greatness. My duty is to the bridge. Each day, I will come get you to make rounds with me. I want your input. My goal is to hone your leadership skills.

"Every night before dinner, as always, we will all congregate in the gym. I want you to observe nightly how we, the gods of Osiriat, perfect our bodies. You will also observe how we respect each other."

They spent three months in this dictated routine. Jupoler questioned them the morning after the third month ended. "What have you discovered about the universe?"

Daphne answered, "It is far too vast to be measured."

John offered, "Its size is unknown."

"What about its origin? What caused it to form?" Jupoler asked.

Daphne was a little perturbed that Jupoler would ask such an impossible question. "We cannot possibly know that."

Jupoler agreed. "Right, but intelligent creatures have always sought an answer. There is no visible answer, so one is invariably created. That answer, without fail, becomes a deity. Osirians think differently. We don't care why it happened; we care *that* it happened. Without it, we would not exist. We give no being the credit. We simply do our best to honor it. Races who elevate gods usually fail. We elevate the process and build on it; that is why we succeed. Any questions?"

Daphne jumped at the chance to ask a question that had been puzzling her since Marsax's class. "Why did you have wars?"

"Good question. It is part of the process of growth. Occasionally, destruction must prevail if growth is to succeed. Destruction rids society of the weak elements. New growth is stronger as a result.

Now, let's discuss what you learned in the gym. John?"

"I observed perfect bodies just like you said I would. What was the point?"

"The point was, and is, that even the gods have to work to keep healthy. You see, they have the weakness inherent in all intelligent life. Intelligence isn't a replacement for strength. Arop taught you a healthy body leads to a healthy soul. This is even more critical to us as gods."

"But what is the purpose of your being gods if no one is to worship you?" John asked.

That question kept Jupoler busy for six months. He kept them with him all day. Each eight-hour day on the bridge, he tested them.

"Observe the vastness of space. How many light years away is that star? How about that one? That galaxy?"

He took them on rounds and ordered them to observe the habits of the gods while he worked. In the gym, he marveled at the physique of his crew.

He could not formulate in words why they were gods without giving away that they were not really gods but, instead, immortal. Finally, he stumbled upon the answer. He invited them to breakfast under the dome.

"I have found the answer to John's question, 'What is the purpose of your being gods if not to be worshipped?' The answer lies in the definition of a God: A being that is omnipresent. A creator. We Osirians, as I explained earlier, disregard the God concept. We are the only race we have found that does this. We believe in ourselves and the abilities of our race. Our race is everpresent rather than omnipresent. We exist on all known habitable planets, and we will find more. What we do when we find them is to create new societies. We have become gods simply by following the definition of what a god is: a creator."

Daphne asked, "But why can't we worship you as gods?"

"Because we cannot control your destinies. We don't have power over your lives. Your life's direction is up to you, as it is for all humanoids. I told you when you arrived, 'god worship leads to dependence on false idols, which leads, ultimately, to destruction.' You must not worship if you are to survive. Tomorrow, I will give you an example of exactly what a god is supposed to be."

The next day, nine months into their classes, they met Jupoler in the gym. "Today, you are going to see a part of this ship that only Arop and I have access to. Follow me."

They followed him to the middle of the gymnasium floor. They walked toward the elevator. Close to the elevator, they turned left down a semi-circular hallway that encircled the elevator. The hallway opened into the pool and small Jacuzzi room. They followed the path past the showers to the computer learning terminal. Jupoler sat at the terminal and typed: Captain gives his permission for Daphne and John to enter room seven.

Instantly, the computer responded in type on the screen: Waiting for approval from co-captain Arop. Bridge, please respond.

A moment later, the word CLEARED appeared on the screen.

The door to room seven slid open. Jupoler motioned John and Daphne in. The door slid shut. The light was so intense they shielded their eyes with their hands. They had heard of mainframes. John remembered seeing one in an ancient movie in which a kid breaks a secret code, stumbles into a non-accessible mainframe, and almost starts a global war.

They were wholly amazed. The room was mammoth, filling one-sixth of the ship. Steel and lights filled the room. One wall housed multiple screens showing every activity taking place on the ship. There were two terminals, one labeled Jupoler and one marked Arop, set up for them, as computer room maintenance was one of their duties.

"You have access to this room for the next year. Ask the computer any question you like. Please break for gym and meals daily. We want you to stay healthy. You could lose track of time because there will be so many questions. I have directed the computer to shut off these terminals after twelve hours of use as a safeguard to your health.

Jupoler left. John and Daphne sat at the terminals. The question the gods feared and the one that plagued the children's minds since day one was the first asked.

The computer gave the appropriate, preprogrammed answers:

"Your parents died in natural disasters. John's parents: volcanic eruption destroyed their tour plane. Daphne's parents: Father died at sea, also due to a volcanic freak accident; Mother died in an earthquake.

The computer lied to Daphne about her mother. It did not know as it was regurgitating the facts as it had received them. Jupoler ordered Daphne's mom killed and entered the "accident" into the logs. All voice records of his order were deleted immediately following their entry.

They visited room seven every day as ordered. They asked inexhaustible questions as every answer created an average of two more questions.

When the year ended, John approached Jupoler. "The computer seems omnipresent. Is it also a god?"

"No, it doesn't create."

"Yes, it does. It created this food we are eating," Daphne pointed out.

"But he didn't create it. The computer only does what it's programmed to do. A god would do things by choice. The computer is an example of what a god can be, not what a god is.

"We have barely over a year left together. I want you to spend it with Arop and me on the bridge. Planex has been training while you were confined to room seven. Report to the bridge in the morning."

They arrived as ordered. Jupoler laid out the schedule for the following year, "Daphne, John, Planex, you will observe each day for the first eight hours. The last four hours of the day two of you will sit in these seats and pilot the ship. One of you will stand behind the seats, giving commands as situations arise. These flights are real. The tests will be simulated. Planex has been through some of this over the last year; he will start as commander. We have entered many simulations into the computer. Remember, the results are up to you. No one can do it for you."

Over the next year, they were challenged with rogue comets, enemy craft, faulty engines, fuel pressure buildups that could destroy the ship, spiraling into planets, and asteroid collisions. These were the minor tests.

Six months in, Jupoler and Arop printed evaluations from their room seven terminals and decided to let the three trainees take full control of the ship. Jupoler and Arop spent this time working on the architectural design to be used as a base for rebuilding the city they knew existed.

They worked in engineering and often sought advice from Uryxs. One evening, as they were proceeding to the gym, Jupoler was attacked. Arop arranged it. Satetan asked Uryxs to linger, and she entered the elevator with Arop and Jupoler. The lift stopped at level two. Vienusia and Marsax boarded. Catching a glance from Arop, Vienusia explained that Mercianiax and Nepeta were already at the gym.

Moments after the door closed, Arop selected "emergency stop." Several voices attacked Jupoler at once. "When are we going to surface? We are ready to breed. May we breed with Johnny now?" Jupoler was taken aback. Unsure of himself, he backed away. Suddenly, he took command.

"You girls, hush! You know the timetable. No, you may not attack Johnny, and you may not indicate that you are ready. He is an Earth male. They develop sexually rather quickly, and I will not have him abused. I will hear no more of this. Arop, take us up!"

At the three-year celebration dinner, Jupoler pointed to Planex, Daphne, and John. "I have secured the future of this ship. These three are three of the most capable pilots I've ever encountered, but there is more to running the bridge. A good pilot also knows everything about his engines. A great pilot knows his ship so well he can take over engineering at a moment's notice.

This is the final step of your training. You will spend the next three years with Uryxs in engineering. Uryxs is going to teach you architecture as his main focus. When you're through, you will possess expert knowledge of the inner workings of the ship. Report to level three tomorrow morning."

The next morning, at the elevator, they met Planex. Daphne pushed the level three button. "What level do you want me to select for you, Planex?"

"No need. I'm joining you."

He noted their confused look. "Jupoler came to my quarters last night and asked me if I wanted to learn about the engines. I said yes. I can't let you guys be the best pilots."

They smiled. John said, "Good! We were hoping you would be allowed to join us; we've come too far together to separate now."

The elevator stopped. They exited into the shuttle bay. The emergency shuttle filled seventy-five percent of the room. Daphne and John looked upon it, awestruck. The first time they saw it, it was in the beginning stages of construction. Planex read their faces. "What's wrong?"

Daphne said, "I never imagined it would be this big."

John added, "Yes, how can a shuttle be that big. It looks like a regular ship."

"It is a regular ship. This shuttle is our emergency backup in case something goes wrong on Earth. Osiriat VI is much bigger."

"But we've never seen it from the outside."

"That's true, John. Osiriat VI dwarfs this shuttle. I'm sure we'll get more time with it later. Now, we must find Uryxs."

He led them around the elevator toward the engine room. Here, they found Uryxs waiting patiently.

"Welcome." He stood strong, solid. His brute force intimidated Daphne and John even though they had beaten him in the ring. He remembered that disaster as he watched them approach.

"This is engineering, the heartbeat of the ship." He waved his hand through the air. "I have looked forward to teaching you its intricacies ever since you beat me in the ring. I could sense your intelligence then. Today, we will tour all of level three. Tomorrow, we go to work."

The next day, when they exited the elevator, Uryxs, waiting for them, thrust tools into their hands. "Take these tools and follow me." They walked to a table and stood over a complete schematic of the shuttle. "These dark areas are complete. These light areas are not. The task is yours. It should take about six months."

The next six months were spent completing the shuttle. Portions of the outer shell were carefully placed and welded to the frame. They assisted as Uryxs fine-tuned the engine. Finally, it was time.

Planex, Daphne, and John sat in the passenger seats. Uryxs sat in the pilot's seat. "Captain, permission to launch?"

Arop was at the helm. "Hold, please. Computer, seal check, level three, shuttlecraft."

"Shuttle sealed. No detectable flaws, Captain."

Arop turned her attention back to level three. "Uryxs, the computer has cleared you. Launch at your convenience. Enjoy your flight."

Uryxs turned on the engine. As it idled, he called the computer. "Computer, raise airlock doors, level three, shuttle bay."

The computer sealed off the rest of level three and then slowly lifted the doors. When all was clear, Uryxs pushed the throttle forward. They rose off of the deck and slowly exited the ship. The airlock doors closed behind them. Uryxs jammed the throttle completely forward, hurling them toward Earth. He encircled the planet and headed back to Osiriat VI. The ship was a speck against the backdrop of space. Quickly, it became gigantic. Now, Daphne and John understood why Planex was surprised when they thought the shuttle was big.

"Osiriat VI is gigantic," John observed.

"Yes, isn't she beautiful? Now you see why a captain, a great captain, needs to know his ship's every detail. This is an awesome responsibility."

The shuttle bay doors opened. They entered nose first. Once the shuttle was inside the ship, the computer sealed the airlock doors. Uryxs turned the shuttle one hundred eighty degrees to prepare it for the next launch and, when it was in position, lowered it to the ground.

They exited the shuttle. Uryxs, last to exit, called the bridge, "Captain, test of shuttle complete. No problems noted. She's ready for service."

"Noted. One of us will come down to inspect it later," Arop informed him.

Uryx turned to his students. Inside, he was beaming. His manner betrayed no excitement. "The shuttle is complete. Follow me to the engine room."

Once in the engine room, he walked to a table and picked up a handheld computer. "This is a diagnostic machine. Watch."

He walked over to a wall and removed a section. He set his diagnostic machine on a pipe running through the wall. A green light flashed, indicating that there were no problems with the system. He then pulled out a wire and cut it. Rerunning the same scan a yellow light on his handheld indicated that there was a system error.

"Look at this. This light means there is a problem indicated. Now, of course, we know where the problem lies because I created it."

He stuffed the wires, still broken, back into the wall. "Now, if we can't identify the problem, here's what we do."

He ran the conduit with his handheld diagnostic machine until the yellow light turned red. At that point, he opened the pipe and found the disconnected wires.

"I want you three to spend the next six months running diagnostic checks on this entire level. The computer will create breakdowns in the system. Every system will be affected. This diagnostic machine will tell you how to repair each individual problem. I will be on hand if you have any questions."

Daphne spoke up. "I have one. What do simulated engine repairs have to do with architecture?"

"Architecture involves planning and building. Taking care of this engine is a basic form of that. Later, we will involve you in real architecture."

Uryxs left them to their task. He went back to the shuttle to await inspection. Later that afternoon, Jupoler arrived.

"Uryxs, I'm here to inspect the shuttle."

They boarded. "My main interest is in the generator and cargo bay."

They walked over to the generator. "Is it fully functional? Will it be able to produce the energy we're going to need to survive?"

"All tests indicate it will. The orbit we've plotted should provide sufficient materials." As they were talking, they quickly found the cargo area.

"Will this bay hold enough materials for the additions?"

"I have made it expandable, like our own shipbays. I have a plan to load it outside of the ship. I'll launch it and cable a lifeline to the ship. I'll then transport all the materials into the expanded bay."

"That's good thinking. Have Daphne and John do the transporting when the time comes." Jupoler turned away and abruptly left Uryxs. Uryxs was not upset. He knew Jupoler's schedule was full and that he did not have time for niceties except during leisure hours.

Daily Uryxs supervised as his students "repaired" the engines. He rarely helped them. After six months, he was convinced they could build an engine if they had to. When they arrived at the engine core, he took time to explain how it worked before he had them run tests.

"You see, the fuel created here runs through these tubes to the thrusters. The fuel ignites in the thrust chamber. What is unique about this fuel is that its waste regenerates when added to water. Here, the fuel waste is collected, and here, this hose transports it out. Down the line here, the hoses merge, forcing the waste and water to mix. The mix creates fuel, which is dumped back into the core. We depend mostly on gravitational pull to travel, so we don't use much fuel. One problem here, however, and the whole ship could be destroyed."

They finished their diagnostic on the core and thrusters. He invited them to the transporter room. Satetan accompanied them.

Uryxs asked Satetan and Planex to step onto two of the four pads. "Later, you two will be responsible for running this system. Let me show you how it works."

They followed him behind a console with a myriad of controls. "This pad controls organic compounds, this one, inorganic. When the item is on the pad you press the button that corresponds with the item. Satetan and Planex are organic, so I select organic. The terminal scans them. It detects inorganic material in their clothing and automatically activates the inorganic pad to run in concert with the organic commands. I then select their destination, in this case, the other two pads. The terminal triangulates both positions. When this green light flashes, I push TRANSPORT. Observe."

Satetan and Planex slowly disappeared and reappeared instantaneously on the other pads.

"Now, when you transport to or from another area, you push this button, and the ship's computer will triangulate and isolate the area. Once isolated, you follow the same steps. You try it. Transport that barrel across the room."

John transported the barrel as asked. Daphne transported it back.

Uryxs was proud of their success. "These transporters provide an important function to the ship. If they malfunction, cargo or people will be lost forever. It is our job to make sure they don't. I want you to spend the next three months running a diagnostic on the transport system. The computer will run simulated problems after the first complete systems check. I will leave you alone on this project. If you have any questions, you'll find me working in the engine room."

The transport diagnostics ran smoothly. The computer-simulated problems were solved easily. Uryxs decided it was time for them to relax.

"You three have performed beyond our expectations. It is time you relaxed. I'm going to allow you to study for the next three months. I want you to spend this time at the computer terminal in the shuttle bay. We have a lesson called Architecture of Osiriat and Earth through the ages. Memorize the material. We will be building in your final year."

Daily, they explored the wonder of the different ages of architecture. The designs they preferred were Greco-Roman. They had durability rarely seen in other designs.

They met with Uryxs in innersolar mapping when the three months ended. He asked, "Did you enjoy the architecture lesson?"

They answered simultaneously. "Yes."

"What was your favorite design?"

They all started to answer, Planex prevailed. "We all prefer the Greco-Roman design."

"Good."Uryxs agreed. "That design Tarus originated when he was assigned to Earth. It is very durable.

I have news. Nepeta has been mapping Earth every six months for the past seventeen years. He has located Tarus' city, Osiriat V, on the southern continent. It is in a sad state of repair. It was constructed of extremely dense metals, but millennia trapped under ice almost completely destroyed it. Your job, over the next year, will be to create designs that will rebuild and reinforce the city."

"How? We don't know how to build. We only know how to repair," John said.

"I will guide you. We will meet over the next six months here in innersolar mapping. Nepeta has built a scale model of the ruined city. We will use this model to develop a plan to rebuild Osiriat V."

"Where will our staging area be? Space?" Daphne asked.

"Yes, we can build it remotely using the transporter. Let's begin."

They walked over to the table where the scale model was displayed. Uryxs asked, "John, what would you do first?"

"First?" John asked, buying a moment by restating the question. "I think I would raise these fallen columns."

"Daphne?"

She did not hesitate. "Yes, that sounds right. Once the columns are raised, we can determine where the walls and roofs rest. Once we have a solid foundation, we can worry about cosmetics such as doors, windows, fountains, and such."

"Good answers. Let's get started."

By hand, they raised the fallen columns. Where columns were missing, possibly ground to sand by the ice, they erected false, paper columns. They used paper to represent the walls and roofs. Uryxs guided them by making suggestions designed to make them think. "Would that look better over there? Is that column for support or decoration? Wouldn't a nice foyer enhance the overall look?"

Their scale model represented a beautiful city, but ruins were still prevalent on Earth. Daphne was curious. "Uryxs, how are we going to build the city remotely?"

"We'll need the model. Bring it to the elevator. We will take it to the transport bay as our guide."

They loaded it and traveled down to level three. In the transport bay, they set it up on a table.

Uryxs asked the computer to bring up the ruined city on the screen. "You can see we have our work cut out for us. Your designs are wonderful, though, and should be easy to implement. This station over here-" He took them over to a workstation that had been sealed off during their diagnostic check. The station housed the tractor beam and the laser cutting tools. "Daphne, you asked how we were going to build the city remotely; here is your answer."

He walked around to a terminal. He isolated a downed column and set the tractor beam to its coordinates. "Observe."

Daphne, John, and Planex watched as the horizontal column became vertical again. "This tractor beam creates an anti-gravity field around the object it wants to move. The object loses most of its weight, and the tractor beam simply moves it to where we want it to go. Now that this column is upright, we want it to stay. This is where the lasers come in. We use the lasers to steady the column. Then, we disengage the tractor beam because we can't transport material through it. I need a hole for the column to rest in, so I transport out the dirt underneath it. The column lowers into the hole. Now, I transport dry cement into the hole and add water. When the cement sets, I remove the laser beams. In this manner, you will rebuild the city. Are you ready to begin?"

They all nodded. Planex attempted a beam successfully, as did John and Daphne. Uryxs, excited that they quickly grasped the process, told them to proceed. "I have every confidence you will succeed. I'm going to leave you now. Build our city."

Uryxs expected the construction to take six months. The building was over in four. He could not believe it. He ran computer stress tests and determined it would stand. The dense metals Tarus originally built with proved resilient. Combined with the material they had brought along, the city appeared indestructible.

Uryxs met with his students. "You have finished two months ahead of schedule. What are you going to do?"

Planex answered for the group. "We finished early on purpose. We noticed that there might be some cosmetic areas to work on. We want to add art to the structure. We noticed faded art on some of the columns."

"What would you choose to represent with this art?"

"We want to cut Osirian scenes into the walls with the lasers. Also, some of the columns are missing ridges."

"Sounds good. Approved."

They spent the next two months casually creating designs in the city. They cut duplicate murals from the ship into the walls. They also cut space scenes, stars, planets, and galaxies and cut designs that they remembered from their childhood, such as boats, cars, and animals.

They spent hours of free time in the gym, swimming and working out. They also spent time visiting the gods as they worked. The majority of the time they spent with Planex. Now that they were older, he taught them what he knew of social interaction and mating rituals of the Osirians.

The night before the final celebration of their completion of eighteen years of learning, they were resting in their quarters. Daphne said, "Do you think we should?"

"I don't see why not. After everything we've been through together, they should be honored that we want them to be immortalized."

"We should go tell Uryxs right now," Daphne suggested. "He is a thinker. He will tell us if it's going to be okay."

Uryxs was surprised and flattered. He contemplated what they told him.

"You better let me announce this plan after dinner tomorrow. If anyone gets angry, I'd rather they were angry with me."

Osiriat VI 2030

Each "god" appeared aged only five years over the last eighteen. Jupoler had lowered the gravity output to acclimate them to the real growth that they would experience on Earth.

After dinner, Jupoler decided a speech was in order on this last formal occasion.

"Daphne and John were already highly intelligent when we saved them. I am proud to say they quickly acquired the maturity and responsibility levels of the children of Osiriat.

"John is twenty-four and, I think you will all agree, as strong-willed as myself. His strong, healthy body reminds me of Uryxs.

"Daphne is twenty-three. She is tall like John. I never thought I would see anyone as beautiful as Vienusia, but Daphne has accomplished this. She even wears her long, auburn hair to her waist like Vienusia. We appreciate them both. I hope they appreciate being chosen?" He had directed his question to them.

They nodded yes.

Jupoler continued. "Would anyone else care to say a few words?"

Uryxs stood and nervously addressed the rest of the crew.

"The children- excuse me- the chosen ones have honored us today. They wish to make the renewal complete. They've taken it upon themselves to rename the planets in this system after us.

"The legend says that the Greek sailor Tarus befriended and memorized the names of the Gods. On his journey home, he was struck ill. When he recovered, his mind had lost the names of the Gods. He remembered there were nine and set himself to the task of naming them. The Greek and Roman royalty, impressed with his story, took these new Gods as their own. Over the centuries, as the planets were discovered, man named them in honor of the Gods. They will be renamed Mercianiax, Vienusia, Marsax, Jupoler, Satetan, Uryxs, Nepeta, and Planex. The sun is to be named Arop. Again, they've done this to honor us."

Jupoler's face boiled. He bolted up.

"Why have you named the planets after us?! Didn't you learn anything in anti-theology class? You are not to worship us!"

Daphne calmly defended their choice. "We don't worship you. We named the planets out of love and respect for you. We have spent the last eighteen years learning from you. Most of our lessons revolved around or were based on symbolism. You've all told us stories of your parents, the Great War, and the qualities they represent.

"We see those qualities in you, their children. We named the planets after you in order to convey to the new generations stories of the beings that rescued us. We hope to instill the values in them that you've instilled in us based on symbolism. We want people to look in the sky, see Vienusia, and say, 'She is why we have beauty and peace in the world.' "

"And what would you say of me?"

Daphne remained calm.

"We would say, 'Do you see that huge planet? That is our lord, Jupoler. He is the most powerful God in the entire universe. All the other planets bow to him. It is he who, along with his sister Arop, our sun, saved our planet from destruction. But beware. He may create or destroy as he sees fit. Honor him always, but never worship him; it's the worst thing you can do.' Can't you see that we want you to be remembered always?"

He was tempted to tell them he was immortal, but if they knew that, they might really worship him, so he settled the issue. "Well, as long as their purpose is for learning and not worship, we'll allow the new names."

Satisfied this subject was closed, he moved on to one he considered more important. "Uryxs, how is the new city coming?"

"Better than expected. Using the designs our genius chosen ones developed in architecture class, we have been able to reinforce the ruined city. When Nepeta found it, we thought it was hopeless."

Nepeta and Vienusia had split up their workload. She took aquarium duties, and he took mapping duties. He had remapped the earth every six months for the last eighteen years. Five years earlier, on the now ice-free continent of Antarctica, he had found the ruins of the fabled city of Atlantis, known to the Osirians as Osiriat V. Humans had been searching the oceans, never imagining they should have been searching the ice. The last group, Osiriat V, built it with extremely dense metals from Osiriat, yet it was almost totally destroyed by the ice. Uryxs was the architecture teacher for a very good reason. Of all the "gods," he was a natural problem solver. His natural patience helped to "lead" John and Daphne in a direction that allowed them to create the designs that rebuilt the city.

"When will it be ready for occupation?"

"Whenever you command, Sir."

CHAPTER 6

RENEWAL

Year 18 A.D. (After Destruction)

The next morning, a general announcement summoned everyone to the conference room. Nepeta's current map of Earth was the subject of the final meeting on Osiriat VI.

Nepeta stood before two maps on the wall. "As you can see from my comparison map of 2012 and the current map drawn in the third month of 2030, there isn't much land left. One new continent has been created. The Andes spine rose as the earth's ice melted, drifting into warmer oceans. The northernmost point of Peru continuously drifted southwest for eighteen years and finally fused with Antarctica, which over the same period traveled due north, the shoreline of the Amundsen sea bearing north toward what was Mexico City. In all of Earth's history, the speed of these continental drifts proves to be an unnatural event, but we must take into account this is the result of two planetary alignments in this system; the first when we arrived and the second just eighteen years ago. The second, combined with the slow-acting changes of the first, caused a catastrophic chain reaction. Earthquakes and volcanic activity under the plates encouraged them to slip into their present positions faster than normal. I believe the process is over and that it is now safe for us to colonize. There are sets of jagged rocks where the Himalayas were located, inhospitable to life. As you can see, the earth is mostly covered with water. I have decided to call this one ocean Galacia because it was created by glacial melts. I have discarded all of the other ocean names."

Nepeta's presentation was over, and everyone turned to Jupoler. "I'm sure we can all agree with the logic of one ocean name. Yet a more important question looms. Has the landing site been preserved?"

"Yes. Your father's crew laid down what the satellites call the Nazca lines. They have survived. We will see huge shapes of animals and other figures. That is where we land."

"Where is Osiriat V from there?"

"A few days walk. We must let the animals go, and then we can walk. We will physically familiarize ourselves with the area."

The next day, Osiriat VI came to Earth. Jupoler piloted the ship. He set the orbital coordinates for atmospheric entry to occur directly over the new continent. The entire crew was gathered in Daphne and John's quarters to observe. A collective gasp arose as the continental details came into view. Miles above the surface, Tarus' Nazca lines appeared. As they lowered, Jupoler changed direction toward the sea. Near the shoreline, two mountains dominated their view. Squared off in parcels, the valley between them stood ready to be planted. Satetan had done her job well, but it was not over yet. Every seed on the ship was to be planted, one type per parcel. The Osirians did not have the ability to change Earth's climate. The success of each plant variety would depend solely on Earth's wish to replenish.

The ship sped out over the sea. It hovered low over Galacia to free the saltwater creatures. Next, it hovered over the only remaining freshwater lake, Lake Titicaca, on the former frontier of Peru and Bolivia, and freed the freshwater creatures. Finally, they headed back to Nazca.

Upon landing, they opened the cargo bays and let the remaining animals out two by two. They allowed the herbivores time to escape before releasing the carnivores. Everyone exited the ship except Jupoler. He took the ship back into orbit, set the coordinates for Osiriat, and set the autopilot to point five percent of light speed. At that speed, it would take two hundred years to reach Osiriat. Jupoler checked the computer to make sure the pertinent information they had gathered over the last thirty years was stored safely. He then launched the twenty-person shuttle into the solar system. It was equipped with a gravitational storage system set to gather the gravity necessary for the immortals as the ship orbited Nepeta and Arop in a continuous loop. They required this shuttle in space. After they established society, they would be leaving Earth. When he was finished he transported himself down to Nazca. Five minutes later, the autopilot started Osiriat VI on its long journey home.

Jupoler gathered his crew for the journey to their new home. Their walk across the countryside lasted one week. They rarely spoke, each quietly drinking in the raw beauty with his eyes. From the Nazca lines, they traveled southeast. Most of the landmass of Chile and Argentina was north of them. Antarctica had moved north, fusing with South America along the now east-west Andes spine.

The Andes, raised high during the recent turmoil, dominated the northern skyline. They often peered into them when they rested, searching out the mountains that held Lake Titicaca, each wondering if the freshwater creatures would thrive and debating if the lake would eventually produce.

A natural harbor that would serve the city well had formed where the two continents met. Mt. Siple sat at the west end of the harbor. The harbor opened east as the continent split, eventually opening to the mysteries of the Galacian Ocean.

Their route brought them to the western foothills of Mt. Siple. Jupoler was leading the group through a pass. He came to a point where he could see the entire valley. He stopped, soaking it all in.

The valley lay between Mt. Siple and Mt. Sidley on the former coast of Hobbes on the former continent called Antarctica. The mountains themselves, until recently covered in ice, were sprouting vegetation, proving that they had found fertile land. To the north, the Andes continued to dominate. The plains to the south would eventually be explored. The harbor intrigued him. He knew once they were settled, the Osirians would gravitate to the water.

He turned back to the struggling group. "Everyone, hurry; I found the city. Come. Look!"

They gathered around Jupoler and stared in awe at the city. Uryx's analysis was correct. Daphne, John, and Planex had built up the city from the ship using lasers and tractor beams. The specifications for the modification of the ruined city had been followed in the letter. The chosen ones truly were geniuses.

Perfectly nestled in the valley, the city's estate houses were massive twenty to thirty-room structures. There were also many small houses. All houses were constructed with marble rubble from the old city set in place by the tractor beams. Estate houses were fronted by columns, grooved with lasers, that held the roofs in place. Estate houses had an open-air entry. One entered between two columns to spring-fed pools and fountains. Over time, it would become customary for guests to wait in these foyers until a resident invited them into the main house. The estates were spread far enough apart so that the empty land could be farmed, producing enough food for the residents of each estate and, eventually, would create a surplus for the city.

Numerous estates, however, were overshadowed. The government offices, grander in scale, rested just above the city on the side of Mt. Sidley, allowing the "gods" to watch over their children. Included in the government offices were living quarters, the community hospital, and the conference room, where all laws would be passed and decisions would be made. No education building existed because all children were to be taught about life at home working the estates.

The city was much too big for eleven people. It could house about one hundred thousand people. Jupoler knew that by the time those population levels were attained, humanity could finally be saved and that the usefulness of the "gods" on Earth would come to an end.

Arop turned to the builders, complimenting them for the benefit of the entire crew. "You did a great job rebuilding the city."

"Let's go inspect your work," Vienusia suggested. She ran toward the city.

Jupoler directed, "In a moment, we will follow Vienusia down into the valley. After we inspect the city's structures, I suggest each group secure quarters. Let's pick smaller houses. I think we should save the estates until they are needed until our families expand."

They wandered down into the valley. Everyone was pleased with their new home. Vienusia was slightly disappointed that they were not moving into the estates, but her wonderful smile demonstrated her enthusiasm for the project, overshadowing any depression she felt.

Each group picked quarters. One group consisted of Daphne and the males from Osiriat. The other group consisted of John and the females from Osiriat. Shelter was in smaller estates, houses with ten rooms, six that would serve as bedrooms. The larger estates would be settled as the families expanded.

Jupoler and Arop met at the government offices to inspect the silos. They had transported enough food for twenty years, after which time they would be allowed to farm, hunt, and fish, which was by law prohibited; they had to give the animals time to reproduce and the soil time to refresh itself, having spent an eternity under ice. The valley was fertile, consisting of finely ground ash and lava from the two nearby peaks. Only one field at the southeast end of the valley was to be spared the hoe, was reserved for soldier training, and soon became known as the Marsax Field.

Two days after they settled, Jupoler and Arop called a meeting at the government building. It was time to establish the rules for running the society. They arrived first, anxious to make a good impression as the leaders of this new community. Jupoler noticed Arop's glow. "How is your new home? Is everyone settled in?"

"I wouldn't say settled in. There will be time to decorate and make it livable later. We've spent the past few days exploring and celebrating our good fortune."

"You do glow."

"You might be surprised, Brother. Vienusia, Satetan, Marsax, and I passionately attacked John the moment we entered the house. We each want to be the first impregnated. Poor John, I think he's exhausted."

"Was there jealousy amongst you?"

"None. John was definitely the right choice. That guy hasn't taken a break in the past two days. I wouldn't be surprised if each of us were already pregnant. Wait until you see how the others glow."

Jupoler paused, reflecting on her good fortune. "I wish I could say the same. I had Daphne pick between us because we must be sure of the bloodlines. I opted out of her choice because I feel I must organize our society. I chose to be last. I don't know who she picked."

"What will the others do during their 'off' years?"

"They will help me set up a society, and when the time comes, they will fish, hunt, and farm."

The door opening interrupted them. John came in. Vienusia was on his right, Marsax and Satetan on his left, all apparently supporting him in his exhaustion. They appeared as if they had broken off their orgy very recently. It was obvious to him that the girls were in love, and John was elated.

They each took their official seats. As they sat, the door opened again. Planex, Mercianiax, and Nepeta sulked in, unsuccessfully masking their depression. Daphne and Uryxs came in next. Arm in arm, it was obvious Uryxs was getting little rest; Daphne was anxious to be pregnant.

Daphne and her men each took their official seats. Jupoler stood, grinning. "It's good to see you all taking repopulation so seriously."

"Jupoler, wait-" Mercianiax stood. " Planex, Nepeta, and I met after Daphne picked Uryxs. We had to refocus our energy. We discussed plans to build and also decided we should rename the city. When we found the others in a free, restful moment, we asked them what they thought. Unanimously, we renamed Osiriat V, Gosirius."

Arop stood. "Why have you done this? You embarrass us."

"We did it to honor your leadership."

Jupoler listened and contemplated the change. He asked Mercianiax to sit and moved next to Arop. "If you are all agreed, we have no choice. Henceforth, this city shall be called Gosirius. I will inform Osiriat when I contact them next.

"Arop, remain standing. We have called this meeting today to explain the rules of this society as laid down by the government of Osiriat.

"First, religion will not be tolerated. Anyone caught worshipping will be banished from the city. Since the city provides all necessities, these criminals will quickly perish.

"Secondly, society will be developed on mathematical principles. Not only will this speed society's evolution into space, but if our society splits and languages change, math will remain universal as it has throughout time."

Arop explained further. "Most colonies our people have founded started with communication in math with the natives, language barriers dissolving over time."

Jupoler continued her thought. "The basic principle of society will be the proven symbol 2π.

"Thirdly, you will all vow to preserve the ideals of anti-theology and 2π because these beliefs will allow humanity to miss the next destructive period."

Daphne and John, the destruction still fresh in their minds, wanting to fulfill their destiny and save humanity, willingly signed the charter, as did everyone else.

Once everyone had signed, Jupoler addressed the group. "People, go now and procreate. You will find plenty of food in the storage buildings and silos. Please inform my office when a baby is to be born. We will all be present at the hospital for the glorious moment. You are all off to a good start. My only concern is that if you mate in two distinct groups, we cannot mix the lines if we are to succeed. Once your children are of mating age, we will allow them to pair."

Procreate they did. John and his harem remained in a constant state of sexual bliss for the next three months. When the girls knew positively each was pregnant, they ordered John to the bachelor quarters. He joined the other males as they worked to improve their city. Six months later, over the period of one week, John became a father four times. Daphne gave birth that week, also. Uryxs was permitted to stay with Daphne for the entire nine months of her pregnancy. They prepared the house for the new baby and made love constantly. When the babies were all born, Jupoler ordered a test. Each child was dipped feet first up to his waist in water. Each one grew a little tail. Everyone was excited. This was indeed a strong race.

Three months after the babies were born, John and his goddesses were again thrust into the throws of passion. Daphne chose Planex and was surprised by his endurance. Once they were pregnant, John again joined the others in their work. Planex stayed with Daphne.

One day, working with the gods, John fielded a suggestion. "I think we should populate more houses."

"Why?" Jupoler asked.

"We will grow out of our little houses too quickly."

"What do the rest of you think?"

Each nodded his approval. Nepeta added, "I think each person should have his own house."

An awkward silence ensued. Mercianiax broke it. "Better give our sisters estates. The way John's going, they're going to need the room!"

John used this moment to press his point.

"I think it will prevent jealousy from rising and will keep our off-spring comfortably separated. We don't want them too used to each other when it comes time to mate. If they grow up like siblings, they may repulse each other later."

Jupoler contemplated for only a moment. "Okay, let's do it: Estates for our sisters, homes for each of us. Daphne will live with her chosen man each year on her estate. I'll order her children to live with their aunts while she copulates.

At the end of twenty years, the city had one hundred new arrivals. The mating of the elders stopped as each woman reached menopause simultaneously. John's goddesses had each given birth to twenty children and Daphne had twenty children herself, four by each god. The women were as healthy as they had been twenty years earlier. The exposure to immortality on the ship allowed their bodies to heal and refresh on a cellular level. The city was prepared for growth. The gods, on their 'off' years, and John had prepared every residence for the new families.

Early on, Jupoler and Arop sensed the problem and worked hard to fix it. They devised a complex plan to keep the bloodlines pure. Each year, as five children were born, the group would renovate a house. When the first group reached the age of fifteen, the first pairing was established. The rules were simple. The children of sibling "gods" could not be paired. The first pairing would be taken from John's four girls and Daphne's one boy. Her one boy was Uryxs' so John's girl by Satetan was not allowed into the pairing and had to wait for a suitable mate, hopefully in the next pairing. The second pairing consisted of John's two girls and two boys and Daphne's one boy. Since this boy was the son of Planex, John's girls by Satetan could now be paired. Neither of the girls were the offspring of Arop, so the pairing ended up being Daphne's boy and three girls of two different ages. The two leftover boys had to wait for another pairing. As complex as it was, the pairings usually went very smoothly. The offspring who had to wait a year accepted their roles as elder children and helped the adults work as they learned to be adults. These pairings went on for twenty years. The children were named after the "gods," and the humans or their names were derived from a mixture. This practice became so inherent that it continued throughout the history of man without his conscious knowledge. People were simply named using the popular, historical names.

By the second generation, Jupoler and Arop were no longer forced to dictate groups. Families were firmly established, taboos rose against marrying siblings and cousins, and genetic lines stayed pure. The second-generation pairings consisted of three people, whereas, with the increased population, the third-generation pairings were truly pairs, and taboos rose against polygamy.

Through all of this, the eleven original parents ruled the city as a team.

Three months into any woman's pregnancy, committee meetings were held to decide where to house the next group. The meetings also covered food and water allocation, and, as always, debates raged concerning the proper time to begin farming and hunting. After all of the children of age were paired, the committee heard public complaints.

Over the next thirty years, the committee shaped Gosirius' growth and direction.

Year 88 A.D.

Daphne and John interrupted the committee meeting. The gods' full attention swung to them. John stated their concern, "We have noticed a problem in this committee."

Jupoler became defensive. "Society has no problems; why would this committee?"

"We are the problem," Daphne said. "Our children are aging, but we are not!"

Mercianiax said, "Jupoler, I think it's time to tell them."

Everyone nodded their heads in unanimous approval. It was time Daphne and John knew.

To Jupoler, it seemed he'd held the secret forever. Accepting his crew's opinion, he allowed the facts to pour out. "When we left our planet Osiriat, we were between the ages of two and seven. Sixty Earth years later we arrived here having only aged ten years. We traveled in hibernation chambers that slowed the aging process. Our mission, however, could run hundreds or thousands of years. As a result, we must not age. It is also our wish not to age, as immortality is our natural state. Our scientists trapped the essence of our dwarf star, Golas, and sent it with us on this mission. As you can see, our bodies haven't aged a day since we turned fifty, and neither have yours. We believe the eighteen years you spent on our ship filled you with the essence of Golas. We estimate your exposure will allow you to live about one thousand years. The exposure was accidental, yet could be beneficial. Should anything happen to us, you can lead society in the right direction."

John gaped and unconsciously blinked. Eventually, he regained his composure. "Why did you wait until now to tell us?"

"We had to be sure that you were really exposed. We felt the news of impending immortality given to a truly mortal person would be too much of a shock. Immortality is our natural state on Osiriat. The ecliptic orbit of our dwarf star, Golas, brings it close to our planet once every fifty years. The gravitational wave effect of Golas and our sun, Sirius, controls the ebb and flow of life on Osiriat. Somehow, this gravitational wave has a negative effect on disease causing organisms and has an extremely positive effect on healthy tissue. Once every fifty years, each inhabitant of Osiriat is regenerated. Due to overpopulation fears we have a law that limits each family to one child, except the governmental families, which may have up to three. Families who wish to reproduce more often volunteer for colonial duty and, therefore, dismiss their immortality with the decision to procreate."

"Are you saying that we can't die?"

"I'm saying you can't die unless you suffer a major trauma."

Daphne asked, "What if we don't want to live?"

"You signed the charter. You agreed to build this society. You must live as long as you can in order to preserve it. If you die, society could die with you."

Vienusia saw the strain on Jupoler's face and decided to take over. "We were there when you needed us. One day, society may feel we've outlived our usefulness. Your lives will be the glue that holds it together. You are becoming leaders. It is your responsibility to live and lead."

Year 218 A.D.

Veon, a fisherman, spent long hours contemplating life. John was his great-grandfather six times removed. He was proud to be of Vienusia's line; she had put the sea in his blood. A male, he had inherited from Vienusia's father, Petex, with no hair except for a few blonde patches on his head.

Veon fearlessly spent his days diving close to the harbor opening. No one had yet dared travel out onto the Galacian Ocean. Although he was from the second generation without the ability to grow a tail, he was a very adept diver. Lungpower allowed him to stay underwater for an hour, sometimes two. His diving ability was further enhanced by his blue eyes, which allowed more light in when he was diving in Galacia's dark waters. One feature of his eyes, which helped him to focus, was the ability to close to slits when submerged. He was sleek and long, which allowed him the hydrodynamics to quickly dive deep.

He enjoyed diving in the off-season. The sport allowed him to investigate fish habitats; to marvel at the massive coral reefs so full of life and vibrant colors. Once, an eel had nearly bitten him when he swam too close to its hiding place, but it had not startled him the way he would be startled today. Another reason he was able to stay under so long was that he had excellent powers of concentration allowing him to control his breathing. Usually, he recited historical stories to himself to help with his concentration:

The lightning, harnessed by Jupoler, was an excellent show. He had ordered Nepeta to torment the oceans; no boat could sail in the torrent. One of the children had angered the gods catching a fish before mankind was allowed to feed off of the land. As a criminal, he was banished for twenty years. Without a ready food supply, he perished.

Daphne and John told many tales to the children. They were fun, scary, and historical. He was frustrated being related to the gods because he could never be one.

Lost in thought over Jupoler's rage, a shape on the ocean floor caught his eye. He decided to investigate, approaching it slowly. As it came into focus, he could tell that it was some kind of boat, but he had never seen one so big. It startled him. He quickly surfaced to breathe.

Gasping, he broke the surface instinctively, inhaling deeply. Veon was wrong about being a god. He inherited his excellent lungpower from Vienusia. Everyone in Vienusia and Nepeta's line had it. Mostly seafarers, they were a main force in the city's economy. He thought about what he might find in the vessel. If it housed treasure, the whole city would benefit, and the seafarers would gain power. Maybe enough power that he would be the first person ever selected to serve on the council with Daphne and John.

Entering the enormous ship, swimming into total darkness, he felt his way around. Eventually, he came to a box and felt around it. Trying in vain to open it, he hit something odd. It gave way, and light flooded the room. Shocked, he knew he would not be able to explain this magic.

Gathering his senses, he continued to investigate. Now that he could see, he looked for treasure. Opening a door, he found not treasure but bones. Human bones? How could they be? This was a question he must ask the leaders.

In the room with the bones, he found a table. Secured onto the table, under glass, was a drawing. He had seen a drawing of a map at the government building. Could this also be a map? It was so different.

Extraction would be impossible underwater. He surfaced, climbed back onto his boat, and sailed west to Gosirius. Over the half-day journey he decided what he must do. Tomorrow, he would visit the government office.

The Request

Veon cautiously entered the god's old committee room. The gods had departed, long before Veon was born, to 'rule from the sky.' Daphne and John renamed the meeting room *THE CHAMBER OF THE GODS.* Anyone could meet with them for a decision on any subject. They knew the will of the gods. He hoped his discovery would land him in this room. He deeply felt society needed representation from all sects. Why should the will of the gods be the final word?

"Veon, what is it?" Daphne demanded.

"Oh, great leaders! I have found a treasure at the Galacian end of the harbor. I was diving and found an ancient vessel. There were human bones in it and-"

John raised his hand to quiet him. "Impossible! You forget we witnessed the destruction of mankind. Nothing could've survived. The gods disintegrated everything."

"Maybe this vessel sunk before the gods intervened."

"Maybe, there were many boats in B.D.," Daphne conceded. "Why did you bring it to our attention?"

"I found a table in the ship that was covered with a picture. It's preserved under glass. The picture reminded me of that map." He pointed to the map of the continent on the wall that Vienusia and Nepeta had drawn so long ago. "It must be valuable. It shows much more land than our own map."

"Can you salvage it?" Daphne asked.

"No. That is why I'm here. The vessel needs to be raised to the surface. Will you ask the gods to help?"

"No. The gods won't help us. We are to survive and work by our own merit. There may be a way to raise it, though. If you find a cloth maker, you may be able to salvage the vessel. A heavy cloth filled with air should raise it. Ask the cloth maker how to fill it with air."

John added, "Go now. Raise it! Let us know when it's done. We would like to examine it. You may have found something important. Good luck!"

The Surfacing

Veon located a cloth maker and explained his situation. He understood the dynamics and built a heavy cloth with a tube apparatus sewn in. It was otherwise sealed. Veon was handed simple instructions on its use and sent on his way. Veon employed a group of twenty friends, boys, and girls, to search for a source of steam. They found a rift leaking consistent steam near the beach where the vessel lay.

They added material to the tube to make it long enough to reach the ocean floor from the steam spring. He took five volunteers and dove to the vessel with his cloth. After the tube was submerged, the others surfaced. Veon, with the strongest lungs, finished the task alone. When the cloth was completely inserted into the vessel, he sealed all but one opening, which he used to push the tube out into the sea. He swam to the surface carrying the free end of the tube with him. The entire process took a day.

Veon surfaced where the diving boat was supposed to be. He saw it docked on the beach, shrugged his shoulders, and swam across the harbor, dragging the tube behind him. When he reached the boat, he secured the tube and waded to the beach. Dusk was upon him. A fire on the beach diverted his attention. He walked toward it, leaving a trail of mud in his wake as he drip-dried.

His friends, some already intoxicated, started this celebration many hours before. They were all proud of Veon, convinced he was going to become a new civic leader.

He found a boy who had not been drinking. "Go to the government building. Ask to see Daphne and John. Inform them tomorrow, the ship will rise."

The boy ran off, and Veon joined the party. He ate and, finally, relaxed. When the party died down, he went back to the boat, untied the tube, waded off to the reef that marked the spring and waded to shore. Following the reef to its origins at the foot of a rift in the surface, he inserted the tube into the rift and sealed it with mud, beginning a process that would change society forever.

The Galacian Sea broke as the sun broke the horizon. The device worked. Ropes were lashed to the floating vessel, and it was beached.

Daphne and John, watching from a nearby rise, now came down to see his discovery. They entered the ship with Veon, found the table, and examined the map. Instantly they recognized it as a navigational map of the Earth of 2012 A.D., known to all citizens of the city as year zero.

John explained to Veon. "This is a map of ancient Earth. The gods destroyed these places. The only land that exists is the land on the map in *THE CHAMBER OF THE GODS.*"

"No!" He refused to believe it. He blurted out without thinking, "This map is a gift from the gods. It was raised out of the sea by beautiful Vienusia and carried to the shore by the great Nepeta's sea. This map is a sign. We must repair this vessel and find these lands!"

John was furious. "Don't you praise the gods. Your actions border on worship, and worship will get you banished!"

"The gods are all-powerful and great!" Veon yelled defiantly. "Their blood flows in us. Maybe they should be worshipped!"

Daphne stepped between them. "Stop, you two! I will hear no more of this nonsense. The land we have is the only land. And you, young man, you will keep your views to yourself! We will take this map and put it in the Before Destruction Museum with the other artifacts that have been discovered over the years. This vessel will rot where it sits. You are welcome to visit and study the artifacts, but I swear if you spread your ideas about worship, you and any followers will be banished."

Listening to Daphne, John collected his wits and calmed down. He put his arm around Veon. Veon shrank away, but John held him tight. "Please, Veon, we love all of our citizens. Listen to Daphne; we don't want to banish anyone."

The Sinners

Veon knew his plan was risky. He gathered fifteen boys and sixteen girls, all ages twelve to eighteen. At nineteen, he had some influence over them. He supervised their secret restoration of the vessel. It was a single-masted, fiberglass ship.

The first day of the project, he gathered the group around him to explain his plan. "You all toured the ship. Hopefully, the problems are obvious. The first job will be to replace any water-damaged walls, ceilings, and floorboards. We will have to cut away that rotten motor and replace the boards over the gaping hole. Volunteers will go to the forest to cut trees. I checked the wheel and rudder when we hauled it in; thankfully, they still work. I need more volunteers. A group must secure food and water and fill the storage area with it. Another group will supply us with plenty of clothing and blankets. Soon, we will have this vessel seaworthy."

Volunteers quickly stepped up. Veon, in an attempt to keep morale high made up stories of the other mysterious lands. He sat in the middle of the work parties at night, retelling his favorite story:

"The land our leaders won't admit exists is green and fertile. There is space enough for each of us to own huge tracts of land. Game, out of reach of mankind all these years, will be plentiful. The gods live on the highest mountain in a palace made of marble and gold. They are waiting for us. They want to watch over us as we grow as a society. I was meant to find the map. We are chosen."

He repeated this story and told others nightly. Soon, everyone believed these stories were true. They were nearly ready to go.

When the work was complete, they celebrated with a beach party. When everyone had eaten and was relaxing, Veon addressed them.

"We have done a great thing restoring this vehicle. I want to encourage each of you to give thanks to the gods. Tomorrow, tour the B.D. Museum. Ask to go on the section of the tour that includes access to the chamber of the gods. Quietly thank the statues of each god. Study the current and ancient maps. See what the gods have done; it will awe and humble you. We will meet here again in two days."

Two days later, they gathered. He stood to gain their attention.

"You have seen the maps. Maybe our leaders are right. Maybe the earth of year zero no longer exists. But I believe islands formed from the jagged rocks that appear as dots on the current map. The stories I told you are true. I say that great Jupoler commanded my eyes to see this vessel. The gods worked through Vienusia to raise it. Great Nepeta brought it to us on his waves." His excitement gathered into a religious fervor. "The gods have sanctioned a journey to the island. Glory to the gods!"

When the crowd's cheer softened, a voice rose above them. "And a journey you shall take!"

Saara was the captain of the Marsax soldiers, the defenders of the land. He represented the perfect soldier, and his men emulated him. The greatest among them, he was the reigning champion of the Marsax Fields, where they trained and simulated battles. He had fiery red hair and green eyes, as any *real* soldier would; after all, Marsax was their protector as well as their ancestor. He stood arrow straight; although of only medium height, he was extremely muscular. His bulging chest radiated an intimidating confidence. There were many Marsax soldiers, each armed with a spear, and each spear pointed at the crowd. They all maintained this posture designed to frighten the sinners.

John and Daphne walked out from amongst them. John said calmly, "Veon, we warned you not to gather in worship. You have broken a sacred article, and as punishment, you shall be set afloat on this vessel. You will not be welcome anywhere on this continent. It saddens me to know you will slowly starve to death on Galacia.

"Here is your map." John handed him the map and walked away without another word. The Marsax soldiers had orders to drag the vessel to water, load it with a week's provisions, and send the sinners off to die. As they worked, Veon defiantly walked over to Saara, who was the essence of power. He was not intimidated.

"Saara, we are childhood friends. How can you do this to me?"

"I have my orders!" He answered flatly. Then, with genuine concern, "Why did you force John and Daphne to exile you? Veon, are you really going to sail for the islands?"

"Yes, I believe they are there."

"But all evidence suggests that they are only jagged rocks, uninhabitable. Veon, if that's true, you will die out there."

"Then I'll die, but I don't believe I'm in any danger. The gods have sanctioned me for this journey. It will be a success!"

Saara clasped Veon's hand. "I will miss you, my friend. Go now. Take your people to die!"

Veon walked away without a word, sad that he was leaving this way, yet sadder that a friend like Saara would choose to stay. He quickly directed his crew to load the ship. The last aboard, he took one last look in Saara's direction and tersely ordered the boat to sail.

As the vessel sailed off, Saara whispered, "May the gods grant mercy on their souls!"

CHAPTER 7

SOCIETY SPLITS

The Gods Intervene

Jupoler noticed a strange blip on his shuttle screen. He called innersolar mapping. Nepeta responded.

"Nepeta, what is that on your sea?"

"It looks like a ship."

"Do you think John and Daphne ordered an exploratory mission?"

"I don't know. Why don't we send Planex to find out?"

"Yes, He's free from pressing duties right now. I will send him in disguise. It wouldn't do for the humans to think he was checking on them."

A general announcement reverberated throughout the ship. "Planex to the bridge, please. Planex to the bridge."

Planex was in engineering running a diagnostic on the shuttle's core. He abruptly halted his work and ran to the elevator. The shuttle was a miniature of Osiriat VI. All departments were condensed into two levels. Fore to aft, the lower level of the ship encompassed the sleeping quarters, food storage, the hydroponics lab, engineering, a one-pad transport station, and the computer mainframe. The bridge, dining hall, innersolar mapping, and a small gym encompassed the upper level. The elevator ran between engineering and the dining area. Planex exited the elevator and walked quickly past the dining hall to the bridge.

"What can I do for you, Captain?"

Jupoler turned. "Planex, good. Look at this. I have discovered a strange blip on the Galacian Ocean. Nepeta and I discussed it. We think it may be a ship."

"That sounds logical. We expected them to eventually wander out beyond the harbor. Historically, they have always had an urge to explore their world."

"I hope you're correct, but they seem to be on a northeasterly heading. I fear that this may be a banishment by sea. They have maps. The banished would know their only hope was the jagged rocks in the northeastern sea. I am sending you to find out."

Planex easily accepted change in his life. "What do you wish me to do?"

Jupoler respected his attitude. He thought that if anything ever happened to Arop or himself, Planex would easily slip into the role of captain or co-captain. His leadership qualities were growing noticeably.

"Find out why they are sailing. I'm going to transport you down to Earth in a boat. Sail southwest until you meet them. When you contact them, coax the truth out of them. Tell them you are from a village to the northeast, an explorer looking for other lands. If they have been banished, lead them safely to the islands."

"When we arrive, will there really be a village?"

"I will take care of that. Any more questions?"

"Yes, why do you want me to help the banished? I thought the banished were supposed to suffer."

"Banishments are also supposed to happen by land. On land the guilty have a small chance to survive. By sea, they are doomed."

Journey to the Islands

Galacia remained calm for the first week. The day of the full moon brought rough seas. At dusk, Veon ordered everyone below. A major storm was on the horizon.

They ate dinner in silence, huddled for comfort as the sea hurled the boat. Sleep came early. The general feeling was that the only way to forget about the storm was to sleep.

Later, when the ship was traveling through the eye of the storm, the youngest members of the group, a brother and sister, woke and decided to go above. Veon and two others were scurrying about the deck, taking advantage of the temporary lull to attend to repairs. They did not see the children.

Veon heard the unexpected splash. He rushed to the side and, frozen, stared in disbelief as the two children, still dressed in bedclothes, seemed to mold to the waves. They were just under the surface, holding onto each other for comfort as if together they would surface, but the wave had them and mercilessly forced them deeper. As Veon prepared to jump in and rescue them, a wave crashed over the deck. He held on for dear life; the taste of salt water brought him back to his senses. The storm was back and, he feared, the children were lost forever.

The following morning, a heavy, gloomy fog enveloped the boat. Veon gathered everyone on deck. "Last night, our youngest passengers disobeyed me. They came topside and were washed into the sea. They are forever lost." Tears flowed. Wails were raised. Veon lowered his head, silently praying to the gods for their safety in death.

Neta, the first person to settle, spoke to the group. She was the food stores keeper and was covered in flour. A distant cousin of Veon, she was born of Nepeta's line. She had Vienusia's webbed feet and hands; however, she acted more like a Marsax soldier than a seafarer. This was Veon's journey, but the supplies and the safety of the crew were her responsibility, one she did not take lightly. She had just completed her daily food inventory, so everyone took her warning seriously. "Those children are a great loss; we must mourn them, yet there may be another great loss. We are running out of food fast, and if we do, we will fail!"

Veon knew he must appear in command or face possible chaos.

"Yes, we will mourn the children. When Jupoler decides to take, he takes, and when he decides to give, he gives. As for food, I'm confident he will provide. I want everyone to fish who's not working on navigation. Neta's right; food won't just appear; we'll have to work for it."

Depression prevailed nine days into their banishment. Fog still shrouded them. Visibility was minimal. Noon brought a break in the fog. Through the haze, the lookout thought he saw another boat. Disbelieving his eyes, he rubbed them and stared hard into the distance. It was moving toward them. He *had* spotted another boat!

"By Jupoler," he gasped. He shimmied down the mast and ran to find Veon. He found Veon and tried to talk, but, out of breath, he could only point. Veon, intrigued by the young man's excitement, followed his finger and looked out over Galacia. From the deck's edge, he thought he saw. . . he blinked hard and looked again. Yes, it was definitely a boat. As it approached, its single occupant began waving frantically.

"Where are you from?" Veon yelled when the boat was barely in range.

"I am Hadim from the islands to the east."

Veon strained to hear him.

"Why are you on this ocean?"

"I seek the land of the gods who created the twenty islands. I was sent to see if they created any other lands." He was getting closer and easier to hear.

"What are your gods called?"

"They call themselves the Gosirian gods. They came from a mythical land called Gosirius. Their leader is Jupoler."

The crew could hardly believe it. The gods *had* settled in another land!

"We are from Gosirius!" Veon confessed excitedly.

"What?! Will you take me there?"

"We can't. We have been banished for worshipping the gods."

Just as Jupoler suspected, Planex thought.

"For worshipping the gods? What is the point of a god if he can't be worshipped?"

"That was our point. You don't want to go to that awful place. Can you lead us back to your islands?"

Planex lied. "I've been traveling for six months in this leaky boat. I can't go much farther. If you will allow me to come on board, I will humbly lead you to my home."

They agreed, and Hadim, a.k.a. Planex, used the next six months to teach them. Their ignorance of the gods surprised him. He taught them of the god's great journey to Earth. Disgusted with the madness they found, they destroyed it and started over. He told stories of the god's great powers, always intriguing his audience. Freshly banished, they were well aware of Marsax's powers. He continually reminded them with stories of the god's early adventures on Earth:

Early man was taught directly by the gods. They lived amongst us. They found humans needed a reason to justify why the gods were gods. These humans used these justifications to educate each other about the gods.

Jupoler was the master of the gods. The people believed he was all-powerful and that he created the universe. His little brother, Planex, was mischievous, always angering Jupoler. Planex was rarely seen because he spent much time hiding in caves from Jupoler's wrath. When the gods left Earth, people related the natural world to Jupoler. When storms came, they'd say, "We have angered Jupoler. Hide in a dark place like Planex so we may be spared his wrath."

Arop is Jupoler's sister. She was thought to be responsible for life's continuance on earth. She was a beauty who shone like the sun. The sun gives us life. The phrase: *the sun shines with Arop's beauty*, indicates that Arop allows us to enjoy life.

Nepeta and Vienusia are the gods of the sea and waterways. Nepeta is easily angered and brings rough seas. He also rules over the ugly creatures of the sea. The phrase: *appease Nepeta, he has encouraged these rough seas,* was meant to stop the rough seas. Appeasing Nepeta caused him to ignore the sea. Then, Vienusia would take charge. The phrase: *thank Vienusia for these calm seas,* was uttered when Nepeta relented. Nepeta and Vienusia worked hand in hand. Her dolphins would chase away his sharks when the people respected the sea.

Satetan is the goddess of fertility. It is she who took the early man by the hand and taught him how to make the land productive. The phrase: *Satetan has provided this bounty,* was uttered at meal and harvest times. It helped explain why the fields produced and kept producing. Satetan had to be praised; on a whim, she could destroy the crops.

Satetan's brother, Uryxs, was lord of the night. Of all the gods, he was the only one to challenge Jupoler. People used the phrase: *thank Uryxs; he has brought the beautiful nighttime sky.* People suspected he fought Jupoler's storms because he knew people were more productive in peaceful weather conditions. When Jupoler's storms became violent, people prayed for his forgiveness and for Uryx's intervention.

Mercianiax is the warrior Marsax's brother. She is war. He is peace. When the gods were on earth to establish a society, Jupoler, knowing Mercianiax represented peace, continually sent him as spokesperson to Gosirius. Whenever he approached, word would quickly spread that the messenger of the gods was coming. The phrase: *follow that star, is a directional message from Mercianiax,* showing how he became the protector of travelers after the gods left Earth.

Neta complained. "But Veon told us they do reside on earth, in a palace on the tallest mountain of the islands."

"Yes, the palace. It's in the clouds that surround the mountain. What I meant is that they are above earth rather than down here on it. They have isolated themselves and wish to have no contact with us."

They finally reached Hadim's land. He was confused because it appeared that the twenty islands were gone. The waters had receded, forming one island. He asked Veon to sail around in order to confirm this. After several days of sailing, they came back to the original spot.

The twenty islands were definitely gone. Jagged rocks, however, still encompassed most of the shoreline. Waves crashed, spray covered the rocks, and Veon wisely sought out a better place to land. As they searched, they admired the landscape. Above the rocks, pine trees rose up the hill and seemed to touch the blue sky. An awe-inspiring mountain rose into the clouds.

They eventually found a beach made up of white, soft sand. A river flowed into the ocean here, and Hadim grew excited. His village was close. They secured the boat. Too excited to unload it, they followed the river Hadim called the Himal. They climbed up the lush green hill it flowed through.

At the top of the hill, where the river started its downward escalation towards the sea, they saw the tall, blue mountain to the north. As they continued, the river flattened out. They passed close to a pine-covered hill on the north side of the path that blocked the view of the mountain.

When they passed the hill, the Himal River valley opened before them; at its head, the lofty snow-capped mountain enshrouded in clouds.

Up the river, to Hadim's feigned amazement, strategically placed to take advantage of the surrounding lands, was an abandoned village. The village was very simple. The enclosures were built out of the tropical materials grown naturally on this island. The group of thatched huts did not seem to have any congruency. As they investigated further, it appeared as if each hut oversaw a piece of land. In the center of the village there was a large hut four times as big as any other. Hadim explained this was used for communal gatherings: meetings, food preparation, and ceremonial dances. He had never seen this place himself. Hadim thought to himself, "My friends, you've truly outdone yourselves."

Veon squatted, pulled a handful of dirt from the ground, and allowed it to fall through his fingers.

"This is a very fertile country. Those hills that surround this valley will bring rainwater to feed our crops. The gods of the mountain provide and watch over us. With this soil and this village, we shall make them proud."

Hadim assured them further.

"You'll not only have crops but there's plentiful game in the forests. Now that the islands are one, the game will be easier to hunt."

"You see, people, the gods have provided!" Veon exclaimed. "The stories I told you on Gosirius; they came to me in visions. How wonderful that they are true."

"Veon, they provided for you and me. My people are gone. I offer you my village as a home. Each couple should find a place to live."

They had naturally come together as couples on the journey. Each one chose a hut and farmed the land adjacent to it. When a surplus was created and stored in the government hut, hunting and fishing parties were sent out to bring balance to the food supply. Temples were built for each of the gods. Continuous prayer blessed this society.

A curious citizen decided to climb the mountain in search of the palace. He fell to his death. Veon found him. This was a bad omen; the gods were sure to be angered. Within the year, the crops began to fail.

Before this disaster hit, society flourished for several years in this valley that was once part of the ancient B.D. Country Tibet. The government assembly was confident that it would flourish again. But the disaster was not over. Game, once plentiful, disappeared. Neta and Veon met in the Temple of Satetan.

"Why has Satetan failed us, Veon?"

"She has not failed us, Neta. She only tests us. The crops fail, but she will revive them while we are gone. We must follow the game into the forest. There, Satetan will guide us on a journey to prosperity."

"How can we be sure?"

"You take one group, and I'll take another. We will go our separate ways. One of us is bound to find game and survive this. We will each return to the village when the gods have given us their sign."

"What is their sign?"

"We will know it when we see it."

Although the people willingly followed Veon and Neta, abandoning the village convinced them of the god's wrath. They thought splitting would give them a fighting chance, but each group became territorial.

Veon settled his people in a large cave on the eastern side of the mountain. In a spacious nook near the rear of the cave, he held counsel. It was from here he sent out hunting and gathering parties and here he awaited their return. First reports showed scarce game, but eventually, game became more plentiful. Herds were reported arriving from the west. Soon, he learned that Neta's people were driving them slowly toward him. Day after day, reports became more desperate.

"Veon!" a hunter rushed into his nook without an invite. Guards grabbed his arms, holding him back. He was not deterred.

"Veon, we have been ambushed by a hunting party of Neta's tribe! Two of my hunters were killed."

"Do you know where they are now?"

"We can find them easily. What shall we do?"

Veon, angry, couldn't see the future in his answer. "Find two of them and bring them to me."

The next morning, the hunting parties clashed. Two of Neta's hunters were captured and brought before Veon. To show his power, without a word, he stood and sliced their throats. His people whipped themselves up into a frenzy. Control was lost. Savagery reigned. A war was fought in the name of the gods. Veon ordered new crops burned. Most of the available game was killed. Water sources dried up or were salted. Famine. Pestilence. As is man's nature, the gods were blamed and soon forgotten.

Planex/Hadim watched in horror. Finally, he approached Veon, whom he considered the more able leader.

"Veon, you must stop this madness. How do you ever expect to gain Satetan's forgiveness if you destroy her bounty?"

"Satetan? What use is she? Can she control the savagery you are witnessing?"

"No, she cannot, but Jupoler can. Don't you see, the more you struggle amongst each other, the further he abandons you. You must make peace to pacify Jupoler."

"If Jupoler has abandoned my people, then so be it. Before I die, I will see Neta killed for her outrages against me."

Hadim slowly turned and walked out of Veon's camp forever. Unable to stop the madness, he finally signaled Jupoler and was transported back to the shuttle. He dematerialized into thin air.

CHAPTER 8

EXILES

234 A.D.

Planex rematerialized on the transport pad in engineering, stepped down, quickly walked past the spiral staircase that led to the computer mainframe housing above him, and hurried through the engine room to the elevator. Once aboard, he selected level one, rose, and exited into the dining area, quickly walking to the bridge directly forward of the dining area.

He burst onto the bridge excited and out of breath. Arop turned to him. "Planex, welcome back. Take a moment. Relax. When you can speak, you may tell us why you returned."

A tense moment passed while Planex caught his breath. Finally, he could speak. "Your suspicions were correct. The boat you saw on Galacia was indeed full of banished people. I did as you asked and reestablished them on the islands. The village you built was ideal."

Jupoler interrupted. "Why were they banished to the sea?"

"Veon, their leader, explained their situation to me. He found a boat in Galacia and restored it. During his restoration, he taught his friends to worship us. Several arguments between Daphne and John ensued. They forbade him to worship. He knew full well the consequences but taught people to worship anyway. Daphne and John decreed they should die in the vehicle that their religion rose around."

"This society you built on the island, is it succeeding?"

"At first, yes. The people believed you sat on the tallest mountain in a palace, watching over and protecting them. Knowing they couldn't reach you, they built temples dedicated to you throughout the village. I tried to gently turn them away from religious beliefs, but they were strong. Crops prospered. Game was plentiful. They truly believed you were helping them. I couldn't get through to them. Finally, I convinced one of the devout to journey to the top of the mountain to ask you to allow them to prosper forever. I knew he would find nothing and report it. I hoped they would give up their religious madness upon learning the truth.

Unfortunately, he never made it. He fell to his death in sight of the peak. Veon and I found him and brought his broken body back to the village. His death was considered a bad omen. The villagers convinced themselves the wrath of the gods would soon fall upon them. All work stopped, and the villagers brought a plague amongst themselves. Any surplus food they had was sacrificed to the gods to appease us. The people, out of food, evacuated the village. They convinced themselves the gods had caused the plague. Unwisely, they split into two groups. They planned to meet again in ten years to reestablish the village. The consensus was if they suffered long enough, the gods would forgive their sin. The gods would then welcome them back into their protection. Each group occupied caves. They sent out hunting parties. The foraging circles widened yearly. Hunting parties clashed. The groups became territorial, defending their territories with their lives. Small battles escalated into full-scale war fought in the name of the gods. They became savages. Famine and pestilence increased. We were blamed. They no longer fight in our names; they fight simply to kill.

This is why I've come back. Our children have forgotten us. They kill each other for food. They have lost all the values we instilled. We must abandon them. All hope for them is lost."

"No. We will not abandon them. We intended for society on Earth to split, but not so soon. This rift must be healed if our experiment is to succeed. What do you think, Jupoler?"

"You're right, Arop. I think it is time to relate this problem to Tarus. Our king is wise. He will know what to do. Arop, you have the bridge. Come, Planex, let's contact Father."

They exited the bridge, walked through the dining area, around the elevator, and entered Innersolar Mapping. At the rear of the room sat the communications center. They sat in front of a huge screen. Jupoler pushed the button marked EMERGENCY CONTACT: OSIRIAT BASE. A few moments later, Tarus appeared on the screen in front of them.

"Hello, boys. You have aged well. What is this emergency?"

Jupoler gave Planex a permissive look. Planex related his story to Tarus.

"Interesting. You have a society that worships you, or rather did, while the original society stays pure. We never intended for society on Earth to split early. If there are different factions, they will never work together for the common good. This banishment by sea, did you authorize it?"

"No, Father," Jupoler admitted. "We expected all banishments to be by land. We did not want society to find the other lands yet. We believe they are not advanced enough to govern more than one area. Banishments are meant to punish, not kill. These people were sent off to their deaths in our name."

"I consider that blasphemy. Wouldn't you?"

"I guess so. Yes."

"Here's what I want you to do. The continent Gosirius sits on an unstable plate. Gravity will force it to drift south into the polar regions eventually. You must take your chosen ones and ten other worthy couples away from Gosirius. Make them reestablish society on the savage island. Accelerate Gosirius' southern drift. Destroy all the inhabitants. They are all guilty of blasphemy because they did nothing to prevent the banishment of Veon's supporters. You must reintroduce the one society concept. You will have no other chances, so a compromise must be reached with the savages. I say allow this religious worship."

Planex was appalled.

"Your own law, Liege, strictly forbids worship. How are we to justify it?"

"While you've been away, we conducted deeper research into mankind's past failures. His belief in many gods seldom allowed for failure. It's when he creates one supreme God that he places total trust and confidence in that he begins to fail. We call it blind faith. He believes so strongly that God will provide the answers that he stops asking the right questions. One God becomes a breakable crutch. Tell them if they wish to worship you to thank you for providing life; they can as long as they realize you cannot control their lives."

"And if one God arises?" Jupoler asked.

"You must stay in the general consciousness. Don't allow yourselves to be forgotten."

Planex and Jupoler watched as Tarus faded away. Quietly, they walked back to the bridge to council with Arop.

She turned to greet them. "What did Father have to say, Jupoler?"

"Well, basically, he said Daphne and John caused this mess, and they will fix it. We will meet with them tomorrow in *The Chamber of the Gods.*"

The gods sat in their marble chairs, etched with representative designs of their individual powers. These chairs remained empty since A.D. 90 when they returned to the shuttle. They left Daphne and John to rule and reestablished their link with the life-giving gravity supplied to them on the shuttle.

Daphne and John sat together, facing the gods in the chairs of judgment. Society was flourishing; why this unexpected visit from the gods?

Jupoler was furious. "You banished thirty-two citizens sixteen years ago. You should've killed them. They found an island that formed in the old Earth area of Tibet and quickly resorted to savagery. They abandoned us and threw out all of the values of a decent society. And now YOU must pay!"

Daphne rose to their defense. "But it's in the charter. Anyone caught worshipping you is to be banished. We have prospered since the banishment, and no one has dishonored you with worship."

"No," Arop reminded. "You were to banish them from the city, not from the land. Eventually, they would have apologized and become productive members of society."

"We banished them to the sea because their religion centered around a miracle at sea. We sent them to die. We never expected them to form a society."

"Right, John, you sentenced them to death. This decision was supported by the entire city, was it not?"

"Yes."

"You did this thing to protect us. We've contacted the supreme God, Tarus. He calls your action blasphemy. You must pay because you dishonored us."

John accepted the will of the gods. "How must we pay? Shall we allow them to come back?"

Nepeta allowed his anger to show.

"No. You shall leave! You must pick ten couples to go with you."

Arop glared at Nepeta, silencing him.

"Where are we going?" Daphne asked.

Nepeta rose again. Arop cut him off.

"You are going to the other land. When you arrive, you must find the savages and convince them to join you in reinstating civilization. The future of the planet depends on your ability to end the savagery and war."

"What will happen to our city, this land?" Daphne asked.

Arop glanced over at Nepeta. "You may now explain, Nepeta."

"Uryxs, Planex, Marsax, and I are going to destroy it. You may explain to the savages that Nepeta created ravaging seas that drove the continent south into Uryxs' darkness. Tell them Marsax killed all that survived the storm, aided by Planex, who killed all who hid in dark places. Tell them the souls of the dead rest with Planex, for he is the Lord of the Dead."

John broke his stunned silence. "Why would you destroy these people?"

"They are blasphemers. They supported your death sentence. Besides, without you, they're dead anyway. When we rescued you, we were under orders to create one society on Earth. My father, the supreme God Tarus, told us that a split society at this juncture will fail. We must destroy Gosirius, and you must spread the story of our power to the savages. Convince them that if they don't rejoin society, they will suffer the wrath of the gods. We apologize, but sometimes good people must be sacrificed for the future good of all people. We trust that you will obey us and that the new society will thrive!"

Jupoler enjoyed observing Arop and Nepeta, but knew he must now intervene.

"The rules are simple. You and the ten couples you pick must remain a core group. Two children each will replace you when you die. You will be a secret society. You will always hold dear the values of Gosirius. You may call yourselves the Gosirian priests. Citizens and rulers may come to you for advice, but you may not reveal your secrets. Again, discourage worship; however, if worship somehow occurs, let it."

Daphne and John were confused. Daphne spoke first.

"Why? One of the first laws you taught us was that worship should never be allowed to form and that if it did, society would fail."

"I understand your concerns. We received word from Osiriat. They will tolerate no more failures. Tarus himself has ordered us to allow worship as long as it's we, the people, worship. When we asked him why the change when our orders had been so adamant, he said that they had reviewed the past failures on Earth and discovered that the people always developed from worshipping the gods who had saved them to several highly complex religions that worshipped one God but differed on their ideas about who that God was and what he wanted from them. This conflict over worship caused each society to break down. He believes that if we are worshipped, our lessons will be preserved and that failure will be assured if other gods arise. In our hearts, we feel worship may be a mistake, but it has been okayed on a limited basis if it will help. We would like you to limit it as much as you can. Tarus has ordered us to allow its formation, and we must obey, but we implore you please be careful.

"Tarus counseled us that we must stay in control if society is to succeed. If any other gods arise society may fail. Go now. You need to find ten deserving, loyal couples. You two should have about eight to nine hundred years left to live. Build the secret society strong. Leave a great legacy."

One week later, Daphne, John, and ten couples sailed for the new land they christened Laarisia to honor the lost continent of Asia. When they arrived, they found the empty village. John and Daphne ordered the group to stay and set up housing. They felt they alone should locate the savages.

"Where shall we go?" Daphne asked John.

"Planex told me the savages have made their homes in caves. Let's walk toward the mountain. We're bound to find someone."

They proceeded quietly. Carefully, they negotiated their way through the forest, marveling at the growth. Forests like this did not exist around Gosirius. Fresh cuts from hardened fern leaves marked their extremities. The smell of fresh growth assaulted their nostrils, much different from the grass and crop growth they were used to. Soon, the smells became repugnant. Human excretions marked the forest floor. They knew they were close.

John thrust his arm across Daphne's chest abruptly halting her. Her questioning glance prompted from him a whisper. "Something is moving in that bush."

He barely completed his sentence when a man rose, spear in hand, ready to kill them. He brought his thrust to a halt, confused. "I know you. You rule Gosirius. Grandparents, why are you here?"

"We have come to save you," Daphne informed him sympathetically.

He rubbed his temple. "This is too confusing. You must come with me. We must ask Veon what to do."

John continued past him. "Splendid, we seek Veon."

They followed the hunter to his cave. People gasped. They certainly never expected to see Daphne and John here. He led them to the rear where a haggard man sat. He was now thirty-five, but appeared fifty.

He heard movement and slowly raised his head. He was frightened, but chose to face his enemy.

"Have you come to kill me?"

John laughed. "No, Veon, We have come to forgive you."

His dead eyes brightened. "Forgive me? Why would you forgive me? I worshipped the gods. Do you forgive me because we abandoned them?"

"No, we forgive you because you were right. We are here to embrace you, to recreate society. Gosirius is dead; destroyed by the gods because of our blasphemous ways. We were informed by the gods we punished you unjustly and that we must reestablish society with you."

"I am ready, but we have abandoned the gods."

"The gods don't wish to be abandoned. They say you failed because you willed yourselves to fail. You feared the wrath of the gods and brought it amongst yourselves."

"The gods will let us resettle the village?"

"They have suggested that you do. Can you gather the other group? It is time we worked together to stop this destructive conflict."

"I think so. We have some friendly contact."

"Good. Bring them to the village. We will accept them with open arms."

Scattered bands of savages slowly came back into decent society.

Once returned, Daphne and John's Gosirian priesthood reeducated everyone about the gods' wishes. When they finished, Daphne found Veon. "What is this group of strange buildings? They appear to serve no purpose."

"They are the temples of the gods we built soon after we arrived. The gods live in a palace on top of the mountain. They watch over us. We must thank them daily, so we built these temples."

Daphne embraced him. "The gods do watch over us, but not from the mountain. Keep these temples intact. We may need them."

Within a few years a worshipping structure naturally arose. All questions to the gods and advice from the gods were received and distributed by John and Daphne. They used the temples to "contact" the gods. They became legends themselves, living longer than anyone had ever thought possible. They found themselves both the leaders of the secret society and society as a whole.

Year 1034 A.D.

Eight hundred years of idyllic peace passed. Daphne and John commissioned mariners to explore Galacia in search of new lands as the ocean slowly receded. Over time they found four new islands in the area Veon's map labeled Switzerland. They concluded that the islands were exposed tops of the Alps and named the area Alpania. Daphne and John sent colonists to the islands. The first island in the Alpanian region was, of course, named Alpania. Honoring the gods for their wisdom in leading society to these islands, the other three were named Marsia, Vienus, and Ciaxian. Colonies were established. Every year, the people came back to Laarisia to participate in the Festival of the Gods. The festival kept the people as one society.

Daphne and John watched the festivals from above. A platform, built specifically for them, was used to entertain colonial leaders during the festivals. In reality this was an inspection tour. Daphne and John's reputation rode on the results. While the leaders of the four new lands enjoyed the festivities, they quietly evaluated the Himal valley. The rice fields, located in the river floodplain, and cereal crops, located on the outskirts and up the hillsides, were green with new sprouts. Harvested crops stood in piles to be used first in celebration, then for transport to the new lands to help sustain them. New lands primarily survived on hunting and fishing. They traded with Laarisia for basic staples. Although their lands could support similar crops, they chose not to plant as trade with Laarisia kept society close and standardized. A few families had begun farming in earnest, but production was nowhere near enough to allow for independence from Laarisia.

The leaders each privately expressed their gratitude to Daphne and John during the festival. They excused themselves from attending the final day of the festivities, as they needed to arrange portage downriver to their waiting ships. Guards were rationing the surplus to the masses. No island would be shortchanged.

John was enjoying crowd watching when he happened to glance over at Daphne. This tenth festival was a joyous event. Why then, John thought, does Daphne look so sad.

"What's wrong, Daphne? You don't look yourself today."

"I'm worried. I was handed the attendance numbers a few moments ago. Something was odd so I had the registrar bring me the numbers from every past festival. Yearly, the numbers have declined, but this year they declined drastically."

"I wonder why? Do you suppose there is colonial hardship?"

"I don't know. I think we should send emissaries to find out."

"Why not ask the leaders?"

"Because they may be here as decoys. If there is a problem, maybe we can help."

Months passed. They waited patiently for results. Many emissaries never returned. Some were sent back dead. Few came back with answers.

Daphne and John sat at their desks in the government house browsing surplus food statistics, when a beaten man burst in. They recognized him as one of the emissaries they had sent to the colonies.

Daphne reached for a towel to wipe the blood from his eyes. "What happened to you?"

"I- I barely return from Marsia with my life. I went there posing as a traveler on vacation. My prying questions alerted the authorities, who accused me of being a Laarisian spy. I was imprisoned. They beat me until I confessed. I pleaded with them. I told them you were only concerned with colonial problems and were willing to send aid. They said they didn't want your help. They want to be left alone. They claim they have broken away from us. They flogged me onto a boat and swore they would kill me if I came back."

Daphne and John sat stunned. Later, three more emissaries, assigned to Vienus, Ciaxian, and Alpania, came in badly beaten.

Daphne was horrified. "What shall we do?"

"I'm dumbfounded. We must summon the gods."

John went to the communication center located in Mercianiax' temple. Jupoler's orders were simple. "We will only speak to you two. After you die, we will only communicate through signs."

John stood in the questioning circle and waited.

On the shuttle, in innersolar mapping, a continuous beep sounded. Nepeta and Vienusia, usually present, were in the gymnasium. Marsax, finished with the food inventory Jupoler had ordered, exited the elevator and walked into the dining area. She heard the faint beep and wondered why no one responded. Curious, she walked through the hallway encircling the elevator and walked into innersolar mapping. There was no sign of Nepeta or Vienusia, so she decided to answer the call.

"Yes. What is your question?" Marsax asked.

"We have a problem. We have established colonies that are beginning to break away from our central rule. We have sent emissaries, most who have been killed. Those who survived told us of a great alliance that will challenge us for power in the world. What can we do?"

Marsax' bloodthirstiness overpowered her rationality. "You must fight! You must make a war on these colonies. Take slaves. Make them suffer for dishonoring the gods!"

Daphne was waiting for John when he returned to the office. "Who did you talk to? What did they say?"

"Marsax. She said we must have a war on the colonies and enslave the survivors."

"But we were sent here to prevent war."

"I brought that up. She said we were brought here to reestablish society and that no one is allowed to break away without being punished. Central rule is the only way to keep us on the right track."

"We aren't prepared for war."

"And they aren't prepared for an invasion. We have four islands to attack. We will need more boats than we currently have afloat."

"I'll order the trees cut. The boat builders will build us dugouts for the troops. What shall we use to transport slaves?"

"Dugouts. For each troop dugout that goes out, two supply dugouts should follow. We will replace supplies with slaves. Call a general meeting. I want all able-bodied men and women trained for war."

Six months later, the war arsenal assembled, Daphne and John sailed. They led their contingent far north and then west. North of Vienus, they dropped south and surrounded her in the night. The troops offloaded. By morning, they were raiding outlying homesteads. Before the colonial government was aware troops had landed, the island was taken. Every citizen was forced into a cattle enclosure. A small contingent of soldiers was left to guard and feed the prisoners.

Daphne and John took Marsia and Ciaxian with the same ease. Alpania, the oldest colony, was bigger than the other islands with triple the population. They planned to take it in a surprise attack.

They surrounded Alpania in the night. When they landed, hordes of Alpanians burst out of the forest to meet them. Those Laarisians who escaped were badly beaten. No one wished to try again. Daphne and John rallied the troops.

Counseling with the leader of each landing, they determined the south shore had the weakest defense. They decided to concentrate all of their force there. They landed and fought all day. By nightfall they had secured the beach.

Alpanian messengers ran across the island gathering troops. Laarisia resumed her attack the next morning. Her troops slashed their way into the forest taking heavy losses as the Alpanians hit and retreated. The Laarisian forces were led into a trap and would have lost the day, but for the reserves John held back. Learning his forces were trapped, he split his reserves, outflanked the Alpanians, and, through sheer luck, captured the colonial governor directing his forces from the rear. His capture forced the island to capitulate.

Many Laarisians died, but in the end Laarisia was victorious. The colonies were depopulated.

Victorious, Daphne and John sent their troops back to Laarisia. The empty boats returned to the islands. Whole populations were slowly loaded and transported to the holding area on Laarisia. The final boats to leave the islands were loaded with Daphne and John and the occupation troops. Wildlife was all that remained on the islands. All humans were once again in Laarisia.

When they returned, Daphne and John ordered their troops to bring all of the slaves to the field in front of their festival platform. Here they informed them of their fate.

Daphne stood. "From this platform we have witnessed many happy festivals. Why did you decide to leave us? We had peace and prosperity.

Did you really think we would let you create your own society? John, tell them how they will be punished for their insolence."

"The great warrior goddess, Marsax, ordered us to enslave you as punishment for breaking away from Laarisia. Most of you will be quarry slaves mining granite needed to build a monument thanking the gods for our victory. The rest of you will be enslaved as either builders or household help. Your first project will be to build slave quarters."

They exited the platform. John headed back toward the government offices. Daphne took his hand and redirected him. "I think we better ask permission to build monuments."

"Agreed," John said, as they headed for Mercianiax' temple.

"Yes." It was Satetan.
"We must speak with Jupoler. We have a judging for him."
"Wait right there," she ordered, tersely.

Jupoler was irritated. "What is this judgment you have for me?"
"We have taken many slaves in the war. We want to punish them and teach them to honor you. We wish to build monuments dedicated to you."

"John, I do not agree with your war. Marsax gave you bad advice, but what is done is done. We were told to expect humans to want to build monuments. Very well, put the slaves to work quarrying granite. Make them transport it to the flat plain by the Himal River."

"How will we know when to quit?"

"Contact me in two years. Uryxs will work up a plan by then. The project may be so massive that the slaves can never quit."

When they left the temple, they noticed the slaves and troops milling about the square. They mounted the platform to once again address the masses.

John raised his hand to quiet them.

"We have a message from the gods. You slaves will be sent to the quarries to gather granite. Most will quarry. A select few will be slated as builders. The elderly will be trained as housekeeping staff.

"Troops, your commanders will meet with us in a moment. You are to be reassigned. Five percent of you will act as a police force as we no longer have outside enemies. Most of you will return to private life as your farms are in disrepair and we have many slaves to feed. Depending on your natural skills, you may be chosen to supervise the mining, transportation, and building slaves. We thank you for your service. Commanders, please assemble in our office."

Year 1036 A.D.

Two years of misery. They were forced to mine not only granite but also salt, mica, quartz, silver, gold, iron, coal, and even jade. A small percentage of workers quarried clay used to build the unsanitary slave quarters. They worked during all daylight hours. At night, they were free, but the people of Laarisia kept them down. They had no rights. Crimes against them were common. Punishment for kicking a dog was more severe than for hurting a slave. Slave men caught alone at night could depend on a good beating; women could depend on much worse. As a result, if slaves traveled at night, they moved in groups.

Daphne and John reveled in the power they had built through victory and stepping on the souls of the slaves. She oversaw the planning and daily management of the mines. He oversaw shipping and work assignments.

Daily, she toured the mines. Mostly, she gave orders to the supervisors. Occasionally, during a tour, she would see a problem and personally order a slave to take care of it. In time, she gained the respect and fear of every slave in the mining system.

Touring the gold mine, she saw reflections through the choking dust of careless flakes left on the ground. She turned to the nearest slave. "Slave, collect these flakes. They are too valuable to lose."

The slave she addressed ignored her.

"Slave!"

No response.

She grabbed his shoulder and turned him to face her. "Slave! On your knees, obey me!"

"Go away, woman. I have important work to do."

"Guards! Take him out of here. He believes he has important work to do. I will find him some!"

At the entrance to the mine, the supervisor was directing ore shipping. Wagons were loudly being loaded. When Daphne came out of the entrance, workers stopped and stared. He followed their gaze and saw one of his workers under guard.

He approached her. "What is this?"

"This is a slave who refused to obey my direct order."

"Is this true?"

"Yes, but it was a ludicrous order. She wanted me to mine dust. Who cares about flakes? I'm mining gold!"

"Nevertheless, you disobeyed a direct order from our leader." He turned to Daphne. "What shall his punishment be?"

"First, whip that scoundrel. Then, assign him to me. His bloodied hide will be thrown into the salt mines!"

Word of Daphne's wrath quickly spread to all of the mines. Now, when she visited, miners went out of their way to please her. Daphne was happier than she ever remembered being in her life. Total control was the most powerful high there was.

Several weeks later, Daphne and John, who had not seen each other because of their respective duties, met in their office.

"John. Why have the trees been cleared at the base of the mountain?"

"That is the new site of our offices. It will be ideal because it looks down upon the village. I diverted slaves to deliver stone to the site."

"How are deliveries going? Have these slaves lowered the production of other material shipments?" She asked, her voice betraying her disgust; after all, she was the production specialist. His little project might put her behind and he had not consulted her!

"No. I realigned their duties. None of the other shipments were affected. My overall plan calls for a group of slaves to ship building materials to the flat plain. I simply diverted some of that material here. I took slaves from the other two groups, those bringing heating materials to the swordsmithery and those bringing treasure to the palace, to help supply us with stones for an office. Actually, there is a stockpile of material already lying on the flat plain. It is time we called Jupoler."

Together, they walked to Mercianiax's temple. When they stood in the circle, a beep sounded in innersolar mapping.

Vienusia quickly answered. "Hello, what is your question?"

"We have gathered the materials Jupoler ordered. What shall we do with them?"

"One moment, please. I'll find him."

They waited a few moments while Vienusia fetched Jupoler from the bridge.

"Jupoler here. Ask your question again, please."

"We have gathered an immense stockpile of materials. What should we do now?"

"You need to make three separate piles. You will set one pile two miles west of the Himal as far north as you can while remaining on the flat plain. I have scanned your material. You might have enough material gathered for this pile. When you gather enough material, you will start another pile five-eighths of a mile west of the Himal River on the same level north as you did the first pile. You will have slaves pace off the distance between these two piles and mark the middle point. You will then use two slaves who will start at each pile at a thirty-degree angle southeast of the first pile and southwest of the second one. A third slave will stand at the middle point and walk due south. Each of these slaves must start simultaneously and pace off three lines. Where the slaves meet, you will build a third pile."

"How will we know how much material is appropriate for each pile?"

"We will let you know."

"What will happen with these piles?"

"You shall see!"

Year 1040 A.D.

Daphne and John contemplated the problem. The slaves were spread too thin. They decided to stop production of precious metals and heating ore. These slaves they reassigned to the movement of the pile of rubble two miles west of the Himal. They now had four groups of slaves: those in the mines, household servants made up of the very young and the very old, office builders, and materials movers.

Finally, pile one was close to completion. Daphne noticed how much time it took.

"John, we restructured our labor force. Why has it taken twice as long for these slaves to move this rubble than it took for fewer slaves to create it?"

"Look at them, Daphne. They are at the point of exhaustion. The slaves we had in the mines weren't used to all of this physical effort."

Observing them work, she could see that although the slaves were miserable, they were resigned to their fate.

One morning, when the slave crew woke, they dutifully expected to move more materials to pile one. Instead, they stared at the awesome sight erected where pile one had been. A gigantic circular monument had appeared while they slept. All the materials were gone. The slaves estimated it would take ten men standing on each other's shoulders just to reach the roof. They formed a human chain, each man hugging the monument; three hundred sixty men were needed to connect around the monument.

The side was decorated with scenes depicting each of the god's special powers. These scenes would be repeated on a smaller scale on each of the remaining monuments. The gods obviously did not want to be forgotten. Later, when a curious slave climbed the hill north of the monument, he witnessed a carving of the sun on the roof. This pattern would be repeated with both a carving of the Earth and the moon on the next monuments built.

They were mystified. Looking for any good in their otherwise miserable lives, they convinced themselves they had built it. Throughout history the slaves would be credited with erecting the monuments.

Daphne and John woke that morning, ate, and walked to the raised platform to watch the slaves transport material. This was their daily habit. They stared at the new monument. A slave, who jumped onto the platform, bounding over the stairs, broke their trance. "Great leaders, do you see what we have accomplished." He pointed toward the monument. "May we now rest?"

John gave him a stern look. "No, you may not. Get back to work. We require a second pile five-eighths of a mile west of the river."

The slave bowed. Slightly depressed because he really had not expected cooperation from his masters, he said, "As you wish." He slowly removed himself from the platform. Secretly, he knew the slaves were powerful. He glanced at it again and thought, *if we built that, we will overcome.*

Daphne looked at John. "How?"

"How the hell should I know! The slaves didn't do it, that I promise you. Let's ask Jupoler."

Jupoler explained. "Yes, we built it from here."

"How?" Daphne asked.

"We will tell you when the job is complete. I'm sure you'll find the process interesting. Now, though, you must continue creating piles. You will know when pile two and three are done when you see new monuments. At that time, I will tell you how it was done and what you must continue to do."

Daphne and John signed off and resumed watching the workers. When the granite quarry was almost dry, they scouted another one. Daphne spent some weeks getting the quarry started. John helped organize the lifting and shipping procedures. Five years of work later, a second monument appeared.

As Daphne and John sat and admired it that morning, another slave approached them. "Lords, we must rest. Slaves will die if they are forced to continue at this rate."

John nodded at Daphne. They had discussed this already. "You may rest for one week, at which time many of you will be reassigned. When your week is over, you will bring us the strongest slaves for the marking ceremony."

"As you wish, mistress Daphne."

He left the platform and melted into the crowd. The slaves spent their week sleeping and relaxing. They wanted to celebrate, but no one had the strength. Extra rations were sent around courtesy of Daphne and John. This week, the slaves dared to grow happy.

Daphne and John waited on their platform. Four slaves approached. Their leader stood in front of them. "Here are the strong slaves you requested. What is their task?"

"One of you will accompany me to the Monument of the Sun. Two will accompany Daphne to the Monument of the Earth. When we are in place, I will send a smoke signal to Daphne. At that moment, we will walk toward each other. When we meet, one of you will wait, and the rest of us will walk back. Once again, when we are all in place, I will send smoke signals. The two slaves waiting at the monuments will travel at a thirty-degree angle southwest and southeast. The slave waiting in the middle will walk due south. Where you slaves meet, a third pile will be constructed."

When this task was completed, Daphne and John addressed the slaves. Daphne, in charge of mining, spoke first.

"We see that you are exhausted. As a reward for your loyal service, we have decided to send you mining slaves back to the mines where your work isn't so laborious."

John added, "You laborers will continue to move building materials to the new site. You will be rewarded. When this task is completed we will allow you a lengthy celebration. We expect the work to proceed slowly since we have depleted your labor force but keep in mind there is a grand reward for your service when this is over."

Less material was moved to the third site. The laborers were at half-strength. The move to took another five years. One morning a third monument appeared, and, as promised, Daphne and John allowed a celebration.

Year 1050 A.D.

The monuments were finally completed. They were three circular monuments set in an isosceles triangular pattern. The biggest one was located two miles west of the Himal River. The Monument of the Earth, slightly smaller, was located five-eighths of a mile west of the river on a direct east-west line with the Monument of the Sun. The third one, the Monument of the Moon, was directly south of the intersection of the first two, as planned. It was very small, only twelve percent of the mass of the Monument of the Sun.

Daphne and John addressed the gathered throng. Slaves dared to smile as they listened.

"John and I promised you a celebration, but first, on behalf of the gods, we thank you for your sacrifice. Demand for mining slaves will be lowered. Those of you who are displaced will be assigned to the plantations. Free citizens of Laarisia have come forward with plans for plantation mansions. Any slave who is a builder will be reassigned to mansion raising.”

The festival to celebrate their years of hard labor began the moment Daphne's speech ended. The miners listened naively as the laborers bragged about constructing the monuments. Vernax, a typical miner, listened intently. His short and stocky frame was covered with years of soot, and his clothing was tattered. Soot was embedded in his hair and skin. Even the whites of his eyes had a blackish tint. Black was all he had ever known in those awful pits. He could recall that long ago, he might have had lighter skin and hair, but that seemed a lifetime away. He rarely saw the light of day, and these stories, however exaggerated, intrigued him.

When the current story ended, he turned to a laborer who stood next to him. The laborer he knew casually he had met Nocix on material pickup days. Vernax stood there quite stubby next to Nocix. He did not concern himself with Nocix's height and obvious upper body strength. Even his clean, good looks could not deter Vernax from spreading his message.

“Your stories are wonderful. They bring us almost as much comfort as our protecting God.”

Nocix was taken by this man's confidence, his absolute defiance of the law. There were to be no other gods than the gods they worshipped! His curiosity peaked. “What protecting God?”

“He protects us from mining accidents. We honor him nightly before we break our bread. We believe he protects all slaves. It was he who allowed you the strength to build those grand monuments.”

“Interesting. Do the masters know of this God?”

“No. He is a secret God. We aren't allowed hope. If they knew of our God, they would destroy him.”

Nocix's eyes brightened. Even the smallest leverage against the masters could bring happiness to all of the people. “Will you tell us more of this God?”

“We will talk of him when we can.”

Daphne and John, tired of watching the slaves celebrate, slipped off to the temple of Mercianiax. The monuments were finished. Jupoler had a promise to keep.

As they stood in the circle, a beep sounded in innersolar mapping. Uryxs answered.

"How may I help you?"

"Jupoler promised to tell us how the monuments were created," John informed him.

"Yes, he anticipated your call. He has sent me to answer since I designed them."

Daphne was unable to contain her excitement. "How did you do it?"

"We used the same process we used to rebuild Gosirius. Tractor beams placed the stones; laser beams cut the designs. We developed the designs over the years while waiting for you to gather the materials we used. We predict the design and magnitude of this project will awe mankind for centuries."

"Do they serve a purpose?" John asked.

"We feel we are losing touch with mankind. When you two are gone, they may forget us. We hope these monuments will serve to remind mankind that the gods rule the planet. There is a message here that will save humanity if they lose contact with us."

"What message?" John asked.

"We cannot reveal it, even to you. It must be discovered. Humanity must save itself; we cannot interfere. I can tell you this; the message is a reminder of our love for you. It may be needed. Even now, your slaves have begun to believe in a god that doesn't exist."

"Shall we stamp out their god?"

"Not directly. We have another project. Perhaps you can work their god out of them."

"What is the project?"

"When you were children, we taught you Earth astrology. We want you to construct twelve statues to surround the monuments, four per monument. The Monument of the Moon will have to adorn it, Aries facing east, Taurus facing north, Gemini facing west, and Cancer facing south. The Monument of the Earth will have Leo facing east, Virgo north, Libra west, and Scorpio south. The Monument of the Sun will have Sagittarius facing east, Capricorn facing north, Aquarius facing west, and Pisces facing south. It is critical to the riddle that Sagittarius stands outside of the circle, ever so slightly offset."

"Why this astrological pattern?"

"It is a signal and warning to future man not to ignore us." Finished, he abruptly signed off, and an astrological book appeared on the floor.

John and Daphne quietly left the temple and walked the streets of the village, trying to decide what to do. A drunken slave brushed by them, answering the question for them. John grabbed him. "Slave! Gather all of the slaves in front of this platform as fast as you can. The gods have an announcement."

The slave broke from John's grip and ran off, scared. Gradually, the celebration noises ceased as slaves quickly poured onto the field. When all the slaves were assembled, John began.

"Slaves, we counseled with the gods. The work on the monuments has only just begun. We have been commissioned to build twelve statues to adorn the monuments. Supervisors find us ten slaves who can carve."

The following morning, the slaves dolefully returned to their routine. The granite quarry cut twelve stones of enormous height. Each was dragged to a monument and laid in place. The carving slaves studied the astrological book. Working together, they carved and raised a statue once every two years.

1074 A.D.

Twenty-four years of mining and construction went into the twelve statues. They were colossal, standing half as tall as the monuments themselves.

The slaves, overworked and tired of constant abuse, built a secret society based on the mining god they now referred to as "the one true God." They talked much of their forty-year plight. They knew they had to escape, but without the support of the metalworkers, they would fail.

Convincing them would be hard. Workers of metals were given nicer houses, better food, women, and, worst of all, slaves. The one true God abhorred slavery. Slaves owning slaves was the ultimate sin.

1234 A.D.

In 1074, the monument complex was finally completed, each one adorned with its own set of statues. Daphne and John did not understand why Sagittarius was ordered offset; they considered it part of the message and dismissed it.

They reorganized the slaves back into their original classifications. Plantation slaves allowed free Laarisians to live in luxury. Household slaves who misbehaved were sent to the mines. Generations of miners lived and died in filth. Material shippers moved between the miners and metalworkers.

Metalworkers were a breed apart. Supplying quality weapons to the policing troops and quality jewelry to the citizens of Laarisia, they were treated almost as equals. Everything they owned was of better quality. They were invited to royal parties. Daphne and John enjoyed their company. Occasionally, one would stand out. Lately, their favorite was a metal master named Ronix, whom they treated like a son, always welcomed, unannounced, at the majestic palace, which had long ago replaced the government house.

Ronix, born into a metalworking family, enjoyed a privileged life. He stood on a dock waiting for the next shipment. From his stance, one would think he was royalty rather than a slave. He oversaw dirty work but always wore a clean toga; the dust ignored him. He could not believe he was related to the scum laborers and miners, his blond hair and blue eyes clashing with the dirty brown-haired, brown-eyed image of a laboring slave. His bulky shadow rested upon the raw ore that had been delivered earlier in the day. As he scrutinized them, he thought, "Well, I do respect them for what they do." They always brought him the finest metals.

His tall, muscular, heavily tanned body shone in the sun, blinding Uria. She could see the familiar look on his narrow face. With most men, it was her jade green eyes and soft brown hair, seemingly untouched by slavery, that attracted them, and she assumed the same was true for Ronix. She looked forward to these days as much as he did. Taller than other miner's daughters, she knew she was beautiful. Her athletic figure would complement Ronix, were she his woman. He insisted she become one of his women, but she protested, citing that the 'one true God' would never allow it. Ronix was speechless that day, but today, she knew he would confront her.

The wagon she rode in pulled to a stop at the dock. He barked to the driver. "Vinx! Fetch those lazy loafers. Hurry up and unload this wagon. I've got a schedule to keep."

Tired, old Vinx's bones creaked as he climbed down to face Ronix. He bowed. He was too tired and old to care how he came across to the masters. Sarcasm came through when he answered. "Yes, Sir. Right away, Sir."

"Now!" Ronix yelled.

Vinx ran off to seek help. Uria, used to this, did as she always did: waited under a shade tree off to the side. She pretended not to notice Ronix approaching as she busily rehearsed her lines.

"Uria! You are a vision of beauty! I've never seen eyes so green. And your hair and face are never filthy. How dare they call you a slave? Oh, Uria. You should want for nothing. Please come to my house and be one of my women!" He finished with flirtatious flattery.

"I told you. The 'one true God' won't allow it."

"Who is this god who would keep you from a privileged life?"

"Why don't you come to my house tonight and find out?" She flirted.

Ronix turned from Uria, realizing he had failed again. His work was second nature; he thought of her all day. At dusk, he walked home, still unsure of himself, bathed and dressed in deep thought. Finally, he made his decision. "If it gets me this woman, I'll find out about her 'one true god'!" He hurried out of his house and walked quickly down the cart road to Uria's.

He arrived at her house early that evening. Typical slave quarters it was a simple clay frame with a tightly thatched roof that overhung so that rain water would drain into the ground gutters, effectively keeping the clay dry and government costs down. The government did not want to waste money replacing existing slave quarters.

It was a simple two-bedroom building with a cooking room and a food storage room. The storage room had two levels; the underground level provided cold storage needs. As he walked in, he encountered an argument.

Vinx, so unlike Uria, was stocky, his brown hair balding, his brown eyes beady. He was still dirty, even though he had his best toga on. Intelligence flowed from his argument; he was not content with slavery.

"Two hundred years! We've been slaves for two hundred years. We were once a part of this society. When we split with them, their gods asked for war. We lost and were enslaved."

"What would you have us do, Brother?"

Vinx gazed upon the crowd to see who had interrupted him. Ury, brown eyes fixed on Vinx, hair dirty from the day's labor, stood patiently, his hardened face inquisitive, that of a believer.

"We must stand and fight!"

"You'll lose," Ronix yelled. He had scanned the entire room when he arrived. No way could these humble slaves win a revolt.

Vinx was perplexed. "Why?"

"I work directly with the military police- you will lose; they're too heavily equipped."

"Then we won't fight. God will find a way to lead us to freedom."

"You expect a newly risen god to fight for you? Don't you realize the nine gods, the life-givers, will destroy him?"

Vinx remained calm. "They cannot. He created them."

Ronix stood dumbfounded. Uria rescued him, taking his arm and leading him outside.

It took him a moment to realize he was outside in Uria's arms. "Your father is a fool. Everyone knows the nine gods are the only gods. No one god created them."

"He did," Uria responded vehemently.

"Do you really believe that?"

"All the slaves do."

"But it goes against everything we've ever been taught!"

"Then we must reeducate you. You are welcome to come back anytime. I want you, Ronix, as bad as you want me, but I will not succumb unless you convert."

"I'll think about it."

He went home and resumed his life. Daily, he analyzed the mistakes these slaves were making. Thoughts of Uria constantly invaded his mind. Despite his concerns, he found himself at her house at the end of the month.

Vinx was calmly preaching.

"The day is near. God will avenge us. The time for many gods has passed. When the gods fall, the fragile crutch our leaders balance on will break. We will be free."

Ronix could not contain himself. "The gods have sanctioned Daphne and John. They cannot fall!"

Vinx calmly replied to Ronix's outburst. "They must. Hermax wishes this harsh slavery to end. He will destroy them."

Ronix left distraught. Uria followed him and tried to calm him. Ronix needed to justify himself. "They are like my parents. I love our leaders. I will not see your father's blasphemy destroy them."

"What are you going to do?"

"I must warn them."

"Please wait. Come next week. Talk to my father alone. If you are not convinced, then you can run to Daphne and John."

"I'll think about it."

He turned and walked away. Uria was too beautiful to lose. He made up his mind. He would grant them one more chance.

The next day, as he supervised the unloading of raw ore at the sword-smithery, he received a surprise visit from Daphne.

She appeared behind him and tapped his shoulder. He turned, expecting a questioning slave. Instead, he found Daphne smiling. "Ronix, I hear you're in love? Who is the lucky woman?"

Ronix was startled. Was it that obvious? He straightened. "She is Uria, daughter of the miner, Vinx."

"Yes, I know of her; she is very beautiful. She approves of your many women?"

"She does not. She won't have anything to do with me unless I promise to give up my lifestyle. I don't know if I can."

"If you do, there will be many tears. I hear the slaves talk. Most consider you a prize because you have our favor. Is this Uria trying to gain our favor through you?"

"I don't think so. She is a simple girl who wants to be happy. I'm sure she thinks her life will improve if she marries me."

"John and I look forward to your wedding. We want to see you happy."

"Let's hope it comes to that. Uria's family has strange views. I don't know if I accept them."

"Can I help?"

He was amazed at her knowing look. "No. I have to figure this out alone."

"When you decide, come to the palace and inform us."

Daphne left. She frequently checked up on Ronix. He was her eyes and ears. If slaves were complaining, he knew about it.

Ronix went back to work. He thought I have to figure this out. When Vinx arrived with his daily ore shipment, Ronix cruelly set him to work, knowing that if anyone knew Vinx's ideals and saw Ronix soften toward him, he would lose his position.

He approached Uria, who, true to her habit, sat in the shade of a tree while her father slaved. "Tell your father I wish to speak to him alone. I'll come to your house five nights from tonight."

"Father will be pleased." Her smile melted him, but he knew he must continue his angry facade or be exposed as a supporter.

Ronix growled. "Tell him he better have answers."

He stormed off to work, leaving Uria astonished.

Ronix's work week was typical. He concerned himself with one shipping error; otherwise, the week ran smoothly. Planning his upcoming confrontation with Vinx preoccupied him.

On the fifth night, as promised, he arrived at Vinx's house. Vinx's sermon ended, and, like a salmon fighting the stream, Ronix entered the house as the parishioners were leaving.

Vinx viewed his struggle as a good sign. "Welcome, Ronix. Won't you join me by the fireplace?" Several of the departing guests looked quizzically toward him, remembering him as the slave who had spoken against their new God.

"Uria, bring our guest a drink."

Vinx reached for Ronix's arm. His smile melted Ronix's defenses.

"My heart filled with joy when Uria told me you were coming. What would you like to discuss?"

"You said last week that the one God created the nine gods. How is it that no one knows about this? How can it be true? How did you discover the one true God?"

"These are many questions, young Ronix, yet they are the same one. Two hundred years ago, God revealed himself to us in the mines. He allowed us to name him Hermax, which means he who arises out of darkness. Before we discovered him, we believed in the nine gods as you do today.

"We asked Hermax why he allowed us to believe in nine gods, as he was the obvious power in the universe. Do you know what his answer was?"

Ronix was slightly perturbed that Vinx would ask such a question. "Of course I don't!"

Vinx chose not to recognize the frustration in his pupil. "He told us the story of creation. He was, in the beginning, a lonely God. The new universe, like a new embryo, created an intelligence to direct its growth. Hermax is that intelligence. But he was alone.

"When he found Earth, he was searching for a planet to create life upon. He began with simple life forms and slowly developed more specialized forms. Intelligence built and was inherent in new life. When he created man, he created a sophisticated thinking machine. He felt that to teach man himself would overwhelm man's neural circuits, so he created the nine gods to raise man. Each god has a special skill he taught to man.

"Hermax is a shy God. He felt he could serve man better by allowing the nine gods to take charge. Man, suspecting there was one God, might forego the teaching of the many gods. Hermax saw the failure inherent in that and hid. He allowed the nine gods power over man.

"When he saw Jupoler rise above the rest, he knew man was almost ready to accept one God. When the gods sanctioned slavery, he knew he had to step in. He waited until the monuments were almost complete to reveal himself because he knows their importance."

"Why does he wait to take over if he is so powerful?"

"He doesn't want to shock man; he wants to be loved and accepted by him. This is why he revealed himself to the mining slaves. He knew they needed hope and the love of a caring God to survive. Our message will reach every level of society. Hermax will prevail."

"Do you really think the nine gods will step aside?"

Vinx noted a bit of concern in his voice as if he felt the story was real and real trouble might be incurred.

"They are guided by Hermax's hand."

He noticed Ronix was visibly relieved.

"They will do his bidding.

"Son, you have heard the story of Hermax. Will you accept him as your savior?"

Uria rounded the corner with the drinks and smiled as she witnessed Ronix's hard shell begin to break.

"I would like to, but what proof do I have that he is real?"

"You will soon see his proof. Our leaders are unnatural. For many centuries, they haven't aged. They upset the natural order. Soon, Hermax will strike them down."

"But I love them. I don't wish to see them suffer."

"Hermax loves them as well. He loves all his children equally and has tolerated endless suffering. If two must suffer so the many may rise from their shackles, he will make two suffer regardless of his love for them.

"I can see you're not completely convinced. I can also see that you love my daughter. You will visit with me nightly. Once I have convinced you of Hermax's superiority and once you have accepted him in your heart, I will allow Uria to marry you."

He left that night confused but came back nightly, as Vinx knew he would. Each night, the truth became clearer, and, as it did, Uria, to his eyes, became more beautiful than ever.

The final night, he burst into the house, ran to a shocked Vinx, and embraced him. "Old man, I have seen the light. May I marry your daughter?"

Vinx was speechless. Ronix heard a dish break and suspected that Uria had overheard his proposal. He boldly approached her and dropped to one knee. "Uria, I am a changed man. I no longer want all my women. I only want you. Will you marry me?"

Vinx interrupted. "Do you accept Hermax forsaking all other gods in his divine presence?"

"Yes, I accept Hermax as my creator and savior."

Uria stepped closer. "Then I shall marry you."

"When?"

"Right now. My father will officiate."

Vinx called in a couple of lingering slaves as witnesses and married Ronix to Uria in the name of Hermax.

They decided she would move into Ronix's house. She rushed off to pack. He counseled with Vinx while he waited.

"Congratulations, My son. Uria is a lucky woman."

"Thank you, Father. While she is away, I wish to discuss your cause. I told you before you can't win a fight. You must simply escape this place. I will speak to Daphne and John. They treat me as a son. I will secure our freedom."

"Do you think you can?"

"I think I must."

Uria entered the room carrying her bags. Ronix took them and led her out across the city to his home. He set the bags inside the door while she waited, picked her up, and carried her over the threshold. He never let her go all night. They made love repeatedly. For all his previous experience, he had never felt anything like this. Finally securing the man she had dreamed of, Uria became an animal, possessive and submissive at once.

He woke early the next day and arrived at the swords smithery as the smiths were starting the furnace. Overhearing their discussion about their sexual conquests sickened him. A truly changed man, he spent his morning drafting a petition to Daphne and John, suggesting they outlaw multiple women for the metalworkers. He cited that quality production would result.

Upon receiving the petition, John asked Daphne, "What is this? Ronix has more women than any of them."

"Not anymore. He's in love. He has probably seen his work improve since he stopped sleeping around. I think it is a good plan."

John sent an order to the shop the following day:

ANY METAL SLAVE ENGAGED
IN SEX WITH MORE THAN ONE
WOMAN WILL BE SENT TO THE MINES.
SEND ALL EXTRA WOMEN TO THE
PALACE TO BE REASSIGNED TO
THE GUILD OF PROSTITUTES.

The metal workers complained to Ronix because they knew he had John's ear.

"Ronix, why should we give our whores back to the soldiers?"

"Because you are slaves. Too long have you exercised a false sense of freedom. Slaves are restricted, always. I can obtain your freedom, though. Join me tonight, and I'll show you how."

Vinx was thrilled with the crowd. Everyone was upset because their women had been taken. Vinx finally possessed the leverage he had coveted these many years.

"So, your women were taken? They may also take your lives. You are slaves. There is only one choice. You must do as Ronix has, embrace the one true God, Hermax."

He explained the power of Hermax. Every one of the metal workers joined. They knew, as a combined force, they could defeat the army.

Their plan was simple: create shoddy military equipment for the establishment while smuggling good equipment to the Hermatics. Vinx approved this plan. Hoping to prevent a conflict, Ronix, a natural leader, volunteered to plead their case to John and Daphne.

The next morning, he arrived at the palace unannounced. He sauntered into Daphne and John's plush office.

John rushed to embrace him. "Welcome, Ronix. It is good to see you. How did your metal workers react to my order?"

"About as you'd expect. They were angry. Many joined the Hermatic movement seeking personal freedom."

Daphne was stunned. "The who?"

"The Hermatics. You've seen them. The slaves with the pick embroidered on their robes."

"Yes. We didn't know what they were. How can these Hermatics supply personal freedom?"

"Their god, Hermax, has promised them their freedom."

"Who is this god who challenges our gods?" John asked vehemently.

"He is the one true God who created the others."

John's anger rose. "You sound like you believe this."

"I do. I even married a Hermatic woman."

Daphne was shocked. "Uria is Hermatic? Why did you not invite us to your wedding?"

"It was a small, spontaneous affair. Besides, I thought you wouldn't approve of my conversion."

Daphne was almost in tears for the love of this man she considered her son. "We don't, but that doesn't mean we don't want you to be happy. It is a pity the slaves threw away the true gods for one false one, though."

"He is not false. He will, in time, require you to release your slaves."

"We love our slaves. Our gods sanctioned them, and we will not give them up. Tell these worshippers of false idols, slaves they are, and slaves they will remain!" Daphne ordered.

"I am a fresh convert-"

"That distresses me," John said, saddened.

"Nevertheless, I am a fresh convert and don't know much about Hermax. I must warn you, though, they say he is a vengeful God. This society will surely incur his wrath if you don't free the slaves."

He was laughed out of the office. Daphne and John, practically crying, had not laughed so hard in centuries. Creating society and running it were not conducive to laughter. They felt euphoric the rest of the day. Imagine a slave, especially a privileged one, having the gall to demand the release of the slaves!

. . . And so it happened. Hermax, the vengeful god, released his wrath on the city. A series of natural disasters brought the city to its knees. Each new disaster brought purges onto the Hermatics.

Daphne and John lost their euphoric attitude. This Hermax, this false god, needed to be punished. The first disaster involved a plague of locusts.

John was furious. "Damn, Hermax. He's ruined our crops!"

"How can we punish him? He is not seen. How do you expect to locate him?"

"We will punish his people. If he wants to ruin our crops, his people will go hungry! Half rations start now until new sources can be found."

Next, Hermax brought incredible rain. They drove away the locusts, temporarily refurbishing the soil for the next year's crops, but soon, there was too much rain, and the palace flooded. A moldy stench prevailed.

John was irate. "He desecrates our palace. I shall desecrate his children! Round up all the palace slaves and throw them into the mines."

Next, a series of earthquakes attempted to topple the city. Two hundred structures fell or burned to the ground. No preference was given to who lived in them. Slave and free alike fell with equal force. Daphne was appalled by the count. "Two hundred buildings destroyed? We will execute two hundred families in response, save the girls. I will send them to the prostitute's guild."

Each disaster was progressively worse than the previous because it built upon the damage already in place. Every purge created anger. Anger created more converts to Hermax. Soon, every slave had converted. John and Daphne saw they were fighting a losing battle. They counseled with the Gosirian priests. According to the gods, they had done nothing wrong. Punishment was ordained based on the phrase: *There shall be no other gods but us.* The priests suggested the direct approach.

So, once again, Daphne and John stood within the communications circle.

On the shuttle, an ancient beep, silent for centuries, sounded in innersolar mapping. Nepeta reacted as if he had heard it yesterday, for time meant nothing to him. "How can I help you?"

John was frustrated. "The god of the slaves; he is taking over!"

"Relax, John. Step out of the circle. I will call a council of the gods."

A few moments later, a beep sounded, and they stepped back into the circle.

Jupoler addressed them. "We are all assembled. Nepeta informs us the slaves are attempting a coup using a false god. Please explain."

"He is called Hermax, and he is a vengeful god. The slaves swear he bore you gods in order to create the living world. They say he is a vengeful god and has created many natural disasters in an attempt to ruin us. We purge his followers, but he grows stronger as he gains more converts daily."

John interrupted. "Is he the god you said was rising so many years ago? The god you said would be destroyed by working the slaves harder? This god seems to have grown as the statues were formed. He thrives on adversity."

Jupoler caught the worried look in his mate's eyes.

"We must discuss this matter. Please wait."

Five minutes later, Jupoler's voice alerted Daphne and John that the gods reached their decision.

"We believe this Hermax is the god we warned you about. We are agreed that you must stop the purges. The natural disasters occurring are just that, natural. They were bound to occur with the changes happening on Earth. This false god, Hermax, will be stopped. The Gosirian priests will take on the task."

John sighed, visibly relieved. "We will tell them. What must we, as leaders, do?"

"You must die. We feel this may bring society back together. The insanity may stop when the reality of your death hits."

"But we have so much to do," Daphne pleaded.

"You have outlived your usefulness on Earth. The Laarisians do not respect you as they once did. They need a jolt of reality. As I said, your death should bring society back together."

A set of pills appeared on the table before them. "Take these pills. Tell your people to set your bodies in the Monument of the Sun. Don't worry; everything will be okay."

Astonished, they stepped out of the circle.

Daphne broke the trance. "I don't believe we've been ordered to die."

"They said everything would be okay. We've always trusted them. We've lived long and accomplished much. If they say it's time to die, then it is. We must not dwell on it. We have work to do. Call in the Gosirian priests."

They returned to their office. A messenger was sent to fetch the Gosirian priest's leader. He arrived quickly. "How may I serve?"

John gave him a stern look. "You are aware of the god, Hermax?"

"Yes, John. No one escapes his vengeance."

"Then you know he must be stopped."

"You are punishing his people. Is that not enough?"

"No, it only seems to strengthen him. We are putting your group in charge of destroying him. We've counseled with the gods. Passive resistance is their answer. If we decrease the burden on the slaves, they may feel they no longer need help from this god. Slowly, the slaves will migrate back to the gods, especially if they see it as a beneficial move."

"We will take on this task, Lords, but why us? We are not the leaders of society."

"The gods asked us to give this job to you because we will no longer be here. They have ordered us to die."

"You cannot die. Society will fail without you."

Daphne ended her silence. "No, it won't. We have established a lasting society. Before we die, we will pick nine people to form a committee that will preserve the ideals, customs, and laws we have laid down."

John added, "I'm glad this subject came up. We must discuss with you our plans for burial."

"I am ready."

"When we die, you will place our bodies on platforms. You may have a funeral procession if you like. We wish to be laid out in the Monument of the Sun. We have chosen this site as our permanent home. We hope this choice will keep our memory alive. As people remember us in our temple, may they also remember the gods who raised us and put us there."

The reality of the situation hit everyone. Holding back tears, the Gosirian priest left, committed to his orders. He felt the heavy burden of the end of an era. He called a general meeting of the priests, which ended in a wail, the outpouring of tears marking the dusty floor.

Daphne and John used the next couple of days to wrap up their affairs. Together, they interviewed fifty people. They made their choices and called back the nine they chose.

John made the announcement. "We have chosen you to preserve our society after we die. We will issue orders to all departments instructing each to obey the laws you create. May Laarisia prosper under your tutelage. Go now. Tonight, send in a doctor, for we will be dead."

When they were again alone, Daphne and John took the pills Jupoler supplied. They spent several hours reminiscing. They had grown over the centuries as close as siblings. He commented on her strength. "I knew you were stronger than I was after you gave birth to twenty children."

"John, you fathered eighty children. Your virility is truly amazing. Do you think we performed so well because of our immortality?"

"Absolutely. I don't think our parents could've reproduced on the level we did."

"That is true. You would think twenty children would have ruined me inside, but after each birth, my body felt regenerated. It was as if the cells were being reborn."

John yawned. "I'm getting sleepy."

"Me too. I think I'll lie down. John, do you think we'll stay together in the next world?"

"That would be nice, but I don't know. Death is the deepest mystery that exists."

Several hours later, the doctor came in and pronounced them dead. The city wept. The Gosirian priests, with heavy hearts, prepared the bodies and the funeral route.

The next morning, a group of priests entered the government offices and came out with the prostrate bodies displayed on two raised platforms. Pallbearers carried the bodies through the city. Freedmen lined the streets, crying. Ordered not to participate, slaves watched from inside their hovels. Near the monument, wealthy citizens and civic leaders lined up to pay their respects. At the entrance to the monument sat the nine new council members, the new rulers of Laarisia. A spokesman stood. "We say farewell to our brave leaders. They entrusted us with the administration of Laarisia. We only hope we are worthy of this great honor. We will preserve the society they founded and spent their long lives improving. They died after a long life and took the secret of their longevity to their graves. When they are at rest in this monument, the entrance shall be sealed. Forever, this shall be their temple."

Tears flowed like rain. Even the normally stoic Gosirian priests cried freely. Solemnly, Daphne and John were laid out on the floor in the center of the monument. As ordered, the entrance was sealed. A great banquet, designed to feed the entire city, began when the seal was placed.

The slaves, denied access to the funeral, rejoiced. Token slaves had been placed at the windows to watch the funeral. The city guard was relaxed, enjoying the funeral and banquet. Only skeleton forces separated the slave hovels from the party, and, in a faux pas' that helped the cause, they were given wine to drink. Their sole duty was keeping the slaves away from the banquet, but the more they drank, the less attentive they became.

Ronix was elected leader of the Hermatians because he knew military tactics. When news reached the slaves of the drunken guard, he ordered everyone to pack their belongings. The slaves had been granted the day off due to the funeral; Ronix's plan to place slave decoys at the windows covered all suspicion that the slaves were planning a major move.

Under cover of the funeral procession and, later, the banquet, the slaves escaped Laarisia. They had an arsenal of weapons; however, they met no resistance except a drunken soldier who wandered to the rear of the hovel town to seek a slave to rape. Found at the wrong place at the wrong time, he was overwhelmed and murdered before he could sound an alarm. He was dumped in the Himal River as the slaves crossed it.

They followed the river to the abandoned harbor. Quickly they commandeered a ship, found a galley slave that knew how to sail, and prayed they would find an uncharted land to hide upon.

They traveled for many days. Daily, Ronix gathered Vinx and two more religious leaders. For hours, they prayed to Hermax, asking him to lead them to salvation.

One morning, they spotted an island near Alpania. They offloaded the ship and sank it, leaving no evidence they were there. Weapons, non-tested in battle, battled the jungle. In the clearing, they constructed a thatched hut village. Ronix ordered a hunt, and when the hunters brought back a surplus of game, he ordered a feast. During the feast,

they felt a great rumbling. Hermax, to protect his chosen ones, surrounded the island with clouds. Hermatia would remain a safe haven
for generations.

The monument was sealed, the banquet over, and the city was at rest.
Lonely soldiers patrolled the streets. Cats chased rats through the empty
hovels. When morning came, and the slaves did not report to work,
society began to crack; order slowly crumbled. Only a combined effort
to locate the slaves could save Laarisia from collapse.

Sometime in the night, Daphne and John awoke. Groggy, they took
in their surroundings. Daphne asked, "John, is this heaven?"

"I don't-"

Before he could answer, they were gone. They rematerialized in the
transport bay in engineering on the shuttlecraft. Sitting on a spiral staircase, smiling at them, was Vienusia.

John was bewildered.

"Vienusia? Are we not dead?"

"No, we love you too much to allow you to die. We brought you
back to reestablish your link with immortality."

"But-?"

Vienusia raised her hand, indicating the conversation was over.

"No more questions."

"Come with me. Everyone is waiting."

They followed her through the mini-engineering room to the elevator, which took them to the waiting immortals.

In unison, a cry rose, "Welcome home, Daphne and John."

Daphne said, "Thank you, lords, for preserving our lives."

Arop said, "You are very welcome. We wish you to join us forever."

"Do you mean we are to become gods?" John asked.

Jupoler admitted, "There are no gods. There are only immortals.
Surely, you must have guessed by now that we are not gods?"

"But why did you portray yourselves as gods?"

"We were ordered to play into human nature. You see, human nature
demands gods. That is why Hermax rose. We saved you from Earth
because, eventually, the followers of Hermax would have tried to assassi-
nate you, and we need you with us."

"Why do you need us?" Daphne asked.

"Because you are humankind's only hope. You will be our contact
with Earth. When the time is right, you will contact the Gosirian priests
and lead society back to us."

CHAPTER 9

EMPIRES

1238 A.D. - 2220 A.D.

THE LAARISIAN EMPIRE

The nine-person committee John and Daphne left in charge took the name Delegatia. By society's unanimous agreement, the Delegatia was the final authority over military, civilian, and foreign matters. There was no leader, only a fair vote. Citizens and military could input suggestions; however, influence and pressure were prohibited. All decisions were the will of the gods, sanctioned by the Gosirian priests.

The Delegatia met one week after John and Daphne died. Everyone spoke at once, each attempting to forward his agenda. Jop listened calmly. Finally, he interrupted the debate.

"Gentlemen, society has rules and laws, which we must all obey. Since the funeral, we have all witnessed these rules wavering. And why do they waver? Confusion. There is no production. The city stands still. Why? Because the slaves fled the country en masse. I believe our first order of business is to send a military expedition out to find these Hermatics. That *must* be the will of the gods! Until we find the slaves, the free men of this society must enter the mines, must learn metalworking, and must farm. We shall pay everyone; after all, they're not slaves."

Everyone agreed. The police force expanded with fresh recruits. Veterans trained them for six months, developing a true military force. Naval ships slowly crisscrossed the Galacian Ocean in search of new lands. Military bases were established on Alpania, Marsia, Ciaxian, and Vienus. On these islands, they caught a few stray Hermatians. These newly conquered lands were populated with adventurous Hermatics who had left the crowded homeland almost immediately. They were easily conquered because they had split from the true faith. As a group, they would not reveal the location of the secret hermatic homeland, and, as a reward for their stubbornness, many found themselves enslaved once again in Laarisia.

The four new military posts, under orders from Laarisia, spent the next one hundred fifty years searching the world for the Hermatians. This push created an economic boom for Laarisia. Ships, weapons, clothing, and food were required by the troops. Freedmen, soon replaced by recaptured slaves, produced materials. Merchants, acting as middlemen, became wealthy by selling to the military bases. They spread their wealth in town at freedmen restaurants and shops. Laarisia became prosperous, propped up once again on the souls of slaves.

Hermatic adventurism continued. The island was isolated, and word of the first enslaved colonists did not reach them. Ever leery of possible soldiers, the Hermatian colonists settled in the hills. If soldiers on patrol ever stumbled upon these hidden enclaves, the hunters would become the hunted.

Fresh slaves arrived in Laarisia weekly shackled in the ship's hulls. Soldiers and civic leaders who had fallen from grace found themselves enslaved as well. True Laarisians turned slaves were allowed pleasant accommodations and were assigned as house slaves who could buy back their freedom in seven years.

As the slave cargo arrived in Laarisia, the military secured the known islands and found six new islands. Named after the gods by the conquerors, Uryxia and Sateland were close to Alpania. Aropia was further west. Across the western sea, ships discovered Andenan, Kashim, and Nepetan. These three islands lay on the Andes spine where the ocean had receded.

Military leaders were given rule over separate lands as a reward for their service. These governors reported directly to the Delegatia. The faraway lands were kept in control through a puppet governing system. A local ruled but was controlled by the closest governor and had no contact with the Delegatia, thus empowering the territorial governors.

The military governors were stationed on Alpania and Aropia. Military clerks were stationed on Marsia, Vienus, Ciaxian, Uryxia, Sateland, Andenan, Kashim, and Nepetan. Clerks were responsible for levying taxes and law enforcement. They reported to the regional governors. Aropia's governor controlled the western islands; Alpania's the rest. Delegatial laws were sent to the governors to be applied to the provincial islands. Clerks on the islands sent the laws to the village leaders. The clerks, completely dependent on the regional governors, in effect, empowered the governors. A strong governor was a threat to the Delegatia. As a result, the Delegatia planted spies in the gubernatorial troops to check the governor's loyalty. If he appeared to be gaining power and preaching disloyal messages, he would be removed. If he remained loyal, eventually, he would be asked to serve on the Delegatia.

During the expansion, the Delegatia sent another group out with the military. Shipbuilders were required to observe ships in action. This observation led to better-built ships and, thus, the development of a strong navy. During the subsequent one hundred fifty-year span, as new ships were built, old ships became merchant ships bringing slaves and wealth to Laarisia. The first ships were two-masted wooden ships fitted with two to three sails per mast. The ships averaged seventy feet long. Sails were used only in favorable winds. Oarsmen provided the main power. These ships housed thirty oars. Besides the oarsmen the crews consisted of ten sail riggers, one pilot, one first officer, and one captain. The pilot wheel was located at the back of the ship for direct rudder control. These ships went to the merchants when the Navy developed stronger, faster ships. The difference in these new ships was three masts rather than two, each rigged with three to four sails. Their length averaged one hundred feet, and they housed fifty oars. They needed three extra sail riggers. As the years passed on and the merchants inherited these bigger ships, it became hard to tell the difference between navy and merchant ships. The Laara ordered the flag of Laarisia to fly from all navy ships, thus eliminating any confusion. Strong military leaders and wealthy merchants eventually put tremendous pressure on the Delegatia. During the last three decades of the expansionism period, through bribes, the Delegatia was expanded to twenty-nine members, most representing the military and merchant classes.

The Delegatia, outgrowing John and Daphne's unused office, built a new meeting hall in the east wing of the palace overlooking the valley of the monuments. The new members included regional governors, several clerks, and many successful merchants. Once a smooth-running machine, the Delegatia found itself bogged down with special interests and infighting. The military men wanted the military to have greater latitude. The shipbuilders wanted restrictions lifted on both production and delivery methods. The merchants, each profiting tremendously from slave labor, wanted more slaves imported to Laarisia.

The core nine members of the Delegatia met in John and Daphne's old office to discuss this dilemma. They feared they were losing control to the mob. After a lengthy debate, Joplo said, "If this is the Delegatia's wish, I will go."

Joplo walked out of the room and, without any preparation, walked out into the village and headed toward the chambers of the Gosirian priests. Joplo emerged early in his career as the spokesperson because of his excellent orations. Three hundred years prior his ancestor, Jop, first issued the proclamation ordering the search for the Hermatics. He was tall, blond-haired, blue-eyed, and a favorite with the women. His receding hairline was an asset, making him appear regal.

Across the village, at the base of the mountain, once thought to be the home of the gods, sat a cluster of houses. Each priest resided there with his family. During the day, the old priests took care of the children, who would one day become priests. The parents of these children were the active, working Gosirian priests. They met daily in an oversized house behind the village, set on a mountain rise.

Joplo walked slowly through the tiny village. When he arrived at the offices of the Gosirian priests, he patiently stood by the door. A child ran in to inform the priests they had a visitor.

Etan, the head priest, came to the door.

Joplo could not wait for introductions. "How can we retain control of our huge empire?"

Etan was the leader of the Gosirian priests. He typified them with his shaved head and his calm spirituality. He was very honest and direct with his answers. He looked up into Joplo's eyes, sensing his frustration. Etan ignored the question, considering it a rude outburst. He showed no irritation. "What brings you to the priests, my Son? Won't you come in?"

Joplo entered the office. Candlelight sent strange shadows bouncing down the halls. A few moments passed before his eyes adjusted. He then saw how simply the priests lived. In each room, he passed groups of priests sitting on straw mats, either meditating or discussing religious problems. They entered Etan's room and sat. "The Delegatia sent me to ask you how we can retain control of our huge empire when our own body fights itself and is in danger of collapsing."

Joplo fidgeted. Etan did not answer him. Instead, he fell into a deep trance. Then he looked into Joplo's eyes. His deep brown eyes resembled an endless hole. They seemed to peer through Joplo into the future. "You must teach the colonies to worship the gods. You must also provide better for your slaves. If you give your slaves better housing, food, education, and a strong belief in the gods, you will quell the threat of other gods rising. Don't follow Daphne and John's example. They squeezed the slaves, and Hermax oozed out of their fingers."

"These things you suggest, they will give us absolute control of the empire?"

"Yes. Why would I have stated them otherwise?"

"What about my other question? What will become of the Delegatia?"

"It may fail. It may succeed. Only time will tell. I really do not know how to help you. This problem I will have to discuss with my priesthood. We may send members to investigate the Delegatia. When we come to a decision, I will seek you out."

"Very well. I will inform the Delegatia of your decisions. I'm sure we would welcome your investigation. Everyone is frustrated with the status quo."

Joplo called an emergency session of the Delegatia.

"The Gosirian priests advise we provide better for the slaves and educate them about the gods. This will enable us to administer the empire more efficiently."

The merchants balked at the suggestion of treating the slaves decently, but the rest of the members outvoted them. In time, they saw the wisdom of this move as production steadily increased.

The military was assigned to and reluctantly accepted their roles as religious teachers. They taught poorly and were soon replaced by the Gosirian priests. They toured the colonies as teachers.

The Gosirian priests, as warned, attended sessions of the Delegatia. The encounter shocked them.

Etan was sent to counsel Joplo. They feared what the Delegatia was becoming. They had enough of this body. Things must change. Joplo found him wandering the halls and invited him into his office. He towered over Etan but remained in awe of the priest. He knew he was not a man to be trifled with.

"How can I help you?"

"As you are aware, we have observed and evaluated your Delegatia. Our findings are shocking. The infighting and bickering at your meetings, the special agendas, are only the tip of the iceberg. We secretly observed your members as they worked privately in the village. We found rampant bribery, corruption, and blackmail. The merchants are sick with power built upon the slaves. The military is sick with the power built upon brute force. These two forces will clash if you do not find a common resolve. We are certain that if everyone aspires to the same goal, the infighting and criminal activity will cease. The Delegatia has simply become too fat. Soon, it will eat away at itself."

"What common resolve do you suggest?"

"You must find the elusive land of Hermax."

"We search daily, my friend."

"You search half-heartedly. They have hidden for three hundred years. It is proven that your slaves will not help. You need to aggressively seek them. Send all military ships on this mission."

"Isn't that overcompensating?"

"No, these Hermatians probably assume you have quit searching. They will drop their guard, and you will win. Now is the time to strike."

"Thank you for your advice, Etan. I will suggest your plan at our next session. Good day."

After roll call, Joplo stood. The restless group calmed. "Lately, I have counseled with Etan, head of the Gosirian priests. He suggested that we come together in a common resolve. The infighting in this body must cease as of today."

An angry merchant rose. "What is this common resolve?"

Joplo was unshaken by this man's anger. "He suggests that we concentrate all of our resources on locating the Hermatians. This will benefit the merchants for we will gain more slaves. The military will benefit when it gains another land to manage. Finally, the priests will benefit because they will be able to prove the superiority of the gods. All those in favor of this action say aye."

All twenty-nine members said, "Aye."

"Good, we are all agreed. Now, I have studied this problem. I don't think the Hermatians traveled far from Laarisia in their primitive ship. I predict their island is somewhere in the Alpanian chain or maybe between Alpania and us. I suggest Zearn, governor of Alpania, be given commission to find this land of Hermax."

Everyone agreed.

The Delegatia sent a runner to inform General Zearn of his orders. Because of his shaved head tainted red from stubble and his medium height, one might mistake him for a Gosirian priest; this was exactly the effect the Delegatia hoped for. If the people of Hermax saw what they believed was a Gosirian priest, they may surrender without conflict.

When the news of his commission to search for the Hermatians reached him, he was shocked. Many times, the Delegatia had praised him as a capable governor, fair and just to the people of the Alpanian region. He sent slaves to Laarisia only out of a pool of lawbreakers. He spread goodwill to the slaves long before the Delegatia made it policy. Before he could begin, he had to research the problem. The Delegatia, anticipating this, sent maps of past voyages along with their messenger.

Zearn thoroughly studied these past voyages. He determined all areas on the map had been explored. Past voyages had noted a strange body of fog east of Alpania. To his surprise, each voyage had sailed around the fog, the sailors superstitious of the unknown. Inside the bank, visibility would be zero, which, predictably, would frighten the crews to the point of mutiny. From that standpoint, he surmised, the captains were right to avoid it.

Zearn believed in an almost dictatorial command. No one would dare protest his decision to sail into the fog when the time came. Fortunately for the crew, yet highly unfortunate for the people of Hermatia, the fog dissipated. Zearn easily found Hermatia. When he landed he saw instantly the people had no will to fight. He ordered his troops to occupy Hermatia without force. No abuse of the citizens would be tolerated.

He waited in his ship's quarters as his troops occupied the island. Reports informed him that the Hermatians were submissive. A map of the island showed a castle where the leaders lived. Here, he would present himself to the natives. When the day arrived, he sent a message to his troops to assemble the populace outside of the castle. As the delegation left the ship, Hermatians streamed in from the outskirts of the island. His impression, as he walked, was that this was a land of peace. The castle was small, more a religious center than a center of power.

He climbed the castle steps to address the Hermatians. Emerald green eyes conveyed a trust to the Hermatians, a sense of fair play they had not expected. Relief shone in their eyes; his imposing figure his hard muscular body, represented the essence of his army. They could have been massacred and knew it. Instantly, he proved that, although a harsh commander, he was an extremely fair politician.

"People of Hermatia. You were wise not to fight. While we are here as an occupational force, I have ordered every soldier to let the citizenry be. Any abuse by one of my soldiers will be met with instant death. I have decided to let you keep your king as long as he accepts the rule of Laarisia. Free you have been, and free you will remain."

The people lived unmolested, as promised. No slaves were taken. The Delegatia felt tolerance would help to keep the peace. People were free to worship, work, and marry, to live life as they always had.

Zearn left a small occupational force on Hermatia and traveled back to Alpania to handle colonial complaints. Hermatia, northwest of Laarisia, was the first island colony run by the Delegatia. They retained their king, but a clerk truly ruled here. When sufficient time had passed, and they were fairly confident Hermatia would not resist, Zearn was ordered to sail to Laarisia.

Zearn visited the island on his way to Laarisia. He visited with the king and was assured that everyone was happy with Laarisia's occupation. He traveled on to Laarisia to accept his reward, a seat on the Delegatia. As a junior member and the conqueror of Hermatia, he was required to oversee the governing of that island.

Zearn sailed back to Alpania with the new interim military governor. On the journey, he explained the intricacies of Alpanian rule.

He helped the new governor set up. Once the transition was complete, he gathered his belongings and sailed back to Laarisia, where he was a hero for bringing Hermatia into the empire. There, he found a celebration. The entire city turned out to welcome him. Before he comprehended what was happening, he was whisked off of his ship, set in a throne-shaped chair, and carried through the city. He accepted triumphal honors, the closest thing to being proclaimed a god, on the flat plain triangulated by the monuments of the gods. His reward was a statue of his victorious posture raised in the center of the city. Forced to retire from the military, he was given a seat on the Delegatia and governorship of Hermatia. He returned to Alpania to formally hand it over to the new governor. Satisfied, he returned to Laarisia to assume his delegatial duties.

He stopped at Hermatia to check the progress of the island. Now, regional governor, he avoided the king's palace, deciding instead to meet with his own clerk.

His clerk was nervous. "I don't care what the king told you. I get the feeling these Hermatians don't respect the gods. They keep Laarisians at a distance as if socializing with us would contaminate them."

"What is their worship schedule like?"

"They worship Hermax three times a week."

"Effective immediately, they will only gather in worship one day a week. Do they have many religious holidays?"

"Too many, Sir."

"We want to be fair. Allow them their holidays, contingent upon them observing ours. Anyone who fails to give thanks to the gods is sent to Laarisia as a slave."

"Will you go with me to inform the king? I'm not sure he'll like these orders."

"He will like whatever I tell him to like. Yes, I'll go."

Together, they informed the king of the new rules. The king was furious but calmed when his advisors convinced him that these rules were preferable to absolute slavery. Before Zearn set sail, his clerk thanked him for establishing his credibility with the king.

He arrived at the Delegatia a nervous, junior member. To his surprise, he became extremely popular, quickly rising to great power amongst the members who stood and clapped when he entered the room, and for good reason. Those who openly opposed him usually wound up dead. Fearing the rule of one man, Joplo approached Zearn with a proposal.

"General Zearn." Weeks overdue, officially he was there to welcome Zearn to his office, the last member to do so. Though he was no longer military, Zearn insisted upon being referred to as "General." "I have a proposition for you. Your appointment to the Delegatia expanded our body to thirty. First, I suggest we cap our number at thirty. Secondly, I think we will get much more accomplished if we work in specialized committees."

"Why are you telling me your ideas? I'm just a junior member."

"Don't be modest, Zearn. I have never seen a member rise in popularity as quickly as you. Your popularity will bring power. This is the third reason I decided to meet with you. I believe ten percent of the Delegatia should form a grand committee. This committee will make final decisions based on the suggestions of the smaller, specialized committees."

"Why a grand committee?"

"It is a safeguard to protect us from one person rising to rule over us all. I propose that the three strongest members form a triangle, as the gods did with the monuments. Our strengths and weaknesses will counterbalance themselves. No one man will rule, and all the interests of the people will be fairly represented and administered."

Zearn thought for a moment. "I would be a fool not to accept your proposition. When will you approach the Delegatia?"

"Next time we meet."

Joplo rose as the business of the day was completed. Others began to rise, but his posture forced them to reconsider.

"Gentlemen, the Gosirian priests were correct. This body is too fat. We cannot effectively rule. I propose that committees be formed to handle certain issues. The committees will report to a Grand Committee.

"I further propose that the Grand Committee be made up of General Zearn, our wealthiest, most popular merchant, Mercor, and myself. The Grand Committee will eliminate waste and protect us from the rule of one person. The Gosirian priests must approve any decision made by the Grand Committee." The Delegatia departed without a word, some mumbling as they left.

The next day, the Delegatia met and unanimously approved the Grand Committee. Zearn and Joplo had spent the last day convincing everyone that the Grand Committee would succeed. Key to the balance was Mercor. He had red hair and green eyes like Zearn, and some felt that opposing him would anger Zearn. Others liked him because of his demeanor, a jolly little man. His unimposing figure invited people to open up to him. An excellent conversationalist, he had a skill most others had forgotten- the ability to listen and, with few words, steer the conversation, allowing people to feel comfortable around him. He was a listener, and, as such, people confided in him a little more than they should. Information was his strength; it would balance the committee.

The Delegatia then formed nine committees, each dedicated to a different aspect of life. Each committee met separately. Once a week, the entire Delegatia met to hear the findings of the committees.

Zearn, Joplo, and Mercor sat in enormous chairs as solutions were presented to them. They would then vote amongst themselves, always contemplating the wishes of the Gosirian priests. The Delegatia and priests sat together to hear the results. Occasionally, the priests would overturn a decision, giving the people the illusion of balance.

The committee of three was indeed perfectly balanced. Mercor gathered information used to make decisions, Joplo informed the people of the decisions, and, if need be, Zearn enforced the decisions, yet it could not last. As in all societies, enforcers who enforce the will of the rulers eventually enforce their own will.

Twenty years later, the Grand Committee dissolved. Mercor, old at its formation, died. Before he could be replaced, General Zearn brought trumped up charges of bribery against Joplo. He was arrested and murdered in his cell.

Zearn gathered a loyal military force around him. They lay in wait while he called a joint session of the Delegatia and Gosirian priests.

He appeared solemn.

"Two tragedies have befallen us, and the Grand Committee, as a result, is going to be dissolved. I am the only member and I will retain the power. The committees will still report to me. Bow, and welcome your emperor, Ruler of Laarisia."

The assembled members laughed and booed. As if on cue, the soldiers rushed in and silenced them. The assembly swallowed their pride and bowed to the new emperor, beginning their descent into puppetry.

"I still seek your advice. I intend to be a fair ruler. Only those who fail me shall be punished."

Zearn, through murder and intimidation, became Emperor of the Laarisian Empire. The Delegatia feared him. The Emperor, however, still relied heavily on the Gosirian priests for advice and did not become the tyrant everyone expected.

The next one hundred fifty years became Laarisia's golden age. Zearn sanctioned scientists to uncover the mysteries of the earth. They discovered plumbing, heating, and cooling techniques. They developed theories on electricity, flight, solar, and atomic power that were never put to practical use. Just as in the earth's B.D. history, religion put a stop to progress. His descendants had kept up his good work until, during his great grandson's reign, the Hermatians rose, finally wielding their ancient swords against their masters.

By 1588 A.D., after only fifty years of Laarisian rule, the Hermatians once again felt like slaves. Visiting Laarisians had more rights than they did. Hermatians were forced to bow to them in the streets. Hermatic temples were outlawed and burned. Hermax worship was allowed only in the home. Anyone caught displaying the Hermatic pick, the symbol of Hermax, in public could be arrested. Arrest meant slavery and deportation to Laarisia.

Zearn, bewildered that the Hermatians did not recognize their good fortune, began restricting them early in the occupation. His one-day worship rule and his order to participate in the festivals of the gods were meant to show the passive Hermatians who were really in charge. These restrictions should have protected the peace.

Unfortunately, a fringe group of troublemakers, used to the freedom they had until recently enjoyed, decided that any restrictions must be protested. They attended the festivals of the gods, as required, but stood off to one side, spreading dissension to those near them. Officially, they worshipped one day a week. In reality, these extremists held private worship services in their homes daily.

Reports filtered back to Zearn that protesters were disrupting the festivals and official gatherings. He decided to punish Hermatian arrogance with a proclamation that all Hermatians must stop and bow to any visiting Laarisian they encountered. Laarisians, fascinated by the newly discovered land, flocked there on vacations. Many decided they would like summer homes there. Zearn allowed them to take any residence they wished, effectively displacing many Hermatians. Laws were handed down, which gave preference to these visiting Laarisians. Laarisians were allowed first refusal in all aspects of life. For example, if twenty Hermatians were waiting in line at a fruit stand and a Laarisian walked up, the Laarisian was served first. The effect of this rule was more religious worship in private.

Zearn's clerk noticed that worship days brought many more Hermatians than when he first began keeping records. He suspected treason, but when he sat through a service in disguise, he heard no sedition from the pulpit or the audience. Confused, he continued to return to services and became friendly with a parishioner who eventually invited him back to his house for dinner. Here, in the privacy of their own home, the parishioners blasted the government, spoke out against the puppet king, and spoke of eliminating Zearn's clerk. The clerk tried not to tremble, excused himself when the time was proper, and sent a message to Zearn warning him of the seditious acts he had witnessed.

Sir:

Worship services in public
appear to be loyal and
legal. I have found to
my horror, they are meeting
places of seditious persons.
These persons, through signals
unknown to us, gather in clusters
in private homes and threaten the
security of the land.

Zearn's face turned purple with rage. He crumpled the message. "Guard, find me a ship. Now!"

Angered, he visited Hermatia personally to stop this rebellion before it began. Because of the evidence, he created the following laws, which he forced the king to implement and post as if they originated from his office:

1. All Hermatians must display the Hermatic pick, the symbol of the god Hermax, on their clothing, residences, and businesses. Any Hermatian caught ignoring this law will be enslaved and sent to the mines of Laarisia.
2. Hermatic worship will be allowed in private homes only. Allowing for large families groups of worshippers may be ten or less. Any group of eleven or more will be severely fined. Second offenders will be enslaved.
3. To ensure that public worship does not take place, I, your king, have asked the occupation forces to destroy all Hermatic temples. They will use the Hermatic pick to reduce them to rubble and burn the remains.

In obedience to these laws, Hermatic picks appeared everywhere. A haze formed over the island as the temples were burned. Laarisians, sickened by what they termed Hermatian arrogance, began attacking local businesses and people. Many Hermatians were ruined. Particularly nasty Laarisians tore the pick off of innocent citizens and turned them into the nearest soldiers as lawbreakers. Though it was an obvious farce, soldiers arrested the Hermatians and sent them in chains to Laarisia.

Hermatians could not fight back alone. A plan was developed. The Hermatian priesthood, out of work except for a few select invites into prominent homes to preach, met to discuss the problem.

"We have lost all of our freedoms."

"Agreed. The pick law only encourages our victimization."

"I am against the burning of our churches, as I'm sure the rest of you are. Hermax must be furious."

"We must fight back."

"We cannot. Zearn took our land peacefully, for we knew we would be destroyed if we resisted."

"True. We cannot fight them in open battle, but if we could get close to the emperor, we might be able to sway his judgment."

"Zearn will never let us get close to him."

"I do not speak of Zearn. I speak of a future Emperor. My plan calls for time. Slowly, we will infiltrate and take over the empire."

"How do you suggest we do that?"

"Simple. You are all invited to preach in local homes, are you not? Preach this. Ask for volunteers for slave duty in Laarisia. Remind them that this is a lifetime commitment. They must openly oppose Zearn's laws, be arrested, and be deported to Laarisia, where they will become slaves for life. Once there, they will infiltrate the slave society. Marry, have children, and, most importantly, reeducate the Hermatic tribes enslaved there. Eventually, enough of us will populate Laarisia, create dissension, and rise in a general rebellion, effectively neutralizing the Empire."

"How will they know when it's time?"

"We will send a messenger. The balance must be correct. There must be too many slaves to handle in Laarisia."

A select few were to protest the anti-symbol law, become slaves in Laarisia, and reeducate the Hermatic tribes. They married into the slave society, spread the will of Hermax, created dissension, and started a revolution. It took one hundred years for the will of Hermax to spread. The revolution was quick and easy. Palace slaves simply secured the Emperor.

Hermatia's founding family of Ronix were civic and religious leaders. Ronixin grew up to look much like his ancestor Ronix. His family was still important in Hermatia. Ronix was the first head priest, and most of his relatives followed suit. They also ran the metal works where hunting weapons were developed. Although they were battle-ready, the Hermatians lost their will to use them when they saw the size of the Laarisian army.

He grew up with the image of the pick his great-grandfather had been forced to burn into the door of both his household and the metal shop. He had a love/hate relationship with the pick. It represented the god he loved and wanted to serve but was a source of pain and prejudice in his society.

He spent most of his childhood angry. He fought off countless Laarisian bullies. One-on-one, he always won the fights, but when gangs attacked, he knew he could hurt one, maybe two, but in the end, he would be defeated.

He spent many years in seminary studying to be a priest. The priests who taught him encouraged him to be strong and to have faith, for one day, Hermax would conquer all evil. He tried, but his bruises often slated his attitude.

He spent many hours at the metal shop working as an errand boy. He befriended one worker who claimed to know how to fight. Through him, he learned to handle a sword. After years of practice, he was a great swordsman.

His arsenal complete, he would bring Hermax back, either by peaceful preaching or by violent overthrow. A double-edged sword, he was confident that any way he struck, he would win.

At a religious service, when it was once again time for the priests to recruit, he caught the fever and volunteered. The next day, he walked up to a Laarisian soldier, a man who, as a boy, had tortured him. His determined look frightened his old foe, and he raised his sword in reflexive defense. Ronixin smiled, raised his hand to his chest, and tore off his Hermatic pick. The soldier, relieved, arrested him. "Ronixin, you scum, I always knew you were destined for the mines."

"I am destined to destroy you."

Angered, his enemy struck him with the blunt end of his sword. He woke up chained to other men on a ship bound for Laarisia, his head throbbing from the clubbing. He did not care. His head swam with thoughts of leading the slaves to victory as Ronix did so long ago.

When they landed in Laarisia's harbor, they were brought on deck. The fresh ocean air burned his nose, a shock after weeks of living in his own foul waste. He was stripped and chained to the other slaves on the deck. The clear blue water below showed the results of past rebellions on deck. Ronixin started as he saw many skeletons shackled together under the surface.

A crewman nudged him from behind. He growled, "That's right, slave. Occasionally, an arrogant Hermatian will upset us before we can deliver him to his new masters. One rotten apple ruins the whole batch, as they say, so off they go, one and all chained like helpless animals, over the side to meet the real gods." He laughed and walked away, leaving Ronixin shivering.

The sun parched them as they waited for the cargo to be unloaded. Finally, they were told to rise. Slowly, painfully, they did. A guard pointed, and they proceeded toward and down the gangplank to the dock below. Here, representatives from each mining guild selected slaves. The ore mines purchased Ronixin, known to hail from a metalworking family.

The guild representative, sensing Ronixin was intelligent, offered him passage up front on the wagon's open-air bench. Ronixin was quiet. His new master mistook his silence for nervousness.

"We have records on you. As all slaves, you will begin your life in the mines. With good behavior, say for about six months, I will raise you to shipping. I particularly want your input on load levels. Eventually, I will have you on a delivery schedule. Your insight into production needs in the metal shop will be invaluable to me."

Within two years, Ronixin, who realized good behavior would propel him far, found himself delivering raw ore to the metal shop. During the lag time, when deliveries were being unloaded, he spoke with the metal shop workers. He offered insights and shortcuts that led to better products.

At the shop's request, he was transferred to their control. He spent a few years on the furnace shaping implements. Eventually, he found himself stationed at the sales counter. Here he met many soldiers assigned to pick up weapons. Knowledge impressed them. They needed intelligent slaves in the palace armory, and because of his contacts, he was selected.

Palace slavery duty was what he had strived for. He lay low and waited for an opportunity to present itself. Knowing the palace slaves as a whole would not trust him if he did not appear to be of solid background, he needed a wife. He frequented the kitchen, and there he found a beautiful woman. She was headstrong like him. She remained clean as if she were above this life.

When he asked, she agreed to marry him. Palace slaves were allowed private ceremonies but were required to marry under the auspices of the gods. This infuriated Ronixin, but she convinced him that since Hermax created the gods, this farce really was watched over by him and, therefore, they would be married in Hermax's eyes.

Once married, he began his work educating her family and friends in the intricacies and realities of Hermax as the one true God. Word that he was a prophet quickly spread through the palace slaves.

Surprised he was considered a prophet, he decided to use the rumor to his advantage. One by one, he directed the palace slaves to arm themselves. Short swords or long knives would do. "On my signal, you will attack the closest soldier. The time will come soon. Zearnanine, the new Emperor, has called a meeting of the guard to announce his policies. We will all be in attendance. It is his wish we spread his will amongst the slave population."

When the fateful day arrived, Zearnanine entered the hall. As the guard compliment stood to applaud, Ronixin gave the signal. The guards were secured, but Zearnanine, quick-witted, ran back down the hall, temporarily escaping the coup.

Ronixin cursed. He ordered his followers to imprison the guards as he ran off after Zearnanine. He searched in vain.

Zearnanine grew up in this palace. He hid well. While he waited, he thought of how he had arrived here, the eighteen-year-old son of Zearnan. His father died at sea, leaving him as heir to the throne. Although the strength and looks of his great-grandfather, Zearn, conqueror of the Laarisian Empire, Zearnanine was much taller. There had been many changes over the last one hundred fifty years and Zearnanine was a product of them. Where Zearn had been friendly to Hermatia, Zearnanine was cruel. He demanded respect for the gods but was wise enough to learn about Hermax's power.

He saw Ronixin hurrying down the hall, frazzled. Zearnanine thought, "He is nervous. He knows his coup is failing. Damn slaves. I'll show him."

As Ronixin passed, Zearnanine flew out of his lofty hiding place and tackled him. He was no match for the older, experienced swordsman. Quickly, deftly, Ronixin pinned Zearnanine.

"Zearnanine, you will abandon the gods and embrace Hermax!" Ronixin ordered, resting his sword on Zearnanine's throat.

"And if I don't?"

He pressed the steel blade into Zearnanine's throat, drawing a trickle of blood.

"Then you shall meet Hermax prematurely."

"The gods will strike you down for this."

"No. Hermax controls the gods. He wishes us free. Your death will be of no consequence to him."

"I have studied Hermax. I feared this day might come," Zearnanine grudgingly admitted. "If I embrace Hermax, what will happen to society?"

"We don't want society to fail. You must remain in control in order for this to work. We want you to release all of the slaves."

"Society will fail without slaves," Zearnanine protested.

"The slaves will teach the Laarisians to work," Ronixin promised. "You must convince all of your governors and troops to convert under penalty of death. The colonies will follow suit in order to avoid a destructive war."

"What do I do if they won't convert?"

"In that case, you will kill them; that is the only choice Hermax offers. He is a vengeful God and will harshly punish any disloyalty."

Zearnanine saw no option but to agree. He saw the opportunity to retain his power through the church. If Hermax had won, so had he.

THE HOLY LAARISIAN EMPIRE

Zearnanine's first order of business was twofold. With Ronixin, his contact amongst the Hermatians, he reorganized society and the military establishment. Ronixin proved invaluable. His talent as a swordsman quickly won him the respect of the military, and his connections with the Hermatian priests helped to soften the blow that society was sure to feel during this time of radical change.

Zearnanine and Ronixin traveled together to the largest ore mine on the island. Zearnanine handed Ronixin an order. "I will gather the freedmen on the surface. You go into the mine and gather the slaves. Here's an order from me to the tunnel masters to allow the slaves to leave their posts."

Ronixin read it twice, then took in the scenery they passed in their coach, scenery he had first seen in shackles. Tears formed at the corners of his eyes. "Zearnanine, it is very decent of you to personally address the workers. Hermax will reward your generosity."

"My friend," this was truly the start of their friendship, "what choice do I have? The fight over religion has dragged on entirely too long. We must come together in a common resolve. The best, and apparently only, God has won."

"Zearnanine, I will counsel with the head priests. We must reward you."

Their conversation ceased as they approached the mine, each one wondering what conditions would prevail here. No one had heard of the coup. The military had not been informed, and since they were the communicative body of society, no one else knew.

After a time, the slaves and freedmen gathered. Naturally, they stood in separate groups, neither wishing to associate with the other. The slaves took advantage of their group security. Their masters braced for rebellion.

Zearnanine addressed them. "I have surrendered the empire to Hermax."

A grumbling arose from the crowd. The slaves shook their heads in disbelief.

"Henceforth, slavery is abolished in the empire."

The soldiers Zearnanine brought to keep the peace were shocked, but had no time to comprehend this change, for a riot broke out. Slaves, full of pent-up rage, struck out at their now former masters. Soldiers stopped the mêlée before the situation spiraled out of control.

The group reassembled, a few bloodied, to listen to Zearnanine's continued speech.

"I'm sure you have questions; concerns?"

A freedman spoke. "Yes, how will we run our operation without slaves?"

"The same as you always have. You have profited from free labor for far too long. I will set fair wages. You will pay your new employees and prosper, for a man who is rewarded for his efforts will put in extra effort. However, this is not where it ends. I want all employees of this mine cross-trained. Miners will become executives and vice versa. I am requiring this in all industries. I feel that the better informed an employee is, the better job he will do. If there are accidents, I want production to continue. Therefore, I wish everyone to be properly educated."

Ronixin and Zearnanine spent the next month visiting each mine, shipyard, farm, and artisan with the same message. A gathering of top military personnel and governors sailed to Laarisia that month under orders from the emperor. They gathered with the Delegatia, Zearnanine's advisor, and the Gosirian priests on the field overshadowed by the Monument of the Sun. The dull buzz of conversation filled the air.

Zearnanine rose. All conversation ceased.

"I'm sure you wonder why you were called back to Laarisia. The rumors are true. I have surrendered in good faith to the will of Hermax, the one true God."

A murmur rose from the crowd.

Zearnanine's raised hand quieted them. "I am tired of the destruction that has resulted from this endless war of the gods. It is time we live together in peace. The Hermatic pick, once the symbol of adversity, is now the symbol of strength through peace. You will all receive new uniforms for your troops bearing the Hermatic pick. All loyal soldiers will wear it. Any soldier who refuses will be considered disloyal and killed. I have learned Hermax is a vengeful God and will not take that insult lightly.

"In order to secure my troop's love for Hermax, I am ordering a project for each colony. In every capital, my troops will receive orders to build a Hermatic temple where the people will be free to worship whenever they like. All restrictions on services are hereby lifted. The freedoms enjoyed by Laarisians will now be shared by all. These monuments, created for the gods, will remain. We must forever remember the creation myth; it is the reason we are here. Though we now realize Hermax guided the creation, the gods' individual stories relate the process clearly."

The group was dismissed. The Gosirian priests saddened Hermax had prevailed, were at least allowed to preserve the story of the gods. They hoped the stories would keep their sect alive. The Delegatia retired to their chambers to contemplate how society would react to one god. Many steps forward in science and medicine were being made in the name of the gods. Would Hermax continue the progress?

The military leaders stayed in Laarisia for a few days, waiting for the new uniforms and contemplating their troop's reaction to the news they were required to protect rather than abolish the one god.

Most troops, used to following orders, accepted Hermax. Their new uniforms bore the Hermatic pick on their chests, which secured loyalty. Pockets of troops, numbering one thousand men, retired to the mountains of Alpania, refusing to convert. Zearnanine heard of this mutinous behavior during an audience with Ronixin. In order to save face, he screamed at the messenger, "Arrest them. Tell Alpania's governor I want one thousand heads to roll."

The governor obeyed. He delivered nearly one thousand heads. He begged Zearnanine's pardon for fifty soldiers could not be located.

These fifty, sensing the futility of their cause, filtered back into society. They found mates and quietly headed back into the hills. They became a savage menace, raiding outlying farmsteads. They hid for generations, teaching their offspring of the gods and a hatred for Hermax. Within five hundred years, they would rise, and once again, Hermax would be challenged.

Zearnanine continued to meet with the Delegatia to discuss public policy and to pass laws. Ronixin, Zearnanine's shadow since his victory, observed these meetings. He discussed the Delegatia's power with the Hermatic priests. One day, they interrupted, demanding to speak to the assembly.

"This body is the instrument of policy, law, and change, is it not?" The head priest asked.

Zearnanine answered, "Yes, this assembly is the honored ruler of Laarisia and her colonies."

"Excellent. We have studied this society. Reports from ex-slaves inform us that you have made advances in science. You have theories concerning subjects such as electricity, solar and atomic power, and human flight."

"That's correct."

"You will ban all science!" He yelled. "Hermax respects the natural world. How natural would it be for man to fly? You must obey the will of Hermax."

The priests felt strongly that Hermax wanted humans to be in tune only with nature. To their satisfaction, a vote was taken approving the ban on all science. To appease Hermax, one more step was taken. All scientists, along with their theories, were destroyed. Society took its first step into the oblivion that would represent a dark time on earth.

Zearnanine, in his agreement with the Hermatic priests, took the name Laara John I. The Laara, for the rest of time, would be the supreme religious leader of the world. A male or female could hold the position.

Females would take the name, Laara Daphne. The agreement was a compromise because, in those first years, everyone was at peace, yet a few colonists still secretly revered the gods.

Informants reported to the Hermatic priests, who now had a temple on Laarisia miles away from the monuments they chose to ignore, that the gods were not completely quelled:

"We stumbled upon a secret festival of the gods in the forest. These people insult Hermax."

The irritated priests arrived at a meeting of the Delegatia. Zearnanine was orating, "And that is why I encourage this body to approve a new ship-building measure-" He glanced over to the door and saw the Hermatic priests entering the room unannounced. He chose to be diplomatic. "Gentlemen, we will deal with this issue later. I believe the Hermatic priesthood would like to address us."

The head priest took his cue. "Thank you for your time Zearnanine, esteemed council members. Hermax is angered. He allowed the Gosirian priests to exist in order to protect the creation myth. We have found they are abusing their power."

Shocked that the priests knew, Zearnanine covered his guilt and innocently asked, "How so?"

"They have encouraged the faithless to revel in a festival of the gods in the forest. We have witnesses who reported this blasphemy. We came here today to order this body to disband the priests! We also came up with a proposition. The Gosirian priest incident upsets us, of course. We feel it is time for the focus of society to change from this group of priests to a real religious leader. We feel the Emperor should take on this role."

After the details of this role were explained, the Delegatia voted. The Gosirian priests would be disbanded as ordered, and the Emperor would become the Laara, the religious leader of the world.

Zearnanine met secretly with the Gosirian priests. He informed them of the results of the vote and that they must disband. They agreed to do so peacefully. Zearnanine respected the priests. His heart burned with pain that they were being treated so. They were the glue that held society together these many centuries.

"I will allow you to meet secretly. Please don't draw attention to yourselves."

Soon, he was called upon by the Hermatic priests. To his surprise, they did not know about the Gosirian priest's secret meetings.

"Holy Laara, we need to retain religious integrity and power in the world. We fear the influence of the old Gosirian priesthood. You have ruled. What is your advice?"

"I'm glad you came to me. I've been pondering this subject for some time now. You took an important step by requesting we build state temples in each colonial capital. For strict control, you must now build minor temples in each town. Once completed, we can use these temples as gathering places for the citizens. Here, we can teach everyone religious history. The boys will be given the choice of the priesthood or the military. Either choice will have religious bearing because the military also speaks the will of Hermax."

"How will these boys choose?"

"Their own egos will choose. Those who want to be spiritually wealthy will choose the priesthood. Those who want to be physically wealthy will choose the military."

"How is a military choice a wealthy choice?"

"I am the Holy Laarisian Emperor. I will proclaim that any officer who retires from the military shall be granted a huge tract of land. He will retain the title Lord and lord over the land and the poor farmers who will work it. Retired enlisted men will supervise or form the lord's guard. Any Navy officer will also be given the choice to be a merchant sailor. The farmers and storekeepers will come from the boys who don't make the cut either religiously or militarily and also from the common men who refuse either choice. There will always be a surplus of commoners. We will give them no other choice. It will be a fair system. The common tenants will tend crops or raise livestock. In return, they will receive a home and fifty percent of the yield. The lords will also keep fifty percent. Both the lords and the farmers will give five percent to the temples. This arrangement will keep the people humble while enriching the lords and the church."

The lords became exactly that. Their tenant farmers were essentially slaves. A lord could take anything from them: food, children, livelihood.

Occasionally, a daughter would be taken and traded to another lord for new lands. The lords who accumulated the most land eventually became kings.

Uryxia, discovered during the first failed search for the Hermatians, instantly held promise. Several deciduous forested peaks dominated the skyline. In the valleys below them, freshwater lakes, continually cleansed with runoff, were surrounded by fertile pasture. Cattle were soon imported from Laarisia, and Uryxia quickly became the dairy capital of the world. Young tenant farmers were given one cow to start their lives. The lords provided bulls to stud for trade. Never wealthy, some tenants owned several cows, but their taxes were ruinous.

Taes was the daughter of a poor tenant farmer in the village of Crono on the island of Uryxia. The family fortune was two cows. Her father knew his son was destined to work the land, so he invested his hopes in his daughter. He neglected to teach her how to work the land, encouraging her instead to explore their world. Every day, she ventured. No farm, no portion of the forest was unknown to her. She, however, was not well known to the citizens of the village. Stealthily, she crept about observing, while those who knew her suspected she was locked away inside her house, learning to be a housewife. In this way, she learned every intricacy of village life. She kept a leery eye out for Lord Rapta whenever she was exploring.

Lord Rapta was lord over Crono. His eyes were new growth green, his hair as fiery as his temper. He was a stocky retired military general who quickly incorporated many lands through shrewd bargaining and pure terror.

Crono was a simple village centered around a Hermatic temple. The temple priest, as was the custom in all villages, took the name of the town; in this case, his name was Cronon. The lord owned ten four hundred-acre estates, each worked by ten families.

Occasionally, he was called to Laarisia to advise the military. Taes hid well in the forest as Lord Rapta and his guard complement galloped away toward the harbor. She hurried to the center of town, where she knew everyone would soon gather. She felt elated as she traveled through the countryside, pitying the poor families she passed. Though her family was in a similar plight, she did not feel enslaved because she did not live her life in the mud.

Ales Lanx was her only real friend, but one she saw far too seldom. They met during services at the Hermatic temple. She only saw her there and on revenue days, when the tenants were expected to turn over fifty percent of their yields. Lord Rapta always provided a feast to lighten the mood of the peasants, and, at one of these festivals, Ales told Taes her entire family history. Today, when the lord left, a tradesman waited for an opportunity on the outskirts of town.

Reviewing the Lanx family history in her head, Taes wandered into the middle of the village in a daydream-like daze. The marketplace was full of villagers, farmers, and merchants gathered to listen to the tradesman weave a terrific story of a new island where a family could take as much land as they wanted, work it, and keep all the profits for themselves. There, his head above the crowd was Ales' father. Taes watched as he hypnotically moved to the front of the crowd.

She could sense, through his body language, that this shy, uninspired man was becoming dangerously agitated. He burst forth out of the crowd and ran home. Taes stealthily followed him.

Farmer Lanx was a second-generation servant of Lord Rapta. His father had been drummed out of the priesthood, forever cursing his family to a life of poverty. He dreamed his whole life of improving his situation, yet carefully avoided the tradesmen and their wild stories of far away fantasy lands. Aware of the rumors, he felt it was better to work in the system. Venturing out could be dangerous. He was tall with an earth brown that penetrated his entire body from his eyes to his toenails, had white hair and was very intelligent and protective of his family. He preferred to hide rather than to be noticed.

Today, however, he had been trapped in the marketplace in the middle of a crowd that was listening to a tradesman speak. Despite himself, he pushed to the front as if some mystical force had moved him. What he heard excited him so that he ran home, scooped up his shocked family, and headed for the coast, leaving the village of Crono behind forever.

Taes followed them until they were safely away. She silently wished Ales luck in her new life and slowly worked her way back home. The sound of galloping horses startled her. She dove into a cluster of bushes in time to observe Lord Rapta's envoy returning home unexpectedly. When they passed, she ran back home, instinctively knowing there would be trouble.

Lord Rapta's daily habit took him to each tenant farm to check productivity and to keep an eye on his tenants. Disloyal acts, real or imagined, were punished severely. Taes warned her family of the lord's return, and they each put on their best work face.

Lord Rapta finally came around. "I forgot my maps. I thought I would have a pleasant visit with each of my tenants before setting back out again."

Her father answered humbly, "Thank you for honoring us, Lord. We appreciate your concern. Hopefully, what you see here satisfies you?"

"Titys, you are one of my most loyal subjects. Keep up the good work. Guard, let's ride!"

They sped off in the direction of Ales' farm. Before her family could stop her, Taes ran off after them. She arrived at the Lanx farm as a messenger rode up to Lord Rapta.

"My Lord, they're not in the village, either."

"Find them! Burn this farmhouse and barn. They have abandoned us, and they will pay!"

He turned. About to ride, he caught a glimpse of Taes hiding in the bushes. She knew she was caught and bravely stood. Soldiers, realizing Lord Rapta had not followed them, reeled and galloped back.

When they arrived at the scene, they overheard him. "Little girl, what do you know of this?"

"Nothing, my lord, I swear."

"Then why are you hiding on this farm?"

"I was hoping to play with Ales. Isn't she here?"

"You know she's not. You will tell me where she went!"

"I swear, I don't know!"

"If you are unwilling to cooperate, you will be seized. Do you understand seizure? First, you will be taken to my palace as a prostitute; second, when we've used you up, you will be traded to another Lord for more land. Is that what you want?"

This was the worst fear of the tenant farmers. They had no rights in these matters. Taes knew her seizure would kill her father. She lowered her head and reluctantly resolved to help. "They went that way," she whispered as she pointed west.

"Good. How easy was that? Now, go before I decide to punish you for stalling me!"

She ran, disappearing into the woods. She did not venture out for days. Her next expedition was taken with her whole family; on orders from Lord Rapta, all tenants were to report to the village square.

A horrific sight met them. The Lanx family hung from a fresh scaffolding, arteries sliced in their appendages. The new wood smell that mixed with their blood sickened her.

Lord Rapta was standing above the dangling bodies on the platform they had fallen from. "This family decided to abandon their farm. You see the consequences of their actions. This horrible thing they did to themselves. As a message to all of you, they will rot where they hang. Because of them, I am late for my meeting with the Laara. Anyone who cuts these victims down will be punished. I leave no guard, but you never know who my spies are. If any of you still have thoughts of leaving, keep this in mind-"

He cupped Ales' chin and lifted her head. Tears ran down her face. She retched at the foul smells emitting from below. "Keep this in mind. I didn't kill this lovely child. She will be my concubine. Don't let your children suffer this fate, for I am a cruel lover. Soon, she will be sold, and I will possess even more land. Imagine your child up here. I have important business in Laarisia. All of you, get back to work!"

Taes watched sadly as the lord marched away, Ales at his side. She, who had once been a glorious representation of the mythical Arop on earth, walked obediently, her head hung low.

The miserable crowd dispersed. Taes' family slowly traversed the path back to their farm. Taes noticed that her father's pace quickened as they approached home. Guessing his intent, she screamed, "Father, no! I barely escaped Lord Rapta's clutches when he found me on the Lanx farm. He will kill all of you and torture me with constant rape. You mustn't."

"No, Taes, I must. Lanx was an idiot. I am not."

"But you heard Rapta, there are spies."

"Spies that will be watching the hanging bodies. No, I am not stupid. I will wait until he is truly away."

Taes ran to the house, crying. She knew she was doomed. The fate of the Lanx family had strengthened her father's resolve.

Ignoring Taes' pleas, he turned to his son. "Onix, my son. Follow Rapta for one day. Make sure he doesn't turn around."

Onix was the perfect choice for the job. At twelve years old, he was still small and skinny enough not to be noticed. Once in the forest, he ran fast as a rabbit to catch up to Lord Rapta. At the slightest strange noise, he would drop and freeze, instantly camouflaged as his entire body, eyes, and hair blended perfectly with the forest floor. Luckily, he inherited his dominantly brown features from his parents, and, of course, he was naturally tan from spending most of his life working in the fields.

Two days later, he came back. "Father, the lord has boarded his transport. I saw the ship launch."

"Then we will head west to the port city of Quota."

Taes wandered to her room and began to reluctantly pack. Her father ran into the room. "Cheer up, Taes, we are going to be free."

"You are going to die, and I am going to be raped. You call that freedom."

"We must try. There is freedom in even making the choice to be free. If we are captured and die, we will be free; all men are equal in death; it is the ultimate freedom."

"Father, you seem to forget. Dying isn't a luxury I will be granted, though; I'm sure I'll wish I were dead, as Ales must."

"I haven't forgotten. I'll make sure we're not apprehended. I told you, I'm not stupid like Lanx. Now, sleep, we leave tonight."

She slept fitfully and woke with a start, her father's hand over her mouth. Slowly, he released her. Reluctantly, she rose, gathered her belongings, and followed her family out the door. She hoped she would never see this place again, for to gaze upon it would surely mean she was a newly bound concubine, probably watching the lord's soldier's burn it to the ground.

She led the family down forest trails she had discovered. They took a roundabout path in case they were discovered because Quota was the logical place to run. They traveled only at night. One week out, Onix took the lead because he had recently been to Quota and knew the terrain. This final week, as she slept during the day, she had a recurring dream. She dreamed they were caught; she dreamed she stood over hanging, rotting corpses. She dreamed of Lord Rapta laughing hysterically as his guard gang-raped her; she started awake.

She trudged on, depressed, tired from lack of sleep. Predominant in her mind were soldiers. She imagined them around every turn, hidden in every bush, waiting to ensnare them. She was noticeably relieved the day Quota came into sight.

Finally, after a laborious two-week journey, they arrived at the outskirts of Quota. The city had expanded quickly. The name originated from leftover old English from the B.D. era. It was the largest trade city in the world. Each merchant had a sponsor who wanted him to make a certain amount of money or trade a certain tonnage. Since everyone seemed to always have a quota, the name was suggested early on and stuck.

From the edge of the woods, she could see the harbor bustling with excitement. Ships from the entire empire were loading and unloading cargo. Taes was amazed. Was it possible there was so much wealth in the world? Were people really free to trade? These questions would have to wait. They found a cave to hide in for the night.

At first light, Titys left his family in the woods and went to search for passage. At the edge of town, he stopped and took it all in. The streets were lined with new wooden buildings, selling variety he had never dared imagine. As he began his walk down the main dirt thoroughfare, he wondered how he would, even with his stocky, strong body, be able to move through the hustle and bustle of the crowds.

He was bumped a few times, but no one seemed to take notice of him, this poor backward farmer. He kept his eyes on the buildings and finally found what he was searching for. Up ahead on the right, close to the harbor, was a mariner's saloon. He went in and ordered a drink at the bar. As he was paying for the drink, he quietly asked the bartender if he had heard any stories of the new land. The bartender pointed out a man who called himself Nepusia. "He's been there. See if he'll take you."

Titys followed his finger to the back corner of the bar. A tall man sat alone with his back to the wall. He was difficult to see, but as Titys crossed through the smoke, his image came clearer. He first noted his sleek, strong body. A stereotypical captain, he had blond hair and blue eyes, as if he were related to the ancient sea gods. Nearer to the table, he began to smell the sea, a sea Nepusia could never truly wash away. The captain sensed someone approaching. As he raised his stern oval face, Titys could see he was very drunk. He decided to try anyway.

"Excuse me, Captain Nepusia?"

"Yeah, what!" He growled.

"The bartender says you can take me to the new land."

He looked him over. He knew he was a farmer; they always approached with that desperate look. Each time, he said no; the risk just was not worth it. "Look, farmer, It's risky and a long way off. You should go back to your lord before he discovers you've gone. Besides, you couldn't afford my price."

That was true enough, Titys knew, but he had not come so far and risked his family's life to hear no. So, instead of turning away, he bravely stood his ground for the first time in his life. "Now you listen, Captain Nepusia. I'll not go back. My lord murdered the last family he caught. I do have money, and I accept the risk. Please come with me and examine my treasure."

The captain, impressed by his character, went with him. They slowly worked their way through town. They fought against the human stream like salmon spawning. In this town, most everyone walked toward the harbor. They trekked quicker in the woods. Captain Nepusia slipped twice, not used to the plant waste that carpeted the forest.

As they approached the cave where Taes and the family were observing their approach, Nepusia slipped again. Instinctively, Taes ran out of the cave to help him up. Their eyes met as he rose. She quivered uncontrollably. His roughness was an overpowering attraction.

They parted as Titys took his arm to show him his treasure. It was a pitiful collection of worthless odds and ends. Titys explained that his real treasure was his family. Nepusia registered almost nothing Titys said; he was transfixed on Taes.

Taes averted her eyes, feigning embarrassment. As she did, the spell broke. He interrupted Titys. "Keep your treasure, old man. I will take you out of kindness."

He spent the night with them in the cave. Before dawn, he woke them. They gathered their possessions and walked through the deserted village to Nepusia's ship.

Diplomacy aside, he had decided to take them with him, not because of the money, but because of Taes. She was sixteen. Her brown hair, eyes, and baby-smooth skin had quickly sobered him. He never sailed without a price. Unbeknownst to the family, his price would be Taes.

That morning, after loading, the captain warned them. "Look, I told you this will be risky. If the Laarisian patrols stop me, you'll all go overboard."

"Understandable, Captain. Let's just make sure we avoid them," Titys suggested.

The family was ordered below decks before dawn. Nepusia finished his final check, untied his ropes from the dock, and drifted into the harbor. Once past the piers, he unfurled one small sail and guided the ship to the harbor mouth. He pounded on the trap door when he cleared the point, inviting the family to come above.

The family walked to a side rail to sightsee. Taes broke away and approached the captain, "Captain, I want you to teach me how to sail this vessel."

"That is a job for men."

"My father is too old. Onix is too immature. Someone on this vessel besides you has to know how it operates for everyone's safety. You will teach me. I am the family scholar."

Nepusia relented. Any excuse to be close to this one was welcome. He began by explaining how the sails were designed to use the wind from behind and from the side. He showed her how the wood meshed plank to plank, allowing for minor leaks that prevented wave pressure from smashing the ship into a pile of splinters.

When he showed her the cargo holds, she dropped her bombshell. "Nepusia, captain, will you stay on with us when we reach the new land?"

"I must sail. It is my life."

She lowered her dress. "Wrong. I am your life. You look through my clothes. You want this body. You shall have it, and you will stay with me. I will never let you go. I have loved you since the moment I laid eyes on you, and I am certain we are destined to be together."

"I can't. I am uncomfortable on land."

"You will learn to love it. Come now. Take me."

As they made love that day, he felt his fate sealed. She was right; he would stay with her. Nature gave them no choice. They continued their secret love making daily.

Titys, concerned that the captain disappeared constantly, decided to look for him. He entered the cargo hold and heard Taes giggling. Fearing he might disturb someone and see something he might not want to, he exited the hold and waited on deck. When Taes and Nepusia come out of the hold, he confronted them.

Nepusia had long prepared for this day. "Thank you, Taes, for helping me inventory our supplies."

"Anytime, Nepusia." A mischievous smile formed on her lips as she walked to the railing.

Titys watched her go. Satisfied she was gazing across the sea, he turned to Nepusia. "Now, you must marry her."

"But-"

"But, nothing. I went to the cargo hold and heard you two. You must honor her by marrying her." Nepusia thought for a moment and, finally, decided to be honest. "I intend to as soon as we land."

"Why not now?"

"Only a ship's captain can marry two people at sea if there is no priest."

"There will be no priest when we land, either. I suggest you make me a temporary captain. I will legalize your love and return the ship to you."

Nepusia agreed, irreversibly sealing his fate to their new island home. The marriage was simple but beautiful. Everyone cried when, as the ceremony ended, a school of dolphins jumped ahead of the ship, their arching rainbows synchronized with the final vows.

Taes moved into Nepusia's quarters. Two days of bliss followed. Then, Onix spotted a ship on the horizon. Nepusia recognized the Laarisian flag. The moment he feared had arrived, yet now that he was married, he could not fathom the option of killing the family.

He had another idea. He lowered the sails and feigned a disability. He then hid the family well in the cargo bay. When he climbed back up to the deck he saw the Laarisian ship was upon him. The crew was in the process of lowering a rowboat. He watched as the sailors rowed to him and secured their boat to his ship. He lowered a rope ladder and welcomed them aboard.

He embraced the first mate. "Am I ever glad to see you!"

"Why are you out here?"

"A strong gale blew me off course. I have no idea where I am, do you?"

"No, we are on a mission to sail due west from Laarisia in search of new lands. Personally, I think we are wasting our time. I think the captain agrees. He will be happy to see you."

The rowboat journeyed back and ferried the captain of the Laarisian vessel to Nepusia's ship. Nepusia repeated his lie. The captain smiled. "You are a godsend. I am under direct orders from the Laara not to return until I find something. Well, a rescue is certainly something. We'll tow you back to Laarisia."

"Great, I'd like that."

A forty-yard rope was secured between the ships. Once secure, they began to sail east. That night Nepusia went below and told the family of the setback. He assured them there was nothing to worry about and then enlisted Onix's help.

Above decks, he whispered, as noise traveled easily over the water. "Onix, take this. We are going to secure you to a rope and dangle it off of the towrope. You need to crawl from ship to ship along the taut rope. When you get to their ship, tie off and lower yourself to the sea. Use this drill and drill three or four holes barely under the waterline. When you finish, climb back over here."

Onix obeyed. The next morning the Laarisia ship listed toward the rear. They signaled Nepusia for help. To their utter amazement, he cut the rope, allowing the last Laarisian ship in this area for the next three hundred years to sink.

Captain Nepusia turned the ship west, returning to his intended route. He spent the next two weeks describing the island to his new found family. Onix was on lookout duty when he spotted land on the horizon.

"Land! Land! Everyone, we have arrived."

Everyone moved forward, stood at the railing, and took in the sight. The land Onix saw was a mountain peak slowly rising out of the ocean as they sailed nearer.

They circumnavigated the island. Four distinct rivers, each with its source somewhere in the mountain, emptied into the sea after watering lush valleys. Forests of pine, a tree they had never seen, choked the foothills and ran partially up the mountain. No settlement was spotted, but Nepusia assured them they had been established.

They chose a wide-mouthed river and sailed into it until they found a good beach to anchor near. Sailing around a bend, they effectively hid the ship from any ocean vessel that might pass.

Captain Nepusia gathered his passengers together to share his knowledge of the island. "I have never explored this island. We should continue to live on the ship as we explore it."

Titys agreed. "Good idea, Captain. When shall we begin?"

"I think they will tell us," Onix interrupted, pointing toward the shore. Slowly, people began to rise from the underbrush and walk toward the shore. They were armed with spears, showing every intention of beating back these invaders.

Captain Nepusia yelled across the water. "Drop your weapons. We come in peace. We have escaped Laarisia same as you."

He climbed into a boat, lowered himself into the water, and rowed to the shore unarmed. Hesitantly, the leader of the natives greeted him. They talked alone for a while. Nepusia wearily returned to the ship.

Titys greeted him at the rail and helped him aboard. "What did they say?"

He glanced at Taes, assuring her everything was alright. She sighed, relieved. "They say they are few. They are scattered in caves amongst the foothills. They have become hunters out of necessity, afraid to farm because out in the open, they may be spotted. I told them Laarisian patrols have not ventured this far yet and that with our help, they would be safe. I asked them to join us to create a stronger society."

Taes asked, "How did they respond?"'

"They agreed. Their leader said they had been waiting for a true leader. I think they have tentatively chosen me."

"Good choice," Titys offered.

Captain Nepusia ordered everyone to prepare to explore the island. As they did, they watched the preparations on the beach. Smoke and the strong smells of cooking signaled a feast. Taes looked up to see the islanders waving them over.

They joined the feast. The leader of the islanders told them to stay put. "Before we left Sateland, I traveled with my master to Laarisia. There, I saw a rare map of Earth made in the B.D. period. When we sailed back to Sateland, I asked a sailor about the many lands I saw on that map. He said Hermax, using the primitive gods, had destroyed them.

"I had my doubts. When I returned home, I told my family what I'd seen. They believed as I did. We quietly enlisted some friends, stole a ship, and sailed blindly into the open sea. I sailed her west toward Andenan. There, we replenished our supplies. I then sailed due north, informing the passengers that we would return to Andenan if we failed to locate land.

"Almost out of supplies, depressed, and ready to give up, we spotted this mountain on the horizon." As he mentioned it, he waved his arm backward in the general direction of the mountain. "I assumed, by the map I had seen, that this was Mt. Rainer of the Cascadian range. We landed and dubbed this island Cascadia."

"Where is your ship?" Onix, always curious, asked.

"We broke it up to make shelters. We used the beams to make steps and secure the roofs of our caves. We intended to build homes, storage sheds, wheelbarrows, and such, but we feared a Laarisian invasion, so we hid the wood and decided to become hunters."

Captain Nepusia thought for a moment. "Tomorrow, we explore the island. Will you guide us?"

"Of course."

The next morning, they began their exploration. They were amazed at the varied animal life. Bears fished for salmon, a delicacy they were told. Creek ponds were dammed up by beavers. Birds and deer sprang forth out of the underbrush as they passed. It was obvious why these people had decided to become hunters.

On the western side of the island, they came across a grassy plain surrounded by forest on three sides and a river on one. Captain Nepusia nudged Taes. "Here, I will build our home and farm. I will sail my ship to this river and hide it near our land."

He asked the hunter if they could use his wood to build their house. "My people are excited. We will help you build a village here to house us all."

They built their village. Some remained hunters, while others began farming. Soon, the entire valley was productive. Taes watched as the hunters brought back many dead beavers. Women skinned them, cooked the meat, and tossed the skins into a pile. When the pile reached an amazing height, she decided to ask what they were doing.

"We are preparing for winter. These pelts, when sewn together, provide the best winter protection available."

They were right. Temperatures turned bitterly cold, and everyone wore fur coats. No one complained. The farmers, who started too late, produced a poor yield. Taes worried until she saw hunters arrive with barrels full of salmon. Wary of bears, the hunters caught enough fish to smoke and preserve throughout the winter. During the smoking process, a pre-winter feast was held. Two bears, who had fought hard to protect their fishing hole, were cooked over an open fire pit. Newly pressed wine from the vineries flowed.

Winter spent indoors was unproductive. However, Taes became pregnant, and Captain Nepusia announced that when spring arrived, he was going to sail back east to gather more colonists. He spent time with Titys and the lead hunter, laying out a plan for immigration. The room was plentiful so everyone would be given a homestead, their eventual success up to them. An underlying feeling of fear was present. Finally, Nepusia voiced everyone's concerns.

"When we arrived, you were ready to defend this land. But had we been Laarisian military, you would have lost. I feel, and I am sure Titys agrees, that if we are to give colonists free land, they must repay us. I suggest we make two year military service mandatory for all new citizens. In this manner, we will have a trained force to fight off Laarisia if she invades. Present citizens will be trained to fight also so everyone can pick up arms to defend this land."

Everyone agreed. Captain Nepusia, over the next ten years, sailed to every island except Laarisia and Hermatia. He lay in wait outside of villages. When the lord left he would venture to the village square, and, as tradesmen did in the past, he told stories of the new land. Then he waited in the harbor pretending to wait for the most profitable load available. Villagers trickled aboard his vessel. The risk was great, so he alone took it to populate Cascadia.

He retired his ship after ten years, sadly watching as it was broken up for building materials. He sat in his cabin one day, flirting with Taes and playing with his kids, when a delegation of villagers arrived.

"Society is growing quickly. We feel we need a leader. You have guided us well throughout our growth period. We are here to ask you to become our king."

Nepusia was dumbfounded. "King? Do you know what that means? You want one man to rule?"

"No. We don't want to repeat the tyranny of Laarisia. We propose a committee of advisors to the king. This committee will present laws, our courts will justify them, and as King, you will enforce them. You will be commander-in-chief of our land and naval forces. Domestically, you will protect the citizens of Cascadia."

"I am honored. Does everyone agree?"

"Yes."

"I must have a governing office. This cabin will not do."

"We have already discussed that. A quarry was ordered opened to shape the blocks to build you a castle. The complex will hold all three branches of government and a prison."

The castle was built over the course of a year. Workers living in temporary shacks outside the walls became permanent residents. Farms sprang up outside the walls; farmers were delighted to grow their produce so close to the market.

Society was running like a well-oiled machine. Nepusia decided to send exploratory missions out into the wilderness. Many discoveries were made.

Mountain climbers, scaling Mt. Rainer, found a multitude of sea-carved caves. King Nepusia utilized these caves by storing food and military supplies in them. He was continually prepared for the eventuality of a Laarisian invasion.

Land explorers found a multitude of minerals, gold, and silver among them. More animals were found: ducks, geese, doves, bass, and many varieties of salmon, all added to the Cascadian diet. They also found a magic powder that they liked to throw into their nightly campfires as it caused minor explosive flashes. Bison were adopted as a domestic food animal. Wolves, well hidden, were seen as beautiful until they started raiding livestock. Professional wolf hunters were recognized by their wolf-skin clothes. They were regulated as controllers, never allowed to harm nature's balance. The wolves kept the elk, deer, and antelope population in check, which provided good grasslands for the bison.

King Nepusia structured the military according to immigration laws. Each immigrant served two years. Any who wished to extend could. All were expected to raise arms if Laarisia invaded.

He also created a small navy. Soldiers who patrolled the rivers to protect the welfare of the landowners manned canoes. Occasionally, they would patrol the ocean close to the beaches. It was felt they were small enough not to be detected by an incoming Laarisian vessel, and if one was approaching, these canoes were light enough to be carried onto land and hidden.

The Cascadian people were so happy with their old king and queen that they decided to honor them. King Nepusia and Queen Taes were asked to attend the yearly closing ceremonies of the committee of law. Taes watched as the lawmakers greeted each other and finally sat as a speaker rose to address the group.

"We are here today to honor our king and queen. The progress this society has made is directly due to their efforts. Without their leadership, we would have remained the savages they found when they arrived on Cascadia. This body has previously agreed and I have been chosen to announce: Henceforth, this island shall be known as Nepusia!"

The king and queen were shocked. The applause startled them. The speaker continued: "We wish to also inform you that your kingdom shall be hereditary. We want every king to take the name Nepusia and every queen to be called Taes. We feel this will provide consistency and strength to our society."

The law committee meeting ended at dusk. Nepusia and Taes were ushered outside. The citizens were celebrating in the streets. An inventor, propelling the magic powder that was still highly misunderstood, created a show of color in the air. These fireworks would be the mainstay of Nepusia's freedom celebration every year.

Captain and King Nepusia died in his eightieth year. He left a fifty-year legacy. All work ceased on the day of his funeral. Citizens watched as his body was marched to the beach, loaded on a rowboat, and tugged out into the ocean. When he had traveled far enough out to sea, the tug captain released the rowboat. As he headed back to shore, smoke began to billow from the king's boat. Slowly, it sank, and King Nepusia, as per his wish, was welcomed back to the sea.

Taes spent her mourning contemplating ways to honor the king's memory. When she returned to work, she ordered the civil engineers to build a wall around the city. She provided plans for a three-tier system that would offer maximum protection in the event of a siege. She knew his major focus had been defense and, in building this structure, she would honor his memory best.

In the last days of her life, she accomplished two goals. She produced plans for a new palace and village complex that would keep builders busy for nearly three hundred years. She also instructed her son and grandson in government policies and encouraged them, above all, to entice and recruit colonists away from Laarisian control.

Cronon was the head priest of the state temple of Uryxia. Tradition dictated he take his name from the town where he first served, in this case, Crono. A typical Hermatic priest, he was determined to distance himself from the former power of the Gosirian priests. Unlike the Gosirian priests, who remained hidden and scared, he was honest, direct, and power-hungry.

After receiving numerous complaints from the local temple priests, he decided to book passage to Laarisia. On the journey to Laarisia, he thought of how his cunning had produced his power. As he landed, he imagined himself wielding his popularity to become Laara. He considered the wizened old Laara weak and held him in contempt. When he arrived at the palace, Emperor Upol (Laara John VI) met him at the door.

Upol was the last Emperor to be spoken of with duality. The first six Laara's were spoken of as Emperor when imperial business was at hand and as Laara when religious business was at hand. This transition was necessary in order for the people to see the Emperor and Laara as synonymous. The next Laara struck the "Emperor" from his name, making "Laara" the most powerful title in the world.

"State your business, Cronon. You better have a good reason for abandoning your post!" Upol demanded.

"Holy Laara, the lords are at their wit's end. They came to us because they can't control their people. Many peasants are abandoning their farms to seek out the island of freedom. This dream of a free country has become overwhelmingly contagious over the last three hundred years."

The Laara's distant ancestor was the mighty Zearn. This Laara was tall thin, and appeared weak to anyone who knew him. He had fiery red hair. Cronon backed up as his green eyes turned red from anger.

"Three hundred years! Why has the Laara never been informed of this outrage?"

Crono cowered. He knew as a leader, there was truly no excuse for his lapse. "I barely found out myself. The priests in the minor temples feared the wrath of the Laara and thus kept it a secret."

"And with good reason. I will employ the military to defeat these traitors. In the name of Hermax, we will conquer this new land. The lords shall tax their people an extra ten percent to help feed the war effort, and these priests who kept the secret for so long- they shall serve as religious leaders of the armies. They will suffer in war for their ignorance!"

Tatan noticed Cronon's worry. He watched inconspicuously from the docks. The guard's commander was signaled. Tatan noticed whispering, then another worried look as the guard's commander called his troops to attention.

Cronon climbed to the top of the gangplank. "I have returned from our Laara's presence. He is on fire concerning this mysterious new island peasants are fleeing to. Commander, prepare your men for battle."

"Yes, Cronon. Are there enough men in my guard?"

"No, I am under orders to enlist the temple priests from each village. The Laara is angry that three hundred years have passed without a report of this situation."

"They will be hard to train, these men of peace."

"The Laara has granted us one year."

Tatan quietly slipped out of the crowd. He entered a store, exited the back door and, when he was sure he was not followed, ran out of town back to his farm.

He was thirteen, considered by peasant standards a grown man. It was as a man he confronted his father.

"Where have you been, Tatan?"

"I was in Quota. I wanted to see Cronon return from Laarisia."

"We have work to do here. Never mind, Cronon. A priest like him would be better left alone. He has the power of life and death over us."

"But we can't ignore him. He has recently come from a meeting with the Laara. He has been ordered to gather troops to destroy the new land of freedom."

"What has that got to do with us?"

"Nothing really, except that I think any soldier left behind is going to turn mean. I'm not going to wait around to find out. I'm going to find passage to the new land and fight Laarisia as a free man."

"Tatan, don't," his father begged. "You don't know what you're saying. Even if you could somehow board a ship and sail to freedom, you'll be killed as a traitor when the Laara tames that island."

"I would rather die a free traitor than a beaten slave!" Tatan yelled as he turned and ran.

"Tatan, wait!"

Tatan ran into the house. His father hurried to stop him but found he had taken a satchel and had run out the back door. Tatan's confused mother burst into tears when she realized Tatan was fleeing.

Tatan did not look back. Normally, he would have hurried straight to Quota, but an instinct warned him to be careful. He stayed hidden in the bushes, slowly making his way to Quota. He heard a noise and hid instinctively. Troops stormed down the road on horseback, looking for any traveler. He overheard the leader say they were under strict orders not to let anyone into Quota.

The four-hour journey to Quota took him a week at this careful pace. He probed the outskirts and found them heavily guarded. Choosing a spot, he waited, and when the guard went to relieve himself in the bushes, he made his move. Stealthily, he crept past the position and into the town. He hid in a barn until nightfall.

At a mariner's saloon, he quietly positioned himself at a back table in a dark corner. He ordered a drink and listened to the conversations around him. Two drunken sailors boasted of the adventure their captain was about to undertake. When soldiers burst into the room, they abruptly halted their conversation.

Tatan, wishing to escape unharmed, picked up a serving tray and walked toward the kitchen. The soldiers made an announcement. "We look for a boy who broke through our lines guarding the approaches to this village."

They searched the room. When they turned toward the kitchen, they saw him enter. The soldier who spotted him thought to himself, "That's odd. I thought they only hired women servers in this saloon."

He moved toward the kitchen. "Hey, you!"

Tatan panicked, tossed the tray at the soldier, and ran. His pursuer tripped, delaying his troops. When he rose, he followed Tatan out the back but had lost him. He reported the incident, and suddenly, every soldier in Quota was searching for the criminal.

He hid in a dry goods store backroom, listening to the sounds of the grunting soldiers running about outside. He fell asleep on a pile of flour sacks. Persistent poking and the sound of a yelling merchant woke him.

"What are you doing here? Are you the criminal the soldiers seek?" The merchant demanded.

"Yes, sir. I'm sorry I hid here. I must leave Quota. I am on a quest to the island of freedom."

The merchant was sympathetic. "Yes, if I were young, I'd do the same. Don't worry, son, you'll reach your ship and you'll do it under the direct supervision of the guard. Come."

He followed the merchant to another room where he was fitted with stock boy clothes and told to join the group of boys that were loading supplies on a ship slated to sail soon. He hefted a bag of flour and carried it onto the ship. He did as the merchant suggested and stowed away in the cargo hold.

The ship was bound for Laarisia. On Cronon's order, a soldier was assigned to it to ensure its course. All escapes to the island of freedom were to cease.

Two days out, two events occurred. Tatan was discovered by one of the sailors who had seen him flee the bar. He told him to stay put; he admired the kid's courage.

The second event allowed the ship to turn off course, westbound toward freedom. Under the captain's orders, the soldier was seized, cut, and thrown overboard. He knew the fresh blood would attract sharks. He wanted this soldier to disappear.

The captain welcomed Tatan as one of the crew. As punishment for stowing away, he made him lookout in the crow's nest, the coldest place on board. This duty was usually rotated, but the captain felt Tatan should suffer the entire voyage.

The journey to the island took longer than anticipated. The captain had only a general idea where it was and, therefore, wasted much time crisscrossing the sea. Many crewmen died of scurvy and starvation. Weakened immune systems carried off men with common colds. Tatan, high above, was immune from this rampant death. He spotted Nepusia.

When he yelled down to deck, only twenty of the original one hundred crewmembers remained.

King Nepusia, when he was informed a ship was arriving, ordered it met. Soldiers rowed out to it. They climbed aboard, met with the captain, and guided him safely into the harbor. The crew disembarked and was ushered to the palace for debriefing. They gathered in the king's audience chamber.

King Nepusia looked over the worn, tattered men. "Who are you? How did you find my island?"

The captain spoke for the group. "We are Uryxians seeking freedom. We are tired of the Laara's imposed feudal slavery. We are tired of being told what we will ship and whom we will ship it to."

"You are welcome to join us in freedom, but you must understand we trade only amongst ourselves. It may be many years before the world accepts us.

"We are a secret, secure society. Our immigration law is strict. Each of you must serve in our military for two years. You will be either landed or water troops; I will decide later. When your two years are over, you'll be granted land. The citizens of Nepusia will help you build homes. You will farm, providing your own food and, hopefully, a surplus for the palace. The surplus and your military training are necessary preparations for the expected Laarisian invasion. We know the Laara isn't pleased with this free land. Do you agree to my terms?"

The captain, taking a moment to consider the offer, thought it would be prudent to agree. "We are weak from our journey. How can *we* serve?"

"Report to our military depot located outside of the palace. You will be assigned duties there. You can serve us by becoming the best soldiers you can. Before you leave the depot, make sure they feed you. My doctors will determine who is fit for service; those who are not will be nursed back to health, but eventually everyone will serve."

The group, minus Tatan, moved toward the exit. King Nepusia, annoyed, did not let his frustration show. "What is it, son? Why do you linger?"

"You mentioned Laarisia's impending invasion. How do you know about it?"

"We have anticipated it since my ancestors arrived three hundred years ago. It is only speculation. I don't have any information about an invasion."

"So you don't know they're coming?"

"Really coming?" King Nepusia was bewildered. Could this boy know more than he?

"Yes, My liege. The Laara has ordered each provincial military force to seek and destroy Nepusia. He even pressed the Hermatic priests to join the crusade as punishment for three hundred years of silence about the mass exodus."

"Thank you for this information. How can I repay you?"

"I was ship's lookout on most of our journey. I have seen your mountain. I would like to be assigned to a lookout position. I'm hoping my family escaped. I fear the worst for them if they stay behind."

"Why did you leave without them?"

"My father is scared and stubborn. After I told him that I overheard soldiers talking about the invasion, his fright blossomed. He believes we will all be killed as traitors."

"The Laarisians will never get that far. Your wish is granted. Report to the military complex." He paused as he scribbled a note. "Hand them this document. It is an order for you to be assigned lookout duty."

As Tatan exited he heard the king yell out, "Guard!"

When the guard rushed in, King Nepusia sat him down. He laid out his plan for defense. Harbor defenses were secure. Siege plans were laid out, and an escape route was planned.

Tatan arrived at the military complex. The sergeant, in change, believing his orders forged, huffed at him. He ordered Tatan to the supply room to be fitted for a uniform. Having stalled him, he sent a messenger to the palace to check the orders because King Nepusia rarely issued orders before a soldier was indoctrinated.

The messenger returned, frazzled. The king had yelled. He did not like having his orders challenged. The sergeant was ordered to treat Tatan with the utmost respect. The sergeant's entire attitude changed. He personally retrieved Tatan and led him to the highest lookout point.

He congratulated Tatan. "Boy, you are in the king's favor. That is rare. How did you do it?"

"I told him the Laarisian forces are preparing an invasion."

"I thought that might be it. Keep a sharp eye out, boy. We've expected them for three hundred years. We cannot be caught with our pants down."

Tatan was fourteen when he escaped his lord. He volunteered for Galacian lookout duty in the hope that his family escaped, also. As the days passed, his hopes waned. He was a small, skinny child with green eyes as sharp as a hawk and so saw the ships before they saw the island. As he counted, his excitement mounted. One hundred ships. The flag of Laarisia. He abandoned his post and ran quickly to the city. When he reached the royal palace, he demanded an audience with King Nepusia. This news was too important to go through channels.

The Nepusia family, being the first to permanently settle the land, had formed a government based on the old kingdoms, yet everyone was free. Each new wave of immigrants added danger to their lives. The Nepusians knew one day Laarisia would strike and prepared by forcing all new immigrants to take two years of military training before becoming citizens. Tatan felt he was prepared to fight.

The palace, where he waited, took three hundred years to complete. When the Nepusians arrived they had built a wooden shelter. From that humble beginning, they consistently added until they had built a magnificent one hundred thousand square foot palace. One thousand acres of farmland inside the walls sustained the castle.

The palace was constructed entirely of stone. There were three sets of walls. The inner wall enclosed the castle. The middle wall enclosed the farmland. Both these walls had walkways on top that extended completely around, allowing fast troop movement in case of an assault. The outer wall encircled the villages that tended the farms. Surrounded by a moat, this wall was the first line of defense. There was a walkway here, too. Every fifty feet, they built battlements where a soldier could easily defeat an invader with his height advantage. The fortifications were well planned, as everyone assumed one-day Laarisia would attack. In case the walls were breached, the castle itself was built for defense. Every window was built as a mere slit. Anyone, in time of war, could shoot arrows at the enemy without fear of being wounded themselves.

Tatan was waiting in the great hall just inside the drawbridge entrance. From this hall, he could see three other great halls. They led to the living quarters, kitchen and dining area, and the prison, respectively. The main hall, which he waited impatiently to traverse, led directly to the throne room and king's council chambers. Finally summoned to proceed, he ran.

He arrived breathless and frazzled. His curly brown hair was a tangled mess, and his clothes were covered in dirt, but the message was important enough for the king to excuse his appearance. "K- King Nepusia. Ships are coming. Hundreds of ships!"

King Nepusia was a direct-line descendant of Captain Nepusia and his Queen Taes. Time had been good for the family. The kings to date had remained as tall and sleek as the captain. This king wore well-groomed, sandy blonde hair that would turn prematurely gray because of the upcoming conflict. His hard blue eyes contemplated Tatan's outburst.

Tatan feared the look, cursing himself for angering this man who, with a word, could take his life. He received a calm reply, for the king saw no sense in scolding the messenger, especially when the message was this important.

"Where? What direction?"

"They sail quickly to our eastern harbor."

"Good. There they will die!" To the guard, he ordered, "Assemble the citizens. To the eastern harbor!"

In the event of an invasion a trap had been set in the eastern harbor. The gathered citizens watched in nervous anticipation as the Laarisian force approached. Would the trap work?

The Laarisian ships, formed in battle groups of twenty, came in too fast. Forty ships blew up in the harbor. When the first twenty hit mines, the second twenty, appalled, could not stop in time.

The admiral in charge of these ships stood next to the general in charge of the invasion forces, proudly watching the textbook approach of the first group of ships. Their command ship sailed with the final group of twenty. This land had been difficult to find, and boredom was taking its toll on the troops. Action was the morale booster everyone needed. Both men smiled, relieved to be finally at war.

Their expressions quickly changed from shock to depression as they helplessly watched. Forty ships and possibly four thousand men were destroyed. They were relieved when the third wave turned away. Survivors from the blast swam to shore only to be killed by vengeful Nepusians waiting on the beach.

Reports flooded the command ship. Criticism of command bubbled from a murmur into a strong demand to return to Laarisia. The easy victory the Laara had promised was not to be. The admiral and general ignored their critics and retired to the captain's cabin to plan their next move.

The decision was reached, and the admiral left the task of informing the men to the general, who stepped out onto the captain's balcony to address the gathered troops. He thrust his finger toward land. "Men, we are here to take that island. It will not be as easy as we were told. The Laara ordered us not to retreat on penalty of death. We must land. The admiral and I have decided to search out another landing site. Lifeboats will be sent ahead to search for mines.

"Once we land, we will ensure our victory. Every ship will be burned. To your backs will be the sea. To survive, you must fight. You will take this island!"

Sixty ships sailed away. The citizens cheered. Bloodied Nepusian butchers from the beach joined them.

The king was appalled at their reaction. He watched the remaining ships retreat. They regrouped and sailed around the island to find a safe place to land. It took a moment to calm the gleeful crowd. Finally, King Nepusia quieted them.

"People, please! There are still sixty ships and no more mined harbors. Prepare for war!"

Forever obedient, the crowd slowly drifted toward the castle complex.

The lifeboats found no mines on the western shore. The Nepusian command watched in horror as the Laarisian ships landed, offloaded, and were ordered burned. This fight would be hard. The Laarisians refused to admit defeat.

A camp was set up on the beach. That night, Nepusians crept in, killed a few guards, and burned the edges of the encampment. The general ordered the area secured. In the morning, he marched troops into the forest. Delaying battles were fought. Regular Nepusian army troops struck and retreated toward the palace giving the guerillas time to prepare their mountain defenses. Thick forests and thick smoke were their allies.

King Nepusia watched the tiny battles from Tatan's lookout post. He was proud of his forces. They fought with a vigor that certainly surpassed their training. Tatan warned him that they must return to the castle. King Nepusia was needed there to command his forces and to offer faith and hope during the upcoming siege.

They used a path Tatan had scouted during his many days in the mountains. It led safely past the fighting. They ran out of the forest, through the gate, and ordered it barricaded.

"What about our retreating troops?" Tatan asked.

"They are under orders to resist until it is deemed futile. At that point, they will head to the hills and join forces with the guerillas in the mountains."

He turned and addressed the general crowd. "Prepare for a siege. I want all active soldiers on this wall. All of you who have served previously continue working. Bring all equipment to the main palace yard for security."

Working as if there was no crisis built confidence in the peasants. When the merchants ran out of supplies to sell, they enthusiastically joined the farmers in the fields. Meanwhile, the Laarisian general hit the outer wall hard but could not break it. He decided instead to study the layout of the palace grounds. Terror would be his weapon. If he could not beat the soldiers on the wall, he would destroy the peasants in their homes. He spent months cutting trees to build catapults and scaffolds on wheels.

Six months into the siege, he attacked again, this time at dawn, to catch the villagers sleeping. He rolled his catapults close, yet out of arrow range, and began lobbing a firestorm at the village. Thatched roofs quickly blazed. Houses built too close to one another caused an inferno to rise. The villagers tried to extinguish the flames, yet each time they made headway, more fireballs fell. Finally, they gave up, salvaged what they could, and retreated into the middle wall complex.

The soldiers stationed on the outer wall were in a helpless situation. If they moved to help the villagers, the soldiers would storm the walls. They helplessly stood as the village burned.

The Laarisian general watched the melee from his perch. When he saw the villagers retreat, he signaled the scaffolds forward. The giant wheeled beasts grunted up the hill, finally resting twenty feet from the wall. Laarisian soldiers poured onto the scaffolds. Full, they continued their slow crawl up to the walls. Nepusian archers killed many before they reached the walls. They were easily replaced. Like ants pouring out of their hill, they overran the wall.

Sensing their imminent loss, the Nepusian force fled through the village toward the middle wall. The Laarisians slowed their pursuit, preferring instead to open the gates; there would soon be time to destroy the fleeing army.

King Nepusia watched the battle from the middle wall. He was impressed by the villager's tenacity when the fire began to fall. He was confident they would run, yet they stood immobile. What surprised him was the loyalty of the new troops. The twenty new soldiers who ended their training only a month earlier fought ferociously. They were the first to draw their weapons and the last to abandon their position against overwhelming odds.

He quizzically glanced at Tatan.

"They fight for their newfound freedom. On the ship, each man stated he'd rather die than return to Laarisia's feudal slave system. This freedom is the most powerful fighting force on earth. Our nation will be great."

The Laarisian force poured through the gap. Men wheeled scaffolds and catapults into the blackened village. The general set up his command post in a partially burned house. It was here he held a general meeting of his officers. The consensus was to mount an instant attack on the next wall.

The general mulled over the opinions, then dissented. "No. I will not attack without the proper information. I want you men to send scouts along the outer wall to observe the enemy fortifications inside the next wall.

I want a full report within the week. Also, I want details to scour the forest for food. I want my troops well fed and rested before we strike again."

King Nepusia, sensing the battle was over, gathered his defensive forces about him.

"Men, I applaud your efforts. I ask only that you defend this wall with the same vigor. If the enemy captures our food supply, we are finished. Go now; your freedom depends on you."

He sent Tatan to gather the villagers. They assembled before him, beaten and disheveled.

"You people are the backbone of our society. I am proud of your determined resistance. It shamed my heart to watch helplessly as you retreated. You have lost your homes, but you shall always have a home in this castle. We have prepared for this moment. I want each of you to harvest our farms and stock our warehouses. When the harvest ends, some of you will continue to work the farms, and the able will be conscripted. I want a major force defending our middle wall. If it falls, we may be doomed."

The week passed uneventfully. Scouts reported to the Laarisian general that, in their opinion, a fiery catapult would not be feasible because there were no structures left to destroy. The citizens, it seemed, had retreated into the safety of the castle.

The general dismissed his scouts. He ordered his officers in. As they arrived, a scout ran in breathless. "G-General!"

"Why do you interrupt, scout? You're one of my food gatherers, aren't you?"

"Yes, General. I beg to report we have gathered much food, however, we've paid a price. Traps these islanders set have killed or maimed many of our men."

The general lowered his head and emitted a low growl.

"General?" The gatherer queried.

"Your report is accepted. Leave me."

His officers found the general depressed. He gathered his thoughts. When the last officer arrived, he addressed them.

"I understand you are anxious to press the attack and end this war. Unfortunately, I cannot authorize that while there are active soldiers to our rear. I have recently received a report that our food gatherers were attacked. Many were killed. I have underestimated my foe, but he isn't going anywhere. I order the siege continued while we flush out the forest guerrillas."

King Nepusia wondered why Laarisia let him breathe. He assumed they meant to starve him into submission. Determined, he drove the harvesters and warehousemen to distress. Weary soldiers on leave from the wall reported the Laarisians were making no preparations.

A year passed in stalemate. The Nepusians took advantage of the lull to plant and harvest three seasonal crops. The warehouses bulged. Wheat, critical to them, was in surplus.

The Laarisian general studied his statistics. The number of natives killed did not match the numbers predicted. Too many were left alive in the forest, effectively neutralizing his movements. What worried him was there was no trace of them. Satisfied he had driven them so deep into the hills that they were no threat to his rear, he called his officers in to lay out his plan of attack.

"I have reviewed our situation, evaluated all reports, and carefully laid out a plan to help us take this wall we face.

"You are partially correct concerning the ineffectiveness of our fiery catapults; they won't be able to be used to terrorize the villagers. Instead, we are going to terrorize the soldiers defending the wall.

"I want catapults stationed at strategic points around the wall. Scaffolds will be stationed beside them. On my order, fire will be flung at the wall. You will adjust the fire until your incendiaries land on the catwalk. Constant fire should clear off sections of the wall. This will allow the scaffolds safe passage. As my soldiers move up, your firing will increase."

King Nepusia observed movement in the Laarisian camp. The war machines creaked. He knew the battle was upon him. He sent a message to the fields: All non-essential personnel arm and proceed to the wall.

Ordered to the wall, they waited beneath it in reserve. They heard the creaking war machines and were the first affected by the constant barrage of incendiaries as they fell inside the compound. After the fire was adjusted, they heard terrified cries from the walls and tensed for battle.

From the inner wall, King Nepusia grew angry as he watched his defenders cringe against the fire. He watched as scaffolds freely wheeled toward undefended areas. He sent messengers to each strategic point, ordering the farmers to scale and hold the wall. Laarisian soldiers poured through the breeches. Once they gained a foothold, the battle turned hard. Overwhelmed, the defenders slowly, reluctantly, retreated off of the wall.

Now exposed, they quickly retreated across the fields, ran through the castle gate, and secured it as the Laarisians approached. King Nepusia ordered the gate blocked. From his observation point, he helplessly watched the Laarisian war machine flood through the middle gate.

Sensing the Laarisian general had no intention of relieving the pressure, King Nepusia assigned most of the people to wall duty and the rest to castle duty. Fighting was fierce. Repeatedly, the Laarisian scaffolds were beaten back. King Nepusia used hot oil barrels and archers defending from the castle windows to stop the Laarisians. A stalemate occurred, interrupted by occasional catapulted incendiaries intended to harass.

The Laarisian general sent a messenger to demand Nepusia's surrender. He refused, determined to fight on, his attitude elevated by watching his soldiers defend their way of life. The stalemate continued as the Laarisians studied the situation. Frustrated by the depletion of his troops, the general decided upon another siege.

Slowly, the Nepusian food supplies dwindled. King Nepusia, realizing Laarisia was waiting him out, knew he should ration the food, but he did not, electing instead to keep his people healthy and their morale high. One night, he ordered the remaining food packed for shipping. He then ordered every citizen and soldier to quietly enter the palace. He led them to the basement to the mouth of the tunnel he had constructed long before the Laarisians arrived. After everyone entered, he sealed off the room and entered the tunnel at the rear of this mass exodus. They exited the tunnel well to the rear of the Laarisians. Unmolested, they walked to the mountains to meet the guerillas.

The first report, the next morning, claimed the castle complex was devoid of people. The general refused to believe it. He ordered the walls slowly probed and met no resistance. Soldiers scaled the wall and opened the gate. The general, once he saw the empty compound, became irate.

"How did they escape?" He wondered aloud.

He never discovered how but did determine that they must be on the run. He left a skeleton force holding the castle and marched out into the wilderness in vain. Finally, he determined his troops were too depleted to face an unknown force. He retreated to the castle complex and sent lookouts to the beaches to await Laarisian replacement troop ships he assumed would come.

A long stalemate began. Each camp licked its wounds. The Laarisians built a temporary village and procured a small vessel they found hidden in the forest near the beach. The general asked for volunteers. Those who stepped up found themselves once again sailing on the Galacian Sea. They were ordered to sail slowly east and rendezvous with any Laarisian vessel.

Meanwhile, King Nepusia set up command deep in a cave on Mt. Rainer. He found more than he expected to find in these hills. These soldiers were a well-prepared, well-trained force who had yet to see true battle. He reviewed the preparations. Caves were connected by an extensive tunnel system. Camouflaged gates were built to hide the caves. When his tour ended, he gathered the leaders of the guerrillas to his command center.

"What plans have you developed to conquer our enemy?"

A brave lad stepped forward. "We figure we should leave them alone until they are reinforced. We are sure the Laara will send more troops."

"What then?" He wondered, leery of allowing Laarisia to reinforce.

"We will harass them, forcing them to stage a seek-and-destroy mission. We will draw them in, cut their supply lines, and execute them."

"I believe the Laara will send troops indefinitely. How can we survive this mass infiltration?"

"We will build traps and snares. We will make them bleed. Their own soldiers will force surrender."

"I hope you are correct. As it stands, I approve this plan. Could work."

The cold, hungry, frustrated volunteers on the boat were ready to turn back when they spotted a mast on the horizon. After they were rescued and fed, they informed the captain of their plight. He set them adrift, freshly supplied, and promised a force bigger than they could imagine once the Laara became aware.

They sailed back. Their message offered a surge of hope to the troops. Morale rose considerably. Men casually prepared for war sharpened their weapons and their skills. The general called assembly.

"I have reviewed all documents. I have found no weaknesses within this culture. Our enemies, I have learned, call themselves Nepusians after their first king and organizer of this society. I know you men are excited to fight, but we must wait for reinforcements. I am confident we can take this island, but I won't risk any lives unnecessarily."

Ten years passed before reinforcements arrived. Minor skirmishes naturally occurred between hunting parties. The invading Laarisians became a parasitic part of the landscape. Nepusian families grew and survived as best they could.

The general met with the new commander of reinforcements on the beach. "Why did the Laara wait so long to relieve us?"

"He experienced many problems. He had to develop a draft. People protested this as an unnecessary war. Minor rebellions flared up across the empire. We've been too busy fighting ourselves to help you. The system the Laara set up is brilliant. Fresh soldiers will arrive here continuously."

The Laarisians marched in full force against Nepusia at the first dawn. True to plan, the Nepusians fought limited engagements and drew the Laarisians further into their trap. At the critical moment, they cut the supply lines and panicked their professional enemy. The lines retreated to the beachhead and, as they did, were unmolested. The Nepusians knew they would regroup and counterattack, so they set snares and traps along every conceivable pathway. The attempted counterattack failed. Each set of traps enclosed soldiers in the middle of groups, creating panic. Panicked troops ran straight into more sophisticated traps. Confused soldiers were killed by Nepusian guerillas.

The Laarisians froze on the beachhead, afraid to march against Nepusia. The weakened force awaited in camp for more reinforcements. General after general landed and forced the men to march. Each succeeding general, questioning the failure of his predecessor, without fail, executed him. This pattern of failure continued for one hundred fifty years until

General Risi arrived, sent personally by the Laara, to end this charade once and for all.

One hundred years earlier, rumors of generals being massacred reached King Nepusia. Old now and understanding he had the Laarisians beaten, he went to his son, who would soon be king.

"You must go back to the castle. Take the majority of the troops. Rebuild the walls while the Laarisians fear us. I will use a skeleton force to repel them should they attack." The next three kings used this skeleton force to repel the Laarisians. When General Risi arrived, the castle was once again prepared for war.

General Risi, as his predecessor did, questioned the general he was replacing. The information was clear and concise. Surprising everyone involved, he spared this man, considering him his greatest asset.

"The problem, as I see it, is that we've been trying to suppress these Nepusians with a show of force. They have beaten us back by turning us against ourselves. I propose we 'play dead.' In other words, we will sit in camp, appearing depressed as if we have given up. During this charade, I will send out one-man teams to evaluate the Nepusian threat."

These one-man teams stealthily searched the countryside. Unnoticed, they discovered the guerilla caves. They also reported the location of the tunnel exit and the occupation of the castle.

General Risi evaluated this information. He gathered his general staff.

"Gentlemen, I am convinced Nepusia has alluded our victory because, in the past, we blindly attacked. I want to try a different tactic. We know where their caves are located. I want you to send five-man squads quietly into the forest. Stealthily, they will position themselves around the caves. The Nepusians, unaware of you, will send out supply parties. Capture and kill these parties. Before they are noticed missing, you may attack the caves."

General Risi's plan was flawless. The bothersome caves were cleared. Now, he could concentrate on retaking the castle, forcing the island to capitulate.

King Nepusia checked the palace defenses. The walls were reinforced, the village rebuilt closer to the middle walls as a defense against firebombs and he reopened the tunnel as a precaution. He worked diligently, waiting for the imminent attack.

General Risi evaluated the castle defenses from high amongst the pines. He respected what he saw and opted not to use the terror methods of the last invasion.

Nepusian soldiers watched as the Laarisians surrounded the outer wall. The attack they expected never came. General Risi continued to evaluate the defenses. He used engineers he had imported from what his men called "the world" to test the strength of the walls. They found, as he hoped, a weak spot.

Now he attacked. The catapult firestorm ignited. Smoke rose and wafted toward the castle. Around the perimeter, Nepusian soldiers laughed as the fire was having no effect. However, one section was not laughing. The Laarisians were bombarding the wall with boulders, and it was obviously giving way.

A runner was sent to King Nepusia. He ordered every available soldier to converge on this breach point. Only skeleton crews were left to defend the majority of the wall.

General Risi observed this redeployment. His ruse was working. In the forest, across from each skeleton crew, hidden scaffolds awaited. Bricks continued to break from the outer wall. Brave Laarisians poured in only to be cut down as they struggled through the breach.

General Risi called off this wasteful attack. The bombardments continued. The weak wall soon collapsed. Once again, the Laarisians charged. Some were stopped, but the wave was too powerful. Still, the Nepusians fought on, miraculously holding their ground.

General Risi initiated phase two of his plan. Scaffolds were wheeled unmolested to the weakly defended areas. The walls were soon breached everywhere. The attackers, who logically should have attacked the village, allowed the villagers to escape. Under orders, they marched to the collapsed wall, forced surrender, and killed every Nepusian prisoner in retaliation for their ancestors.

King Nepusia watched the massacre in horror. He met instantly with the villagers who had escaped. "Many a fine, brave soldier died today to preserve our freedom. You are now the defenders of this land. You will defend this wall until the odds force you to retreat to the castle. There is no dishonor in living."

The Laarisians gathered to lick their wounds. As they did, the Nepusians condensed their resources into the castle. There, they prayed for victory.

General Risi decided a long siege would weaken them further. King Nepusia had no intention of sitting idle. He sent special troops through the tunnel to harass Risi's supply lines and attack his rear. They never returned.

General Risi efficiently attacked the second wall. King Nepusia, sensing disaster, ordered his troops into the castle. He was a firm believer in living to fight another day.

General Risi, knowing he had the Nepusians on the run, kept up pressure on the wall. Laarisians quickly learned to use the wall defensively as castle archers cut them down in the open. Nepusians on the wall further harassed the Laarisians with boiling oils.

General Risi, angered, ordered firebombs. Some firebombs struck the oil barrels causing massive explosions and confusion on the battlements. He then ordered the scaffolds moved forward and pressed his advantage.

King Nepusia, overwhelmed, ordered all citizens and troops into the tunnels. He sealed the entrance behind them and hurried to the exit. The scene there dumbfounded him. The entire fighting force of Nepusia was surrounded. All hope of victory gone, he awaited General Risi's arrival, praying to himself that the guerillas may still save this land.

General Risi arrived some hours later. He spoke with a subordinate who pointed in King Nepusia's direction. The general moved toward the king, arm extended, hand open.

King Nepusia quizzically took his foe's hand and shook it. General Risi spoke first.

"Rarely in one's service does one meet so worthy a foe. I am honored to finally make your acquaintance, King Nepusia."

"As I am yours, Lord." The king bowed. When he rose, the look in his eyes betrayed his thoughts.

General Risi read the look.

"You may wish to know your guerillas in the hills have been neutralized."

Shock passed over King Nepusia's face.

"Yes, Nepusia, we captured that force long before we attacked you. You see, I wished no enemy at my rear. The failure of my predecessors I did not wish to repeat."

"Are they dead?"

"To a man. I was ordered to destroy all resistance to the Laara."

"Will you kill us?"

"No. The Laara has different plans for your army. She respects your courage and your citizen's ability to hold us off these many centuries. She wishes you to become a province within the Holy Laarisian Empire. You people came here to be free, and she has no wish to abolish your freedom. She has issued orders to allow your government to continue. She asks only a ten- percent tribute and, this, only to support the occupational troops we will station here.

"She also wishes to build Hermatic temples here. What god do you worship?"

"We worship no god. I'm sure my ancestors arrived here believing in your God, Hermax, but over time, the pressures of creating this society squeezed the god concept out of us."

"The Laara will be disappointed Hermax didn't survive, but he is no concept. I assure you he is very real," General Risi warned. "Expect missionaries to arrive to educate your people. If you surrender now, I am authorized to guarantee your government's survival and to help you rebuild."

King Nepusia counseled with his leaders. All options were discussed. Some saw no choice but to surrender. Others saw surrender as a way to buy time. King Nepusia sought an audience with General Risi, capitulated the island, and signed the surrender.

General Risi, victorious, secured the next vessel bound for Laarisia. He spent the next six months at sea imagining the Laara's face when he delivered the news.

The boat docked. General Risi bounded off. In his excitement he almost tripped over two crewmen securing the boat to the pier. He yelled out an apology as he ran. Arriving at the Laara's palace breathless, he sat on a bench to regain his composure. A guard, recognizing him, ran to fetch the Laara. When she was ready, he was asked into her audience chamber.

General Risi found the Empress depressed. He was very disconcerted. He was short and powerful, emulating the great Zearn in his appearance and every movement. The scar traveling the length of the right side of his face made him look harder than he actually was. The Laara, the first woman ever in the position, was his source of strength. She stood taller than most men, effectively humbling her commanders. Her pleasant demeanor, along with her curiosity for detail, forced honesty from them. Her auburn hair turned fiery red whenever she was upset. He looked her over. Her hair was normal, so he took a risk.

"Laara Daphne, why are you depressed? We won! Nepusia is ours! I have their surrender in my possession."

She stared blankly through dull green eyes at the General. Slowly he backed up as her eyes changed to a dark jade and as her hair began to appear as if it had caught fire. She snapped out of her stupor, angrily shaking the papers in her hand.

"What good is a victory over one land when eleven lands blame me for war and are leaving the Empire?"

"What news is this? Provinces cannot blatantly leave the empire. Where are the soldiers to stop them?"

"They are non-existent. The provincial militias were deleted to skeleton forces because of the war. The soldiers were overwhelmed by armed uprisings worldwide. A few, a very few, returned to Laarisia alive. I have only Nepusia and Hermatia left. I haven't the strength to force the others to stay. What do we do now?"

Shocked by her pleading tone, Risi attempted to calm her.

"Maybe we should ask Hermax. He will provide."

Laarisia took on the task of converting Nepusia. Laarisia and Hermatia became religious centers. They barely focused on military issues necessary to quell Nepusia.

General Risi, sent to Nepusia to gather fresh troops for Laarisian duty, found an armed rebellion in progress. He went to the king.

"What do you know of this rebellion?"

King Nepusia slowly rose from his nervous bow.

"They are two of my commanders who were dissatisfied with the surrender. They claim I should've fought to the death. They are rogues. I do not support them," he replied vehemently.

"Will you help me find them?" General Risi asked, in a tone that the king interpreted as an order.

"I am a servant of the Laara. You don't need my help. They hide in the caves."

General Risi attacked the caves immediately. The rebels fought valiantly and refused to surrender. Agitated, he ordered the caves sealed. One month later, stragglers emerged from a hidden cave Risi had not found. They avoided all troop concentrations and surrendered to the king, hoping for a lenient judgment.

The king astonished them.

"You exercised your freedom of choice when you decided to rebel. With that choice comes responsibility. You knew the punishment you would receive if captured. You cannot hide behind my robes. I have no choice but to turn you in. Guards!"

The rebels found themselves in General Risi's care. To show goodwill toward this king, he loaded them on his ship for trial in Laarisia. Two more transports were loaded with freshly conscripted soldiers. These troops, after training in Laarisian combat theory, would become the main force of Laarisia, forever guarding her from attack.

Three months into the journey, the rebels were weighed down and tossed into the Galacian Sea because they "mutinied." This was the official report. The Nepusian troops suspected it was a ruse. Beaten rebels, their spirits broken, could not have possibly revolted. They knew better than to protest. Who would believe them?

Laarisia remained a religious center only for one thousand years. The nations of the earth became thirteen separate societies. The fortunes of war frowned on Laarisia. Her only influence lay with Hermatia and Nepusia. But Earth repairs itself. When a forest recedes, another on the opposite side of the world will suddenly thrive. The same is true of man. When a dominant society recedes, another will rise. Invasion of Laarisia was imminent. The Laara enlisted the Nepusian troops for protection. The Nepusian guard successfully kept invading hordes at bay until. . .

In each kingdom, the farms were generally abandoned. The masses drifted toward tribal life. Few farms held the kingdoms together. In Alpania, the tribes grew stronger daily. They first raided the farms, then the temples, and eventually the castles.

Typical of warlike societies, a strong leader who claimed Jupoler or Arop's lineage naturally arose. Axiax of Alpania was a natural warrior. He wore his fiery red hair in a great mane, had a wild, three-foot-long beard, and often flew into rages. His face turned as red as his hair, cowering those around him as he appeared a man with a flaming head. Watching strong men blanch when he pounded his fist on the nearest table, often breaking it in two when his anger flared, pleased him. His green eyes reflected the honesty and integrity most warriors expected. Though famous for his rages, his opinion was worshipped because people knew he was honest.

He was born on an isolated farm, intertwined with the scrub brush at the edge of the forest, on Alpania. His father's farm was overseen by a lord who owned a loose confederation of farms, none near enough to justify a village, spread throughout the island. News rarely reached them. They were content to farm, not realizing that farms were being abandoned nationwide.

Axiax developed quickly. His father assigned him tasks meant for bigger boys to encourage his developing muscles. Axiax's quick temper worried his parents, so they kept him busy from dawn until dusk. Planting in the spring included plowing and picking work, which developed his upper body. His father planted a variety to keep the family healthy. Axiax developed strong hands picking grapes, olives, and varied citrus fruits. He developed his famous sword swing using a scythe on wheat and hay. Bales of hay carried to the shed for their two cows strengthened his legs and back. Milking them, he often drifted off into daydreams. He wondered if women's breasts were hard and strong or would they melt in his hands? The last day he saw his family alive, he was sent to gather wood in the forest.

Joyously, he ran off into the woods. The two-hour task would take all day. His father was lenient. He worried his father would be enraged if he dawdled during a simple task like wood gathering, but knew his mother's smile tempered his father's attitude. He always returned from the forest with small game. Hunting satisfied his desire to be a warrior. Farm life was not for him. Although a farmer's boy stood almost no chance of joining the military, he was determined to try.

When his game bag was full and his duffle bag full of wood, he decided to head home. At the edge of the forest, he stopped and stood still, like a deer sensing man is near. His own senses told him something was wrong. Suddenly, the sound of galloping hoofs filled his ears. Melting deeper into the bush, he was astonished to see many men on horseback riding toward his home. What could they want?

He decided to find out. Dropping his load, he maneuvered through the forest to the point closest to his house. His mother and father stood in the doorway, defiant.

A soldier demanded, "Peasant, your choice is simple. Quit this farm and join our tribe. We will feed you and clothe you. Your life will be much better because of us."

The farmer yelled. "You! I've heard rumors of your kind. Bullies molesting the land, defying the government. I'll have no part of it!"

He turned away.

"Then you shall die!" The soldier slashed at the farmer's leg with his sword. Not a deadly blow, but one designed to cripple him. Axiax, shocked, stifled a scream.

"Take him. Lash him to that tree so he may watch what happens to those who defy us."

As they dragged him away, Axiax's mother tried to run. Two soldiers stopped her and held her tight. When the farmer was secure, they dragged her to him. They cut off her clothes, raped her repeatedly until she died, and burned the house down. The farmer was burned alive. His tears of anger could not douse the all-consuming fire.

Axiax froze, his temper flaring. He was helpless but imprinted on his brain each man who had caused him pain. Laughing, the soldiers rode away.

Axiax, only ten, tearfully buried the remains of his family. Enraged, Axiax followed the soldier's trail with each step, planning his revenge.

Weeks passed. He watched as they raided more farms. The pain he witnessed deepened his resolve, though he never buried the dead, fearing the raiders might backtrack and realize they were being followed.

One night, the tribe camped. Axiax snuck in close and stole a sword. The next morning they sent out a wood gatherer who never returned. Axiax killed him. The first taste of death excited him. Worried, he buried the sword and ran well ahead of the advancing column; he knew they would be on guard and that any further revenge would have to be taken from the inside.

He formulated a plan, stopped, and waited. When the group found him, he feigned excitement.

"You are a wandering tribe! I am an orphan. I wish to join you."

Their leader glanced through him. "We have no need for boys."

"Of course you don't, but I can hunt, gather wood, and scout. I'll do any job. Please let me join you. I am an orphan. I have nowhere else to go."

"It is a rough life, boy," he warned. "But if you're adamant, then so be it. Ride with us. Watch and learn. Soon enough, you will grow into one of us. If you don't, you die. Understand?"

"Perfectly, Sir. I'm ready!"

Their leader sent him to the corral. He was given a weak mount, sensed it, but did not care. He climbed up, spurred his new horse, and rode off to his destiny. In camp, he was told to hunt, cook, clean, gather wood, and stay out of the way; he was forced to watch the wagons during farming raids. When he showed all signs of becoming one of them, they gave him his own sword, knife, and leather shield. The leader saw great potential in him and took him under his wing; he taught him blade-fighting techniques until he was an expert. His first sexual experience was the gang rape of a farmer's wife and daughter. Strange, he pondered afterward, that his own mother's torture never entered his mind. And why not? Because he was becoming more ruthless daily. Due to petty insults directed at him from jealous tribesmen, swordfights and knife fights ensued. He soon eliminated many of the enemies on his revenge list. This was perfectly legal within the tribal system. Unspoken law required every insult to be backed by the sword.

When Axiax was eighteen, he approached his mentor at the campfire. Already scarred from his many fights, this boy, with only a stubble of a beard but a killer by nature, openly insulted the leader of his tribe.

His mentor, the confident, uncontested leader of the tribe, smiled a toothy, ruthless grin. He remembered his eighteenth year as the year he had challenged and beaten the previous leader. He still had a few tricks up his sleeve. If Axiax was suicidal, so be it.

He stood, raised his sword, and bellowed, "You dare challenge me! Very well. I shall enjoy this. I will miss you when you're gone."

They walked out to an empty field covered with a fine mat of grass. Simultaneously, they drew, beginning combat without a word. They were equal fighters. Axiax had learned well. Yet, as any good master would, his had held back a few tricks.

Axiax, face freshly scarred, hands and legs bleeding, devised a trick of his own. Wandering in the forest in search of wood, he had found a natural pit in this field. He covered it with a mat of grass for later use. Now, he steered his opponent toward it. Axiax thrust as his opponent fell into the hole. The force of the fall, combined with the thrust, drove the sword completely through him.

Axiax rose victorious. The tribe bowed before him, unanimously accepting him as their new chieftain. He ordered the tribe to return to its base camp. Here, in a final act of vengeance, he trumped up disloyalty charges against the remaining tribesmen to whom he owed retaliation and ordered them caged and burned alive as his father had been.

His actions were a mystery, and he gave no one time to evaluate them. Farm raids bored him. He decided the real threat to their nomadic way of life was the Hermatic temples. A general order to raid village temples was proclaimed.

No one protested. Everyone hated Hermax and every idea he represented. The tribe had revived the ancient gods. At each temple, the priests were given one chance to convert. None did. All were killed, and their temples razed.

Axiax's thirst for blood was not satisfied. He coveted control of the entire kingdom. His ego insisted he become king of the Alpanian tribe, ruler of the island. They razed the land. The king sent out soldiers, but it was evident he did not see the Alpanian pagans as a threat. Ruffians, yes, but not a threat.

Axiax faced two obstacles if he was to rule over the island. He must take the state temple and the castle. The goal was really one and the same, as they were located in the same complex. A direct military assault would not work. A plan was devised. He ordered troops to dress up as Hermatic priests and pilgrims. They were to walk dejectedly to the state temple and demand entrance and protection as pilgrims.

His entire force entered the castle walls unmolested. They took up their assigned positions, disrobed, and, as soldiers, killed everyone in sight. Axiax was admitted after the slaughter. He walked into the castle, found the throne, and sat. The defeated, dejected king was brought before him.

"I have waited my entire life to meet you. My father was a farmer and a loyalist. He told me many times what a great, powerful man you were. Yet here you are, defeated, at the hands of a simple peasant's child. Your kingdom was weak; mine shall be strong. I am King of Alpania now. You! You are now seafood. Take him away!"

His first days as king were anxious. The tribe was commanded to cease all raids and to help rebuild the farms. Society would need a steady, guaranteed food supply. The true warriors, ruthless haters of farmers, protested. Assuring them they would not be bored, he granted them the castle compound as a practice field and promised them they would soon go to war.

The state temple was converted into a place of worship for the gods, honoring them for their help in his success. He sent a messenger to Laarisia to inform the Laara that he was dissolving all political ties. The Laara issued a formal protest but took no decisive action.

For three years he developed Alpania in his image. He traded only within the Alpanian island structure, hesitant to venture too far out to sea lest Laarisia strike. He built trust amongst the neighboring governments. When he sensed the time was right, he called forth his patient soldiers.

"Men, you have stood by while I developed this kingdom. You have kept order where chaos might have prevailed. You begged me for another war; I now give you one."

A cheer arose.

"I have worked hard for three years to gain the trust of the island kingdoms that surround us. The time to strike is now. General Maar will lead you on a little island-hopping expedition.

"We will begin with Marsia. I will promise them several shiploads of goods as a gesture of goodwill. Your troops will bring the goods. When the ships land, you will disembark and secure the harbor. From there, you will march against the minor Laarisian force that governs the island."

The conquest of Marsia was quick. Ciaxian and Vienus combined forces but were also quickly overrun. Uryxia and Sateland accepted bribes and secured positions in the Alpanian government rather than risk war. Once conquered, they each remained a part of the Alpanian Empire throughout all time. Axiax achieved his empire. He proclaimed it was the will of the gods.

Axiax rose because he was a risk-taker. He was covered with battle scars earned as he almost single-handedly carried each battle. With his tall muscularity, wearing skins of violent animals, and the club he slept with, he was an imposing figure no one dared defy. Comfortable covered with blood and dirt, an evil blackness and the rank scent of death accompanied him wherever he went. People to shrank away from him. He held his people together through superstition, magic, and the threat of violence. In each land that had broken from the Empire a great sorcerer arose that spoke the will of the gods.

Axiax counseled with his court sorcerer. The wise man, realizing Axiax's imperial longings, thought for a moment. He then advised, "You must attack the enemy of the Alpanian Empire."

"Laarisia?"

"Yes."

"But they are too strong."

"No, they are weak. You shall see."

CHAPTER 10

THE DARK AGES

2220A.D.-3220 A.D.

The all-encompassing Alpanian tribe was leery of Laarisia. Axiax knew his sorcerer was right; the only way to fill the people with confidence was to march on Laarisia herself. He excused the sorcerer and sent for General Maar.

General Maar protested. Although shorter, his appearance emulated Axiax. Like Axiax, he wore a scar on his right cheek. This scar, however, was not won in battle. One night, they had all been drinking in celebration of their latest victory. Suddenly, Axiax turned from jovial to serious. He wrestled Maar to the ground and demanded he pronounce his loyalty. When he did, Axiax sliced his cheek open simply to see if he would seek revenge. Maar cried out in pain, but he passed the test of loyalty, swearing his love for Axiax for all to hear. His loyalty caused him to be a good advisor, which is why he disagreed with Axiax.

"But Axiax, Laarisia is too powerful. Armies who attempt invasion are beaten and enslaved."

"I don't agree. They have lost most of the Empire and with it their strength."

"But their military-"

"Is away in Nepusia trying to control it. Laarisia is virtually undefended. I have revived the nine original gods. It is time to force Laarisia to give up Hermax and to reestablish the Gosirian priesthood. We will set the world on the right religious course."

"If Laarisia is defenseless, as you say, then we must march quickly!"

Axiax ordered General Maar to prepare for battle. He was made responsible for troop counts, supplies, and morale. Runners were sent to each provincial island. They carried orders recalling all but a skeleton occupational force. The recalled forces were to confiscate supplies from their charges, load troop ships, and wait in port.

In Alpania, merchants gladly donated supplies to the cause. Morale at the docks and in the cities was high. Axiax never lost a battle, and now, he would take Laarisia, securing the world for Alpanian trade domination.

Two weeks after Axiax made the decision to invade Laarisia, he boarded his command ship. He spent a day reviewing his invasion plan. That day, ships from the western provincial islands arrived. At dawn, they sailed east, met the other ships, and turned southeast toward Laarisia.

One hundred ships carried two hundred men per ship. These twenty thousand troops were well equipped. On the second day out, General Maar escorted Axiax on a weapons inspection tour. He expected to see short swords, shields, and clubs, but General Maar had a surprise in store. Maar pried open a crate while Axiax impatiently waited. A gleam caught his eye. He reached in, pulled out a weapon, and chuckled.

"What's this?"

"That, Sir, is a Hermatic pick, the symbol of the god Hermax. Our blacksmiths forged twenty thousand of them. Each man will carry one into battle. It will appear as if Hermax is taking vengeance on his own people."

"And if the Laarisians feel betrayed, you think they will quickly turn away from Hermax?"

"That is my hope."

"General Maar, you are truly gifted. Before we land, make sure every man has received and been trained in the use of these picks."

"Yes, Sir."

Three days later, the Alpanian fleet sailed unmolested to Laarisia's main harbor. General Maar supervised the troop offloading. The buildings were abandoned. The first lucky troops were quartered there, the rest in tents. Axiax was housed north of the city in what appeared to be the mayor's official residence.

From his residence he had an unobstructed view of the monuments and government offices of Laarisia. He smiled as he looked toward the hills. Trails were being cut through the waist-high grasses. People, as they always did, were fleeing the expected onslaught of his army. Usually, he would order them hunted down. This time, however, he was going to grant them amnesty. Those who returned would be sent as slaves into Laarisia's mines. Those who did not would receive no mercy. He would eventually scour the hills.

These thoughts occupied his mind when he caught a flash out of the corner of his eye. He turned to see a lone figure slowly approaching his camp, head held high. He crossed the great plain, dwarfed by the monuments behind him.

He was a distinguished-looking man. His eyes appeared sky blue against the background of his snow-white hair. He approached with unprecedented confidence, unprecedented because people typically ran from Alpanian troops. Axiax rode out to the crazy man with every intention of making him the first casualty of the battle, but as he approached, he saw that this was a foolish old man, tall with a confident gait. Axiax dismounted, still with the intention of striking him down, walked up, club raised, then lowered to the ground. There was a domineering presence emitting from this man's eyes. Axiax unconsciously dropped his club and greeted this man.

"Who are you?"

"I am Laara John the seventh, the Holy Laarisian Emperor."

"Why do you risk your life walking alone into my camp?"

"You will not harm me. I wish to talk to you about sparing Laarisia. Please, may we talk?"

Axiax stood dumbfounded. This man was braver than any he had ever known, including himself. "Of course," he answered obediently.

He ordered a command tent moved up. Axiax and the Laara talked for hours.

General Maar, busy coordinating the landing, did not see Axiax leave camp. Occasionally, he would look north to Axiax's command house, impatient for battle orders. He had been so engrossed he had not glanced north for two hours. When he finally did, he was stunned. Beyond Axiax's quarters, his command tent was set up. Maar fidgeted. Axiax knew better than to approach the enemy front alone. The imperial guard was nowhere to be seen. In a rage, he stormed off north, leaving a lieutenant to finish.

When he reached the command center, he found the imperial guard engaged in a game of dice. His face turned purple with rage.

"Where is Axiax?"

A bored private looked up. "Axiax is in his command tent in conference with a stranger who approached our lines."

"He what! Is he alone?"

"Yes, Sir."

"Is he crazy? You men, up! We march on the command tent."

The game of dice continued. No one moved.

General Maar was dumbfounded.

"When I get back, you will all be arrested and probably executed!"

He stepped twice toward the command tent. The private who had just answered him was upon him in a flash, a blade resting on Maar's neck.

"I don't think so, Sir. We are under strict orders to not allow Axiax to be disturbed, even by you. My orders are to kill anyone who dares approach the tent."

Maar was aggravated by the attack.

"Everyone here outranks you. Someone arrest this man."

Slowly, the bored dice players rose. A major offered, "No, Sir. It is you who are under arrest. This mere private outranks us all. Axiax made him his personal aide. We are not only powerless to help you; we don't want to. When you see who walks out of that tent, you'll understand. Come now; join us at our dice."

"I will not," General Maar answered obstinately. "This is an outrage."

The major shrugged his shoulders.

"As you wish, Sir."

He nodded to the private, who lashed Maar to a post in view of the command tent. Axiax left standing orders to restrain him because he was sure Maar would try to 'save' him.

General Maar, the sun beating down upon him, sweat stinging his eyes, glared at the tent. What was Axiax up to? Why hadn't he been consulted? At the very least, he should be privy to this meeting.

When they emerged from the tent Axiax kneeled, asked his blessing, and apologized to the Laara. The Laara touched Axiax lightly on the head, forgiving him, turned without a word and walked back toward the city. Axiax returned to his command post. When he saw General Maar, he stifled a grin.

"What happened to you?"

In one motion, he cut the ropes.

"I attempted to reach you. These men arrested me. I insist they all be executed!"

"Denied. They were under my orders. I did not wish to be disturbed."

"While you did what? Who was that?"

"That, General, was our adversary, the Laara. He is a fine man. A worthy opponent. General, forgive these men. Go back to the harbor and order the troops to reload. We are leaving."

General Maar angrily reproached Axiax.

"Sir, why do we retreat? We have them, sir!"

Axiax spun violently towards Maar. "Don't you ever question my judgment. It is my wish that Laarisia be spared."

"But-"

"General, attend to your men!"

When the Gosirian priests saw the Alpanians retreating, they came down from the hills and begged Axiax to take them to Alpania. Until now, they had been in hiding, they explained. They knew he was sympathetic to them, and they wanted to leave. He granted them passage because they would only make him stronger once news of his retreat spread.

The soldiers could not believe Axiax backed down. They came to the conclusion that the Laara had convinced Axiax that Hermax and the nine gods were equal. Maybe Axiax was too humbled and embarrassed to talk about it. Historians would wonder why he made his decision for the rest of time.

The one thousand years that defined the dark times were stagnant. Records did not survive intact. The sparse records that did survive tell of the plight of Axiax and that of Linx, the great sorcerer who brought forth Aropia from obscurity to master of the world court.

Jupoler watched with detached excitement as the Alpanians revived the gods and marched on Laarisia. Like every Alpanian, he longed to know what the Laara said to change Axiax's mind. Whatever it was, it allowed Hermax to rise in Alpania, sharing equal time with Jupoler and the gods. Soon, they would again fade into myth. Why was Hermax so powerful? What was this inherent human need for one all-powerful God?

Jupoler watched for centuries as mankind enveloped himself in a dark time. Wars, pestilence, famine, and Hermax. No matter the circumstances, Hermax offered hope, and yearly, he became stronger. He saw he must do something to end this destructive cycle before the myth of the gods disappeared.

He studied Earth's history, particularly the Dark Ages, and here he found his answer. Calling upon Uryxs, he ordered him to Earth to begin a process designed to end Hermax forever.

"Uryxs, as you know, humans have almost forgotten us. I have studied this and decided we must rise again."

"How can I help?"

"I have found a monument in the sea west of the island they call Aropia. I will recede the sea two miles westward to expose it. Quickly, humans will discover it. You will be there to explain its purpose. Tell them it is a sign from the gods.

"They have a great need for sorcerers down there. You are to become the sorcerer, Linx. The name means you are linked with us, but no one will know. Keep your communicator on. You are obviously not a magician but will be seen as one because we will initiate 'magic' from here."

Uryxs bowed. He returned to his quarters where Arop had laid out his costume and gazed upon it in wonder. He tried it on, checked himself in the mirror, and chuckled; he did not think this costume would bring him respect, though he knew Jupoler had done his research. He would soon see how effective it was.

One night, while Jupoler receded Galacia, exposing the monument, Uryxs transported to the surface. Bitter cold met him. The sea winds cut into his skin. He gathered his cloak tight. In the moonlight, he watched as the monument was exposed. He decided to sleep in the forest, found an ideal cave, and hid there until locals discovered the monument.

He dreamed of Tarus creating this simple monument. Telltale signs showed that lasers cut the granite, formed the road, tractor beams set the beams in place, and, as the other monuments on earth, mankind arrogantly gave himself credit for the accomplishment.

The village of Maram in Aropia was near. Not yet a port city, it sat three miles from the ocean. Aropia's landscape consisted of hills and valleys. There were no significant mountains. Northeast of Maram, several hills drained into a natural lake, itself drained by a small river. The river traveled north of Maram on its way to the ocean. The land was continually wet. It rained or snowed three hundred fifty days a year. A small island, all land was cultivated. Corn, potatoes, wheat, and barley grew as easily on the hills as they did in the valleys. Maram thrived because it was surrounded by bogs. North of town, the river fertilized the land during flood season. The ocean to the west provided fish and kelp. South and east of town, sedges, and heaths grew up in the bogs. Wildlife hid here. The hunting was spectacular. Sphagnum at the bog's edge died yearly, compacting with the other plant debris to form peat. Maram harvested the peat and supplied all of Aropia. Still a primitive land, Aropia was the best kept secret in the empire.

One day, a discovery was made. As the confused citizens gathered around it, a strange hooded man approached. He carried a walking stick taller than himself, which housed a crystal within its knotted wood top. Short yet powerfully built, his pale skin and white hair made him appear to be near death, but his brown eyes showed he was very much alive. Behind those eyes sat the brain of a serious thinker. He drew back his hood, revealing his twisted, grotesque face. A collective gasp rose from the parting crowd.

"Why are you people gawking at my stones?"

A brave lad pointed toward the stones. "Your stones? Did you build this?"

They were huge monolithic stones situated in a circle one hundred feet in diameter. Several were connected on top by other monolithic stones that lay across the two standing stones. Within the circle of stones, there were the scattered remains of other monolithic stones. Some lay flat, and a few stood tall. Every stone in the enclosure was covered in seaweed, as the structure had only recently surfaced. Outside the circle, a sea-carved two-foot wide ditch surrounded the stones three hundred forty feet in diameter. At the northeastern area of the ditch, there was a break. A faint road seventy feet wide extended about two miles, ending at the sea.

He worked his way into the center of the circle of stones.

"No, the gods built it. When mankind failed to understand it, the gods sank it into Galacia."

"How do you know this?"

He raised his staff to the sky.

"I am the great sorcerer, Linx. I know the will of the gods!"

Lightning struck, and the people cowered.

"What is it for?"

"At the moment, it is for you to clean. You will understand its function eventually," he suggested.

"We have no time to clean this structure. We must attend to our crops and to the hunt."

Linx glared into the crowd. "I understand, but as I said, I know the will of the gods. If you ignore your chores and clean this structure, the gods will make your crops ten times more productive; however, if you decide to ignore the will of the gods, famine and pestilence will rain down upon you."

"The God Hermax will protect us," came a voice from the crowd.

"I have heard of this god, but you must think. What good is one god against the nine who created these stones?"

Linx, confident that he had persuaded them, walked through the crowd into the woods. Slowly, they moved toward the stones and began to work.

Linx watched for weeks as the villagers cleaned the stones. They first concentrated on the seaweed. When it was cleared, they began work on the two-foot ditch. Daily, they removed sand until they had dug three feet down and hit solid packed dirt. There were fifty-six holes in the dirt that were filled with shells. The shells were excavated. The final project involved excavating sand from the path that led to the sea. As the men excavated, the women made jewelry out of the shells. The whole process took two months.

Jupoler was correct. They were receptive. Once it was cleaned, Linx walked back to the site.

"Good. Good. It looks great. The gods will be pleased."

"What is its purpose?" Someone in the crowd asked.

"It represents the gods. It was put here to help you. Since it will give accurate time and seasonal readings, you will be able to progress as a society. Each spring, you must have a festival to honor the gods."

He explained to the villagers the history of the gods, then ordered, "You must revere the gods at these stones and forget about the false god, Hermax."

Soon, the weak memory of Hermax faded. The nine gods kept their promise, and prosperity, such as the villagers had never dreamed, rained down upon them. The nine gods prevailed because these poor people desperately needed something to believe in.

Years passed. Linx had spoken the truth. The crops yielded ten times more every year than they had before the stones were uncovered. Each year's festival was grander than the previous year. The gods, their myth always alive, rose again. Hermax, perceived as a false god, was regulated to myth. In time, Hermax remained only in isolated temples whose priests had little or no contact with Laarisia.

During the Nepusian war, each province slowly broke from Laarisia and Hermax, relying instead on the gods and their sorcerers for guidance. Order crumbled over time as society scraped by. Aropia was the most depressed land. Endless wars were fought. No one emerged victorious. A powerful leader was needed.

Near the end of the Dark Ages, Aropia emulated Alpania. When Axiax abandoned his attack on Laarisia and rescued the Gosirian priests, he started an unforeseeable chain reaction. He re-established the major Hermatic temples on each island. In the villages, he allowed the people to continue to worship the nine gods. Some thought this was a result of his negotiations with the Laara.

This was not the case. He wrongly thought that the religions could co-exist. The Hermatic priests, stationed once again in central temples, received secret orders from the Laara to eradicate the gods. A war of retaliation ensued. Farmsteads burned, and parishioners were attacked on their way home from Hermatic services.

Axiax died trying to promote the peace. A series of progressively degenerate rulers followed. Religious abandonment proceeded. Contact was forbidden outside of the Alpanian nation. The loss of Hermax and Laarisia was a loss of guidance. The nine gods were not a physical presence, and chaos ensued. Society, weakened by chaos, slipped into famine.

Aropia, when it embraced the gods, experienced several prosperous years. Jupoler provided highly productive crops. He assumed he was doing the farmers a favor. His theory was to allow them several good years, each ten times better than the last. When I stop helping them, their surplus should carry them through any bad years, and the experience will allow them to discover good farming techniques.

He was wrong. The yearly festivals depleted any surplus. When he pulled his support, failure was imminent. Each year, crops yielded less. Landowners failed at an astonishing rate. Opportunists purchased the land, enslaved the farmers, and became minor barons. Ten baronies sectioned off Aropia. Border conflicts were constant. Backroom deals abounded. Everyone saw that the baronies must be united under one king to reestablish the peace. Baronies began to ally, and the conflicts became more intense. Farmers, caught in the middle, suffered miserably. Once prosperous Aropia, Laarisian leadership absent, became the most depressed land on earth. Jupoler, sensing the people might turn to Laarisia for help, contacted Linx. He hoped the other nations would follow the example Aropia was going to set.

In each land, a king arose. Aropia, as the stones became an integral part of everyday life, became Stonland. Its kingdom was representative of the others, weak and tumultuous.

Linx evaluated each baron and reported on his relative strength to Jupoler. Acting on Jupoler's orders, he situated himself as the personal sorcerer of the baron of the district of Maram. He encouraged him to invade the other baronies. Linx, through Jupoler, handed him many victories. A northern baron vowed to stop him. He was the last baron to be defeated but witnessed the battle and saw that sorcery had overcome his troops. He saw he had no choice but to bow to the baron of Maram. He must accept him as king of the land or die. A treaty was signed guaranteeing him his lands in exchange for support of the king's policies. Aropian custom dictated he provide a feast for his new king's army. During the feast, the king, drunk, cornered his new ally's wife and forced himself upon her.

She fled to her husband, weeping, demanding justice for this unprovoked attack. The fragile peace Linx established was shattered before it was a day old.

The king begged for Linx's help and promised him anything, if he would only grant him victory. In the ensuing battle, the baron of the north was destroyed. The king took the defeated baron's wife as his prize. Nine months later, she birthed a son. The king was ecstatic. He left her to supervise the gathering of flowers for her room.

While he was gone, Linx stole the baby. Upon his return, he found his wife screaming. He dropped the flowers and, in a rage, swore revenge against Linx. His trail was easy to follow. He lost it, though, as Linx hid in a cloaked field created by Jupoler.

The king, alone, yelled, "Linx, where are you? Bring me back my baby!"

Assassins, loyal to the north, followed the king. They attacked and murdered him, sending Aropia back into chaos.

Linx named the child Herme. He hid him in a cottage deep in the woods.

As the sun set upon the Dark Ages, Linx presented the boy, whom he claimed as the direct descendant of John, to the warring barons. Herme appeared to be an exact duplicate of John. Linx watched from afar as he grew. He was skinny and mischievous. During hunting games, he led others well. Extremely athletic, he moved as fast as the rabbits he hunted during the games. All those who knew him trusted him. His abilities caused Linx to mentor him. The majority were convinced that Herme was descended from the gods; only he could be king because all kings must be divine rulers. Not everyone was convinced.

The small lordships and baronies surrounding the city of Maram allied themselves with Herme, for they remembered Linx as a great savior. The remainder of Aropia united against Herme's forces. These seven remaining baronies distrusted Linx, his treachery twenty years past never forgiven. They would never accept a mere boy as king.

Linx's strategy was simple. He advised Herme to march his entire force north to his father's old enemy's barony. Herme's troops laid siege to the palace. Two weeks passed as rolling platforms were built. When all was prepared, Herme signaled the attack. Anxious to prove himself, he fought braver than anyone. The baron, better equipped and more experienced, routed Herme's forces on all fronts. Dead lay in the moats. Fires sent a depressing haze over the field. Herme ran across the front, attempting to inspire his men. As the battle turned disastrous, Herme found himself isolated. Turning toward the castle, he saw the baron directing his victorious troops. He slipped into the moat, swam across underwater, and rose into a tangle of reeds. He spied the baron standing alone watching the battle, cornered him, disarmed him, and ordered him to swear allegiance.

The baron spat.

"Never! I will not swear allegiance to a mere boy. You are not even a soldier. You have taken no blood oath to protect the land."

Herme pondered that, then offered his opponent his sword.

"Rise, my lord. Take my sword. Give me the blood oath yourself. Then, as a valiant soldier, you will swear allegiance to me."

Jupoler heard this banter as Linx stationed himself close to Herme.

The baron took the sword offered with every intention of striking Herme down. As he raised the mortal blow, Jupoler fixed his tractor beam on it. The baron stared at his arms as they involuntarily were forced to give Herme the blood oath, establishing him as protector of the land.

"You are indeed protector of this land, my liege. I humbly accept you as king."

"And I accept you, great baron, as leader of my military. I've never seen anyone fight as well. Will you join me at Maram castle?"

"Yes, my liege."

With Linx and Jupoler's help, Herme won the land. Aropia united as one land. The barons voluntarily came to Maram, the new capital, and together they protected the land. The gods were worshipped at the stones. Through their example, the stones became the center of the nation's belief structure and life. The barons, under orders from Herme, renamed the land Stonland.

As Herme grew tall, society grew prosperous. Crops rarely failed. People everywhere prospered. Herme became more powerful with each passing day. He reestablished the system of lords to appease the barons and took the ten percent himself.

The defeated barons, now lords, at first simply military advisors, were asked to create what Herme named *The Council of the Lords*. This council ensured that he, or any future king, would respect the people. Any decision made by Herme was first presented to the lords. In this way, all citizens were ensured a fair and impartial government. He reestablished contact with the other nations, and for years they all prospered. Linx counseled him as the kingdom prospered. One year, failure settled in as it naturally must, and Herme called for Linx.

"Why are the crops failing?"

Linx knew it was because the shuttle was at its farthest orbit from Earth; therefore, Jupoler was out of control.

"Satetan must be ill. When she is well, the crops will prosper again."

"But the crops in all of the nations are failing."

"Satetan is very sick," Linx stated confidently.

Herme was not so confident. Disgusted, he dismissed Linx. Leaving the lord's council in charge, he set off on a quest for answers. One week later, deep in the forest, he stumbled upon a dilapidated Hermatic temple. As he entered the temple, he yelled, "PRIEST!"

A startled priest came around the corner. He wore a brown robe that represented the calm, content lifestyle of the Hermatic priesthood. His frazzled hair was bowl cut. The King's yelling had disturbed his sleep. He had fallen off of his bed and was quite angry.

"Quiet, my son! What do you want?"

"I am king of Stonland. My reign has been prosperous, but now the crops are failing. Why can't I stop it?"

"Because you believe in nine gods instead of the 'One true God.' The one true God is punishing you," he stated flatly.

"But my sorcerer Linx says Satetan is sick--"

"Silly superstition, my liege. You must ask Hermax's forgiveness. Only then will your crops succeed. You have had false prosperity that you believed the gods were providing, but it was actually Hermax. He is all-powerful. It was he who made your crops fail. Occasionally, he does this to humble man. His hope was that you would journey the land in search of the truth. He led you to me. He has created a worldwide famine. Every country seeks answers from their king. The answer lies with Hermax. You must go to Laarisia and beg his forgiveness."

"Thank you."

As he turned to leave, the priest asked him, "What are you going to do?"

He felt confused. Life, so clear days ago, seemed a mirage.

"I don't know."

He commandeered a ship and sailed to the port of Maram.

The sea relaxed him. On his way back to Maram, he made up his mind.

He stepped off of the ship at the port of Maram as soon as his security escort arrived. He settled into his throne and summoned Linx.

Linx bowed.

"My liege, I trust your journey went well?"

A grin spread across Herme's face. "Yes, very well. I met a man who proved to me how wrong we've been to follow your advice. Guards!"

Guards appeared and arrested Linx. Herme ordered him marched to the stones.

"You may call upon your gods, there. You are hereby banished from Stonland."

"But-"

"Take that scum away! Order the council to gather."

A messenger ran off. Within minutes, the council was gathered in the throne room. They heard what happened to Linx and feared for their lives. Herme sensed this.

"Please, relax. I have called you to tell you how my journey went. I found a way to refurbish our land. This famine was brought on by our belief system. Since I perpetuated this system, I deem it only right that I repair the damage. At dawn, I sail to Laarisia to beg the Laara's forgiveness. While I am gone, banish the gods and embrace Hermax."

Linx abandoned at the stones, contacted Jupoler, and was mercifully transported to the shuttle. Jupoler missed Linx's dismissal because of the shuttle's distant orbit.

"Uryxs, why have you returned?"

"I have been banished. So have you. As we speak, all the kings from every island have landed on Laarisia. They intend to beg the Laara to allow them to worship Hermax."

Jupoler was not angry. He was, however, disgusted. He bellowed in front of all the gods, gathered to welcome Uryxs home.

"That's it! I'm done trying to help these people. Tarus was wrong to ask us to try."

He thrust his finger toward Uryxs.

"You will contact the Gosirian priests! Tell them we are done with humans. Let them know it is up to them to find a human who will unquestionably support us. If they don't, I'm afraid they're doomed. Look at this prediction Vienusia made."

He slid a diagram over to Uryxs. Uryxs grasped its meaning immediately and gasped.

The morning after Herme banished Linx, he left on a quest to Laarisia. When he arrived, he set off on foot to the Laara's palace. It was a chance he had to take.

He set up camp outside. It was winter, yet daily, he knelt in the snow, waiting for the Laara to acknowledge him. Within a week, eleven kings of eleven lands, begging the Laara's forgiveness, joined him. Laarisia and Hermatia were not represented because they had never given up on Hermax. Herme called a council of kings and found they all quested, all conferred with a Hermatic priest and all decided to embrace Hermax.

The Laara, angry, came out after two weeks and asked to speak privately to Herme.

"Why do you disgrace my palace?"

Herme bowed.

"We have come to ask the great Laara's forgiveness. Our kingdoms are failing without Hermax. We all want to convert back to Hermatic ways."

The Laara knew he had them now.

"Hermax will accept you back, with conditions. I want the Hermatic pick carved into your stones. All nations will abolish all religions. You are to reestablish the feudal farming communities with a ten percent yield donation to the church. Also, you won't make a political move between kingdoms, including marriages, until you consult the Laara! Go. Talk to the other kings. If you all agree to the conditions, you shall be granted prosperity through Hermax' will."

The kings truly had no choice. Most kingdoms had a farming system in place. They taxed twenty percent because they did not want to give up their ten percent. The gods faded to myth. The Gosirian priests, still residing in Alpania, were disbanded. The Laara requested they be sent back to Laarisia. They became monument maintenance personnel as the Laara realized they were an integral part of religious history. The only rule the Laara imposed on them was that they were to wear their hair in the bowl-cut style of the Hermatic priests. This ruling forced them to conform to his will.

CHAPTER 11

KINGDOMS

3220 A.D. - 3620 A.D.

Political and religious control of the world returned to Laarisia. The kingdoms were separate states, except Alpania, which ruled over five provinces. True to their word, no one made a move without the approval of the Laara. Stonland eventually broke the pact, becoming the first to trade with Nepusia because of a daring man named Captain Edion.

King Herme was hungry for a trade monopoly and bypassed the Laara to establish one. Nepusia seemed the ripest target. Trade began after he requested a meeting with Captain Edion, a true explorer. Of medium build, short for a captain, the king wondered how he commanded so well. His body was browned from the sun. Most of his life had been spent at sea. Naturally calm, his sailors knew if they crossed him, he might explode. What truly made him a good commander was that he listened to and respected the opinions of anyone on his ship; in return, he expected them to listen to him, as he made no decision until weighing all the available options. Calm, with an inquisitive look that telegraphed his disbelief that the king actually requested to speak to him, he appeared before the throne.

"Captain Edion, you have sailed to Nepusia. Do you think they would be willing to trade with us?"

The captain ran his fingers thoughtfully through his rich golden beard. He stared disbelieving, his hard blue eyes studying the king's face.

Such a simple question. Was this really why he was summoned here? Though he thought the answer was obvious, he quickly shared his opinion with the king.

"They have spent one thousand years doing business with Laarisia and Hermatia only. I think they are anxious to open new relations."

"Good. Load three ships with trade goods and sail to Nepusia. Sit in their harbor until you have made a good trade."

Maram merchant ships were sleek and fast, the first to dispense with oar power. Measuring two hundred feet long and thirty feet wide, they had three masts, each fitted with three enormous sails, also a one-sail mast at the head of the ship, and a cross mast (or rudder sail) above the pilot's station. The design was simple. By cutting the rudder sail at a forty-five-degree angle, the pilot could turn the ship full sail into an oncoming wind. With synchronic timing, the front mast was cut into the opposite angle, forcing oncoming winds to circle behind the mainsails. The oncoming wind was, in effect, reversed, allowing the ship to make headway. Because of this innovation, the wind no longer controlled the direction of the ship; the pilot did. These ships achieved greater speed than any other ships in the world. The water-to-deck height was thirty-five feet, except at the captain's quarters located above the massive rudder and behind the wheelhouse at a height of fifty feet above the water. This was where the captain lived, observed, and addressed the crew. His perch fifteen feet above the deck gave the impression that he was indeed larger than life.

Captain Edion succeeded. Nepusia trapped animals for food. When he saw them, he convinced the citizens to let him have the skins. He spread his wares before the Nepusians. They surprised him, for they wanted nothing of value. They gave up their extremely valuable skins for shell necklaces Edion intended to give as gifts at the conclusion of the trade. The people of Stonland paid a premium for processed skins. Stonland remained cold most of the year, and before long, fur was the fashion. The trade monopoly Herme dreamed of made him fabulously wealthy.

For years, this trade continued under Laara's nose. Eventually, when Herme's monopoly was discovered, the Laara decided to legally grant Stonland exclusive rights to trade with Nepusia.

The Laara, concerned about rumors that Stonland had taken action without consulting him, arrived one day unannounced at Linxiton Palace. He was ushered to the throne room. Here, he confronted Herme.

"Herme, I have heard rumors you trade with Nepusia. You know they are restricted to business dealings with Laarisia and Hermatia. Why do you interfere?"

"I apologize, Laara. Our wish was to make Nepusia feel welcome as an important nation of the world. We meant no harm and certainly did not mean to interfere. We trade them for skins. What is the harm in using a commodity that was only being wasted?"

"You're right, of course. Hermax does not want us to waste. This trade, is it profitable?"

Herme was unable to hide his true feelings. "It's astronomical!"

The Laara thought for a moment.

"Herme, I disagree with the way you opened trading. You should have come to me for permission. As punishment, you will pay both Laarisia and Hermatia a portion of your profits. To guarantee we all profit, I am hereby officially granting you monopolistic rights to trade in furs with Nepusia."

"Why are you being so generous?"

"Because, on the one hand, I want to punish you, but I can see your business will profit all parties involved. I will not go to the expense of training another nation in the fur trade when you are already experts. I will not restrict you as long as you pay your tributes."

Stonland was to send twenty percent of either merchandise or cash to Laarisia and ten percent to Hermatia in return for a trade monopoly with Nepusia. Stonland protected its monopoly militarily. The Laara looked the other way as long as the tributes flowed. Other nations traded with each other but learned never to approach Nepusia.

Captain Edion sailed with a military escort. He soon decided to demand a tribute to Stonland from each foreign ship he encountered. When he returned home after collecting the first tributes, he gave the treasure to Herme. Herme was so pleased with his new fortune that he passed a law: All ships would demand tribute. The kingdom soon became the wealthiest of all.

Andenan, Nepetan, and Kashim traded only among themselves. Their ships stayed close to the shoreline, rarely encountering Stonland ships. When they did, they immediately paid the tribute.

Captain Nies of Alpania spotted a Stonland ship in distress one afternoon. He directed his crew to sail to her rescue. When they tied onto the disabled ship, they were assaulted. Captain Edion apologized for the ruse. He said they stopped all ships this way the first time. Any ship encountered again knew to stop and pay tribute or be destroyed.

Alpania was by far the largest kingdom, as it also incorporated the provinces of Marsia, Vienus, Ciaxian, Uryxia, and Sateland. Captain Nies, of Alpania proper, reluctantly paid the tribute because he was caught off guard. Sailing back to Alpania, he had to put down a crew mutiny because they thought he was wrong to pay the tribute and should have fought. This tall, blonde-haired, blue-eyed man was not used to being questioned by his men. He was proud, and pride lost him his left hand, which he replaced with a hook. He personally executed each man who had revolted by slicing his neck with his hook. By the time the ship reached Alpania, he was in a constant state of red-faced anger, having long ago surpassed hatred.

When Captain Nies docked, his first order of business after securing the ship was to demand to see the king. As he entered the throne room, he noticed that it was newly decorated. Everywhere, the walls were covered with the antique short swords and leather shields Axiax had used to conquer all of the Alpanian provinces.

Hanging with the sets of swords and shields hung many Hermatic picks. Until the battle was called off, these picks were to be the main weapon used in destroying Laarisia. The floor was covered in a variety of animal skins, just as Axiax's command tent had been. The young king had been busy hunting while Nies sailed and he suspected, now, that was why King Surat's expression beamed. His appearance made Captain Nies sick. This portly, jolly, pig-nosed ruler with his dirty body and dirty brown hair did not seem to notice the captain's disgust and welcomed him back with open arms.

"Captain, how good it is to see you again. I trust your voyage was magnificent?"

When his embrace was not returned, King Surat backed away and, finally, noticed Captain Nies's look.

"Why do you look so angry?"

"King Herme of Stonland has demanded a tribute from all vessels his ships encounter on Galacia!"

The king's normally pale face turned beat red with anger. "He what?! What makes him think he can do that?"

"He claims to have the best-equipped navy in the world. He threatens to sink any ship that doesn't pay. What are we going to do?"

Surat pondered this new development.

"Everyone will pay the tribute."

"But, it's an outrage!"

"I know. No one is to protest until I speak with the Laara. You will transport me to Laarisia at once."

Two weeks later, King Surat was in Laarisia. He found the Laara watering his private palace garden. The Laara's appearance unsettled him. This once great man was bent with age, hands shaking as half the water he poured spilled to the floor. He was senile, as Surat soon found out.

"Holy Laara, King Herme of Stonland has taken control of Galacia. He-"

"Impossible! No one owns Galacia. It is the property of Hermax."

"Nevertheless, he forces tribute from all ships he encounters. Have you given permission for this?"

"No. I was unaware."

"What can we do?"

The Laara thought for a moment.

"Don't pay it."

"He has threatened to destroy our ships if we resist."

"Then don't sail. Surat, I have solved your problem; now you must help me solve mine. Do you think the purple flowers look better on the north or south side of the garden? Shall I have a slave dig them up and move them so you can compare?" He asked innocently.

"No, Laara. Please don't bother them. I'm sure whatever you choose will suffice. I must go now. I'm very tired."

He left the palace as confused as ever. The Laara was, as he admitted-truly unaware.

King Surat sailed back toward Alpania, feeling frustrated by the Laara's apparent senility. Two days outside of Alpania, his ship was intercepted by a merchant ship from Stonland led by Captain Edion and his military escort. As the ships approached, King Surat told Captain Nies his plan.

Captain Edion demanded tribute as he approached the king's ship.

"I will pull alongside and tie up to you. Prepare to be boarded."

Captain Edion's military escort kept back. Like cats, their posture indicated they were ready to pounce.

Once tied to Nies' ship, his crew poured aboard. Captain Edion, the pilot and his first mate, stood at the wheelhouse, observing the onslaught.

King Surat let the merchants aboard. When they were all on board, he ordered the crew to restrain them. The crewmembers closest to the Stonland ship ignited and untied it.

Captain Edion and his two companions desperately tried to put out the fire. The ship, engulfed in smoke, was the signal his escort was waiting for.

The military ships moved in. As they approached, all crewmembers of Captain Edion's ship were murdered. King Surat ordered spears and arrows to be launched and successfully beat the Stonland fleet.

Captain Edion watched helplessly as each ship was captured and sunk. Captain Nies made no move to rescue survivors. Those who made it to his ship and begged for help were cut down. Horrified, many tried to make it to Captain Edion's ship. Most drowned. Those who made it had no time to rest. They were given the task of extinguishing the fire.

Laughing, Captain Nies ordered his ship to retreat. He let Edion's burnt ship limp away as a warning to Herme.

King Herme was furious.

"What! How dare Alpania oppose me!"

"They are well-armed and excellent fighters, my liege. They have inherited the trickery of Axiax. We should leave Alpanian ships alone and harass the easier Andenan/Nepetan/Kashim trade route."

"No! I will not give Alpania free passage. If I do, they will become stronger and more of a threat. No. We will attack!"

"How? We have to get too close, and they are excellent archers and spearmen."

"I'll tell you how. We traded Nepusia for a magic powder they mine. My scientists figured out how to harness its properties. Come outside. I'll show you how it works."

They walked out to the courtyard. The captain saw a model ship on a pond in the distance. They stopped at an iron tube that had a string protruding from its rear. Captain Edion thought the whole contraption a ridiculous joke and began to laugh.

The king kept a straight face. He slyly asked, "What's so funny?"

"What good is a tube like this against arrows and spears?"

"Observe."

The king lit the string. Hiss, hiss, BOOM!

The captain was shocked. A lead ball shot directly into the ship and sank it. He turned to the king in disbelief.

"In about one year all my ships will be fit with many of these propellers. No navy in the world will stand up to us; if they do, they'll be destroyed!"

In that year, Alpania grew bold and began serious trading with Nepusia. They also discovered the powder and put it to good use. Captain Nies, under orders from King Surat, sailed a military escort of ten ships alongside an expedition of five trading ships. Captain Edion used a five-ship escort and one trading ship economically loading the escorts with merchandise. Neither man was aware the other had discovered a use for the Nepusian powder.

When the inevitable clash occurred, Captain Nies and Captain Edion were en route to and from Nepusia. When he saw the Alpanian merchants, he predicted they were slow and heavy. He ordered his merchant ship to fall back and plunged toward the Alpanian group.

Captain Nies duplicated the move. Head first, the two battle groups converged. Almost upon the Alpanians, the Stonland force turned broadside and fired its propellers. The Alpanians had developed an adjustable catapult system and sent burning explosive charges hurling through the air at Stonland's ships. The propellers shot faster and more accurately, allowing them to win the day.

Every Alpanian military vessel sank. The Stonland forces surrounded and boarded the merchants. They carried mini propellers designed to be fired by hand. Men who put up a fight were shot down. Alpania quickly surrendered. Her ships were stripped. Every defeated sailor was ordered to sail with Captain Nies. He was allowed to limp home, as Captain Edion once had. As he sailed away, the vengeful Captain Edion fired and sunk the Alpanian vessels. As an afterthought, he fired on Captain Nies. He hoped to cause a fire such as he had faced the year before. He succeeded. An oil barrel was hit, split, and ignited. Captain Edion laughed as Nies' crew scurried about. He noticed Nies calmly staring back at him and knew war had begun.

Determined to end the escalation, Laara Daphne VIII personally visited Stonland. She was still a teenager, forced into office when the old, senile Laara died. He had let the empire slip through his weakness. Weakness would be her first challenge. Her pink-tinted white flesh, just a trace of baby fat, and soft, perky breasts, she knew, showed off her young age, and people associated youth with weakness, especially when a leadership position was involved. She was, however, tall, which helped to offset the appearance that she might be just another weak Laara. She dominated every meeting she attended in Laarisia and Hermatia. She was direct, determined, anxious for peace, and determined to promote it herself. Inside, she was a warrior, as her outside appearance showed. No one realized that red hair and green eyes meant someone's ancestors were from the warrior class; in this age, it was instinctive. She arrived at King Herme's castle in the full regal robes of her high office.

"Herme, I am here on two accounts."

"Which are?" He wondered, bored.

"News has filtered to me that you continue to demand tribute from all ships you encounter on Galacia. Per your agreement with our beloved deceased Laara, you must stop, as you have not cleared this policy with me."

Herme's look was far away.

"And your other point?"

"Hermax is upset that you've started a war with Alpania. He has asked me to tell you to withdraw."

"I will address your first point. I demand tribute as insurance that other nations will not approach Nepusia. When a ship is boarded, it is searched. If Nepusian goods are found, I tax them heavily. If they are not, I take a small tribute for my time. I have done this without your permission for two reasons. First, I have the strongest navy in the world and can. Secondly, I have a trade monopoly contract with your office. You are not strong enough to stop illegal trade. I am. I will protect my monopoly militarily if I must. You are welcome to ten percent of my tributes, but I will not stop.

"Now, your second point. Alpania has attempted to break my monopoly. Many of my people have died protecting what they consider right. Laara, I appreciate your concern for the Alpanians; however, the scum has dishonored my kingdom and will be crushed. If you and Hermax can't accept that, then you can both go to Hell!"

Herme's voice unbalanced the Laara. In shock over his outburst, her voice trembled.

"If you truly refuse to accept Hermax' will, your country will be banished."

"Then banish us. I have a war to fight. You are excused!"

Daphne VIII rushed out of the castle crying. She quickly sailed to Laarisia where she cut off all relations with Stonland.

He was determined that banishment by Hermax would not affect him. King Herme was found at the stones requesting Jupoler's advice. He willingly abandoned Hermax and wished to reestablish his link with the gods. Although Herme would lead his land to them, Jupoler ordered the gods to ignore him. Jupoler felt he was not a true believer. His war-hungry nation readily cast Hermax aside. No mere god would dictate their lives. They quickly and conveniently forgot that the nine gods had led them to misery. The Hermatics were forced to flee to the deep forests once again.

The war was going well. The two months of banishment had not hurt the kingdom. Herme saw a fidgety man coming. The man who approached had a small, wiry frame and mussed-up curly brown hair. He walked, always, like a man with important news that could not wait. Even from far away, Herme saw the man's quick, awkward gait.

He knew Xar, his administrator, was coming. Intelligent enough, but Herme did not like the way he nagged him into action. He pretended to be in deep meditation; surely, the little man's request could wait. Maybe he would get the clue and go back to wait at the castle for Herme's return.

Contrary to Herme's wishes, Xar kept coming. This news could not wait.

"King Herme-," Xar interrupted.

"How dare you interrupt my prayers!"

"Forgive me, Sire, but this is important."

"Don't you ever find anything unimportant? What could be more important than my worship?"

"The kingdoms of Alpania, Andenan, and Nepusia are landing soldiers on our eastern coast. Our banishment caused the others to join Alpania. They believe we are finished without Hermax's support. Even now, they march toward Maram!"

Herme was paying attention now. He was sorry, though he would never admit it to this little man, sorry he had yelled. This was indeed important.

"In what strength?"

"There are many thousands, Sire. Andenan has united with Kashim and Nepetan; each is now a province in the Andenan government. They are second only to Alpania in force. What are your orders?"

He thought for a moment.

"Set up propellers and gun troops in all of the passes. No matter what force they have, they won't beat our firepower. They'll quit before they ever reach Maram. Also, send the entire navy to Hermatia. We will lay siege to the island until they surrender."

Xar performed as ordered. As expected, the invading land forces could not penetrate the passes. When they received word of Hermatia's siege, they retreated and sailed off to save her.

Herme won the land battle with the threat on Hermatia. He knew the passes would not hold forever. When the invaders retreated, he sent word to the navy to free Hermatia and surround Laarisia.

A runner found Daphne in the palace.

"Laara, you must come to the roof now!"

She followed him up the stairs and onto the roof. What she saw astonished her. The harbor was full of ships flying Stonland's flag. He informed her that Stonland had laid siege to the island.

"Find the commander of those forces. This war stops now!"

Recently promoted, admiral Edion, entrusted with the fleet, met Daphne in the palace.

"Take a message to Herme. The war is over. He may continue the tribute system and have sole military jurisdiction over the Nepusian trade route."

"What of the Andenan and Alpanian threat?"

"I will order them back. Tell Herme he has won. He may have his gods."

When the message was received, the war stopped. The Laara would not allow Laarisia to be dragged into the war. Daphne the Eighth forgave Stonland. Gradually, she sent missionaries to Stonland to secretly rebuild the Hermatic temples.

Herme's son, Herme II, was a disappointment, the complete opposite of Herme. He was round and pathetically uncoordinated. Herme, disgusted, daily ordered him out of his sight, and, as a result, Herme II spent many days of his youth exploring the forests of Stonland, quickly learning that his green eyes and sandy blonde hair combined with brown clothes camouflaged him well. He became a great hunter and through hunting, developed athletic prowess. One day, he stumbled upon a Hermatic temple. He lay low for a few weeks, watching their habits. Eventually, he exposed himself, befriended them, visited often, and secretly converted. When Herme died, Herme the Second became king, embraced the Laara, abolished the tribute system, and brought great peace to the world. The world looked to Laarisia for religious leadership and, thanks to Herme the Second's generosity, Stonland for economic and military leadership.

Herme the Second's peace gesture led to the birth of the arts. Alpania quickly became the art center of the world. The Laara commissioned statues and paintings representing the Hermatic struggle. Enormous cathedrals replaced the state temples. The original gods, over the centuries kept alive through myth, were painted on the ceiling of these temples. The clothing of the gods consistently bore a Hermatic pick, representing the one true God's power over them. In the temple of Alpania, Herme the Second's son Noxon, sixteen, the mirror image of his father, and Surat's granddaughter Ursia, fifteen, were to be married to secure the peace. Noxon fell in love with Ursia the moment he laid eyes on her. She had a perfect, breathtakingly beautiful body and dressed to accentuate it. Fair-complected with bright blue eyes, her long blonde hair fell loosely over her breasts. The wedding was huge. The couple took up residence in Linxiton Palace in Maram. Soon after, trouble began.

Linxiton Palace was a five thousand-acre estate on the outskirts of Maram. It was built to honor Linx soon after he brought Herme to power. It served not only as the royal residence but the center of government itself, and also housed the dungeon of Maram.

The well-manicured grounds included the lord king's farms, his forest, and many mazes. From Maram, one traveled, usually by coach, along a private road. Iron entrance gates would open only on the king's order. Once past the gates, one was awed by the majesty of the place. Like the castles, it was an immense structure surrounded by a moat. What caught Ursia's eyes were the towering pirouetted spires with high windows that surrounded the palace, breaking the wall every fifty feet.

As they approached, a drawbridge came down. They rolled in through a high arch and came to an abrupt stop. Unlike other castles, this was one building. They exited the coach. The driver backed it up and took it to the royal stables.

She now saw the reason for the high windows. When the sun hit them just right, they cast rainbows throughout the main hall. Once inside, there were three paths to take. The grand staircase led to the royal residence, which, along with guestrooms, encompassed the entire third floor. Halfway up the stairs, veering right, one would enter a hall that led to the second-floor government offices. The entrance to the grand staircase was off to the right of the entrance. The archway/hallway it created led to the king's throne room, royal banquet hall, and entertainment center. Every wall of the hallways and staircases was decorated with either paintings or sculptures of the gods. If one came across a painting of the stones, he knew he was near Linx's old quarters. If one came across a painting of Linx holding the boy Herme above his head, he knew he was on the way to the throne room. The dungeon encompassed the basement of the palace. The entrance was just off of the throne room, as the king was the final judge in all matters.

As Noxon gave Ursia the grand tour, King Herme the second met with King Surat.

"I only ask that my people be able to settle in your lands."

"Give me time," King Surat begged, "all of my provinces have rebelled because of the royal wedding."

This was the moment. He coveted Uryxia. Previous to the engagement, when he was first introduced to Ursia, King Surat's royal escort had led him on a tour of the islands. None stood out in his mind except beautiful Uryxia. One thousand lakes dotted the mountain landscape where rains continually fell. River outlets flooded the valleys, creating rich farmland. Although the fields were fat with cattle and sheep, he sensed the roaring rivers, harnessed, would produce great power. Uryxia was the jewel of Alpania.

"I will help you quell the rebellion for a price. I want the province of Uryxia."

Herme the Second sent forces to Alpania to quell the rebellion. The rebellion started when the news traveled that Alpania and Stonland were going to ally through marriage. People were happy Herme the second promoted peace, but they distrusted him solely as the son of Herme. The annexed Alpanian islands had assimilated the pride of Alpania into their respective cultures. They were fiercely independent and considered Alpania a world power greater than Stonland. When news of the alliance reached them, each island revolted.

Marsia, Vienusian, Ciaxian, Sateland, and Uryxia formed militias who gathered in the mountains to train. The citizenry lived as normal, betraying nothing. The militias gathered arms and practiced for months. When the day came to invade the capitals, they were welcomed with open arms. Messengers ran to Alpania to report the loss of each island. King Surat was in the process of unleashing his navy when Herme offered his help.

They formulated a plan. Their combined navies surrounded each island. Massive troops landed in the capitals. The rebels ran to the hills. The loyalty of the provinces was reestablished through martial law. Occupational forces were left to keep the peace. Surat sent the combined armies into the hills, intending to flush out the rebels. Most rebels perished. Few snuck through the lines, living to fight another day.

Once the threat was quashed, King Surat, true to his word, allowed Stonland to annex Uryxia. Surviving rebels quietly emigrated to Uryxia, for they sensed there would be another opportunity to fight.

Noxon and Ursia spent their first months of marriage housed in Linxiton palace. When the rebellion ended, Herme the Second came to them.

"I have taken Uryxia as a prize. I offer it to you as a wedding gift."

Noxon was flabbergasted. He had no desire to live in Uryxia; besides, Ursia was in love with the palace. He knew, however, better than to cross his father, so he showed no emotion.

"Where shall we live, Father?"

"The castle is empty. Servants await your arrival."

Ursia, properly silent, turned red and stormed out of the room, surprising Herme.

"What's wrong with her, son?"

"It is nothing, Father. She loves it here. I'm sure she doesn't want to move. I'll talk to her."

"You do that, son. If she gives you trouble, tell her she is welcome to stay here, in the dungeon."

"There's no need to threaten her, Father. She is a good woman. She will see her duty. I'm sure she will calm."

Noxon left his father and found Ursia hurriedly packing. Her entire attitude had changed.

"Ursia, why are you excited?"

"Oh, Noxon. I admit I was angry with your father when he ordered us to move, but on my walk home, I realized this is more than we could've hoped for. Here, we would've been and prince and princess sitting idly by watching the kingdom governed by your father. Now, we are going to rule!"

She closed the last trunk.

"Call the servants. Tonight, we sail to our destiny."

That evening, they set sail for Uryxia. The captain took Noxon to one side to warn him.

"You must expect resistance when you land."

"I do. Father sent guards and a relief occupation force to contend with it. They will meet us when we land."

The captain saw he need not worry. They navigated the harbor unmolested. When the royal couple walked down the gangplank, the crowd cheered their arrival.

The road to the castle was lined with well-wishers. Noxon and Ursia wore permanent smiles. This assignment was going well. Taking no heed of the captain's warning, they soaked up the beauty of the island; it was the most beautiful of the Alpanian provinces. Snow-capped mountains, rivers, lakes, forests, and simple people dominated the landscape.

Once inside the castle, the administrators greeted them. Noxon and Ursia were ushered to the throne room and told to sit. They were briefed on Uryxian customs, laws, and lifestyles and were offered suggestions on governing these unique people.

Noxon thanked them. "I have orders from father. He expects me to govern his way."

"We will review your father's wishes, but we recommend you listen to us. We don't want another rebellion."

"Too late." An administrator turned away from the window. "The castle is surrounded. I believe we are under siege."

Noxon and Ursia ran to the window. What they saw astonished them. The very people who had welcomed them sat with scowls on their faces, weapons in their hands, and an arsenal stockade to reinforce them.

Noxon yelled, "Betrayal!"

He paced for a few minutes. When he stopped, he announced his decision.

"They have betrayed us. We must betray them." He looked to the head administrator. "Call a truce. Ask them if we can rid the castle of the loyalists to their cause. Amongst the exodus, we will hide a messenger. I'll plea to Father for help."

The rebels agreed upon the exodus. They knew the extra fighters would boost their cause. The messenger Noxon sent boarded a ship headed for Alpania proper. He claimed he had relatives there and was tired of fighting. Once in Alpania, he was free to sail to Stonland unnoticed. He quickly gained Herme's attention.

"Double-crossed! Poor Noxon and Ursia are trapped. Guards! I sail for Alpania at once!"

Herme the Second's entire fleet sailed to Alpania. He met with King Surat. Although he was concerned for his granddaughter's safety, he refused to commit troops for political reasons. He told Herme attacking an island so recently under his control would cause dissent in his other provinces. Rebellion was fresh on his mind. Herme understood and, although he did not need to, asked Surat's blessing to raid Uryxia.

With Surat's blessing, King Herme the Second sailed to Uryxia. In the main harbor, he destroyed every ship he found. His troops landed and, before they attempted the castle, destroyed the town.

The rebels sent runners to investigate the smoke. They came back with terrible news. Herme's entire force had landed. The rebel leaders met, decided the fight could not be won, and offered to surrender.

Herme the second accepted the surrender. He arrested everyone and systematically murdered them. His excuse: "I will have no more rebellion. I have cleansed this island. I will send colonists from Stonland to repopulate it."

Noxon was appalled. He saw now that Uryxia would be run as a puppet of Stonland, as his father wished.

While rebellion and massacre occurred in the east, Nepusia boldly moved south. Because of the trade monopoly, they developed an alliance with Stonland. Laarisia was forced to relax restrictions upon them. They were finally free, after more than one thousand years of religious-based rule, to pursue their own interests. Stonland heavily influenced these interests. Trade monopoly profits built a superb navy and army. Intelligence from Stonland indicated that Andenan annexed Kashim and Nepetan, yet they still traded only amongst each other.

Years before, King Herme the First forgave Nepusia for its attack on Stonland when he realized their hand had been forced by Laarisia. Herme, however, wanted Andenan punished. Nepusia prepared to accomplish this while remaining friendly with Andenan. Years after Herme died, they were finally prepared.

With the world's focus on the war in the east, Nepusia's armed forces quietly slipped out of port. They ravaged the Andenan sea lanes. They easily conquered Kashim and Nepetan for news of the invasion, offered by escaped merchant ships, created a panic and they were abandoned. All citizens fled to Andenan.

When the Nepusian force landed at Andenan, they found it heavily fortified. Terror filled the beach as each yard was purchased with more blood than they could afford. The Andenan force struck and retreated. Angrily, the Nepusians followed them.

When the Nepusians were drawn far enough inland, soldiers charged out of the hills. Outflanked, the Nepusians fought a bloody retreat. Few made it back to the ships. Nepusia's imperial dreams were crushed. Many men were unaccounted for. They never attempted another invasion. Law regulated the military, desperate to rebuild, to homeland security.

After Herme the Second massacred the rebellious citizens of Uryxia, he met with the Laara.

"Herme, I understand why you committed genocide on Uryxia. You must understand there have been formal protests, and I am confident other nations will attack you. Hermax will reward you for your sin."

Herme stood arrogantly, staring ahead. "Let him. I am ready,"

"Herme, my entire purpose in life is to keep the peace. I will do what I can on a religious level, but rage will not be blinded by religion. I am depending on Stonland to stop these destructive conflicts. You have heard by now what happened to Nepusia?"

"Yes, Laara."

"They gambled and lost. You are proven the strongest nation in the world. Being the best, you have a responsibility to promote the peace."

"I will try, Laara. I am old and tired of fighting. I truly want to leave my son a peaceful world."

Herme the Second did try, but countries continued to attack his ships. Eventually, peace came, but Stonland found there was not much profit in peace. On and off for the next three hundred years, wars raged.

Stonland never started them. Instead, she goaded others. They were purposely difficult in trade negotiations and masters at destroying their own ships. They always blamed the "enemy."

Peace was only known in the remotest areas. Observing the destruction and chaos a poet, Noplod, decided to write historical plays about the old empire's violence. A graying, middle-aged man, his ancient ancestry was of the slave farming class, as evidenced in his younger days by his brown hair and eyes. His recent ancestry was of the merchant class, so although he had not experienced oppression firsthand, the battle reports still angered him and were his inspiration for becoming a playwright. Short height, bald head, and eccentric ways made him look the part of a royal fool rather than an educated man. Always late, running to his destination, he seemed confused about where he was most of the time. Anyone else would have been long ago banished as a fool. His plays saved him. They were equally funny and sad, yet always ended tragically. Unwittingly, he kept the myths of the gods alive, becoming so famous that he was asked to perform each new play for the Laara and the council of priests. His stories were revered through time, reproduced in child's plays, local theater, and seasonal festivals where troops would dress the part.

Each successive Laara received protests. They pleaded with Stonland but were too weak to make a difference. Hermax was failing them.

Stonland's kings, without fail, pleaded innocence to the Laara, swearing they were only protecting themselves. They claimed they were actually stopping wars before they got out of hand.

Stonland attempted what Nepusia had failed to do three hundred years earlier. Andenan was venturing too far out with her merchant fleet. Stonland decided to make her pay. Andenan would "attack and sink" a Stonland merchant. This atrocity would be followed by Stonland's invasion of Kashim.

After the quick, victorious battle of Kashim, a warrior named Celes was walking through a tiny ruined village, lost deep in thought. The stone buildings stood ruined, like soldiers frozen in a surprised, obscenely grotesque gesture. Roofs were mostly gone. Smoldering structures stood with one or two walls. He was glad the people had surrendered before street-to-street fighting began. Celes knew if it had, he might be a disfigured body lying next to one of these walls.

The few roofed buildings may have been ideal to house the refugees, but the commander had insisted on building a prison camp to further humiliate the losers. Celes thought it unfair but would not contradict an order, so as a form of self-punishment, he decided to tour the village. Not a true warrior; his entire makeup was that of a seafarer. He was not aware and had always wondered what the longing feeling was whenever he was on a troopship headed to battle. Joining this game as an investment, his goal was a lordship. As he negotiated the rubble, a shimmering glint, tall, strong, blonde-haired, blue-eyed, armor-plated, dirty, weary soldier with blue sky in the background. He had never seen a mirror before, and the image intrigued him.

"My god," he thought, "could this creature really be me? Has it been so long since I was clean?"

Throughout Celes' military career, he searched for and kept all mirrors that he found. In his experiments with them, he found them useful in both starting fires and blinding the enemy in battle. In retirement, he was granted lordship of a fine village in Stonland. He spent his life experimenting with mirrors, beginning by giving a mirror to the blacksmith of his new manor, asking him to discover its origin.

A few days later, Celes was out disciplining one of his tenant farmers. The farmer seemed distracted and Celes turned to look. He saw him before he heard him. Nyxs made him laugh. His short, stocky, muscularly powerful, deeply tanned body was meant for blacksmithing, not running. His bowed legs gave him the appearance that he was tripping down the hill.

As he came closer, Celes finally heard what he had been yelling.

"Celes! Celes, sir!"

Celes waited patiently for Nyxs to catch his breath. "What is it? "

"I- I- I finally figured it out. This is a highly polished piece of metal enclosed in glass. I think that's why it reflects so well!"

"I can see the sky in it. Do you think it would allow me to see great distances?"

"I don't see how Sire."

Celes, forever experimenting, developed a tube fitted with a few mirrors and glass at each end. He took it to Nyxs.

"Look into this across the valley. What do you see?"

"By Hermax! I see horses grazing, two males and two females. How does it work?"

He handed the tube back to Celes.

"It's a system of mirrors that actually brings objects closer to you."

"Do you have another?"

"No, but I'm going to make one. It's going to be rather large. Do you think you could make a stand that would elevate it, rotate it, and hold it? It will probably be close to three hundred pounds and twenty inches in diameter."

"I'll get to work right away, sir. When you're finished, may I have this small one?"

"Of course."

Celes built the tube and mounted it on Nyxs' stand. He surveyed all the countryside that he could. One night, after dinner, he decided to gaze at the sky. He "discovered" five planets of the solar system. He named them Mercianiax, Vienusia, Marsia, Jupoler, and Satetan, lest mankind forget the mythical gods. Only the Gosirian priests knew these were already the names.

CHAPTER 12

THE AGE OF SCIENCE

3620 A.D. - 4120 A.D.

Celes' written account of the numerous new stars and planets he viewed launched humanity into an age of exploration, invention, and discovery. Science blossomed. Celes was the scientific leader of the world, yet led a reclusive life.

He spent years studying the skies. He confirmed that the stones truly acted as a clock, both seasonal and daily.

He spent several weeks camped out near the stones. The path the sun took would, yearly, predict the equinoxes. As he studied, he realized the sun's path was not determined on its own; it was determined by the Earth. This tangent recorded he had irrefutable evidence of the movement of the heavens. When he returned home, he shared his theorem with Nyxs.

"Nyxs, come here. You must see what I've discovered."

He laid out a map for Nyxs, who immediately saw the intelligence of his prospect.

Celes watched Nyxs for a reaction.

"What shall I do?"

"Sire, this is too important. You must go to the Laara."

"How? No one meets with the Laara unless they're important."

"Go first to Maram. I will watch over your lands. Speak to the head priest there. He will get you in to see the Laara."

Celes traveled to the temple of Maram. Located in the center of Maram sat the twenty thousand square foot cathedral. Eight columns, each one hundred feet high, braced crossbeams that, in turn, supported the granite roof. An ambitious artist carved larger-than-life depictions of the mythical god's parents, their likeness based on imagination, one per crossbeam. Outside, the roof and outer walls appeared as one piece. The roof lay at a forty-five-degree angle, and the walls stair-stepped to the slight overhang, resulting in a perfect congruency. At the front of the building, the entrance consisted of a fifty-foot arch and doorway. Within the walls of the arch were carved eight sculptures of eight gods, each looking up to the top of the arch to the figure of Jupoler. Jupoler himself sat with down-set eyes in submission. Above Jupoler, Hermax, hidden, rested his pick on Jupoler's shoulder, for he was in control. Outside, the front wall was covered with many hundreds of tiny Hermatic picks carved to appear that they were about to fall upon anyone looking directly up at them. The door was decorated with a sculpture of Ronix leading the slaves to Hermatia under Hermax' watchful eye. Upon entering, one continued to be impressed with the art. The sculptures carved within the walls were of Veon's mythical escape, the slaves emerging from Laarisia, the enshrouding of Hermatia, Hermax raising the slaves from the mines, and, of course, the nine gods groveling at Hermax's feet. Nine stained glass ceiling windows each depicted a battle between a god and Hermax; each god was defeated. Fifty rows of wooden benches led to a raised pulpit. The Hermatic pick encompassed a majority of the wall behind the pulpit.

Celes found the head priest. He was on his knees, facing the pick, praying. When he rose and turned, he found Celes kneeling behind him, waiting.

"Rise, my son."

"Your eminence. I seek your counsel."

"What can I do for you, my son?"

"I wish to meet with the Laara. I have made a fascinating discovery."

"You are Celes, the scientist, are you not?"

Celes bowed to hide his embarrassment. The fame that came with his simple discoveries upset his modesty.

"Yes, your eminence."

"I am glad you are here; it saves me the trouble of locating you. The Laara has heard of your good works and wishes to meet you."

"Excellent! My information is vital. I came here seeking your approval. Do you wish to review my theory?"

"No, I will not covet the Laara. Since he has requested you, I see no need to review anything. The Laara knows what he wants."

"How shall I get to Laarisia?"

"I will write you an authorization to meet with the Laara. The pass entitles you to board any ship bound for Laarisia."

He handed Celes the pass and led him to the door. They shook hands.

"Good luck, my son."

The next day, he boarded a ship bound for Laarisia. As he sailed, the odd feeling returned; his senses heightened as if the salty sea air was opening his mind. He became one with the sea creatures, gulls, and rolling waves. This oneness with the Earth motivated him.

Confident, he strolled off of the ship in Laarisia and was ushered immediately to the Laara. After a formal introduction, in which the Laara expressed great pleasure at finally meeting the great Celes, and Celes assured the Laara that this was not a social call, the Laara turned to the business at hand.

"What is it you have discovered, Celes?"

He couldn't contain his excitement. "The mariners are wrong. The planets rotate around the sun."

"Impossible! Everyone knows God made the Earth the center of the Universe!"

"But Laara, I have proof."

Celes laid out rolls of paper at Laara's feet.

The evidence was astonishing and, the Laara feared, most likely correct. He pondered a moment. "I will exhibit your proof to my council of priests. They will decide."

Two weeks later, Celes was dead, burned at the stake as a heretic for claiming the Earth revolved around the sun. The Gosirian priests, protectors of the truth, wept. Unable to expose themselves, they stole his proof and returned it to Nyxs.

Nyxs, upset, determined to prove Celes correct. He made and presented eye tubes to every captain of every ship that sailed into the Port of Maram. Within five years, the Laara received numerous reports from mariners that the Earth revolved around the sun and was forced to absolve Celes. He decreed that all heavenly bodies would now become "of Celes" or "Celestial." He then requested all of Celes' papers and built a museum featuring his work near the palace in Laarisia.

Science evolved as the new art form. Inspired by Celes, inventions appeared everywhere. Moveable type printing was developed. Better ships were built, and the globe was finally circumnavigated. Because of Celes, mankind could safely sail anywhere with the moon and stars to guide him.

The first circumnavigational voyage originated in Stonland. The ship, Nevon, was staffed with a science officer, as was every ship. The science officer, Phaol, had no duties on the ship. The crew teased him for his stumpy, awkward appearance. His unkempt clothes and messed up brown hair were far below navy standards. They were respectful of him, however, because he had the captain's ear. Phaol was so awed by the plants and animals they encountered that he kept a pictorial diary.

Phoal was an inspired youth from Stonland, born during the great wave of enthusiasm caused by Celes. A natural artist, he drew everything he saw. His father, when he caught him drawing, beat him and ordered him to stop wasting his time. Thanks to the invention of movable type, he was able to learn to read and kept abreast of all new discoveries. He worked hard on the farm during the day read until all available light disappeared. Although not formally educated, he was reluctant to stay on the farm with his abusive father. He ran, at age sixteen, to the port city of Maram.

He walked through the city in a daze, amazed at its size. Sailors, sensing he was naive, followed him and, in a back alley, shanghaied him. When he woke, he found himself assigned as a cabin boy on a ship. He did not let his method of employment bother him, for a ship meant adventure and exploration.

He quickly became the captain's pet. Although he tried to hide it, his knowledge was exposed. The captain, learning his helper was brilliant, depended on his advice. Were the crew aware, there would be a mutiny.

Phoal's services were so appreciated that he was allowed to leave the ship to tour the island when they reached Laarisia. This was unheard of. The cabin boys never left the ship. Since women were not allowed to sail, cabin boys were normally used for entertainment, sexual or otherwise, and sailors did not want these facts exposed; therefore, they remained on board as slaves. Several sailors commented on this strange breach of protocol, and rumbled, mutinous whispers circulated.

Phoal was impressed with Laarisia. He toured the monuments, the palace, and the Museum of Celes. Unopposed by men like his father, he sketched everything he saw. When he returned to the ship, he showed the captain his drawings. The captain was impressed. He knew this boy's brilliance was being wasted so he promoted him on the spot to science officer. Aware of the rumblings, he kept the promotion secret. When the ship returned to Maram, the captain was ordered to report to the Nevon, a ship that the king expected to circumnavigate the Earth. Suspecting this would be a historical voyage, he asked Phoal to come along but abandoned the rest of his crew, choosing instead to allow the king to hand-pick one for him. The crew accepted Phoal, as they had no knowledge of his past. They teased him because they needed sport. Phoal sketched every breed of plant and animal they encountered on both land and sea.

After the journey, the captain encouraged Phaol to continue exploring. "Start on Stonland. I'm sure no one has ever recorded the landscape as you have. Keep it up, and soon you will be working for the king."

Phaol traveled around Stonland and added to his pictorial diary all the plants and animals he encountered. One day, he stumbled upon some people digging in a pit.

"What you got there?" He asked, using the local backwoods dialect.

One of the diggers held up a monstrous bone. "Don't know. Huge, isn't it?"

Phaol camped in the woods near the pit for weeks, watching them dig and occasionally touring the site. When the bones were finally extracted and arranged on the ground, he drew a picture of them. He drew intricate pictures of each one. The teeth reminded him of lightning- the symbol of Jupoler- so he christened the creatures Jupolorians. Jupolorians were thought to have been huge, powerful, and violent. Residue of cement was found, and they assumed the Jupolorians were also builders, but this was dismissed because of their tiny hands, which appeared more adept at tearing flesh and less adept at building. Maybe they had overtaken a city and lived in the houses?

Phaol went back to Maram and studied his diaries. He spent years carefully classifying all animals in groups. Due to overwhelming proof, he lumped man and monkeys together, causing great religious controversy. The high priest of Maram, when he found out about Phaol's lies, went to the Laara.

"The scientist, Phaol, says man came from monkeys or, at the very least, is somehow related to them."

"Ridiculous!" The Laara yelled. "Everyone knows Hermax created man through the original nine gods. Tell this Phaol to quit spreading lies!"

"He is published, Laara. We can't stop him."

"Yes, you can!"

The Laara thought for a moment and then ordered the priest to carry out his plan. "Gather up all of his books and pile them around a stake. Burn this heretic, Phaol, while you're at it."

A scientist named Haden spent his working life pondering ways of improving farming techniques in order to free the people employed by the lords. He cut a poor figure. Dark, stout, bald, about five feet tall, he lived a hard life. When his children reached working age, his lord, a rare kind of lord, allowed him to come in from the fields and perform "soft" labor tasks. Haden, finding the work easy, had too much time on his hands. Anxious to give his children a better life than his, he began his work inventing better farming techniques. His seeds improved yields. He invented machines to do the work, which freed the farm workers. The capital cities soon bulged with displaced farmers looking for work.

The Taria family was one such displaced family. Haden's farming improvements, meant to help the poor farm workers, actually increased the lord's profits and hurt the farm workers. Many lords evicted their tenant farmers, who were displaced to the cities.

Tepex and Pinodol Taria thought their lord kind, and after hearing rumors of eviction, they went to plead their case.

Tepex approached the lord, hat in hand, the posture of a beggar. The lord acknowledged him.

"Tepex, why have you left the fields?"

"Yes, Sir. Sorry, Sir. Begging your pardon. The wife and I wonder that is, do you plan on keeping us on?"

He was taken aback. "You have been loyal. Why do you ask?"

"We have heard the machines Haden invented are superior, and landowners are evicting their tenants."

"I do not know this, Haden. I will investigate, but let me assure you, no machine can replace your loyalty."

His lord researched the rumor. He wondered at the sanity of mass evictions but, approved when he saw the profit potential, promptly returned home and dismissed his entire labor force. Tepex's anger boiled. His glare alone called his lord a liar. The lord glared back, shaming Tepex and, unknowingly, saved his own life as Tepex's courage drained.

Tepex was tall, brutish, balding, and beginning to gray at the temples. Still, he could not believe he had been let go. Hadn't he always been loyal? His brown eyes focused on Pinodol. She was still beautiful and, though a half-head shorter, was a perfect contrast to him. Her blonde hair and blue eyes had passed to his children. Her youthful hourglass figure intact, she was beginning to form crow's feet around her eyes. She had supported his every decision but did not really understand farming. His children had a hard time understanding it also and seemed to be excited for the upcoming change. They were unaware their restlessness was genetic; they belonged to the sea.

A pan boiled over, and her quick reach brought him out of his meditation.

"Pinodol, you are so beautiful. Look at us; we're almost too old to start over."

"Relax, Tepex. I hear the cities are booming with opportunity. We will be able to find something. You're smart. We'll survive."

"You have accepted this?"

"I have no choice. Neither do you. We must tell the children it's time to go."

They gathered their possessions, including their fourteen-year-old son Wilix and the tall, blossoming sixteen-year-old Obvia, and headed for Vienusian, Alpania's capital city.

They traveled several days past farms devoid of human life, cluttered with machinery. They wept at the change. Machines harvested, baled, and sorted produce quicker than humans could. When they crested a hill and saw Vienusian, Pinodol wept for joy.

"Here lies opportunity. This city will be our savior."

They followed the road, drowned in a sea of refugees. A sea of people, more than they ever expected to see in their lifetimes, crowded around them, each soul listlessly traveling onward. Tepex attempted to stop people, but everyone was in a daze, transfixed on their destination.

They found several nice places to live, but there were no vacancies, so they continued deeper into the city. The country fresh air was replaced by black soot that curtained the buildings. Eternal night ruled the inner city. People threw slop into the street from their windows. The stench gagged them. Tepex had almost given up when a kind man directed him to a vacant apartment. They had little money. The place was a hovel, but it would have to do.

Tepex announced as they quickly unpacked their meager possessions, "I am going to go find a job."

He found one within a couple of days. He was a delivery runner for a produce stand. The job depended on tips, and he barely made enough to pay the rent. Daily, he inquired, of anyone who would talk to him, about available work. He soon realized there were too many people and not enough work. The highest-paying jobs were in the ironworks and textile mills, but someone had to die for a job to open up there.

Pinodol attempted to cheer him. "Tepex, we must have money. I will find a job."

He was too tired to argue.

Pinodol took Obvia with her. They did not have to go far to find work. The kind man who found them a place to live owned the building. Pinodol saw him in the lobby and approached him.

"Excuse me, kind sir; can you direct me to a place to find employment?"

"Look no farther, Madam. I need two women to help clean my apartments. You two can work for me."

They took the job. For several weeks, they worked, making ends meet. Every day, they came home covered in filth. Too tired to clean up, they slept where they collapsed.

The dirty work did not diminish Obvia's beauty. She worried when she caught the landlord stealing glances at her. Pinodol told her she was imagining things.

Obvia's deepest fears came true one day. Pinodol suggested they clean apartments alone since they were paid on a per apartment basis. She agreed, but as she worked, she kept the door open for safety. In the event of an intruder, she would call out to her mother.

She was busy cleaning a bedroom when she heard a door close and decided to investigate. The landlord stood blocking the door. He jingled coins in his hands.

"Obvia, how would you like to make some honest money?"

Innocently, she asked, "How?"

A crooked, evil grin formed on his face. "Strip off them clothes and get in bed. I'll show you how."

She betrayed no shock or fear. She simply turned, to his great surprise, and walked to the bedroom.

His crotch instantly stiffened. He walked in a stupor toward the bedroom. "Could it really be this easy with this one?" he thought. He had been confident he would get her, but he assumed she would be tougher to wear down.

These thoughts filled his head as he collapsed to his knees. Pain racked his mind. He held his stomach and reached for the broom, amazed that it had hurt him. He could hear her running down the hall.

He slowly regained his composure.

"Bitch, you'll be back. All you whores come back. I'm reality!"

The next day, Obvia and Pinodol worked together. The landlord, in obvious pain, said nothing and avoided them. He knew in his heart she would come to him for money. He could wait.

Wilix saw immediately that this life was worse than working for the lord. He went to Tepex and offered to walk him to work.

"Dad, this life you have chosen for us is wrong. We live like pigs. I can't stand it."

Tepex lowered his head in disgrace. If his own son noticed, what of others?

"What can we do?"

"I have noticed there are plenty of positions available in the army and navy. Many young men are joining to escape this festering city."

Tepex agreed that this was probably best. He knew each of them would be better off alone. Wilix tried to join both the army and the navy. He was refused by both.

Depressed over his failure, he dragged himself back to the apartment. As tired as he was, Tepex thought it was his duty to console his son.

"They wouldn't take you?"

Wilix stifled his anger.

"No, they said I was too small, wasn't from a proper family, and had no education."

Tepex was genuinely concerned. "What will you do? Would you like me to put in a good word with my boss?"

"No. I'll think of something. I'll make so much money that I will buy my way in as an officer. Then I'll punish those who attempted to hold me back."

"But how, Son? This city is full of poor people, people with almost no chance to improve themselves. There is no hope."

"I will walk the streets. I'll listen and learn. There must be an opportunity out there somewhere."

True to his word, he walked the streets looking for honest wages. He found nothing but intolerable, oppressive work. He slid into the role of loafer, another lost face in a sea of lost, miserable faces. He was forever aware of his surroundings. One day, he witnessed a theft. Another loafer stole a coin purse and ran. The incident happened so suddenly and professionally that the victim did not notice his coin purse was gone. Wilix followed the thief with his eyes, judged where he might be going, and met him there.

When he arrived, the thief was casually counting his newfound wealth. Wilix startled him.

"I saw you take that purse."

The thief growled. "Go away, urchin, it's mine. I stole it fair."

Wilix felt a small surge of fear, then realized he should not because he had no intention of fighting this stranger.

"I don't want it. I want to ask you how you became so brave. Isn't crime punished severely in this city?"

The thief settled back against the wall, comfortable now that he realized Wilix was no threat, possibly a new colleague.

"Hunger. That's what creates a thief. And yes, they will harshly punish you if you're caught. I work alone. It's easier to stay undetected that way."

"This time, you stole coins. How do you get money if you steal valuables?"

"There are a few back alley dealers. If you're interested, I'll show you around," the thief offered.

Wilix indicated he was, and the thief gave him the grand tour. That day, he began his short-lived career as a thief. His first attempts were coached by his new friend, who quickly abandoned him when he felt Wilix understood the game.

Several months passed. Wilix provided well for the family, but not too well, for he was saving his money. Tepex suspected his son was a thief, but his full stomach forced silence.

Wilix went to the bank one day to withdraw money. It was time to bribe the military and become a man of rank. He carefully hid his money and exited through the rear door, thieving instincts making him paranoid. Determined to make it to the military headquarters without being accosted, he walked the streets overconfident. Thieving, unbeknownst to him, was habitual; the false belief that no one would ever catch him ruled his subconscious. He walked by a produce stand and politely helped himself to an apple. As he took the first bite, the vendor yelled, "Stop! Thief!"

His reflexes took over, and his feet ran before he could offer to pay. He had no plan of escape, a perilous situation to find oneself in if one is a professional thief. He ran toward the harbor, hoping to lose his pursuers in the warehouses.

Running for his life and finding no visible shelter in the warehouses, he jumped onto a ship and, rolled into a wooden leg; looked up into a distinguished man's face. The man he landed under was tall and strong. His dark green eyes and fiery red hair jutted out from under his captain's hat, plume an albatross feather. The man was laughing a bellowing laugh, showing his fierce teeth. Wilix was reminded of a wolverine he had once seen and feared violence would soon be upon him. Instead, when he finished laughing, he grabbed Wilix by his shirtfront.

"Thief, this is your lucky day. You're hired."

He and the rest of his crew broke out into hysterical laughter. And that is how Wilix became a pirate serving under Captain Wolv, the Wolverine.

Tepex was finishing a delivery on the docks when Wilix flew by. When he saw him jump onto Wolv's ship, he knew he had lost his son. When he returned home, he told the family. Tepex and Pinodol were brokenhearted. Obvia tried to cheer them up.

"At least he has a chance for some kind of a life."

The moment Wolv's pirates unlashed the ship, Wilix began his adventure at sea. Captain Wolv personally escorted him on a tour of the ship. He evaluated Wilix as they walked and decided he should begin his career as a galley boy. Wilix accepted his job obediently, relieved to be free of the pestilent city.

He performed his duties exceptionally well. Captain Wolv promoted him. He took the boy's training upon himself. He taught him to use swords, guns, cannon, and deceitful tactics. Soon, Wilix joined the other mates, swabbing decks and manning the crow's nest.

When Wolv sensed merchant ships were scarce, he conducted land raids. Isolated villages by the sea were prime targets. During one of these raids, Wilix had his first sexual experience. Women were herded onto the ship like so many cattle and systematically raped. Wilix was forced to participate or be killed. He did so willingly; his hatred for the cities was intense. He enjoyed inflicting pain on these villagers.

News of Wolv's escapades reached the Taria family in Vienusian. Tepex and Pinodol collapsed. They were severely overworked. The added pressure of a son gone bad killed them. Obvia, depressed, turned to her landlord for help. He called the death wagon, as was his civic duty. Toward Obvia, he was not so kind.

"You'll have to move out of here. With your parents gone, you haven't the money to stay."

"Where will I go?"

"There is a fine house I run. It's for single women only."

"A whorehouse, I suspect."

"Yes, my love and I will be your pimp. You can be hired only after I have a taste," he grinned, showing her his rotten teeth.

"I'd rather take my chances on the street."

"Your choice, but you'll be back."

She left the apartment behind, thoroughly disgusted that her life had come to this. She found odd jobs but had to sleep in alleys.

As the weeks passed, her situation deteriorated to the point of desperation.

Hope sprang forth in the form of Wilix. Unsure of her vision, she blinked hard.

"Wilix!"

He turned to see the street urchin she had become. "What's happened to you?"

"Mom and Dad died, and I was thrown out. You are a pirate. Do you still have the money you were going to use to join the military?"

"No, sister. Captain Wolv allows no possessions on his ship. He took my money the first day. He said it was payment for my passage."

"Can you ask him to return it? Look at me. I'm filthy and homeless."

Wilix, for the first time during this reunion, truly examined her. Despite his feelings, he knew what he had to say.

"He would sooner kill me."

She was desperate.

"May I serve aboard your ship?"

"He allows no women. I'm sorry, sister. If I were you, I'd go to the Army or Navy and volunteer to be a nurse. I have to get back. Good luck."

He left her to her tragedy. She took his advice and applied to be a nurse but was rudely turned away by the head nurse, who informed her women of her ilk were not welcome in the service. She wept freely.

She was backed into a corner and knew it; she wandered the streets in an aimless depression. When she found herself back in front of her old apartment building, she involuntarily walked in, found the landlord's apartment, let herself in, removed her clothes, lay on the bed, and waited. When he came home, he was confronted by the shock of his life. This naked woman he had once propositioned begged, attempting to hide her nervousness.

"Careful, I'm a virgin."

Careful, he was not. Clumsy and hurtful he was. However, forgetting her moment of pain, she concentrated instead on the fact that two minutes later, he was done. Giggling to herself, she asked, "When do I go to work for you?"

"Right away. Get dressed, and I'll take you to your new home. We really must get you cleaned up and powdered like a proper whore."

Obvia was an instant success. The men who frequented the whorehouse waited in line for her services, excellent as they were rumored to be. Long lines formed on the weekends. Her average customer base was five a day, ten on weekend days. Her success pleased her pimp but also created somewhat of a dilemma; if the other girls could not work, profits were actually going to decline.

Her reputation spread throughout all quarters of the city. One client, an admiral, secured her for an entire weekend. The weekend ended too soon.

"Would you like to end this charade? I have a spot for you as ship's whore on my flagship."

"I thought women weren't allowed on ships?"

"For you, my dear, an exception can be made."

For a modest fee, he purchased her from her landlord. The landlord wanted more, but the admiral assured him that if he did not accept the deal being offered, his establishment might be raided. He knew he was losing the best whore he had ever known, but no one whore was worth a raid.

She acclimated to sea life quickly. Every day, she slept with the admiral. She slept with seamen only as a reward. She was an incentive for better work.

She learned that the admiral's main mission was to stop piracy. After a particularly intense night of lovemaking, she informed him that her brother had been forced to serve Wolv and asked if he could attempt to save him. The admiral lost in the afterglow, agreed.

Wolv was the most notorious pirate on the high seas. Laarisia insisted that pirates, especially Wolv, be stopped. Stonland and Alpania were allied for this purpose, but the admiral wanted to catch Wolv first to prove Alpania's superiority at sea. The information from Obvia was interesting, but could it be used?

Typically, the Alpanian and Stonland navies showed up after the pirates raided. The admiral interrogated victims tirelessly and wove a story together that accused Wilix of many atrocities. He did not appear to be the innocent Obvia protested he was. Wilix was being groomed to take over when Wolv perished. The facts were plain. He knew in his heart he could never keep his promise to Obvia.

Wolv, overconfident, began to strike in a pattern. The admiral, in advance of Wolv, planted information at his next suspected target, a merchant ship bursting with gold bound for Andenan from Laarisia. His overloaded flagship sat low in the water. All naval markings were taken away, and merchant flags were hung.

Wolv took the bait, approached the "merchant" quickly, fired a shot over the bow, and demanded surrender. They complied, slowly raising their white flag. Wolv and Wilix climbed into a longboat and rowed across. From the sea, they demanded the ship drop sails and prepare to be boarded. When the "merchant" complied, they rowed back. Once aboard their own ship, they brought her alongside the "merchant" and lashed the ships together.

The "merchantmen" feigned fright as the pirates poured on board. Unarmed and placid, the pirates let them be. At the precise moment, the admiral signaled his men to cut the ropes. As they did, the ship's sides opened up, and twenty-five propellers pummeled Wolv's ship. It sank in seconds.

Unarmed "merchants" secured weapons they had stowed. The pirates, knowing they were beaten, dropped to their knees and asked for mercy like the cowards the admiral knew they were.

Obvia watched the scene from the safety of the admiral's cabin. Before her eyes, she saw that every pirate, including Wilix, was about to be hung. She lunged at the door only to find the admiral had locked her in, she assumed, for her safety. She watched helplessly as Wilix fought against the rope, twitched, and, finally, stilled.

She confronted the admiral.

"Your brother was Wolv's assistant. You are a whore. I respect neither. I am not obligated by passionate promises."

She reached to slap him. He caught her hand.

"Mind your manners, lass, or you may find yourself a gift from me to the crew. I'm sure the rape wouldn't last very long. These men are rough; you'd be dead within the month."

They caught Wolv on the western ocean, terrorizing the Andenan and Nepusian islands. The admiral once again camouflaged his ship and set slow sail for Stonland, hoping to mop up more pirates, but word spread fast. Without a leader, the pirates faded into obscurity. Never again would a leader such as Wolv rise. The remaining pirates would be captured, surrender, or become land lovers hiding in the hills scattered across the world.

Obvia stewed privately for six months. She continued her role of ship's whore. She would give the admiral no excuse to punish her, which was a real possibility since he had raged on more than one occasion:

"You are the sister of a criminal. I should've killed you along with him, but frankly, the men would rebel; they need their motivation."

When they landed at the port of Maram, he disembarked to inform both the king and the high priest that Wolv was dead. Obvia asked to come along to do some shopping. He agreed because she was beautiful, and he wanted to make other seamen jealous. He left her in a dress shop and never saw her again.

She left the backway and ran down the alley deep into the center of Maram. When the admiral returned and discovered her treachery, he conducted a half-hearted search. Failing to locate her, he visited another whorehouse, found one to his liking, and "purchased" her using the same threats he had used to "purchase" Obvia. He took his new whore back to the ship and was on his way.

Obvia hid in the alleys for a week, surviving on whatever she could find or steal. She finally decided it was safe to leave. Her last night in the alleys she was bitten on her ankle by a rat. Painfully, she hobbled to a whorehouse and requested work. She was very pale, obviously sick. The madam took her in; as a patient, not a whore. Twenty-four hours later, she died. One week later, the entire enterprise was dead, as each whore had come in contact with her. The disease was highly infectious, and each client that week was equally infected. Whole families perished. Sailors infected destroyed whole crews.

Overcrowded, the capital cities bred disease quickly. Soon, it was in all the kingdoms. One-quarter of humanity died before it was stopped.

Medical science greatly advanced because of the disease. The dead were examined. Warehouses were piled with bodies as too many died to be buried efficiently. Several of the warehouses were burned. The high priest of Alpania ordered his surgeons to rescue a few dead bodies before another warehouse could be burned. They stored the stolen bodies in an empty, cold storage food cellar.

The high priest decided against Hermax and allowed secret experiments on the bodies. Each was systematically stripped of flesh. Muscles, bones, and organs were studied and named. Four bodies into the experiment, the disease source remained mysterious, but its effects were numerous and catalogued.

A surgeon familiar with Celes' work decided to use an eye tube to examine the bodies. He saw a blurred vision of the components of the blood. He decided to add extra power to the tube by fitting an extra glass in front of his eye. What he found amazed him. Cells he never imagined existed and riding piggyback on them, a parasite he was sure came from rats, for a multitude of dead rats had appeared at the same time humans began dying. He studied dead rats and found the parasite.

The findings were reported to the high priest. He knew that killing all the rats would be impossible, but relocating them was an option. Single-handedly, he initiated a garbage pickup service and dumped the refuse well away from the city. The trick worked as the rats followed the refuse like a magnet. Diseased people were quarantined. The disease ran its course. Unable to find a host, it faded away.

The high priest convinced his surgeons were brilliant and allowed them to experiment on live people. Doctors discovered more about anatomy and began to perform preventative operations. Celes' journals on glasswork allowed doctors to isolate germs using his tube theories. People no longer died of minor wounds, and medicines were discovered that ended and even prevented symptoms. People began to put glass in front of their eyes to correct weakened vision.

The kingdoms of Nepusia, Andenan, Stonland, and Alpania each commissioned explorers to investigate the seas and discover new lands. As pirates were no longer a threat, exploration, at first, was peaceful. Every country shared goods and services designed for exploration. The problem arose not when countries claimed ocean territories but when they defended them from trespassers. Pitched battles were fought over perceived ocean territories. To avert another costly and destructive war, the Laara called the four kings to Laarisia.

The Laara was a sensible, compromising man. He appeared, as he should, domineering in his robes. He laid the law down to the kings.

"I will not have another destructive war. Wasn't the plague enough? No, we will avert war right here and now. I have a map of Earth here and I am going to split Galacia based on your kingdom's size.

"Andenan, you have three provinces in the west. I grant you the entire southern portion of Galacia. Stonland and Alpania, since you were once connected by marriage, you get the entire northern Galacian Ocean, except the one thousand-mile diameter that surrounds Nepusia, which I am obviously giving to Nepusia. You will fish, explore, and maintain these areas. Any treasure or land found in your regions will belong to you. I will accept no more fighting over territories. I order Stonland to give Uryxia back to Alpania as a peace gesture. Finally, Laarisian and Hermatian ships will be granted free access to all of Galacia! Are we agreed?"

It was not a question; it was an order. They all agreed. The territory allegations were too generous to ignore.

Nepusia's territory the others deemed small, but the king was thrilled. It would help secure his borders, and he was granted what he knew to be the finest fishing waters in the world. Trade in seafood would enrich his land and increase his power and standing in the world.

In 3959, farming machines and ships that had run on steam for three hundred years were improved. The Jupolorian dig in Stonland was long ago abandoned. Now, years later, new workers were assigned by the museum to dig deeper in an effort to find older bones. The scientific community felt that understanding their past would ease their future. The accepted belief was that the Earth held many surprises. None were more surprising than the black, thick substance that oozed out and filled the pit they were working in. Testing a sample brought to the surface, they quickly determined it was flammable. Stonland discovered the black substance ran machines faster and more efficiently than steam could. Every vehicle was reequipped with "black" engines.

Miniature "black" engines were affixed to horse buggies. These horseless vehicles retained the name buggies but soon picked up the nickname "bugs." Horse roads quickly became "black" roads, named after the engine leaks that soon covered them. Celes' drawings showed a man in flight. Scientists invented more powerful engines and affixed them to a winged "bug," and Celes' dream of one-man flight became a reality. Suddenly, Mankind was moving faster than ever before. Mass production was introduced, and rough airports were developed.

Stonland produced all of the known "black" liquid. No one protested because King Jopol sold it cheaply. Eventually, all engines ran on the liquid. Once everyone became dependent, prices became outrageous. Nepusia, Andenan, and Alpania's kings met secretly.

The tallest of the three was King Syal of Nepusia. He retained the blue eyes of Nepusia's reigning family but dismissed the surname Nepusia as he felt it confused foreigners now that Nepusia was a world power. Citizens dismissed his choice as a rash decision of youth, yet he appeared older because of a facial scar. Won in a youthful swordfight, his black beard would not grow there. The flaw made him appear angered, although, normally, he was serene. When he became truly angered, he turned domineering and temperamental. Enraged, he yelled, "These prices are outrageous!"

"I agree. Something must be done!"

King Sikm of Andenan, slightly taller than King Rasu, had black hair and brown eyes. His normal attitude on any issue was to remain calm. However, when King Syal's fist pounded the table, he was caught up in the moment and voiced his concerns loudly.

King Rasu of Alpania hosted the meeting. He was short and fat, yet his muscle tone could still be discerned. His intelligent brown eyes, his balding brown hair, his pig nose, and big ears made him look less the king and more the jester, yet he was an excellent schemer. He called these other two to Alpania because he wanted leverage. If he could solve their mutual problem, he would own them. King Rasu let the others vent. When they were finished, he paused to create suspense.

"Relax, gentlemen, something will be done. As I see the situation, we, as independent countries, need to explore our own lands to try to find more liquid sources. I have already sent spies to Stonland to research how the 'black' is discovered and developed. We are certain that, since it originates in the Earth, it must have geological signs that point to it. Our solution is to depend on King Jopol's greed.

"I know King Jopol well. His greed will be his downfall. Buy the liquid, pay the price. Don't complain. I have my best scientists building faster ships, bugs, and flying machines. Buy the liquid in bulk. When we have superior equipment, we will attack Stonland and secure the liquid. King Jopol will grovel at our feet."

They agreed to be patient and to meet again when King Rasu felt the time was right.

Within two years, Stonland found itself involved in another war. King Jopol was ready. The money he had made from the "black" sales had resulted in funding for and the development of rocket and atomic technology. Stonland's superior firepower quickly won the war.

He launched his rockets at every capital city of his enemies. In naval combat, he fired torpedoes and missiles at the enemy from a range they could not defend and effectively destroyed every naval vessel he contacted. Nepusia's capital had the misfortune of being located near a dormant volcano. When Jopol's rockets struck the inner cone, a chain reaction was set in motion. A sea of lava and ash burst forth. The people of the city fled. Those who fled by boat into the harbor were boiled alive as the lava turned the harbor into a cauldron. Wooden ships burned quickly, and their passengers perished.

Simultaneously, the kings surrendered their forces to Stonland. King Jopol had the other three kings brought before him. Even the Laara was present at Linxiton palace.

King Jopol was tall, blonde, blue-eyed, and angry as hell. He had an enormous upper body, and through his clothing, his guests could see it twitching. His normally jolly face and pleasant disposition were gone.

"What happened?! I feel I was very generous to each of you with the 'black.' You had to have it all, I guess. Well, now you have nothing! You will each be provinces in my new world government. Stonland will dictate policy. Stonland will own Galacia. Laarisia no longer dictates policy. As a concession to Laarisia for not condoning this war, I leave her religious rule over herself and Hermatia. Any province that disobeys me will automatically be destroyed."

What began as a dictatorship became a republic overseen by a world council. There were five senators and seven representatives, and of course, the king of Stonland. Representatives represented the wishes of Marsia, Vienus, Ciaxian, Uryxia, Sateland, Kashim, and Nepetan. Senators represented the whole of Nepusia, Andenan, and Alpania, with senators from Laarisia and Hermatia to lend a moral balance. The senators of Alpania and Andenan spoke and voted for their seven representatives. The king could overturn a vote of the senators. Senators and representatives could overturn the king with a unanimous vote of twelve.

Posted in all government offices, all schools, and many homes was a list of the rules that governed the world:

KNOW ALL CITIZENS:

1. Stonland is the center of the world.
2. Stonland owns Galacia:

    a. all trade will be taxed to support the World Council.

3. The World Council is your buffer against a dictatorial government.
4. The World Council weighs all recommendations of the king.
5. The world council consists of:

    a. seven representatives, one each voted into office from Marsia, Vienus, Ciaxian, Sateland, Kashim, Nepusian and Nepetan, and

b. five senators, one each voted into office from Laarisia, Hermatia, Nepusia, Alpania, and Andenan

    1. The senators will vote on the will of their representatives, who shall not have a vote on issues unless a unanimous vote is needed to overturn a decision of the king. This would be the case if the king vetoed a vote of the senators.

6. Senators from Laarisia and Hermatia have no representatives to work with. They may, however, consult the Laara on any issue. They will add integrity and morality to the council.
7. All citizens of the world will obey all rules and laws set forth by the council. They are provided for the good of all. Violators of the law will be fined, imprisoned, enslaved, or executed, depending on the severity of the crime.

This was the strong republic the chosen one was born into in 4124.

CHAPTER 13

THE CHOSEN ONE

4124 A.D.- 4196 A.D.

The Gods watched the atomic war in complete disgust. It seemed man would plunge himself head first into oblivion, and there was nothing they could do. They went about their business daily, hoping beyond hope that somewhere, a human would come to his senses. One day, Nepeta and Vienusia completed their yearly analysis of the sun. Shocked, they called a meeting of the gods.

"Everyone, almost 25,000 years ago, our people came here," Nepeta began. "They predicted the sun would change and gave themselves what they called 'a great year' to colonize Earth. As you may remember from our training, a great year is just over 25,000 Earth years."

Jupoler, forever impatient, asked, "What is the point, Nepeta?"

Vienusia stood and said, "The point is: We have been studying the sun since we arrived, and colonization is now out of the question."

"Why?" Arop asked.

"Because the changes our people predicted, however slight, will serve to eradicate all life on Earth."

A stunned silence followed Vienusia's cold prediction.

Planex broke the silence, "Our poor children. What will they think, that their own God smote them?"

Uryxs, naturally depressed, said, "Then we have failed."

"No! I refuse to believe that." Jupoler cried. "How long until this disaster hits?"

"We think less than one hundred years."

"Everyone, forget your assignments. We must watch Earth closely. Our new mission is our old mission, to find a pair of humans who have the strength to succeed with us in space."

The short atomic war occurred in 3964. King Jopol alone dictated policy for ten years; then, in 3974, he allowed the republic to form. The World Republic was the most secure government in recorded history. One hundred fifty years later time had proven it the best. Into this republic, a child named Taval-pan was born in 4124. His name meant son of Taval. Pan added to a boy's name and Pul added to a girl's name had become a very popular name form in the last fifty years.

He was born into the representative's family from Nepetan, historically a state within the grand province of Andenan. When the atomic war ended, Nepetan's royal family formally surrendered to King Jopol. In all his new provinces, King Jopol disbanded royal authority; however, he did not abuse them. He knew these royal families held the secrets of the land, and, therefore, he tapped them for information. Absolute rule was tempered by the advice he sought from the ex-royals. A delegation from Andenan, which included Taval-pan's great-great-grandfather, the dethroned king, counseled and eventually convinced Jopol that a representative form of government would work in his favor. Hesitant at first, he gave the newly formed Senate minor duties. Aware of the test, they performed admirably and became a fair governing body the world could depend upon.

The representatives worked in the Senate house. The provinces they represented honored them, referring to them as senators. Nepetan's senatorial, ex-royal family was elevated by the citizens of the island. They were treated as if they were still royalty. The faith of the people reverberated through the Senate chamber because the representative, his comfort provided, was open to policy suggestions given by those who provided it.

Taval-pan lived in the senatorial mansion of Nepetan through his fifth year. He grew up playing and learning on the balcony of his bedroom at the rear of the old castle. His home rested two-thirds of the way up the side of the highest mountain in Nepetan. It overlooked the capital city, the commerce center of the island. Scars pocked the neighboring mountains. Though not nearly as wealthy in natural resources as Kashim, Nepetan supported a flourishing gold, silver, and copper mining industry. Raw iron ore was shipped worldwide. Most metal could be traced back to Nepetan. He watched loggers slowly deplete the forest. On the plains and foothills, he observed grains, rice, beans, and potatoes, as well as domestic livestock, flourish. He gained great respect for his home through his mother's teaching and longed to learn about the rest of the world.

His mother provided this education while his father exercised his senatorial duties in Stonland nine months of the year. His father, the representative Taval, worshipped him. During his off time, they were constant companions. He took Taval-pan with him around the island as he counseled with leading citizens. By the time he was five, he was acclimated to people and comfortable around strangers. When Taval spotted this quality, he knew it was time.

Returning to the mansion after a fishing trip, Taval broached the subject.

"Taval-pan, it is time for you to join your contemporaries in boarding school."

"What's that, Daddy?"

"It's a place you go to live and learn. Every child goes to school. This one is the best."

"Is it far away?" Taval-pan asked, worried.

"Yes, Son, it's in Andenan."

Taval-pan used to his father's travels, accepted that.

"What kind of kids will I meet?"

"You'll meet all kinds. High quality, really. The school is reserved for senatorial offspring and the wealthy."

"Will I learn about the whole world?"

"Yes."

"You say it's in Andenan? Will you or Mommy be there?"

"No, Son. You must go alone. Don't worry. School is arranged on the same schedule as the senatorial sessions. You and I will see each other as much as we do now."

Taval-pan prepared for the challenge. His mom taught him basics that summer, giving him a foothold in the educational process. As the summer came to a close, he packed his belongings. On the final day of summer, his parents escorted him to the harbor.

Taval-pan boarded a ship bound for Andenan and Taval, a ship bound for Stonland. As women had throughout time, Taval-pan's mom waved and cried as the two ships pulled away. Taval-pan barely registered his mother's presence as he and Taval stood at their railings, staring at each other. When it was clear Taval's ship would turn east, Taval bowed to his son. Taval-pan yelled, but the ocean noise made his message barely audible to Taval.

"Father, I love you!"

Taval-pan grew apprehensive when he realized he was alone. He did not fear meeting new people. His fear was Andenan, the power center of his island world. Something that big scared him to death. Would he adjust? Would he fit in? Would the other kids like him? Would he get lost?

These thoughts dominated his journey until, finally, Andenan appeared on the horizon. He ran to the rail to watch it approach. The closer it came, the calmer he became. Andenan was just a mountainous island, very similar in design to Nepetan. What he thought might be the senator's home sat on the mountain overlooking the harbor.

The ship maneuvered through the harbor, eventually docking near customs. Taval-pan went to his cabin, secured his luggage, and joined the slow-flowing disembarking herd. When he reached the dock, he found, to his surprise, a lady holding a sign that said Taval-pan.

"I am Taval-pan."

She peered down at him.

"You see those children, go sit with them. I'll be along in a moment."

He walked off toward the children, smiling. None were rich kids he had wondered about. These were all children of the representatives of each island. The leader of the group seemed to be the oldest boy from Andenan. He and his siblings came along to make everyone welcome.

Then, Taval-pan asked what they were waiting for.

"The children of Kashim are just arriving. We must go as a group to the school."

Taval-pan made small talk and waited politely. He noticed the lady with the sign coming toward them. Behind her lagged a boy, and follow-ing him was-. Taval-pan gasped. The girl following was the most beauti-ful he had ever seen. He rushed up to meet these children of Kashim. He quickly acknowledged the boy and then ran to the girl.

"Hello, I am Taval-pan, sole heir of the representative of Nepetan."

Shyly, she said, "I am Miska of Kashim, daughter of the representative of Kashim."

These two, who would not know real love for many years, somehow instinctively knew that they were destined to be together. Taval-pan took her hand, which she shyly gave, and led her to the waiting children. After the introductions, the chaperone led them to their new home. A ranch house in the country, it was a serene, ideal setting for a boarding school.

Realizing they had a week until school started, Taval-pan and his two male companions fashioned poles and found a stream to fish. The day half gone, they decided to explore. In the heat of the day, they found the source of the stream, a pond nestled amongst a meadow and a few large trees. They decided to swim nude, not realizing the girls had followed them. Taval-pan experienced his first embarrassing moment when the girls, as girls will, took their clothes and exposed themselves to the boys. The boys bravely chased the girls and recovered their clothes. The situation, which should have angered the boys, somehow brought them closer to the girls. They had "bared all" and, henceforth, were a tight-knit clique.

As school progressed each year, this clique acknowledged others as a courtesy. They, like their parents, became natural leaders of the school.

They strutted around campus. Required to wear togas and dresses embroidered with the hermatic pick, each leader sewed their island flag onto their clothing to set them apart.

Taval-pan's love for Miska grew with each passing day.

He was highly inquisitive and a fast learner. He quickly arrived and stayed at the top of his class throughout his career. The sons and daughters of Andenan and Kashim, his closest friends, were a tight social unit. They realized that if they could work together now they would have a smooth transition working together as adults.

Taval-pan was tall for his age. He had blonde hair and blue eyes and especially liked Miska who reminded him of pictures he had seen of Vienusia. He thought it silly that he should relate her to a mythical goddess; after all, their school uniform promoted Hermax rather than the gods of legend. She liked Taval-pan's muscular body and brilliant wit. Once she became dedicated to him, she stayed dedicated to him, as was the nature of Kashim's women, for the rest of her life. They learned together the struggles of mankind throughout the centuries. They were taught peace. Their daily chant was: WAR IS SENSELESS! UNITED IS THE WAY! EVERYONE PROSPERS! EVERYONE GAINS!

Every free moment found them together. Each year, when they went home for three months, they wept and promised to write letters often.

Taval and Taval-pan still toured the island, but Taval knew his son was detached. He did not say anything until his seventeenth year.

"Son, each year, you seem more detached. Have you decided where you are going to go to university?"

Taval-pan came alive.

"Oh yes. The University of Stonland. They have the finest history department. I intend on becoming a historian." Then he sulked again. "But what of Miska?"

"The girl from Kashim? Simple. Take her with you."

"Impossible, Father. She is loyal to Kashim. I don't believe she'll ever leave it."

"Nonsense, if she loves you, she will go."

His last year at school was magical. Miska was dedicated to him. One weekend afternoon, on a picnic at the isolated pond they had discovered as kids, she bared herself to him, and they made love in the tall grass. They were never embarrassed by the act and took precautions; they made love as often as they could, using the first time as justification.

When the semester ended and graduation was over, the true test of their love began.

Miska innocently broached the subject. "Are you going to marry me, Taval-pan?"

"Not yet. First, I must graduate from the University of Stonland. Then we can be married."

A worried look crossed her face.

"Will I not see you for four years?"

"No. Miska, you don't understand. I want you to come with me."

"Impossible, Taval-pan. I'll not leave Kashim, especially if I'm not married. I will wait for you. I'll write you all the time."

"It won't be the same. Please come with me?"

"No!"

She ran home, warm tears flowing.

Taval-pan and Miska, for the first time, spent their summer together vacationing first in Kashim, then in Nepetan. When the summer came to a close, Miska helped him pack and escorted him to the harbor. There was a long kiss, and the promise to write renewed.

He boarded and, repeating his actions as he had at five, stood at the railing as the ship departed. He did not release his grasp until he lost sight of Miska. Nepetan was still in view as he left to find his cabin.

Miska, sobbing, boarded her ship for Kashim. She arrived home and began the long process of learning to run the household from her mother. She spent her days longing for Taval-pan's letters. She wrote him before his letters arrived. His letters were frequent the first year, then tapered off, then stopped altogether. She was not worried, though. The tone of his final letter told her he was immersed in his studies. Like any good woman of Kashim, she waited.

Stonland amazed Taval-pan. The modern city of Maram made Andenan appear provincial. It made Kashim and Nepetan look like backwater countries. He found the university, settled in, and immediately began his studies.

Studying hard to become a historian, his first major class was the History of Science, concentrating on ship-building theories as they related to man's expanded ability to control his world. The first boats had allowed little travel between islands; mostly they were restricted to encircling their own islands. As the wind and water current mysteries were solved, ships grew bigger, and captains became more adventurous. In this period, the Alpanian islands were discovered.

Laarisia's war against rebelling Alpania forced greater innovations in shipbuilding. A new class of cargo ship, the Slaver, was unveiled. Many slaves were brought to Laarisia. Slavery segued his studies into construction theory, which was just that, theory, for no one could isolate how the monuments were built.

Little was known about the slave revolt and subsequent founding of Hermatia. That a slave revolt occurred, there was no doubt. Records were "lost" to avoid embarrassment. The Laarisians did not want future generations to know how completely they had failed.

The periods known as Laarisian Imperial and Holy Laarisian Imperial were, scientifically, still dominated by ship-building advancements. This occurred because, in this water world, transportation was the key to communication. Feudalism, a new form of slavery, kept great minds restricted. Only a free mind is inspired to invent; therefore, military officers were prone to invent.

History of science class took an exciting turn at the end of the dark ages. Celes' glasswork and theories propelled man into a scientific age. Feudal lords began to search out the "minds" that existed on their lands. One lord, tired of the many hours of writing records that consumed him, commissioned one of his tenants, a blacksmith, to develop an easier writing method. Thus, moveable type was invented. This revolutionized communication. Not only could correspondences be sent with unalterable messages, but also the common man could now easily be educated.

The section on animal anatomy and classification was possible because of Phaol's work on the Nevon. The monstrosity called Jupolorians that they studied at the Museum of Maram fascinated Taval-pan. That such creatures could ever exist on such limited amounts of land astonished him. He nor his professors would ever realize the earth was not always made up of islands. They visited the spot where Phaol was burned. The world now accepted evolution, and the professor wanted to instill in his students what a rash decision it was to murder Phaol for his beliefs.

"A man's beliefs, whether you agree or not, are sacred in our society. Burning this poor man was a symbol of the dark times, times. Hopefully, humanity will never revive."

The section covering Noplod's plays was meant to be entertaining, an easy way to familiarize students with history. Taval-pan found this to be his hardest class to understand because it was taught in the ancient language of kings Noplod's era used. The class counted as a foreign language. This was the only way to teach a foreign language, as everyone on earth spoke the same language. It was meant to challenge the students, as it was truly a dead language. Taval-pan knew mastering this class was important, though, because one never knew what one might uncover in the field as a historian. He buckled down and became expert enough that he dreamed of Noplod's plays in his sleep.

Haden's inventions and the disease/displacement they created were the subject of his next session. They were taught two major points. One, inventions usually freed up mankind and allowed him to advance. Two, for any action, there must be an equal reaction. Farming techniques displaced the farmers to the cities and factories. Factories produced while destroying the people they depended on to work. When diseases ran rampant, medical science beat them, opening the door for greater diseases. Medical science was just that, science. Like any other field, progress was limited by new, regressive situations that had to be solved lest a newer, more powerful plague be produced. The anatomy and physiology of the human body intrigued him, and he knew instinctively that he had better memorize it. He was certain he would find ancient bones that he must classify in ancient villages.

A mechanical science section dealt with the discovery of the black. The magical black liquid allowed society to advance so rapidly that it soon outgrew itself. Bugs, planes, black-based machines, and ships dominated the land and sea. The atomic war was now known to be a blessing in disguise because, although much damage was done and many lives were lost, those left realized how precious the earth was and slowed production so as not to scar it any worse.

His last section dealt with religious history. Covered were ROYALTY, which justified itself through religious, genealogical lines, LAARISIA AND HERMATIA: the homes of true religion, and RELIGIOUS MYTH: the basis for religious philosophy.

Royalty and religion were a proven source of comfort to the common man. A ruler was divinely installed; that divinity was the glue that kept the commoners loyal, leverage intended to keep each generation in chains. Whether royalty was truly divine or not was beside the point. What the people chose to believe equaled how deeply they could be deceived.

Everyone in the school was a Hermatic, so Laarisia and Hermatia's contribution to the world of religion was skimmed over. Taval-pan was not very concerned with this lack of coverage. He assumed one day, like any true Hermatic, he would make a pilgrimage to Laarisia or Hermatia. He might even catch a glimpse of the Laara.

Religious mythology was a comical section. The students were awed that mankind could have ever taken these nine gods seriously.

The professor erased any lagging confusion.

"You must think. Forty-five hundred years ago, Hermax was not known; he had not chosen to present himself. Little was known. Lightning must have frightened primitive man, unpredictable floods, and babies being born. 'Why are these strange things happening?' He cried to the heavens. Hermax, the creator, heard his plea and sent his nine personal messengers to help. These nine "gods" assumed the characteristics of natural phenomena, controlled them, and calmed man. Of course, he revered them. They had saved him. You students think the mythical gods are comical when, after all, they are and were necessary. Without them as a base to build upon, Hermax could never have risen."

Taval-pan was so impressed by this speech that he chose and titled his graduate thesis Mythology vs. True Religion. He argued, as the professor had, that the mythological gods were necessary in their day and for the contribution of Hermax's religion. They were mankind's link, but Hermax was the one true god. Taval-pan's evidence proved this inconclusively. Anyone who tried to refute it was branded a fool. His thesis found its way to the Senate. Many of the members took Taval to one side. Lucrative offers were made.

After graduating, he was summoned to his father's office. A secretary ushered him in. Taval sat behind his desk, engrossed in a report. He looked up to find Taval-pan standing at attention.

"Sit down, Son. We need to talk."

Taval-pan obeyed.

"First, I want to congratulate you on your graduation. I have been reading your thesis. It is a masterful piece of work. Actually, it's the real reason I asked you here. Every one of the senators and representatives read it. We showed it to the king and he has expressed a desire for you to work for him."

"In what capacity?"

"He wishes to employ a world historian. The job entitles you to free worldwide passage. The king is interested in securing records of both past and present events. Once compiled, this history will serve as the official version our children will learn. The king feels understanding the past is the key to the kingdom's success."

Taval-pan was confused. "Why is he offering the job to me?"

"He enjoyed your thesis. Your research was impeccable, which is the quality he hopes to see in this job. Also, I convinced him this job would prepare you for taking my place."

Taval-pan saw the advantages and accepted the commission. He spent an average of two years in each state and province. He gathered the historical record of all the old kingdoms, starting with the most recent one, Nepusia.

He dug into Nepusia's past. A sailor from Alpania, searching for an easier trade route to Andenan, decided to travel the northern ocean. Lost at sea with only ancient instinctive memories to guide him, he stumbled upon a new island formed as the ocean receded around the Cascadian mountain range. From a deep, recessed part of his brain, the word Cascadia surfaced. He did not know the word or that it was an ancient memory. He rested on the beach for days, gathering his strength. Finally, he decided to explore and found a very fertile, open, free land. Excited, he sailed back to Alpania, where he told his tale to anyone who would listen. Colonists slowly trickled to Cascadia. The promise of free land was too great a lure to deny.

When Captain Nepusia's party arrived, they found the island sparsely populated and in dire need of order. The Nepusian family became royalty, but treated their subjects as free men with free will. As a result, by the time Laarisia attacked, an enviable loyalty had formed. Nepusia's defeat and subsequent rule by Laarisia was a period of religious expression.

When Stonland made her wealthy in the fur trade, she built up her military. Still loyal to Laarisia, she allied with the rest of the islands to attack Stonland. When Stonland was victorious, she was the first to negotiate a treaty and trade agreement, yet she was simply buying her time as she was destined to ally against Stonland in the future. Currently, one hundred fifty years after the atomic war, the island was still recuperating from the chain reaction caused when Jopol's missiles targeted her dormant volcano. Her one thousand-mile ocean territory was finally recovering. Underground volcanic chain reactions drove away many fish.

He spent two years in Andenan. Andenan, Nepetan, and Kashim were considered "new" islands. The receding ocean had exposed three peaks on the continent formerly called South America. A starving, dying merchant ship that had been blown southwest, terribly far from Stonland, located Andenan first.

The men cheered when land was sighted. Once ashore, they prayed for salvation. Tired, they swore they would never sail again. Against merchant tradition, they had smuggled five whores on board. These women became the mothers of Andenan. They named the island as Cascadia had been named. From the depths of their collective minds, an ancient memory of the long-forgotten Andes range surfaced. Andenan, meaning "Andes rising" suggested this new land would thrive.

Generations later, brave boys, disregarding their elder's fear of ocean travel, set out to explore. They found another island close by that they christened Nepetan, after the god of the sea. Upon their return to Andenan, they gathered colonists and started a new, separate society.

Close to Nepetan was another island. Explorers from Nepetan found gold and other valuable metals there. Miners were stationed there, and when enough was gathered, trade relations were opened with Andenan. The island of precious metals was such a cash cow for Nepetan that it was nicknamed Kashim. The name stuck when settlers arrived to service the miners.

Later in the history of this region, Andenan, feeling that they had fathered each society, invaded both Nepetan and Kashim. Defenseless, their quarry surrendered and willingly became provinces in the Andenan Empire.

About the time Stonland opened trade relations with Nepusia, Andenan decided to explore the north. The sailors had no idea Nepusia was there, and when they found it, they made a few good trades. But Stonland was strong and drove the Andenans south with their threats and tribute system.

Andenan isolated itself. Except for minor correspondences with Laarisia, it had no contact with the outside world. When they learned of Axiax's defeat, they were relieved, suspecting he could have been a threat to their peace. When the Nevon circumnavigated the globe, they became internationally recognized. Rumors of the islands were now confirmed.

Andenan society held a grudge against Stonland because they had not been allowed to expand and explore. When the Laara called for arms against Stonland, they graciously replied. When Stonland beat back the combined forces, Andenan instantly sent a representative to Maram to seek out a fair trade agreement.

The agreement was accepted, and, like Nepusia, Andenan experienced a new prosperity. Kashim's wealth was kept a secret for two hundred years. When Stonland found out, they invaded. Kashim was destroyed, and Celes was advanced. Andenan became a quiet, obedient province waiting patiently to attack Stonland. Stonland's powerful atomics forced Andenan to seek a lasting peace.

Nepean was a homecoming for him as he already knew the history. He casually spent his days writing his report on the Andenan Empire. The archives in Andenan were so complete that he felt visiting Nepetan and Kashim before writing his report was a useless gesture. After finishing his report on the empire, broken down into three sections detailing each island's history, he took a four-year vacation.

Nepetan was home, a home he had been away from too long. He spent leisurely days rediscovering the island and lounging on the beaches with friends. Although relaxed, he was frustrated. By royal order, he could not leave Nepetan for two years. Being so near to Kashim was torturous.

When his two years finally ended, he rushed to Kashim. He immediately found Miska and renewed their relationship. Those were the best two years of his life.

Kashim duty extended his vacation; most of his time was spent with Miska. She showed him a world he was unaware existed. Their love grew deeper daily. He was the historian, yet she supplied most of the information he gathered in Kashim. When his two years were coming to an end, he sensed her depression. Their expedition took them far inland. When she sensed his brain was full, she found a meadow. They picnicked and made love. After a slight rest, they explored the land. They came upon a ruined village. Miska's smile vanished.

"What's wrong, Miska?"

"You are going to leave me to explore Stonland! What do you think is wrong!?"

"Let's get married. You can come with me."

"I love Kashim. I'll not go to Stonland unless my brother dies and I'm forced to become Kashim's representative. I will only go there to help Kashim and Andenan proper."

"I don't understand. I love you. I always have. Why won't you marry me?"

"I love you, too. It breaks my heart to see you go, but go, you must. It is your destiny. I must stay true to my beliefs and true to Kashim. My family and my land need me here."

"Why do you hate Stonland so vehemently?"

"Look at this village. Stonland's army did this."

"It was war. Troops destroy."

"Yes, it was war, an invasion of an innocent, unthreatening nation. When these people surrendered, the commander imprisoned, tortured, and massacred them. Many of my ancestors died here. History tells us Celes walked away from this battle a changed man."

"Yes, he discovered the mirror here and became the father of modern science. Something good did come out of this battle."

"One good man will not change my feelings toward Stonland. It is a treacherous society. The republic will falter one day, and society will come under Stonland's boot."

The walk back to Miska's house was tense. Neither said a word. Tav-al-pan, having spent considerable time in Stonland, knew in his heart she was wrong. Miska, realizing he had to leave, struggled in vain to think of a reason for him to stay.

They embraced one last time. He broke the silence.

"You know I have to go."

She fought back her tears.

"I know; please don't ever forget me."

"I won't." He awkwardly turned and walked away.

The next day he boarded a ship to Stonland. As it traveled through the harbor and out onto Galacia, he kept watch on Kashim. As it disappeared, so did all his hopes for a life of love. He stifled a tear, walked to his cabin, made minor adjustments to his Kashim journal, and slowly accepted his fate. The king wanted an honest, forthright report, and though Stonland would look bad, he was determined to rewrite it, for he felt history denied would repeat itself, and the world needed a steady republic, not a tyrannical empire.

His arrival in Stonland was another homecoming. His father met him at the ship. They drove through Maram to Taval-pan's quarters.

"Son. King Jopol the Fourth understands you will be his guest for two years. He doesn't want you to spend every moment researching. He has offered you twenty assistants, most of who've been at work for a few months, to gather your information. Within a month, the king wants you to write a concise history of Stonland for his review. If he is satisfied, the remainder of your stay will be spent observing the Senate in action. Is this okay with you?"

He sensed his father's question was really an order. "I would like that, Father. I will finish in a month."

"Good, Son."

They approached his new residence. Assistants were milling around outside.

"Who are they?"

"These are your assistants."

Taval-pan thanked his father. Taval sped off to the Senate. Taval-pan introduced himself to and dismissed his assistants when he discovered they had completed all of his research. He saw immediately he would finish on time.

One month later, he sent, by messenger, a concise outline of the report on Nepusia, Andenan, and Stonland to the king. Stonland's read:

STONLAND: PRE-HISTORICAL

Discovered by Alpanian merchants. Originally named Aropia after the goddess, Arop. Insignificant island of farmers and fishermen who worshipped Hermax.

STONLAND: DARK TIMES

Aropia became Stonland in honor of the magical stones found on the outskirts of Maram. Linx, sorcerer, and spiritual leader, brought society in contact with the nine original gods. Gods are all-powerful and considered real. Hermax is too quickly forgotten. They appointed Herme king, bringing prosperity to the land. The gods betrayed man. Linx was banished by Herme. Herme sought out the Laara and reestablished the Hermatic religion. Herme himself secretly worshiped the gods.

STONLAND: THE RESURGENCE

Stonland was the first to trade with Nepusia. They introduced an "at sea" tribute system and backed it up with propellers and guns. Stonland goaded its neighbors into a world war, which ended in a stalemate. The country officially banished Hermax. The Laara sent secret missionaries to Stonland. Herme II embraced Hermax, and as a result, the gods disappeared, forever demoted to myth.

STONLAND: REPUBLICAN TIMES

The great scientist Celes brought light to the world.

Inventors displaced farmers.

Industry and pirating thrived.

The plague threatened to destroy the earth, and, as a result, medical technology improved.

The world is circumnavigated.

The Laara assigned ocean territories to the nations of the world to prevent future conflicts.

The "black" was discovered and distributed by Stonland, thus creating world dependence and wealth for Stonland.

Andenan, Alpania, and Nepusia, angered, invaded Stonland.

World War was averted as Stonland used atomics.

All countries united under King Jopol of Stonland's dictatorship.

Jopol formed a republican Senate consisting of a representative and senatorial body designed for balance. Worldwide, freedom prospered.

THIS IS AN OUTLINE ONLY; CONCISE REPORT TO FOLLOW.

Several days later, King Jopol IV received and read the preliminary report. Satisfied, he asked Taval to begin bringing Taval-pan to the Senate.

After turning in his historical report, he spent time with his father and King Jopol IV at the king's request. The king was younger than Taval. At forty, he had retained his powerful build and blonde hair. Most leaders, with the pressure of world rule, would have gone gray years ago, and normal men of medium posture tended to grow portly around forty. The king shrugged away his good health, complimenting his senators and representatives for keeping world order. It was a world in which he could relax his rule, thereby keeping his youthful appearance. The king felt that all of the future representatives and senators should see the government in action so they would not be hopelessly lost when they took over; thus, he spent time with Taval-pan.

They took him to the Senate daily to observe. The senate chamber was located in a hall of Linxiton Palace. Taval-pan would always remember the first time he entered the Senate and saw, across from him, the senator and representative's chairs. They were set in a semi-circular pattern facing him. To his left were seven marble chairs, and to his right were five. The king's chair sat in the middle. The king's chair, larger and more comfortable than the rest, was decorated with pictorial scenes from every country engraved in marble. The senator's chairs were larger than the representative's chairs but not quite as large as the king's. Each of the twelve chairs was decorated with scenes from its represented country or province. Directly in front of the king's chair was a podium used for presentations to the senatorial body. On the walls hung portraits of the great kings of Stonland.

After two years of constant exposure to the Senate, Taval-pan was ready to venture on to his Alpanian assignment. The chambers left quite an impression on him. He knew he would remember them as he spent the next ten years in Alpania, less than two years in each province. Each time he was exposed to a legal problem he would imagine the glorious Senate solving it. He could not wait to join them. This was the effect the king wished to achieve.

Taval visited him in his quarters as he was preparing to leave.

"So, you're off to Alpania?"

"Yes, Father."

"Are you excited?"

"Oh yes! Alpania's history is deep. I'm especially interested in the power struggle with Stonland. I must find out why they failed to hold Stonland back."

"Yes, we would appreciate your insight in the Senate. Alpania commands a large part of our body, and there is always underlying tension. Maybe your research will help us control it."

"Father, I want to thank you for everything. I know it was you who convinced the king to give me assistance so I could see the government at work."

"Did you enjoy your visits to the Senate?"

"So much that I can't wait to work there if you'll excuse my saying so."

"Not at all, Son. My father did the same for me. It's only natural that you want to see me retire and take over. That was my goal. Personal feelings don't matter; the greater good of society does. Now, come, let me give you a ride to your ship."

Taval drove Taval-pan to the docks.

Their goodbyes were cordial, as each expected to see the other soon. As the ship left port, Taval-pan found his cabin and began to plan how he would attack the problem of Alpania. By the time he landed in Quota, he had it worked out.

He was met by a representative of King Jopol IV and taken to what would serve as his home and headquarters for the next ten years. Provided on the walls were detailed maps of Alpania and her provinces, Marsia, Vienus, Uryxia, Ciaxian, and Sateland. Gazing at the map, he confirmed his decision. Each land would be visited by boat explored, and, always, he would return to Alpania. Once he had explored each island, he would concentrate on Alpanian history, and, here, he would write his report.

Ten years quickly passed. He wrote in his journal the following report:

ALPANIA AND HER PROVINCES

I will begin with the provinces, although they are only secondary to this report. They exist, as a body, to supply food and manpower to Alpania. The impression I gather is that Alpania was settled first. Restless citizens explored Galacia and found the other five islands. These islands, at first independent, were populated by farmers. Villages did not exist. When Alpania invaded, ambitious generals formed farm collectives based out of control villages. This was the first attempt at lordship, a concept that quickly spread across the globe, affecting all islands save Nepusia.

The farmer and the land became property of the lord. Religion, first based on the gods and later based on Hermax, was their only outlet for hope. Eventually, industry took over, and these poor, unskilled farmers were forced into the cities. The vacated land was now home to machines. Plague destroyed one-third of displaced Alpanians. Of those who survived, many became enslaved in the factories while others learned a craft, hoping to become independent businessmen. Still, others joined the military to escape the cities.

Now, I focus on Alpania proper. Her history parallels the founding of Laarisia or, rather, the civilizing of Laarisia by Daphne and John. Upon civilizing Laarisia, they ordered their ships to explore the surrounding ocean. Alpania was the first land discovered and settled. The other islands were found but, as I pointed out earlier, were not settled en masse until Alpania decided to colonize.

The Alpanians enjoyed prosperity in the beginning. Then, growing cocky, they broke relations with Laarisia. Laarisia attacked, and slaves were taken. Alpania's records were lost or destroyed, leaving a historical gap of a few hundred years.

We do know that when it became a productive land once again, it was filled with Hermatics. A small tribe, worshipping the ancient gods, lived peacefully beside these Hermatic farmers. Then, one day, the reasons are unclear; this tribe rose and massacred the farmers.

The infamous Axiax was a Hermatic peasant boy. When his farm was destroyed, he dismissed Hermax as a protecting god, followed the angry tribe, learned of the gods, and murdered his way into a leadership position. He swore vengeance on anything Hermatic.

Under Axiax's rule, the tribe became more ambitious. They attacked and conquered each of the present Alpanian islands, Hermatia and Stonland. Stonland was a savage place quickly abandoned by an overextended Axiax. He knew of the Andenan islands; we can be sure he would have attacked had he not felt overextended in Stonland. His plan to attack Nepusia was abandoned to concentrate on Laarisia.

He ruled his empire with an iron fist. Hermatia, representing everything Hermatic, was destroyed. Few Hermatians escaped to Laarisia, but those who did told such horrible stories that Laarisia, all-powerful, began to fear this little tribesman. Only the Laara remained confident.

The Laara knew that adversity was the key to Hermax's strength. In his heart, he knew the gods were weak and would cower in fear if a strong man rose to face them, especially a religious leader representing Hermax. (Please note that this is only an assumption. No one knows why the Laara faced Axiax or how he convinced him to retreat).

When Axiax felt he had the colonies controlled, he planned his attack on Laarisia. His faithful servant, General Maar, whom Axiax had cut to test his loyalty, protested such a dangerous move. Axiax argued that Laarisia was too preoccupied with Nepusia and, therefore, weak. Based on this new insight, General Maar supported Axiax's plan completely.

His troops were excited. They had never lost a battle and did not expect to start now. They willingly set up camp on Laarisia's beach and awaited orders. When the orders came to get back on the ship, they were shocked and surprised. General Maar summed up the troop's feelings when he confronted Axiax. Axiax told him to obey orders or die and, to his dying day, never revealed what the Laara said to convince him to retreat. He accepted the Gosirian priests. Their sanctuary on Alpania was secured until such time as Laarisia again became the dominant country and religious ruler of the world.

When Axiax died, he left an empire ruled by his hereditary family. When Laarisia regained control, his family easily converted back to Hermatic ways. Through trickery and violence, they kept the Alpanian Empire together; only Hermatia escaped as a peace gesture to the Laara.

The province developed parallel to Stonland and should have been more powerful because of its resources and manpower. But Stonland had one resource besides- ingenuity. Alpania was late in its attempts to trade with Nepusia. A few good trades whet their appetite until they were stopped cold by Stonland's naval tributes. A few ships smuggled goods out of Nepusia, and this is how Alpania discovered gunpowder when Stonland did. Again, ingenuity saved Stonland. Their propellers and guns beat back Alpania's fire catapults. Alpania became subservient to Stonland's wishes and lost Uryxia.

Up to date, Alpania and Stonland were on-again, off-again allies. Alpania bided her time until Stonland lost favor. Ironically, when Stonland was banished by Hermax, Alpania, once a staunch supporter of the gods, rallied the attack on Stonland in the name of Hermax. Again, they rallied troops when Stonland hoarded the black. Atomic damage caused them to quickly surrender and willingly join Stonland's empire.

End of report

Ten years of living in Alpania matured him. The arts still flourished, and when he was not tied up with his work on provincial islands, he took advantage of the culture Alpania had to offer. Countless museums, plays, musicals, and inland tours transformed him from a wild-eyed youth to a mature, confident, Hermatic adult. His sense of responsibility grew as he witnessed how delicate life was.

It was with a heavy heart that, in the summer of 4169, he set sail for Hermatia. Hermatia was primarily a religious center and, he was afraid, would not inspire him the way Alpania did. On the voyage, he had time to ponder his situation, and as he did, his excitement built. At last, he would visit a land that would prove his graduate thesis. This proof, he thought, would strengthen his position in the Senate when he arrived there to work. The Senate: the climax of a successful career.

Hermatia's rich history nourished the soul of a Hermatic. With a light heart, he stepped off of the boat and went straight to the temple.

The state temple of Hermatia was built in the shape of a Hermatic pick. The main entrance was at the head of the pick. Entrance doors were twelve feet high and six feet wide. Carved into the doors was the creation story. Hermax, unseen, except for a hand wielding a pick, directed the nine Gods to go forth and create humanity. As he passed the entrance, he saw doors to his right and left. The left led to the priest's chambers; the right led to the seminary classes. Both areas were embedded in the head of the pick. Directly ahead of him was a massive hall. As he passed through the entryway, the temple ceiling opened to fifty feet above him. On the sidewalls, at the twenty-foot level, plain glass windows were spaced every six feet of the six-hundred-foot hall. There were also several fifty-foot-long windows in the middle of the roof. In every overhead window, there was a black Hermatic pick painted so that any source of light, day or night, would cast shadows of the pick on the floor of the temple. People were to have no doubt who controlled this sacred place.

He walked the hall's center aisle, taking in the mural scenes that dominated the walls. There, again, was the creation story. There was the rise of Hermax. Over there was the destruction of the nine gods by Hermax. As he came to the halfway point, the murals gave way to portraits. Starting with Laara John I and ending with the current Laara Daphne XV.

He reached the pulpit area where a priest was lost in prayer. While he waited, he took in the grandeur of the scene. The pulpit was raised high above the seats yet was comparatively small, shadowed by a Hermatic pick that rose from the floor to the roof. Taval-pan, seeing this place, wondered how anyone could have ever doubted Hermax.

"Hello, my son."

The priest brought him out of his stupor with a fright, for he imagined the sound came from the inanimate pick itself. The priest's brown, jeweled robe complimented his hair and eyes. He wore a Hermatic pick necklace; bejeweled and gaudy anywhere else, it seemed natural on this spiritual leader of men.

He bowed.

"Father. Where may I find the head priest of Hermatia?"

"I am he. Who are you?"

"I am Taval-pan. King Jopol the Fourth sent me here on a five-year mission to gather Hermatia's history."

"Wonderful! I'm so glad you arrived here safely. I was just praying to Hermax that you would. Please, come with me to my chambers, and I will begin your lessons."

They walked to his chamber. The priest wasted no time. When the door shut, his first lesson began.

"We first came from the land around Alpania. Our ancestors foolishly broke ties with Laarisia, were conquered, and became slaves. The rulers, John and Daphne, drove the slaves hard. When John and Daphne died, the slaves escaped. Ronix, who was led by Hermax, led them to this land. The grateful people made Ronix their king and head priest. He ordered the people to take their unused weapons and explore the island. They brought back plentiful game and had a freedom festival. Hermax surrounded the island with fog as they dined."

"How did the fog really form?"

"Do you doubt Hermax, my son?" The priest was surprised.

"No, but there must be a scientific explanation."

"If you search, you will search in vain."

Choosing not to heed the warning, Taval-pan did a search.

The island wilderness lay unchanged since Hermatia was first populated. The population was small; any attempt at largesse was denied when the citizens were taken to Laarisia as slaves. The freed slaves were distributed to islands around the globe. Few found their way back to Hermatia. Hermatia remained a center of religious purity. He met many fishermen and hunters, who, to a man, took only what they needed to survive from the land. In this way, a balance existed, allowing the island to thrive.

Into this overgrown, forested island, he thrust himself for the next ninety days. He circled the small island many times, first scouring the beaches, then the cliffs and caves, then the forests, progressively working his way up to the central, dominant feature of Hermatia. It was at the peak of this mountain that he found the answer he sought.

He first took in the view. The sparsely populated beaches were a flurry of activity. Fishing boats stood in line waiting to be unloaded. Groups of women cleaned the fish while others lay them on racks to dry. Hermatians learned early that unsuccessful fishing trips outnumbered successful ones. Preservation insured against starvation.

His eyes followed the beach inland to the overgrown forests. He knew from his journey that, although it appeared overgrown, it was a highly productive area. Here, crops were not planted in rows but purposefully set in tiny clearings. Wheat, corn, potatoes, and cotton were planted this way. Pickers worked in teams, each assigned to a specific plant. Twenty pickers often picked four or five plants in a one-hundred-square-foot area.

From his vantage point he could see clearly the meadows that housed livestock. These animals instinctively felt safe in the meadows and were always led deep into the forest for slaughter lest fear of the meadows should arise.

The meadows near water held no livestock. They instead were flooded to produce the perfect environment for rice.

Poppy fields began where the tree line gave way to the mountain. Important in opium production, Hermatia developed the first anesthesia in the years following the plague, allowing doctors to operate safely.

He realized after a few days that he stood on an extinct volcano. He determined that it had steamed out within two hundred years of the arrival of the slaves to Hermatia. It continually smoked, and the smoke, cooled by Galacia, had formed a cloud of steam around the island. He reported his findings to the head priest.

"You see, my son, Hermax, killed that volcano in order to hide Hermatia."

Taval-pan conceded that the priest would never accept the scientific explanation. He then asked the priest a question that had bothered him his entire life.

"Why are the Laaras always named John or Daphne?"

"That is an excellent question, my son. Most people don't have the courage to ask it. When Zearnanine was forced to create the Holy Laarisian Empire, the priests wanted him to remain in control. They allowed him to change his name to Laara John because they knew it would help secure the loyalty of the troops and the common people. It was decreed that the Laara should be named John or Daphne, depending on who held the position throughout time."

"But why John or Daphne? Weren't they evil to Hermatics?"

"No matter. They are the original children of Hermax. All of us came from them. They were the most powerful rulers the earth has ever known. The Laara, having their name, would command respect from the kings and commoners forever."

Having explored the island thoroughly, he spent the remainder of his five years interviewing the head priest and sometimes lesser priests of Hermatia. Occasionally he would take a break and venture out to the meadows. There, he daydreamed of Miska. Busy as he was, he could not erase her from his mind.

Toward the end of 4174, he wrote the report he would one day present to the Senate:

HERMATIA

This wholesome, religious country was discovered and founded in the year 1234 by a group of ragged, worn-out, close-to-death escaped slaves from Laarisia. It appears they were well-armed but did not have to fight their way out of Laarisia due to a well-timed escape. The whole of "free" Laarisia was mourning the deaths of Daphne and John, the original children of Hermax. These confused children worshipped the nine gods of mythology and created slavery, which Hermax rose to destroy.

Ronix, led by Hermax, found Hermatia. He blessed the land and ordered his people to use their unused weapons to hunt game. A feast was held to celebrate their freedom. According to legend, Hermax enshrouded the island with fog during the feast. I find this debatable as in my study of the island I found proof that the glorious mountain that commands the island was once a volcano that died or "steamed out" about the time the island was settled. The hot ash and lava, when it came in contact with the Galacian Sea, would have created a fog dense and large enough to hide the island. The head priest of Hermatia believes this was Hermax's plan. As I have stated, it is debatable.

Hermax kept the island hidden for one hundred fifty years. A free farming community developed. The memory of slavery in Laarisia was fresh in the minds of the populace when General Zearn invaded. General Zearn shocked them. He treated the Hermatians like the free society they were. He offered no threats as long as the community allied themselves with Laarisia.

General Zearn was a good administrator, but he could not overcome the hatred and prejudice the Laarisians felt toward Hermatians. Against his better judgment, he let slip by him laws that the king of Hermatia was required to enforce. They were not enslaved but were dictated to, which was nearly as bad. Knowing they would be enslaved if they broke the law, selected Hermatians flaunted it to be sent to exile in Laarisia. Here, they intermixed with the slaves, engineered a common uprising, and secured Laarisia for Hermax.

Laarisia and Hermatia now co-existed as religious centers of the world. Laarisia would never again impose her values on Hermatia; instead, she would seek Hermatia's input on all issues. When Laarisia conquered Nepusia, Hermatia adjusted to sharing the responsibilities.

Laarisia was responsible for the military control of Nepusia. Hermatia was responsible for the religious indoctrination of the populace. This task was more difficult than it sounds. Most families had come from religious backgrounds, but religion was quickly discarded as they became buried in the work that needed to be accomplished. Prosperity was so great that religion never again gained the foothold it needed. Historically, hard times encourage religion's growth. Religion thrives on hope and these self-sufficient people simply did not need hope.

The Hermatians set up schools and built churches in a massive attempt to teach everyone. If people would not come to town, they would go to the people. The Laarisian military forced anyone they could find to enter the school system.

Once backward Nepusia restarted down the correct path, Laarisian administrators developed the government. They left the working democratic system alone. Their main goal was to introduce Laarisia and Hermatia's opinions. Nepusia would become a vital force in the planned allied triumvirate.

The triumvirate solidified over the next two hundred years. Nepusia sent supplies to Laarisia and Hermatia in lieu of troops, which they were forbidden to employ when Axiax was terrorizing the east. Eight hundred years later, when Nepusia decided to trade with Stonland and Alpania, politically, they stayed close to the triumvirate.

During these years, Hermatia remained the pure religious center of the world. The first grand temple was built here. The brilliant structure was used as a model for Laarisia's later Grand Temple. When Stonland laid siege to Hermatia, the priests and populace prayed for a miracle. Hermax granted one when he had the Laara end the conflict.

After the Galacian fighting, Hermatia won free passage of the entire ocean, but this did not amount to much revenue since she was not a trade society. Her missionaries, however, could now travel safely. When the countries of the earth allied against Stonland during the last war, Hermatia was determined to stay neutral. King Jopol rewarded her by offering her a senator's chair. The advantages of this position were understood immediately. Now, Hermatia would have a voice in world law. From this platform, they could heavily influence the world in favor of Hermax.

End of report

Taval-pan asked the head priest for his opinion on the report's accuracy. Although doubt concerning Hermax was present, over all he enjoyed the presentation and deemed it worthy of the Senate.

"Taval-pan, you have been with us five years. I assume you are ready to travel on to Laarisia, yes? I have taken the liberty of securing your passage on a seminary boat. It is loaded with priests who will be confirmed in Laarisia."

Taval-pan was genuinely surprised.

"Thank you. When does it depart?"

"In two weeks."

"Good. I want to revisit the interior of the island."

Taval-pan spent the next two weeks meditating in the forest. As usual, when he was not working, images of Miska came to him. Thus far life had been fulfilling, but not complete without her in it.

He boarded the sleek Laarisian cruise ship in the spring of 4174. It was a pleasant voyage of true believers. The intellectual religious conversations stimulated him. Still, he sensed there was an inherent weakness to being overly religious. Not being prepared militarily to defend your country strictly for peaceful, religious reasons would invariably leave society open for attack. Mentally reviewing Alpanian history, he realized this was exactly how Axiax had risen. Near the end of the voyage he pretended he was Axiax to determine how Axiax would have related to these priests. He knew not one of them would have completed the voyage.

Axiax detested priests and would have thrown them all to the sea. Why, then, did he spare the Laara?

When the ship arrived, the harbor was a bustle of activity. Taval-pan saw none of it. So deeply was he involved in his Axiax fantasy that he saw only an empty, abandoned city, the citizenry fleeing into the hills. He disembarked at the head of an imaginary compliment of soldiers. In his mind, he heard shouted orders as he was drawn to the monument erected to Laara John VII celebrating the "defeat" of Axiax. He kneeled, slowly forcing his mind back to reality. Here lay the eternal question: Why did Axiax retreat? He pondered it as he rose.

"Impressive, isn't it?"

He turned and looked into her green eyes and saw her gray hair and her robes. He knew at once it was the Laara Daphne XV.

Shocked, Taval-pan dropped to his knees and bowed.

"Stand up, Taval-pan. I have been expecting you. I received a message from our divine ruler, Jopol the Fourth, that you would be arriving from Hermatia. How long will you be with us?"

"I am assigned to Laarisia for ten years. When my tour is up, I am to report my worldwide historical findings to the republican Senate."

"Ten years. Good. Come with me."

"Please wait, Laara. Before we go, I have a question."

"What is it, my son?"

"I have been contemplating this moment, and I wonder: Do you, as Laara, know why Axiax retreated when he had Laarisia in his grasp?"

"No one knows. I am afraid Laara John the Seventh took that secret to his grave. He felt the world would be better off not knowing. His priests finally convinced him enough time had passed and that the information was needed to protect the peace. He went to bed one night scheduled to reveal the secret the next morning but died in his sleep."

"He left us with a great mystery."

"Yes. Maybe you will uncover the truth as you research. Now, let's go."

Taval-pan was fifty years old. The climb to the city was strenuous, but he did not let his strain show in front of the much older Laara, who moved with graceful ease as if she were floating along the path.

They traveled the same route Veon and later Daphne and John had used when Laarisia was first discovered. They walked across the plain to the river, along the river constantly rising in elevation. Through the forest, they wandered. At one point Taval-pan saw in the distance a snow-covered peak. It quickly disappeared behind the dense forest, but Taval-pan gasped for air, suddenly realizing how far he may have to climb. He was amazed that the much older Laara was not winded. Over the next hour, they passed many cascading waterfalls. As the Himal River plowed toward the ocean, Taval-pan kept his mind occupied with the water. He knew the river was the ending and the beginning of a great cycle. When it emptied into Galacia, it was reborn. Evaporated salt water formed clouds, which blew over the island. These clouds dropped moisture in the form of snow or rain onto the mountain. All streams led to the Himal, which came to life high in the mountain. He reflected that life was much the same everywhere. For each living organism to survive, something had to die, and the earth, like the sky that embraced her, would reuse all that returned to her.

His thoughts were interrupted as they scaled the last slight rise. Before him lay the great high plain of the Himal River. Here, the river calmly flowed through countless pastures. The tranquility he felt justified to him why this place had been picked to build the monuments as well as the Grand Temple and palace. It overpowered the senses. He felt he knew why it lasted as the center of civilization for so long.

They continued walking across the plain toward the Grand Temple. Life was surprisingly simple here. Farmers attended their crops; fishermen set their nets. He stared, amazed that the original village still stood. It was refurbished every ten years in an effort to maintain the simple life.

The Laara directed him quickly to the Grand Temple. Taval-pan stared in awe. There were three buildings. Each one was built in the shape of a Hermatic pick. The heads converged, forming a courtyard. He was to find out later that the building on his right was administration and priest quarters, and the building on his left was reserved for local services: preachings, weddings, and the naming of infants. Ahead of him was the Grand Temple. Its doors were exactly the doors he had seen in Hermatia; however, here, above them, was a balcony the Laara sometimes used for public addresses.

"What's wrong?"

Daphne saw the look of wonder on his face.

"The temple. It's magnificent! I thought the temple in Hermatia was beautiful, but this temple is awesome."

"Come on. I'll show you the view."

They walked through the massive doors. He noticed the artwork on the walls was similar to that in Hermatia. Here, however, there were statues of each Laara rather than portraits. Here, there was no window in the ceiling. Instead, there was a gigantic mural. The Gods, dressed in white robes and dresses adorned with Hermatic picks located near their feet, were busy creating mankind. They arrived at a staircase and climbed to the roof. Once on the roof, the Laara showed him the entire city and valley below. His eyes caught the monuments across the Himal River valley.

"It's true. The monuments do appear to represent the Sun, Earth, and Moon."

"Daphne and John are buried in the monument that represents the Sun. The Sun is all-powerful and life-giving, as were they. This is why all the Laaras take their names."

"How did you know-?"

"The head priest of Hermatia told me. Come, you have much work to do."

He spent his first few years in Laarisia at the Grand Temple. Daily, he interviewed the Laara. He gathered the complete history of the church and the Empire from her. Unfortunately, she lacked a workable knowledge of Laarisia before the slave revolt. He feared all memories of the first Republic might be lost. Nearing the completion of his temple duty, he decided to confront the Laara.

"Laara Daphne, you have provided me with generous information concerning the history of your religious empire. Judging from what I have collected from other regions, this information will cement our beliefs about our past. The only item I feel is missing is what life was like during the first Laarisian Republic. We know Veon found the island. We know Daphne and John ruled and enslaved others. We know the slaves escaped. But what was life like? Why were they here? Where did Veon come from? Why did Daphne and John rule so long?"

"That is knowledge I do not possess; no one does. When Daphne and John died, society's focus changed. There was a fervor. Public opinion demanded the slaves back. Many lands were discovered, and man began to look forward. The past was all but forgotten."

"How can past knowledge simply vanish?"

"Nobody cared anymore. We wanted slaves, wealth, and land. The past wasn't important to society then, but I do believe it was important to society as it was happening. It's true there are no written records, but I have always wondered if the monuments have a message, if they contain a written record."

"Do you think I should investigate them?"

"Yes, I do," she answered in her natural, commanding tone.

He spent six years researching the monuments, yet no clues to the first republic were found. The evidence he gathered referred to times when mankind perished and would probably perish in the future. Through mathematical measurements that seemed to universally rest on 2π, he gathered proof that the monuments thought to represent Earth, the Sun, and the Moon only also seemed to represent the star Sirius, its dwarf, and a planet in the system. The monument pattern seemed to be laid out *exactly* as that system would appear in 4296 A.D. Though representing another system, the monuments also seemed to be an exact map replica of the Earth's dimensions, made at a time when mankind did not have mapping technology and could not have possibly known the size of the Earth! The twelve statues that surrounded the monuments intrigued him. One in particular, named Sagittarius, faced due east and was out of line with the others, almost as if it were reaching east.

During his ten years gathering information in Laarisia he became an eccentric, older man. As he reached sixty, he began balding on top, his gray hair growing long on the sides only, his beard long, shaving a time waster. The daily dress was a white robe and leather sandals with leather binders that laced up his shins. The constant excavations left his robes frayed and tattered at the fringes.

In his last year, he received permission from the Laara to enter the Monument of the Sun. What he found mystified him. Everywhere, there were references to the nine mythical gods. What was noticeably missing were bones or any evidence that anyone had ever been laid to rest here. He went to the Laara, concerned.

Her answer to this strange mystery was a little too convenient.

"Well, obviously, Hermax took Daphne and John to spend eternity with him."

Taval-pan bravely countered, using a familiarity few would dare. "I disagree, Laara Daphne. All evidence in the monument seems to point to the legitimacy of the nine gods. Maybe they took Daphne and John."

"Taval-pan, you know the gods are just a myth. You proved that with your own thesis. Maybe the bones dissolved over time."

"Maybe. But I still believe there would be traces of them. Some sort of residue, clothing, fabric pieces."

"If Hermax took them, why would he leave any evidence behind?"

Taval-pan left, dissatisfied. The Laara would defend Hermax to the end. All of his evidence pointed to the validity of the nine Gods. As a historian, he felt he had no choice but to report his findings to the king and the Senate.

LAARISIA

Most of what I can say about Laarisia has been summed up in my previous reports. Veon, famous in religious chronicles, discovered Laarisia in the year 218. We know only that Daphne and John ruled Laarisia, took slaves, and died, at which time the slaves escaped. I was, unfortunately, not able to fill in this gap in time or the gap from zero to 218 A.D. The prehistory of Laarisia was carelessly lost in the confusion of Daphne and John's death. I can say, with absolute certainty, this: The slaves DID NOT build the monuments as theorized. I will present my evidence directly to the Senate to support this claim.

Laarisia has been the leader of the world politically, militarily, and religiously the thousands of years since she was founded. In my evaluation of why one island should so dominate I have drawn two conclusions: location and resources.

Subheading: location

This island sits at the center of a web on the Galacian Sea. This meant travel and discovery were simplified; her people were magnetically drawn to each successive island. Currents changed as islands emerged allowing voyagers to easily locate new lands. Each new land, populated with Laarisians, naturally remained under Laarisian control. Alpania was the first to revolt, and the citizens were enslaved (refer to Hermatia priest testimony, not Laarisian records: destroyed).

Subheading: resources

Early in its history, Laarisia is thought to have been very wealthy. Many mines, abandoned and current, point to vast riches in gold, silver, jade, and building/decorative materials such as granite, quartz, mica, iron, and coal.

These early riches allowed the populace to trade and grow. Ships were built, and upon them, discoveries were made. As each new island opened, so did trade opportunities. Soon, a wealthy merchant class arose. To protect this class, a strong military complex arose. When Hermax took over, systems were already established to keep religious order.

As the world expanded, shipping and new lands were discovered, and the responsibility for welfare fell to Laarisia. She used Hermatia for moral support, and her judgment was enforced militarily. The weight of her military was never felt as hard as it was in Nepusia.

The occupation of Nepusia weakened her and left her open to attack from Alpania. Nepusia was another major source of wealth, and when Stonland found it, they became all-powerful. Laarisia was subjected to moral religious rule over a small portion of the world. Religious policies originate in Hermatia or Laarisia but are posted by Laarisia.

End of report

He spent his last few days in Laarisia, sitting in his room reviewing his summary report of each island. He decided to write summary reports instead of complete reports because he did not want to read his words to the Senate; he wanted them to be curious enough to ask him questions so he could convey his feelings. Reading over the reports now he made a few changes. They would serve as a proper outline. He knew each verbal report would take significant time, and he wondered how much the busy Senate would tolerate. He decided to ask Jopol the fourth when he returned.

The Laara accompanied him to the docks. He detected the faint hint of an ocean storm in his nostrils. On the horizon, he thought he saw tiny, cumulous clouds forming. Their goodbye was pleasant until she gave him her warning.

"Laara Daphne, you have been a wonderful teacher," Taval-pan began. "The wealth of information I collected; I don't believe I could have done it without you."

"I'm sure you could have, though the years you spent researching would've been longer. I must say, I'm a little worried about you, though."

He was bewildered. "Why?"

"Are you set on including the nine god's relationship to the monuments in your verbal report to the Senate?"

"I must tell the truth; present the facts as I see them."

"I understand, but please be careful. Opinion against the mythical gods runs high. You may find yourself in hot water with the Senate."

"I'll survive. King Jopol the Fourth expects controversy from my research."

They embraced one last time. He turned, walked up the gangplank, and soon sailed to Stonland.

They sailed directly into the storm he had sensed earlier. The Galacian Ocean tossed his transport like a toy boat. He had a fleeting thought that Hermax was warning him, but resolved to present his report to the Senate based only on facts, religious controversy be damned. Cautiously, the transport entered Maram harbor. Frazzled, Taval-pan disembarked.

Upon arrival, he went straight to the palace and demanded to see the king. He was expected and sent directly to the throne room.

The king ignored him for a moment, then looked up.

"Can I help you, peasant?"

Taval-pan, surprised, silently evaluated the king.

"I am no peasant. I am Taval-pan."

"Taval-pan! What has become of you? You are dirty. Why do you appear in my chamber unshaven, wearing a torn robe?"

"Excuse my appearance, Lord; I have been working extremely hard in Laarisia."

"Yes, Laarisia," he said absently. "Listen, we must get you cleaned up if you are to report to the Senate. As you appear now, they won't take you seriously."

"I agree. May I ask you how I am to be presented to the Senate?"

"Your father and I have discussed this. We feel the Senate can spare one to two hours a day to hear your reports."

Taval-pan quickly calculated in his head.

"At that rate, I will be reporting to the Senate for five years."

The king was mildly amused.

"You have that much information?"

"Yes."

The king thought for a moment. "Well, we can't spare more time. This shall be an enjoyable five years. It will be good to have you back amongst us."

"Yes, Sire," Taval-pan agreed, beginning his bow.

Taval-pan excused himself and left for his room to prepare for his first report on Nepusia.

The following Monday, clean and professionally dressed, he arrived at the Senate. He took a seat in the guest lobby and waited as they debated shipping laws. Galacian territories, defined hundreds of years earlier, were being questioned. Taval-pan found the process interesting. When the debate ended, King Jopol the Fourth stood.

"Gentlemen, we have a guest today. Please welcome home, Taval-pan."

They mumbled and nodded their approval as he rose and walked to the podium. He cleared his throat. "Thank you, my lords. I am Taval-pan, King Jopol's official world historian. I am freshly returned from a thirty-five-year research mission sanctioned by you in which I was assigned to rediscover each island of the Earth. My first report concentrates on the island of Nepusia. Geologically, it consists of. . . ."

He talked for two hours. Every day the Senate met, he addressed them. He dissected each land methodically, covering every aspect of an island's growth, from its geological formation to its colonization to its present culture and importance in the world. He wrapped up each section with his personal insights into the society represented and offered suggestions on how it could improve to mesh with Stonland's current foreign policy, fuel for future senatorial debate.

Five years flowed past as he reported his findings to the Senate. He began by reporting on all of the states and then the provinces. The provinces made up of several states, created an interesting dynamic. The senators paid rapt attention and asked deeper questions when he discussed provincial rule. Every day, he went home and poured over the information that he had gathered in Laarisia. Mathematically, it made sense. It was finally time.

Alone in his room contemplating, worried, he realized the last five years of presentations had been uneventful. The Senate body listened politely, never disagreed, and seldom asked questions. When they did interrupt him, they merely asked for clarification or deeper insights. So far, Taval-pan has reported the known history as it was written and taught. Today, he would enter the realm of the unknown and was apprehensive; he knew he would be on trial.

Entering the Senate, prepared for battle, should one arise, he listened casually to the senatorial debate, trying to judge who would oppose him and planning his reaction. When his time arrived, he rose and slowly walked to the podium.

"Today, I will report to you on my last duty- Laarisia. Most of you know the history already, so I'll not dwell on it. What I wish to discuss with you is the mystery of the monuments and the validity of the original nine gods."

A short, fat, badly combed over, bald senator stood up, abruptly terminating Taval-pan's prepared speech, and yelled at the king, demanding to be heard. Upon the king's approval, he fixed his beady little eyes on Taval-pan and used a powerful, booming voice meant to unnerve him.

"Trivial! Everyone knows the monuments represent the Sun, Earth, and Moon. The slaves, with Hermax's help, built them. The nine gods are a myth; your own master's thesis proves it. Why do you waste this government's time on trivialities?"

Taval-pan was undaunted. "I spent my whole life taught to believe as you do, Senator Reesar. At first I didn't believe it either, but I've been inside the Monument of the Sun. All artwork represents the gods. There are no references to Hermax."

Senator Reesar yelled, "Blasphemy! You dare question the validity of the one true god? Hermax is omnipresent; of course, he resides in the Monument of the Sun. I don't have to enter it to know that. If there is artwork inside representing the false gods, it must have been meant to seal them away. King Jopol, do we have to listen to these lies?"

King Jopol contemplated Reesar's outburst.

"Thus far, I hear no lies. Senator Reesar, you helped unanimously vote Taval-pan onto this mission. You are out of order. You must sit down and listen. When Taval-pan is finished, we will decide what to do."

His scowl threatening permanence, Reesar reluctantly obeyed. King Jopol motioned to Taval-pan to continue.

Taval-pan was hesitant to begin again.

"I have a report here on my mathematical calculations. I welcome this Senate to pour over the details. Send it to the best mathematicians. What I've found is this: Those monuments represent Sirius, its dwarf star, and a planet in the system as they will appear in 4296 A.D. They also form a map of the earth made when mankind didn't have any idea how big earth was. The artifacts and statues I researched all seem to point to one thing- mankind will be destroyed in 4296."

"Are you certain?" A calm voice asked.

Taval-pan turned to the sound. The representative who had spoken, except for his gray hair and graying blonde beard, was the spitting image of Taval-pan. He smiled.

"Yes, father!- I mean Representative Taval. Hermax has failed us. We must rely on the gods in order to survive."

A mumble arose that King Jopol the Fourth quickly suppressed. Annoyed that he had lost control of the Senate, he glared at Taval-pan. He knew there had to be an investigation into these allegations. He instructed Taval-pan. "You will appear before us in one year. You will not discuss your 'facts' with anyone. I will not have the citizenry panicked without proof. In one year, we will decide this issue."

Taval-pan, ever obedient, bowed.

"Fair enough."

One year later found him in the Senate again, anticipating the king's decision. During the last six years, he had groomed himself and dressed properly, hoping the Senate would take him seriously. Had it all been wasted time?

The king addressed Taval-pan as the assembly looked on.

"Hermax will not destroy mankind. He is a loving, charitable God. We thank you for your report. Our mathematicians don't agree with your assessment. Our scientists are convinced the artwork within the Monument of the Sun was created to bury the nine gods."

Taval-pan scanned the room. The faces were expressionless, except Reesar's, who beamed.

"Daphne and John are with Hermax. You will go back to Laarisia and gather proof that Hermax is the one true god. You will apologize to the Laara for insulting her. Good day."

Taval-pan was shocked. All the evidence was there, but the scientists refused to see it. He sulked out of the Senate. Aimlessly walking down the street, he was stopped by Taval.

He grabbed Taval-pan's arm. "Son, the king's ruling is for the best. The important thing is you presented all the evidence you found. King Jopol is honored to have you on his staff. He confided in me. If you follow his orders and spend the rest of my life proving Hermax is real, you will secure my vacant Senate seat. If you do not, I will be the last representative from our family to serve. You must succeed, or he will ruin our family."

"As you wish, Father."

"Good. Now, when does your ship sail?"

"Tomorrow morning."

"Excellent. Once you've packed, join me for dinner. I feel we won't see each other for a long time."

Later, on the ship to Laarisia, Taval-pan contemplated his father's plea. He knew he had to prove Hermax real to preserve the family's honor. It went against everything he had learned, but once he was in the Senate, maybe he could secure change.

The ship docked, and Taval-pan disembarked. He was secured by a compliment of Stonland soldiers who escorted him to the Laara's palace. The soldiers forced him to his knees in the Laara's presence.

"Speak!" The captain of the guard demanded.

Taval-pan sighed and attempted to rise but was held in place by the captain. He obediently spoke.

"Laara Daphne, I am here to beg forgiveness from you, Hermax, and the good people of the planet I sought to defraud."

"Get up, Taval-pan. You are a good soul who was simply misled by what you thought were the facts. King Jopol told me you were coming to apologize. There is no need. You are forgiven. You have my permission to search the island. Your past research has shown us how important it is to prove Hermax is indeed real. Go now, bring me proof."

Taval-pan, shed of his escort, sulked out of the palace, depressed. He considered himself a pitiful sight. He was a sixty-six-year-old man who had apologized to the Laara like a guilty six-year-old. He knew he was right but did not know how to prove it; he knew he must to preserve the family's honor.

"But Hermax isn't real," he said aloud to no one. "I will 'prove' he exists for the good of the world, but privately, I will worship the nine gods. They are valid, as my evidence proves. They are the creators, the reason we are here. I know I'm right, and no royal scientist will prove me wrong, but for myself, I need rock-hard evidence. Where to find it?"

As he was leaving the Laara's temple, his mind contemplating what he must do, he looked across the Himal River to the monuments and said to himself, "The year I spent researching you, I ignored the maintenance staff. I will interview them as my last resort."

After changing into one of his old robes, a determined walk took him to the monument center, where he sought the maintenance supervisor. As he approached, he was surprised to see a tall man staring in his direction. The man appeared to be in his seventies. As Taval-pan got closer, he became aware that those serene brown eyes, indeed, were watching him, smiling. The man's head was shaved, gray stubble barely visible.

"Welcome back, Taval-pan. We have patiently awaited your arrival. I am Solgas, the supervisor of this entire complex and the keeper of the Monument of the Sun. Later, you will meet Lunagas and Gaiagas, the keepers of the Monuments of the Moon and Earth, respectively.

"Why have you been waiting for me?"

"The gods told us you had questions concerning these monuments. We are here to help. Come."

He gestured toward the Monument of the Moon.

Taval-pan was shocked. "You communicate with the gods?"

"Yes"

"May I?"

"Eventually. Be patient."

Taval-pan noticed the statues surrounding the monuments all had Hermatic picks painted on them.

"If these monuments represent the gods, why are there Hermatic picks painted on the statues?"

"When the Gosirian priests were disbanded, Hermax destroyed the gods. The people wanted to tear these monuments down, but the Laara stopped them. He told them it would be sacrilegious to destroy Daphne and John's chosen resting place. He suggested that they take it into possession for Hermax by painting these picks. The Gosirian priests were sad at the time as they could not stop the vandals, knew the gods would be angry, and that man's fate was sealed."

"And did they seal man's fate?"

"Yes," he stated bluntly, without any trace of regret.

Worried for mankind, he followed Solgas into the Monument of the Moon. They descended a staircase into an underground lair. A musty odor replaced the fresh air he was used to. His eyes slowly adjusted to the dark. Then, gradually, he began to see dim lights around the interior.

"What is this place?" Taval-pan asked, amazed.

"You are in the chamber of the Gosirian priests."

A shocked expression appeared on Taval-pan's face as his brain processed this wholly unexpected information. Several thoughts raced around in his mind. What Gosirian priests? They were outlawed centuries ago. If they were Gosirian priests, why would they live in a monument?

He took it all in. The monument was built in a circle, and around the outer edges were ten shelters. He later learned that six people lived in each one. There seemed to be no space. He wondered how they could stand it, but everyone seemed to be content.

Confused, he said, more as a question than a statement of fact, "But the Gosirian priests were outlawed centuries ago."

"That's true. At the end of the Dark Ages, the Laara disbanded us and then hired us as monument maintenance personnel. We have been a secret society ever since."

"You said before that you're here to help. What can you do?"

Solgas' face beamed. "We can save you."

"How?"

"Listen to me as I explain life to you. You will want to join us, I'm sure. You are a historian. You know the entire history of mankind as it has been taught to you. Let me fill in the gaps.

"The first 'gods' were the ancestors of the 'gods' Hermax destroyed. They came to earth twenty-five thousand seven hundred seventy years ago in the age of Sagittarius. They had been watching Earth for many years and determined that each astrological sign rose in the vernal equinox for two thousand one hundred sixty years at a time.

They decided to help the hairy, violent, yet intelligent race we call man to prosper. Since it was the dawning of a new astrological age, they related the age to the sun. They observed mankind's meager progress for seven hundred seventy years. When the 'gods' decided to intervene, man excelled. That first growth period, or sun, lasted about four thousand years before disaster hit. The 'gods' saw the disaster coming and saved two each of animals, plants, and man. There have been disasters over time. Each time a new set of 'gods' rescued life on earth in order to start over. The 'gods' gave plenty of warning each time, but mankind wouldn't heed it because he'd always forgotten the 'gods,' preferring instead to revere newer gods and the religions they brought forth. The fifth sun was destroyed in our year zero, and the sixth sun rose to a new set of 'gods' soon after. Daphne and John were the humans saved during the destruction.

"The 'gods' aren't really gods at all. They are an immortal race from the planet Osiriat in the Sirian system. The current 'god's' goal was to rescue mankind in year zero and make sure they averted the next disaster that will happen in 4296 A.D. as the new age of Sagittarius begins. The monuments representing the Osirian system as it will appear in 4296 were the clues they placed that only now you have discovered. You see, if mankind fails this time, the 'gods' won't be able to save the race. The first 'gods' measured our sun and determined it would change significantly in the next age of Sagittarius, twenty-five thousand seven hundred seventy years in the future. They called the cycle a great year and gave themselves a great year to save mankind. They weren't expecting five setbacks, yet anticipating the possibility after the first one, they advanced man a little farther each time.

"Because of the sun's change, all life will be eradicated, and Earth will have to start anew. Even the Osirians can't stop it. They are the only hope for mankind.

"The original plan demanded that mankind never worship the Osirians as gods because each disaster warning was ignored due to the blinding effects of religion. The plan worked for two hundred years and then failed due to man's inhumanity to man, as demonstrated in the story of the banishment of Veon.

"The Osirians were forced to accept their roles as gods to attempt to control man. They allowed worship even though they detested it. Man destroyed all hope through war and slavery. The false God, Hermax, arose, and mankind was seen as lost. Periodically, the old gods rose, but Hermax continually found a way to beat them.

"We Gosirian priests have isolated ourselves these many centuries, breeding for the purpose of holding the truth and preparing for your arrival. We knew one day, a human would question the validity of Hermax.

"We know you have tried to convince your government that the signs point to the gods and disaster. You must stop. They refuse to hear you. If you wish, the Osirians have granted you passage back to Osiriat, where you will become immortal. If you wish to bring a family member or a mate you are welcome to. It is now 4190. You must return as 4195 comes to a close, or we will leave without you. Jupoler's original orders call for him to return home as soon as mankind understood the signs and could save himself. It saddens him that only you believe. He calls you Taval-pan, the chosen one."

Taval-pan felt mystified and vindicated. He was too much the good historian to let it bring him down. After all, Solgas' tale proved him right.

"I had no idea man's history was so long."

"Do you wish to be saved?" Solgas asked for clarification.

"Of course. There's nothing here for me anymore."

"Then return to this chamber before 4195 ends."

He finished his work in Laarisia in 4192, having spent two years exclusively at the monument complex interviewing Solgas, Lunagas, and Gaiagas, men he judged to be true historians. Their information was gathered over the centuries as a defense against Hermax. They were fortified behind his words, ammunition in case he ever fell to the gods. Taval-pan wrote a glowing report concerning the validity of Hermax that he personally handed over to the Laara. He sent a copy to Jopol, who released it as a pamphlet, circulating it worldwide as the gospel truth. Thanks to Taval-pan's tireless effort, Hermax was solidified, and, as a result, man's fate was permanently sealed. Taval-pan enjoyed sealing it because, after he was discredited by the imperial scientists and discovered the nine gods were indeed real, he ceased to want to be involved with the earth. There remained one set of humans he wished to save.

He wrote his family in Nepetan that he was coming home. He arrived by boat six months later. Flight was becoming fashionable, but he did not yet trust it. Six months on a slow boat allowed him time to reflect on his life's work. He would never serve on the Senate, and, being an only child, his family name would die out. Convinced he was progressing toward a greater reality, he wondered if the Osirians truly could grant him immortality. Miska was his one constant thought. Their entire youth and middle years were wasted; he would now offer her eternity.

He rented a bug at the harbor rent-a-bug store, drove home, and parked a few blocks away; there were parked bugs clogging the street near his house. Annoyed, he slowly walked toward home. Everything was exactly as he remembered it. He had seen a world of change, yet this little corner lay untouched. The closer he got to his house, the more concentrated the bugs became.

Continuing on, it dawned on him that all of these people were at his house. He walked up the walkway to the front door and, with a sigh, opened it. He was hit immediately with the strong smell of alcohol. His eyes burned from the unexpected draft of smoke that blew past him. There, in front of him, was a huge banner that said ***WELCOME BACK, TAVAL-PAN!*** Hundreds of people were talking and dancing; most were intoxicated, their once-white robes and dresses covered in food and drink.

A group of less intoxicated people welcomed him and said the party had gone non-stop for a week. After all, Taval-pan had been gone for almost thirty years. Finding a place to sit back and relax, he watched the party and let people come to him, disappointed only by the absence of Miska. Watching them, he solidified his decision to save these people.

When things settled down, he gathered them around to tell his tale of the gods and the pending disaster. His tale took two hours to tell. Cousin Tarta painted the scene. When he saw the fresh canvas, his jaw dropped to the floor.

Tarta was covered in colors from the party and from his paints. Taval-pan had never really cared for him as a child. He had always thought him a bit too cynical. The painting was red with different shades of bright yellow and dark orange swirls forming what appeared to represent a massive explosion. Taval-pan himself was in the red forefront, the explosion behind him, bound to overtake him. His long white hair flared up the sides of his head, accentuating his baldness. His beard was flowing, his torn robe flapping in the breeze as he ran, arms raised high, warning everyone to run away. He wore sandals with leather laces wrapped up his shins that made his run look awkward.

When his senses returned, he approached Tarta. He towered over his fat, dumpy cousin, who looked up, smiling. Tarta had an evil, cynical smile that Taval-pan knew only too well.

"Tarta, what's this?"

"Your father warned us you might come here with that crazy doomsday story. When I heard you telling it, I felt the need to paint this. It's a fool prophesizing the end of the world, a little too late."

Everyone laughed. They laughed harder still when Taval-pan asked if he could keep it. He was sure the Osirians would not mind. He needed a reminder of man's stupidity if he was going to leave him behind. Disgusted, he excused himself, went outside, and walked down to the beach.

He curled his toes in the moist sand and thought, "On this shore, I'm in isolation. No one I love believes me."

He then turned his attention to the roaring waves and yelled, "Tell me sea! You, who have seen eternity. Do the Osirians lay sweet plans for me?"

No answer aside from the sea's roar. He thought he heard "Miska" in the whisper of the spray as it dissipated on the rocks. "Yes. Miska. She has always been my rock, my hope for the future!"

The next morning, he woke early, gathered his bags together, negotiated the sea of humanity that lined the living room floor, and walked outside to retrieve his bug. He loaded it and then moved it closer to his house. Quietly, he opened the front door, found Tarta's painting, and took it to his bug. His family and friends proved quite a disappointment. He decided to check into a hotel for the remainder of his stay.

Brooding in his room, mesmerized by Tarta's painting, he came to a decision. Obviously, he would not be able to save his family. He would try, however, to save Miska and convince her he was right. If Miska laughed at him, there would be no hope for his future.

His decision was made; he packed a few clothes, secured the room for a month, requested no service or cleanup, and ran down to the harbor. There, he purchased a ticket and boarded a cruise ship for Kashim. When he arrived, he ran to Miska's childhood home, hoping she might still live there. To his relief, she answered the door.

"Taval-pan!" She shrieked, delighted.

"I have come for you," he declared.

"And you shall have me."

She took his hand and led him to the bedroom. Their lovemaking was the most passionate experience of their lives. When it ended, they lay on the soaked bed and swore to never leave each other again.

She had inherited the house. She had never married; instead, she waited these long years for him to come to his senses. They spent a week in bed rediscovering each other.

One day, she rose and decided it was time for them to go outside. She took him touring around Kashim. Each day, they picnicked in a different locale. While she entertained him with the sights, he entertained her with his worldly adventures.

During one picnic, she reflected, "I was a fool to stay here. Long ago, I should've married you. The sheer joy of sharing your adventures would've been worth any sacrifice. All those years wasted that we could've been together."

"We are together now. That's all that matters."

Then, the fateful day came, the day he ran out of stories. He only had his Laarisian experience left to tell her, and he feared her reaction. Miska saw the fear blossom on his face.

"What's wrong, Taval-pan?"

"I am afraid I'm going to lose you like I've lost my family and friends."

She caressed his hand, assuring him.

"Why would you say that? You know I'll never let you go."

"You might after I tell you about Laarisia."

"Yes, you haven't yet told me of Laarisia. Could things have been so bad you think I would leave you?" She asked a slight mixed tremor of worry and hurt in her voice.

He was silent for a moment.

She clutched his wrist.

"Taval-pan, we've been through too much. I want to know."

He looked at her, contemplating.

"Miska, you must promise me to keep an open mind. What I'm about to reveal will shock you. I reported it to the Senate and it shocked them so bad that the king discredited me and forced me to renounce the facts. Will you keep an open mind, Miska?"

She was suddenly quite worried.

"Of course, Taval-pan. I trust you with my life. You can tell me anything. My god, what is so bad? Please tell me?"

"Okay, I have told you about my worldwide travels. What I haven't told you is that as a scientist, I began to doubt Hermax when I toured Hermatia."

"Why would anyone doubt Hermax?"

"Please, Miska, no questions. This is hard enough as it is," he pleaded.

"I felt my belief in Hermax wane when I discovered that a dying volcano created the steam causing the fog that hid Hermatia in ancient times. When I took my case to the head priest, he discounted the facts. He assured me Hermax killed the volcano to hide the island. I grudgingly accepted his decision, but a seed of doubt had been planted.

"In Laarisia, I spent many wonderful years at the Laara's palace, where she taught me Laarisia's view of world history. She encouraged me to tour the monuments and permitted me to enter the Monument of the Sun. That was a life-changing experience.

"As you may know, The Monument of the Sun is the final resting place of Daphne and John, the founders and leaders of Laarisia in its infancy. These are the leaders who, through their cruelty, woke Hermax. He rose to fight the tyranny of slavery. The entire history of the Hermatic religion begins with them.

"You can imagine my shock as I entered their tomb and found no evidence they had ever been buried there. I found no evidence of Hermax. What I did find were references to the nine gods. There were statues etched in the walls, paintings, and scrolls detailing their time on earth, overwhelming evidence that they had been here. I was convinced Daphne and John were buried elsewhere and that this place was a shrine to the gods. How Hermax emerged from these monuments was still a mystery.

"I didn't report this shocking news to the Laara because I wanted solid evidence to back up my thesis. I began an investigation of the monuments themselves. What I found astonished me. I took measurements and found that every time I applied 2π to my calculations, wonderful results appeared. I found that the monuments were laid out as a scale model of the earth at a time when man had no knowledge of the earth's size. They also seemed to represent the stars Sirius A and B and a planet that should orbit through them.

"Now, with all the evidence I had, I approached the Laara. I told her that Daphne and John weren't in the Monument of the Sun and never had been. She insisted that Hermax had taken them to be with him, and that's why no physical evidence of their entombment remained. I didn't bother her with my other evidence because her opinion obviously wouldn't be turned.

"Five years later, I presented my evidence to the king at the Imperial Senate. That august body was in an uproar. The disturbance I caused obviously upset King Jopol. He ordered me to be silent for one year while his scientists poured over my material. They found no proof that Hermax was a false god or that the nine gods were real. King Jopol ordered me to return to Laarisia, apologize to the Laara, and spend the remainder of my career proving Hermax was real. If I refused, he promised to ruin my family. So, reluctantly, I accepted defeat and 'proved' Hermax valid.

"I obtained all of my information concerning Hermax from the Gosirian priests."

She paid rapt attention because, in her heart, she needed to believe him. Yet this news sent a shock wave through her.

"Yes, Miska, the Gosirian priests. They survived as the monument maintenance staff. I was as shocked as you. Anyhow, they spent centuries compiling facts concerning Hermax's validity so that when the nine gods attempted, finally, to rise, they could use his words against him.

"They took me under their wing and told me the truth. This may be hard for you, but I need to tell you. Hermax is a false god. Slaves, as an avenue of hope, created him. Their faith was based on fabrication. By faith's definition, they accepted what they could not see, what they perceived to be true but could not prove. Hermax was described through metaphor, allegory, and exaggeration. The real gods, who had incidentally spent time on earth raising humans, were used in creation stories and added weight to the new faith. The stories helped the slaves process the unthinkable. Problems arose when mankind began to believe literally in the stories and relegated the gods to myth. On their own, the slaves escaped, but they decided to thank Hermax, and with their validation, he grew into the mega god he is.

"Not only is Hermax a false god, but, and this may be even harder to take, there are no gods at all, not even the original nine are truly gods. They are from a planet called Osiriat, the very planet the monuments refer to, if you know how to decipher them. They are an immortal race who has tried to save humankind from destruction five previous times. Apparently, each time man elevates them to gods, he discards them for new gods, refuses to see the signs they've placed, and perishes because he loses his way.

"The next and last period of destruction is going to happen in 4296. The monuments warn us. The statue called Sagittarius is offset to the east because at the dawn of the age of Sagittarius, the sun will change, and all life on earth will be eradicated. We expect a different form of life to evolve, but mankind will be lost forever. The Osirians have offered me and a mate passage to Osiriat and the promise of immortality. Well, what do you think?"

"Taval-pan, I've always wondered why we relied so heavily on one god. I know you. If you believe these facts in your heart, then they must be true. If you're proposing, then yes, I will marry you and leave this planet. To spend eternity with you is more than I ever dreamed possible."

She held him tighter than ever. Together, they sighed.

Two weeks later, they finally married. The ceremony was held in the state Hermatic temple. Taval-pan invited all of his friends and family. Some snickered, wondering aloud how Taval-pan could anger his precious nine gods by marrying under Hermatic auspices. Taval-pan did not care. He was determined to present a popular front to protect his father.

His father asked, "Son, where will you honeymoon?"

"We are going to honeymoon and live in Laarisia. I have the Laara's invitation. She holds no ill will toward me. She has pardoned me and reserved an apartment in the palace for us."

"If you have her blessing, you are in good hands, Son."

A rented bug took them to their ship. They sailed first to Nepetan to retrieve Taval-pan's belongings, then set sail for Laarisia. Miska was shocked when she saw the painting and then laughed when she understood how foolish it portrayed mankind.

The Laara welcomed the new couple with open arms. She set them up in their own apartment and invited them to a banquet in their honor.

At the banquet, the Laara ushered them to one side.

"What are your plans?"

Taval-pan, knowing the question was really directed at him, lied. "I plan to live on each island for one year so I can show this wonderful woman my life's work. Then, I suppose, I shall be called upon to serve in the Imperial Senate."

The next morning, they set out for the monument complex. Taval-pan carried his painting under his arm. Solgas welcomed them.

"Do you think the Osirians will let me take this aboard?"

"They are reasonable. I'm sure they will," Solgas assured him.

"Solgas, this is my wife, Miska. She is coming, too."

"You are lovelier than his description. When can you join us for training?"

"Give me a week. The Laara must see me prepare to sail."

One week later, Taval-pan loaded a bag and told the Laara he was taking Miska on an extended tour of the island. They headed toward the monument complex and were never seen again.

It was 4193. They trained with the priests for one year. Miska learned to decipher the mathematical facts Taval-pan had uncovered. They were given descriptions of the nine gods, taught their personalities and habits, and the history of their time on earth.

CHAPTER 14

ESCAPE

The major focus of their studies was Osirian culture and history. They were taught the basics of Osirian life, including plant and animal species, hunting and fishing techniques, and languages. Realizing that to survive in their new home, they must understand it and its culture, they delved into their studies.

Solgas interviewed them as the year came to a close.

"Do you feel this year has been educational?"

They looked at each other. They had discussed classes every day. Taval-pan answered, "You have taught us well, but this has been a tough year."

"Things are bound to get tougher when you join the Osirians. They have ordered training here to stop. Soon they will send for you. You require sufficient onboard training before departure."

They wandered the halls of the Monument of the Sun for a week, wondering when they would be called. One night, as they slept, they were suddenly beamed to a dark room. As they awoke, a beam of light shone on them from above. A voice commanded, "Do not move!"

"Who are you?" asked Taval-pan.

"You shall see!" The voice answered.

One by one, the light shone on each "god."

"I am Planex- Lord of the dead!"

"I am Uryxs- Lord of the night!"

"I am Nepeta- Lord of the sea, Galacia!"

"I am Satetan- Goddess of fertility!"

"I am Jupoler- Lord of the Universe!"

"I am Marsax- Goddess of the warriors!"

"I am Mercianiax- Messenger of the Gods!"

"I am Vienusia- Goddess of love!"

"And I am Arop- Goddess of light!"

The voice, Jupoler, spoke, "At least that is what mankind first thought. You have been chosen because you thought to question the validity of Hermax. We are aware that you've spent the last year learning about Osiriat. You will now spend time with each of us learning in depth about Crystalia, Lonix, Isoloquat, and Gosiria. Each country speaks a different language, which your teachers will use."

Arop added, "We have two more people for you to meet."

The entire room lit up. A man and woman walked out from behind the Osirians and introduced themselves as Daphne and John.

Taval-pan recovered first.

"How is this possible? Why aren't you in the Monument of the Sun?"

John explained. "You have been asking that question for many years. Our 'deaths' were the catalyst of your faithful choice. Because of the lack of evidence, or rather the overwhelming evidence of the gods, you chose to abandon Hermax. This is possible," he continued as he waved his hand in front of himself and Daphne, "because we never really died. Our deaths were staged. The event was engineered to strengthen society's belief in the gods. The Delegatia's goal of locating the escaped slaves held Laarisian society together; the gods thrived. But, alas, man's nature couldn't be turned, and one god eventually rose. We have waited centuries to meet you. The Osirians granted us immortality for saving mankind, as they will you."

Vienusia interrupted, "Daphne and John, like the nine of us, are your ancestors. Their job will be to prepare you for space flight."

As ordered, Taval-pan and Miska spent the next two years learning about space travel. Four months were spent exclusively with John and Daphne. John and Daphne beamed them from place to place to acclimate them to the process. They showed them the hibernation chambers and ordered them to hibernate for one week to get the full sense of the process.

After the hibernation experiment, they spent every day in the mini-gym, gaining strength for the journey. The gym was housed in a clear dome-roofed room where, when they were not working out, they were required to study space. From Earth to Sirius/Osiriat, they knew every obstacle. Beyond the parameters of their flight, they knew every star. Navigational knowledge was critical in the event the computer failed, and they were forced out of hibernation to guide the ship.

When Daphne and John finished training them, they were assigned to Uryxs and Satetan. For five months, they were taught basic engineering, again as a precaution against computer failure. When they mastered engineering, they focused on farming theory. The humans, like all Osirians, would be required to farm. Uryxs concentrated on harvesting techniques, while Satetan concentrated on the mechanics of fertilizer, planting timing, and soil qualities.

Next, they were assigned to Mercianiax and Marsax. Their job was to teach them both hunting techniques and self-defense. Hunting techniques were necessary because they would have to supplement their diets with meat, but self-defense?

Miska, curious, asked Marsax. "Why must we learn self-defense when we will journey to a planet where we are welcomed?"

Marsax had anticipated this question.

"Miska, when you hunt the animals of Osiriat, you will not be welcomed by *them*. They will try any means possible to halt your attack, so you must be able to defend against them. Also, we are always prepared to journey to other planets, and there, you will have to be prepared for any eventuality."

They excelled with Mercianiax and Marsax and, at the end of five months, were assigned to Nepeta and Vienusia. Nepeta and Vienusia helped with the aquatic training and breathing exercises. They spoke to them in their high-pitched, chirping language as they taught them about sea living.

Every day, they met in the pool that was next to the gym. Nepeta and Vienusia ran aquatic computer simulations projected into the water. At the end of five months, Taval-pan and Miska were prepared for any aquatic event.

Their final five months of training were spent with Jupoler, Arop, and Planex. Jupoler was usually indisposed, in communication with Tarus preparing the rendezvous. Arop was left to captain the shuttle. This meant that most lessons fell to Planex to teach. He was responsible for drilling Osirian custom into them. The chief concern was that the humans might somehow offend the natives. In the entire span of Osirian history, a race was never purposely brought back to the home world.

Training in custom and ritual was the most challenging. One false move and Planex would make them begin again. The months were tedious, but they were not spent alone. At mealtimes, everyone would gather. Taval-pan and Miska were spoken to and required to answer in four different languages. They could not shake their accents, but Crystalian they used flawlessly, as chirping and clicking were easier to imitate than the spoken word. When 4196 arrived, they were ready to leave and as well-rounded as any Osirian they traveled with.

They were on hand in 4196 when the Gosirian priests were brought aboard. Over time, the "gods" had built up the shuttle to be able to house about one hundred people. The priests were overjoyed to see Daphne and John, whom history claimed were dead.

Solgas fell to his knees, weeping.

"My lords, we have spent centuries humbly keeping your will alive. We were certain you were dead even after Taval-pan found that you had never been housed in the Monument of the Sun. What is this miracle that allows us to see you alive?"

John answered, "First, welcome all of you loyal Gosirians. We are flattered that you kept our will alive, especially through the adversity we know you've encountered. What is this miracle? Know first that we never really died. The Osirians put us to sleep. This is the great reward. You have served the Osirians well, as we did, and you have been granted, as we were, immortality and a new home on the planet Osiriat. All you sought to defend has remained pure; however, the humans who chose to ignore you are impure and cannot be saved.

"Two things you must know on this ship. First, this room will house you. Soon, Uryxs will send you materials to build your shelters. Second, we are still your leaders. If you need anything, see us, and we will send your request to Jupoler. Once you've settled in, the Osirians will be down to meet you. Gradually, before we depart, our leadership will no longer be useful, as you will be dealing directly with the crew."

Sixty years earlier, Osiriat VI launched again from Osiriat. Its mission centered on collecting and analyzing earth data. Jupoler stayed in consistent contact with Tarus over the centuries. As the end neared, their contact was more frequent. Tarus had to equip Osiriat VI correctly for the rescue.

Jupoler and Tarus' conversations revolved around a waiting game. The Osirians knew how to speed through space; however, they had not done much to improve communications. Being immortal, time did not affect them, so they let sound travel at its normal rate.

Jupoler's group was the first to stay away from home for so long. As the earth year 4100 approached, Tarus decided he wanted better contact with this group, so he sent probes out to drop sound relay stations every one light year away from Osiriat. Earth was eight point seven light years away, requiring eight stations. These relay stations dropped the signal travel time down to three hundred sixty-five days.

In 4187, Jupoler's time, Tarus sent him a message.

"Son, Osiriat VI was sent back to Earth in 4136, your time. The onboard computer pilots it. When it reaches you, its speed, factoring in declination, will be point zero five percent of light. You are aware, I'm sure, of how terribly fast this is. Once it reaches the Sol system, it will arrive in your location in forty-four days. I have equipped Osiriat VI with the materials you requested for rescue. I leave it to you to judge the safest way to transport to the ship. By the way, were you able to save anyone?"

One year later, Jupoler was on the bridge when he heard a beep indicating an incoming message. He read the message and then downloaded it into the shuttle computer with the command: PROGRAM THE CORRECT COORDINATES FOR SUCCESSFUL TRANSPORT TO OSIRIAT VI. He then sent a message back to Tarus.

"Father, here I sit in the earth year 4188. Received your message. Thank you for equipping Osiriat VI. The computer is working on the transport problem. We will rescue sixty people from the Gosirian priesthood. We are studying humanity and believe we may have found someone to save. Will advise when we have secured. Jupoler, out."

Tarus read the message one year later. He returned to his work. A response was not necessary; he trusted Jupoler to keep him informed.

Jupoler discovered that his computer could plot where they were going to be in 4196, but in no way could it judge the transport sequence with only half of the information. He relayed this message to Tarus: "Father, my computer needs the assistance of the Osiriat VI computer to plot the transport coordinates. I realize we are going to cut it close, but if the Osiriat VI computer is the same one I used 4000 years ago, I have every confidence we will succeed. I have received a message from the Gosirian priests. One human male and a possible mate have denied the false god, Hermax, and are scheduled to join us. Their training commences in two years. We will leave at six. Jupoler, out."

As Osiriat VI neared, the co-captains called a meeting of all aboard. The Gosirian priests consisted of ten families of six people each. They held the meeting in the Gosirian priests' quarters, in the most spacious part of the ship. Here, the Gosirian priests were spread out and, as a result, more comfortable than they had been in the Moon monument. The room was square in shape. An old cargo bay, it held ten shelters, five shelters on each of two of the walls. The remaining two walls were devoid of structures. One wall contained a bank of windows allowing a magnificent view of space, and the other wall was decorated with a mural of Osiriat, the separate countries, and the Osirians as children playing at home. It was here everyone now gathered to hear Jupoler speak.

"Osiriat VI, the ship that first brought us here, has been sent back to Earth to take us home. My father, Tarus, has equipped the computer with all of the knowledge necessary to find us.

"When the ship reaches this solar system, it will not slow down. When it reaches us, it will be traveling at point zero five percent of light speed or three million three hundred forty-eight thousand miles per hour. I have called this meeting to discuss our beam-out policy.

"Uryxs and Satetan, our engineers, will build a transport bay for all seventy-three of us in this very room. When I give the order, everyone is to proceed to this transport bay with haste. Remember, Osiriat VI won't slow down. If this split-second beam out is to work, everyone must cooperate."

Jupoler sent the coordinates to Osiriat VI as it approached the planet Planex. The signal traveled quickly toward the ship and was intercepted as it reached the planet Jupoler. Osiriat VI held half the puzzle, and when it received the information relayed by the shuttle computer, the puzzle was completed. Several days passed as it carefully analyzed every scenario. The disastrous ones were discarded. The allowable parameters were narrowed until one avenue of escape was isolated. This process was completed as the ship neared Marsax's orbit, and it immediately sent the coordinates to Jupoler.

Jupoler responded to the beep from Osiriat VI with lightning speed. He nervously stood by as the onboard computer analyzed the message. He had been monitoring Osiriat VI and knew it would quickly reach Earth. When the time and transport coordinates came up, his eyes widened. He pushed the intercom button and calmly ordered, "Everyone to the transport bay. Now!"

They gathered as ordered and waited; the adults were nervous, the children playing at their feet, blissfully unaware of the looming danger. Everyone watched the monitors as Osiriat VI appeared. Jupoler quickly glanced at Uryxs, making sure he held the transport remote, a necessary piece of equipment, as no one would be at the controls.

Jupoler had his own remote. As Osiriat VI rushed by and they began to beam out, he activated it. One minute after they were all safely aboard the ship, the shuttle blew up.

The shuttle pieces, now space junk, orbited Earth for the next one hundred years. They were silent witnesses to life's imminent collapse. Eventually, their orbit decayed, and they became the sole inhabitants of Earth. Time would slowly bury them. Hundreds of thousands of years later, a new experiment in life would begin. Eventually, erosion would expose the pieces, and it would be life's only link to the failed human experiment.

The new passengers on Osiriat VI did not witness the shuttle's destruction as they were traveling fast away from the area. By the time the shuttle blew, it was not even a dot on their sensors.

Jupoler satisfied everyone was onboard, made an announcement, "Everyone will proceed immediately to the hibernation chambers. Each family of six will go with one of the Osirians, Daphne or John. They will show you how to enter stasis. When you awaken, you will be near Osiriat. I want to personally thank you for staying loyal to us. I am needed on the bridge. Good luck!"

Once on the bridge, he turned off the autopilot and guided the ship toward the sun, Arop. Arop was to be used as he had used the dwarf star Golas to slingshot the ship toward home. He realized, however, that this star did not have the gravitational pull he needed. The computer would know.

"Computer, what speed will we accomplish by slingshoting around Arop?" Jupoler asked, attempting to solve the problem.

"I estimate about ten percent of light," the computer answered mechanically.

"We need more. How can gather more speed?"

"I anticipated that problem on the way to Earth. You must end the slingshot maneuver around Arop by heading toward the planet Nepeta. You will then slingshot Nepeta, releasing the ship toward the planet Uryxs. Again, you will slingshot Uryxs, releasing the ship toward the planet Jupoler. Slingshot around Jupoler toward Sirius."

"How much speed will we gain?"

"With these moves, you will max out at fifteen percent of light."

"What if we use Satetan also?"

"No. Satetan is a wasted step that would achieve the same results."

"So, at fifteen percent of light, it will take one hundred twenty years to get home?"

"That is correct."

The ship housed seventy-three hibernation chambers. All were in use except Jupoler's as they began the slingshot maneuver around Jupoler.

"Computer, what is your present speed?"

"Thirteen percent of light."

"Are you sure this maneuver will gain us two more percent?"

"Positive."

"Will we have speed declination as we travel to Osiriat?"

"I have enough fuel to maintain fifteen percent of light for many years. As the years go by, my fuel consumption will increase. It is predicted that when I run out of fuel, the dwarf star, Golas, will take over and pull us into the Sirian system at fifteen percent of light."

"When will you wake me?"

"I am to wake you prior to Golas' gravitational pull becoming too strong to escape."

Jupoler was satisfied with the plan.

"Computer, give me fifteen minutes before you activate my hibernation chamber. I am going to check your airlocks."

"Thank you, Sir. Have a good sleep, Sir," the computer said politely, indicating to Jupoler that it could handle things from here.

Jupoler excused himself. As promised he checked the computer main frame airlock. He took one last look at his hibernating passengers, wondering aloud if they would be safe for the next one hundred twenty years, then went to his hibernation chamber, undressed, lay down, put on his facemask, and waited. At the appropriate time, the lid closed, latched, and began to fill with water. Seconds before he fell asleep, he felt it. This time, it was no dream. He really felt the slingshot effect as the ship reached fifteen percent of light and headed home.

Hibernation is not conducive to dreams. The brain and body shut down to about one percent of activity. This is barely enough, with feeding tubes, to keep a person alive. Certainly, the brain cannot dream, as all of its imaginative functions are stifled. The rush Jupoler felt as the ship accelerated to fifteen percent of light caused his hibernation chamber to malfunction.

He laid down too late and the rush caused his brain to increase activity rather than relax. Theoretically, dreams are quite impossible, but he experienced them. His childhood, mission training, time spent on Earth, and time spent above it, forever orbiting around Nepeta and Arop, flashed through his mind. The computer fought to correct his chamber and succeeded in shutting down his body but not his brain. It finally shut itself down, much to the computer's relief, for if it did not, he would be killed when his brain ran out of material to review. The rush would, however, affect Jupoler when he arose in one hundred twenty years.

DEBT OF GRATITUDE

One hundred twenty years later, he woke, still feeling the effects of the rush he experienced as they left Jupoler. The water quickly drained from his chamber, and the hatch opened. As it did, he heard:

"Captain, to the bridge, please. Hurry, please." Through his groggy state, the computer reminded him he had a job to do.

As he stumbled off to the bridge, he felt a strange sense of deja vu. Immortal, the passage of time did not affect him as it would a mortal. The computer's voice remained unchanged over the last forty-two hundred years, adding to his confusion. Through his haze, he thought he was reentering the Sol system. By the time he arrived, he had walked off the feeling and realized he was home. He took control of the ship, turned it hard right toward Sirius, and waited for Sirius to break Golas' gravitational pull. The moment it did, he again pulled the ship hard right and headed home to Osiriat.

The Gosirian priests, Osirians, and the other four humans woke and were ordered to the transport bay. Jupoler noticed that they had all aged twenty years except for, of course, the Osirians and Daphne and John. All were groggy. Jupoler began his welcome home speech.

"When we land, you will be welcomed to Osiriat by the royalty, my parents, Tarus and Elysia. There will be a celebration to honor our success. You know our customs, so you should enjoy it."

Solgas, the first to come out of grogginess, was genuinely concerned.

"What is going to happen to us?"

"That is a matter for the king to decide. I'm sorry I can't be more specific; they've told me nothing. Everyone, please return to quarters, gather your possessions, and brace for landing."

They landed, and as Jupoler promised, there was a major celebration. The celebrants filled the royal hall, and the Osirian royalty sat as they had sat before the launch of their children. Individually, the elders welcomed their children home.

"How was the hunting, my boy?"

"Excellent, Father. Marsax was as powerful as always. She formed an army on Earth."

"That's my girl!" Wolvernix said.

Oblivia stroked her lightly. "Did you enjoy having babies?"

"Oh, Mother. It was so wonderful. I never thought I could feel an emotion as powerful as hunting. I taught them self-defense but was saddened when my children destroyed themselves."

Petex and Dolphinia greeted Nepeta and Vienusia with hugs and kisses.

Dolphinia asked, "How did you like the sea?"

Vienusia smiled. "It was so diverse. There were some areas that were too dark to venture into. They made me long for Osiriat."

Petex asked, "Nepeta, did you enjoy your duties?"

"Oh yes. Their animal population was much more diverse than ours. It's too bad they couldn't be saved."

Cronix and Sate showed no emotion to Uryxs and Satetan; none was expected, as it simply was not in their nature.

Cronix spoke for both of them. "I trust you performed your duties adequately on this mission?"

Uryxs answered, "I did my duty. Engineering never ran better on any ship, and when it was time to populate the earth, I performed well."

Satetan said, "Mother, I had twenty children. I taught them well. Their crops succeeded more often than not, but I am so disappointed. We should've been able to save them. They turned away from us and wouldn't heed the warnings."

Tarus and Elysia warmly embraced their children. Planex was slightly apprehensive because he barely remembered them, but quickly livened when Tarus whispered in his ear that he was always his favorite child.

Elysia asked, "Arop, did you handle your pregnancies well?"

"I did my duty and produced fine children. Somehow, though, they became unruly and, as a result, have destroyed themselves. Our failed efforts sadden me. Only Taval-pan and Miska renewed my hope. Forty-two hundred years into our mission, two good, reliable humans were finally born."

Jupoler said, "Yes, they are a miracle. Father, why didn't you tell me space would hold such wonderful adventures?"

"Because my adventure failed and, though it was wonderful, I didn't want to taint your experience. Planex, what did you do on Earth?"

"I was a jack of all trades. I helped everyone in their work and befriended the chosen ones. It was I who trained them; I, they turned to when confused. Jupoler sent Uryxs and me to Earth to try to correct humanity when they faltered. In this respect, we failed, but, as Arop pointed out, at least we have two who survived."

"Yes, I would like to meet them later. Jupoler, give them an important job; they deserve a reward."

"How can I-?"

"You'll see. "He directed Jupoler's attention back toward the party.

Tarus waited until the celebration wound down, then announced:

"Fellow citizens. This mission was a success, and, as we promised, your governors and royal couple hereby relinquish their duties and turn them over to our children!"

The applause roared like angry waves breaking on a stormy beach. A hush fell over the crowd as the nine new rulers rose.

Jupoler spoke for the group. "We accept this honor if it is the will of the people."

Again, the audience roared. They adored humble rulers. Jupoler's raised hand quieted them.

"The governors of each land seem to be brothers and sisters. I decree that when they marry, they shall rule as a team.

"Arop and I are your new king and queen, but this is improper. I will deal with it in a moment. First, we have the problem of Planex. He has always been a prince. When he marries, I shall grant him the governorship of Gosiria, freeing the royalty for more worldly tasks.

"Arop and I have discussed the awkwardness of a brother and sister rule and have come up with a solution. We wouldn't be here except for the efforts of two humans, and, if you will, I would like to bring them up. Daphne. John. Please come forward."

The audience politely applauded as Daphne and John rose from their seats and proceeded over the bridge. Jupoler and Arop came out to stand opposite of them.

"We have a solution to this awkward brother/sister rule," Jupoler said. Together, they asked, "Daphne, John, will you marry us and rule this planet with us?"

Daphne and John were momentarily shocked. They soon recovered and answered yes, causing great applause. The wedding took place two weeks later.

The ceremony was held in the reception hall. Tables were removed in favor of benches. Two thousand people attended. The governing families and the guests of honor, Taval-pan and Miska, sat in the front section. John and Jupoler stood upon the moat bridge awaiting their brides.

Trumpeters signaled the bride's entrance. As they entered the hall, everyone gasped. Arop, dressed in white, shone bright as the suns, as she had as a child. Daphne, also in white, added to the impression that the dual suns were present on the planet. Their trains consisted of rhinestones that shone brightly as a Crystalian tail would in the sea.

When they reached the top of the bridge, they each took their future mate's hand and walked forward to Tarus. He began the ceremony with an observation, "Never in Osirian history have couples known each other for thousands of years before they married. These will be happy unions, for they must truly know each other.

"Do you men take these women as your brides, to love, cherish, and honor for all eternity?"

"We do."

"Do you women accept this challenge to spend all eternity with these men?"

"We do."

He whispered, "Turn to the audience, please." When they had, he announced, "May I present the new kings and queens of Osiriat?"

Wine flowed to the fountains as the women said, "We do," and the audience roared their approval.

The humans were given a deserted island in the Lonix chain that they named Earthia. The Osirians turned out in great numbers to help them build a village. They saw it as an excellent opportunity to interact with another species.

Taval-pan and Miska were elected to govern the village. Any requests or problems were to be directed to Daphne and John, who were granted the governorship of Earthia. Jupoler and Arop wanted their spouses to have important jobs. What could be more important than helping the humans?

The Gosirian priesthood was officially broken up since there were no longer "Gods" to protect. The children, who, during the journey, had become adults, were asked to pair off and mate. Jupoler gave the humans five years to develop their society. It was to this developed society the governors, Daphne and John, were sent to with orders from the king and queen. Daphne and John were seated comfortably in Taval-pan's house.

John began, "You know Earth history, and you know these people spent over twenty-five thousand years trying to save mankind. You also know that they colonize many planets. Their colonization efforts have revealed another humanoid race at the beginning of their development.

"You should know our rulers feel that you owe them a debt of gratitude. You are hereby ordered to pick eight people whom you believe will excel in space. They need to be in the twenty-five to thirty age group."

"Where are they going?" Miska asked, concerned.

Daphne knew the answer would sound better coming from her. She put her hand on John's knee and squeezed to quiet him. "We're not sure. Our rulers will tell them after the training."

As always, the entire village turned out to bid their governors farewell. Soon after they were gone, Taval-pan visited four males and four females. He asked them to take on the mission. None hesitated. They were sent to Gosiria for training. They trained on the ground and in the space station training facility where the others had trained as children. Two years passed. They found themselves in the same hall where they had their arrival celebration. Their destination was announced. It was named to honor the retired royal couple.

The speaker continued:

". . .And you eight have been chosen to repay humanity's debt to Osiriat. Planet Elysia in the Tarus system has an emerging race of humanoids that need our help.

"You will be seen as "gods." Encourage that belief, but do not make the mistake of your saviors. Keep absolute control, but don't let religion form. You were rescued, but religion was Earth's downfall. Many millions died because they believed in the false god Hermax.

"Remember, when people refuse to see the inherent danger, religion blinds and becomes the great destroyer. Humanoids kill and die in the name of false beliefs.

"If you complete your mission and save the planet Elysia, you will return as heroes and rule Osiriat!"